UNKNOWN CALLER

YELLOW SHOE FICTION
Michael Griffith, Series Editor

UN KNOWN CALL ER

A NOVEL

DEBRA SPARK

LOUISIANA STATE UNIVERSITY PRESS
BATON ROUGE

Published with the assistance of the Borne Fund

Published by Louisiana State University Press
Copyright © 2016 by Debra Spark
All rights reserved
Manufactured in the United States of America
LSU Press Paperback Original
First printing

DESIGNER: Michelle A. Neustrom
TYPEFACE: Sentinel, text; Gotham, display
PRINTER AND BINDER: Maple Press

LIBRARY OF CONGRESS CATALOGING-IN-PUBLICATION DATA
Names: Spark, Debra, 1962– author.
Title: Unknown caller : a novel / Debra Spark.
Description: Baton Rouge : Louisiana State University Press, [2016]
Identifiers: LCCN 2016009623| ISBN 978-0-8071-6469-3 (softcover : acid-free paper) |
    ISBN 978-0-8071-6470-9 (pdf) | ISBN 978-0-8071-6471-6 (epub) | ISBN 978-0-8071-
    6472-3 (mobi)
Subjects: LCSH: Man-woman relationships—Fiction. | Interpersonal relations—Fiction. |
    Marital conflict—Fiction. | Domestic fiction. | GSAFD: Love stories.
Classification: LCC PS3569.P358 U55 2016 | DDC 813/.54—dc23 LC record available at
    https://lccn.loc.gov/2016009623

For Cilla and Eliot, best of friends

The past is never dead. It's not even past.
—WILLIAM FAULKNER, *Requiem for a Nun*

The present contains nothing more than the past, and what is
found in the effect was already in the cause.
—HENRI BERGSON, *Creative Evolution*

It is quite true what Philosophy says: that Life must be understood backwards. But that makes one forget the other saying: that
it must be lived—forwards.
—SØREN KIERKEGAARD, *The Diary of Søren Kierkegaard*

CONTENTS

PART ONE

1

MAINE NIGHT

IT IS TWO IN THE MORNING when the phone rings. "Damn," Joel says.

"Sweetheart," Daniella groans, meaning nothing particularly tender, just saying the word to put the world on pause while she figures out what's required of her.

"I'll get it," she adds, though there's really no point. The call isn't for her.

In normal families, a late-night call means only one thing: tragedy. A drunken mishap. A car crash. A heart finally giving out. Maybe a decapitation or a roadside bomb, the twenty-first-century offering, as it does, an escalating range of horrors.

But the Pearlmans are not a normal family. When the phone rings at 2:00 a.m. at their house, it is always *her* calling. From Geneva or Paris or London. They can never be sure where she's taken up residence, only that the call will be long-distance and unpleasant.

THE PHONE RINGS A SECOND, then a third time, sounding unaccountably mad, as if gauging the mood of the caller and comporting itself accordingly. Daniella hurries to the dresser where the phone sits. She means to catch it before Ben wakes, though one more ring and the machine will pick up, and there will be a fuzzy recording intoning, "Elvis has left the building. Elvis has left the building," after which Joel's voice will say, "We're not here. You know the drill. After the beep." But of course electronic barriers do not dissuade this caller. At the sound of the tape clicking on, she will hang up and try again. If Daniella and Joel simply unplug the phone—which they are disinclined to do, since what if someone truly needs them?—the woman will ring Joel at work tomorrow, and there he doesn't have the luxury of failing to answer. They've tried new numbers over the years, unlisted ones, but she always finds them.

"Joel?" the woman on the line inquires, perfectly polite, though Daniella's groggy hello is plainly not male.

There was a time when the woman wouldn't speak no matter who answered. She just hung up. Then called again. And why, Daniella always wondered. Because she couldn't bring herself to talk? Because her purpose had been merely to bother?

"No," Daniella says sleepily now, keeping her voice mild and unsurprised. "I'll get him." It is the only exchange she has ever had with the woman. "Guess who?" she mouths to Joel.

The woman—she has a name, Liesel—was Joel's wife for five months, nineteen years ago. She doesn't call as often as she once did, but now when she does, it isn't to hang up but to accuse.

"Stop yelling," Joel will say, and "I don't know what you want from me." Sometimes he just lays the phone on the bed, and Daniella can hear Liesel's angry cries, though she can't make out the words.

"What does she yell about?" Daniella has asked on more than one occasion.

"What doesn't she yell about?" Joel says. "You abandoned me. You don't care. We could be starving, and you wouldn't care." He shrugs, defeated and maybe—just slightly—amused. The whole thing is ridiculous.

JOEL AND DANIELLA DON'T have curtains on their bedroom windows, which face their fields, and it seems—can this be mere coincidence?—that Liesel always calls when the moon is high and full over the tangle of weeds and wildflowers there. Tonight there's a three-quarters moon, swollen like a harvest moon, a big white clown's nose in profile, poking the sky.

Two parallelograms of light decorate Daniella and Joel's bedspread. As a girl, Daniella used to follow the nighttime shapes as they skirted across her bedroom whenever a car passed. She'd felt unaccountably moved by the traveling light. Now she is too far out in the country for such a thing. The shapes are steady, her room orderly, her husband standing and pulling on the pair of boxers he has left on the floor.

For five months Liesel lived here with Joel, and there are times when Daniella thinks she should feel her presence—the former lady of the house!—but she doesn't. Instead she senses the chicken farmers whose barn burned down in the 1950s, and before them the superstitious people who put a worn black shoe—a women's decrepit lace-up—in the kitchen wall, apparently to ward off evil spirits. Though her mind generally doesn't tend to the dark, Daniella has had the bad thought that the shoe was all that remained of a woman trapped behind the walls for being, in someone's estimation, a witch. Daniella first came to her home as Joel's architect; she worked for the firm that did his kitchen remodel. Though she loves her home in its current form—walls painted yellow, green, and mauve, original art hanging everywhere—there's something about its history that she wants to avoid.

"What? *What?*" Joel is now saying then shouting into the phone. Daniella shushes him and whispers, "You'll wake Ben." He waves impatiently, a brusque "leave me be" gesture, but he must share her concern, for he goes downstairs. Through the floor, Daniella hears the rise and fall of his voice, but no specific words. She is curious about what has made him stay on the line—normally he hangs up within minutes—but she's too lazy to get up to listen. And maybe it's just as well. Not that Joel tends to be bothered by Daniella's interest in his affairs. If this were a call about a patient, he'd tell her the whole story once he hung up, but he has dealt with the Liesel phase of his life by pretending, as much as possible, that it never happened. It embarrasses him, Daniella suspects, such a striking mistake in judgment. "Often in doubt, but never in error," he likes to mug with doctor friends. But actually he's rarely in doubt. If she has a complaint, and she doesn't really, it is that her husband can be a bit of a know-it-all.

Daniella drifts back to sleep, then is woken by Ben. "Ma-ma," he cries out once, panicked, and though she knows this is a cry from a bad dream, and he has not in fact woken, she goes to his room, kisses his warm cheek, straightens his blankets. He is beautiful in sleep, soft cheek pressed to the mattress, thumb having fallen out of his mouth, though at six he is probably too old for this comforting, bad habit. Daniella hasn't pressed the issue. The one time she did, Ben told her that sucking his thumb and touching his pillowcase—he loves its over-laundered softness—made "an excellent combination," as if the pillow were a fine wine he'd decided to pair with his thumb.

Heading back to bed, Daniella sees that it is now 2:42 a.m. Joel has been talking for over thirty minutes. What exactly do they have to talk about?

When Daniella next wakes, it is to Joel shaking her. Her glasses aren't on, so she can't read the red blur that is the digital clock across the room. "Guess what she said?" he asks, and there is something simultaneously eager and cautious in the question.

"What?"

"Liesel says she's sending Idzia here. She says we're taking her for the rest of the summer."

"Oh, my God." Daniella sits up then says it again. "Oh, my God! Joel!" Idzia is Joel's seventeen-year-old daughter. Joel has never seen her, not once and not for lack of trying. "She's . . ."

But before Daniella can formulate her question, Joel says, "She's coming next Friday. Flying into Boston. Liesel's already bought a ticket."

"God," Daniella says, trying to absorb this information. "Well, wait. Why now? What did she say?"

"She doesn't say. She just says she's coming."

"What are you going to do?"

"I'm not going to let her go back. That's what I'm going to do. She gets here, and I'm going to keep her here, save her from that lunatic."

Daniella doesn't think he's serious, but she's not sure. He can't take Idzia from Liesel, of course, and even if he could, the girl is grown now. Still there is a small part of her that warms to the idea, that thinks, "A second child!" Daniella miscarried before she had Ben, then several times after. Uterine cancer a year ago and the ensuing surgery seem to have sealed Ben's fate as an only child. Daniella thinks about adoption but Joel is set against it, convinced they'll end up with a child with all sorts of problems.

It is the Sunday of Fourth of July weekend. In a few hours, Daniella and

Joel will get up and shop for the gathering they've planned. "So . . . *this* Friday," Daniella says, trying to piece together what must happen now. "Can you cancel your patients?"

"I'll have to. I can't send you to pick her up."

"No," Daniella admits, though she wouldn't mind.

Joel is always in surgery on Fridays, so she wonders how he will pull this off. There is so much to think through. If Idzia is going to be here for the summer, what will she do? Joel is at work all day, Daniella half days, and they can't just leave Idzia home with nothing to do but feed their four chickens.

"You don't even . . . How will you recognize her?" Daniella asks.

"That's what I said to Liesel. I said, 'Will I have to hold up her name? Like I'm just her taxi and not her father?' And you know what Liesel said, that crazy bitch, you know what she said? She said, 'You'll recognize her all right. She's a little monster.'"

"No!"

Joel nods.

"That must be it, then. They're not getting along, so that's why she's sending her."

Joel shrugs.

"She might be a good mother." Even as Daniella says this, she realizes she has a vested interest in Liesel *not* being a good mother, in the possibility of being the fairy stepmother, that oxymoron, someone who will rescue Idzia from the horrors of her life, though she has always imagined Idzia's life as less horrible than peripatetic, perhaps appealing for not being staid.

"I better get some sleep," Joel says now, and Daniella signals her agreement by pulling up the covers.

She has just started to fall asleep again when she hears Joel say, "What are we going to tell Ben?"

THERE SHOULD BE a simple answer, and the simple answer should be: the truth. But what exactly is the truth? The plain fact is that by the time Joel married Daniella, Liesel no longer felt like a previous wife. Not after all that happened. After all that happened, she just felt like a nightmare girlfriend. The nightmare girlfriend with the baby, though it initially occurred to Joel that Liesel could be lying, that there might be no baby.

Why, after all, should there be? He'd heard not a word till, five years after she left, Liesel called to ask for money. And by then there was no baby but a child, a child whom he wanted to see.

"No," Liesel had said. "That can't happen."

"What do you mean that can't happen?"

"Idzia is mine."

"Uh," Joel had said. "Sounds like you're telling me she's mine, too."

Was Liesel afraid he would try to take the child, use Liesel's eccentric past against her? He didn't know, but he wasn't going to send money to support a child whom he couldn't meet.

So Liesel tried to divorce Joel in France, even though they already *were* divorced. The whole thing never made sense to Joel, but she somehow succeeded. She and the French courts agreed on a settlement, which he didn't honor, so now he was a criminal in France. "What are you going to do?" Daniella had said as all these legal machinations were going on. They'd been given to understand that Joel could be arrested if he went to France. "Not go to France, that's what I'm going to do," he said. After all, he had a legal divorce in America. She could hop around the world and become a citizen of whatever country and divorce him for sport, if she wanted. He didn't care, though he could imagine Liesel, in animated mode at a party, saying, "Finally, a reason for foreign travel!" And when he pictured her like that, making fun of herself, eager to entertain others, he could almost imagine loving her again. Almost. But not quite.

IT IS DANIELLA'S IDEA to go to a child therapist for advice, and Joel livens at the suggestion. *Yes, someone else will decide what to do.* The only time he's been in therapy was for his "crackup"—though only he calls it that—after his marriage to Liesel ended. Part of him thinks therapy is bullshit, but there's a bigger part that respects those with credentials.

Making an appointment on short notice turns out to be no small feat. At their Fourth of July party, Daniella and Joel secure a few names of child therapists. Most of their friends are surprised to learn that Daniella is Joel's second wife, Ben his second child. Predictably they act surprised at the novelty of the situation. *God,* they say. Or *I can't imagine.* Joel's sister, Amy, up from Boston for the party, manages to land in most conversations where Liesel and Idzia are discussed. She confirms Joel's opinion of his former wife as insane. "God, he'd be miserable if he'd stayed married to her," she says. This is true, Joel knows. All the more so because Joel *would* have stayed married. He is the fiercely loyal type. He would never leave a woman to whom he'd promised himself, even if he found himself unhappy as the years wore on. "Thank God for Daniella," Amy repeats to Joel's friends. It has been Joel's family's refrain through the years. In getting divorced, he'd dodged a bullet and won a woman far lovelier and smarter than Liesel.

July 4 is a Monday. On Tuesday morning, while Joel is at the hospital and Ben at camp, Daniella calls around for a therapy appointment. In the end, there is only one therapist who has an available slot, and that only at 5:30 p.m. on the 6th, which won't work. Daniella and Joel will have Ben with them then, never having found a reliable babysitter and not quite having the kind of friends, despite their many years in Maine, with whom you can drop off a child for a few hours. Joel will have to go alone.

ON WEDNESDAY JOEL FINDS himself in a windowless waiting room in a building on Commercial Street, the road that runs along the bay in Portland. Later, Daniella and Ben are going to drive the twenty minutes from home and meet Joel for pizza at Flatbread, a harborside restaurant with views of fireboats, a big plus for Ben. Also in the waiting room is a father, bland and defeated as any career insurance man, sitting next to a boy dressed in black, a heavy silver chain hanging from a hidden loop on his pants. The boy has done himself up in whiteface, then painted black triangles under his eyes and purple lines bisecting his cheeks. Ziggy Stardust on a smooth-cheeked adolescent face, still pudgy with childhood fat. What if Joel's daughter is the female version of this child? Multiply pierced, earlobes distended with studs, furious and ready to believe Liesel's version of what happened? *How could you abandon me?* she'll want to know, when it was Liesel who did the abandoning. He has asked Liesel for a picture. He has asked many times over the years, but also two days ago, so he'll be able to recognize Idzia at the airport, but Liesel hasn't sent one. She just says, "You'll know. You'll know." She sounds more weary than angry when she speaks. And Idzia, Joel thinks. Isn't she terrified? Flying to America to meet a man whom she knows only as the person who pays so little child support? Joel knows this is how Liesel has represented him. She says in her spiteful late-night voice, "She knows. She knows who you are."

Just the thought of explaining who he is to the therapist already feels exhausting, because under what circumstances does Joel not sound like a bad guy? Well, the true circumstances, Joel wants to answer himself, but even so. He knows he appears the *schtoonk*. The few times he has told people about his first marriage and his invisible child, they have asked questions that suggest he has not behaved as he should, that he should have fought harder for his daughter, got on a plane, flown over, risked arrest and insisted. But insisted what? He couldn't kidnap the girl.

THE MIDDLE-AGED WOMAN who ushers him into her office is far kinder than Joel is expecting. Her name is Sally, and she wears the bright-colored, oversized clothing that Joel associates with the morbidly obese, though she is quite slim, her manner mild in contrast to the exuberance of the clothes. Her skin is pale and papery, a face passing out of middle to old age, where wisdom (Joel hopes) resides. He tells his story and then leaves her with his question: "What should we tell Ben?"

"Huh," the woman says, chin in hand, but not out of hesitation. She smiles and tilts her head and starts to speak, but Joel says, "The one thing I haven't said is he just . . . he's . . ." Still quite sensitive, he wants to say.

"Tell Ben that Idzia is a friend. Don't say she's a half sister—"

"But . . ." Joel starts to interrupt with the perhaps obvious observation that this will be a lie.

"No, no," Sally says, holding up her hand. "That way, if she doesn't come back after the summer, he won't be disappointed."

Sally speaks with such confidence that Joel is reassured, although there is part of him that can't believe she would say this. Is she a crackpot, too? Still, perhaps the truth isn't as important as protecting people. In his line of work—"I'm afraid you have prostate cancer"—truth and protection have generally been the same. You can't act to help yourself if you don't know what you have. But it is true that sometimes—"I am afraid you have stage 4 kidney cancer"—there is no way to help oneself, and it is unclear what protection might be.

"But Idzia will be offended, of course, if I ask her not to tell. Insult to injury and all that."

"That's true," Sally says, as if only just considering this.

Maybe he will tell Ben that Idzia is "a sister from a long time ago." That has an almost fairy-tale feel, as if she's a special treat rather than a dark secret. "Maybe that will satisfy?" he asks Sally.

"Maybe," she allows.

"You know," he says, no effort to keep the edge out of his voice, "if I knew what to do, I wouldn't have come here."

"Well," she says mildly, "really you have to figure out what you most want."

"What I want," he says, "is to do the least harm, and I want you to tell me what that might consist of."

"Oh," she says, again evenly, apparently practiced in the art of disappointing. "I can't do that."

And so the session ends. A complete waste of money and, what Joel cares about more, an hour of his life. Still, there is just enough time before dinner for Joel to go back to his office and check his email and take one last look at whatever files are left on his desk. His practice, urologic surgery, is in a two-story brick building just down the street from Maine Med. The building was built in the 1970s, and "It looks it," Daniella always says, unhappy as she is about the wall-to-wall carpet and wood paneling. Joel doesn't really care how dated things look, since the office has what he most wants: a short walk to the operating room.

Once Joel gets to his desk, he finds an email from an unknown address: station4@uclh.nhs.uk. He doesn't open it, of course—no need to court a computer virus—but then he notices the subject line, which reads, "This is Idzia." So he clicks, and there she is. His daughter.

WHAT CAN YOU TELL from a photograph? That she is a girl with a round face and straight, thin hair pulled back into a loose ponytail. That she is smiling, squinting skeptically, and holding up a small kitten to the camera, as if it is the kitten, and not she, who is the point of the photograph. *It is a joke,* she seems to be saying, *this displaying of oneself for the camera.* She appears to be sitting on a bench, perhaps in a city park, and she is wearing jeans and a scoop-neck T-shirt with some sort of unzipped sweatshirt over it. He has the urge, as he examines the photo, to pull the sweatshirt closed, to neaten her up. The T-shirt dips low, her cleavage—she is curvy like Liesel— clearly visible. Her clothes look comfortable, and he can discern no jewelry or rings, nothing that would suggest she made an effort for the picture. She seems older than seventeen. Not grown by any means, but no youngster. Not a high school girl any longer. Definitely ready for university, though he has no idea if she *will* attend university come fall. He expects there is something planned—a job if not school. Otherwise why would Idzia's return date be set so firmly for the end of the summer?

He can't even begin to guess what sort of girl she might be.

The email has a one-word signature: "Bertie." Joel flashes on a youthful Dick Van Dyke playing Bert. That was the name, wasn't it? Of the chimney-sweep in *Mary Poppins?* Why would Liesel get someone else to send the picture? And who is Bertie anyway? Her boyfriend, presumably. Her boyfriend with an email account, which Liesel uses because she doesn't have one herself? That would be like her: acquiring someone to help out. So why does he feel so jealous? After all this time? Shouldn't he be thinking, "Poor sap. He's stuck with her now." Only he doesn't feel that way. He knows what it is like to care for Liesel. He knows what it is like to love her. It was her leaving that he didn't like. It was only the way she was *after* that he hated.

He calls Daniella, who must already be in her car, because she doesn't pick up, a precaution they have agreed on. And he's glad, actually, that she doesn't answer, because he needs some time to think. How much does Idzia know about where she is going? Will Liesel describe the farm as she remembers it? And what will Liesel remember? Her five months in Maine took her from late November into April, not exactly the state's best months, and it had been a winter with so much snow, the house always cold, the renovations (the new windows, the insulation, the kitchen) all in the future.

Does Idzia even want to meet him?

Yes, yes, Joel supposes—people search out their parents. Adopted children find their biological parents. They need to know.

He looks back at the screen, slides the photo to his desktop, then prints it so he can show Daniella at dinner. He emails back, "Got the picture. Thanks." There are two other emails that Joel has to answer then delete-delete-delete. He gets rid of all the messages. He likes an empty "Inbox." Nothing more on his "to do" list.

What would he say if someone asked him what Idzia looks like?

The truth, of course. The unpainful truth. He'd say exactly what he believes. She's beautiful.

PULLING OUT OF THE DRIVEWAY on Thursday afternoon, Joel starts a CD. He is always listening either to an audiobook or NPR. He isn't comfortable with silence. Back in medical school, he'd wake and immediately turn on the apartment's TV and dress in front of it, not something that seemed weird till his roommate commented on it. When Ben was a baby, Joel would push him on the swing while chatting on his cell. "Just multitasking," he'd shrug when Daniella caught him at it.

After fifteen minutes, Joel ejects his audiobook, an exposé of the food industry that is basically just making him want to puke whenever he eats chicken so maybe he's had enough of the book anyway. It doesn't seem that he should be "entertaining" himself while on the way to meet his daughter for the first time. But as he pulls onto I-95, he can't quite figure out what to do. He turns on the radio, but it is that afternoon program that plays snooze-inducing oldies, the one with the host with the unbearably whiny voice. He snaps the radio off and starts to run ridiculous conversations through his head.

"Idzia, you can ask me anything you need to ask . . ."

"Idzia, I want you to know that I have always loved you . . ."

"Idzia, your mother and I . . ."

"So, Idzia, what kind of music do you like?"

And then he wants to scream. There is no part of him that can even begin to imagine what the next twenty-four hours will be like.

Perhaps the hours will simply fail to unfold? He has had this thought before when unable to imagine the future. When he was ten, his parents had taken him and his sister to Puerto Rico. The idea of it had seemed so fantastic at the time that he assumed the plane would have to crash on the way. Picturing a hellish accident was somehow easier than imagining himself in such a different place.

"I wonder what she's like," Daniella had said once, many years ago, after a late-night phone call.

"What she's like? Liesel's a bitch." But that wasn't quite true. She was more crazy than bitchy.

"No, no," Daniella had said. "Your daughter."

He *didn't* wonder what she was like. Or he'd stopped wondering. At the time, his daughter would have been eleven, and Ben not yet one. Joel was documenting his son's life with a vigilance that even Daniella thought a bit much.

But Ben is Joel's son, and there has been nothing to disrupt their bond. Joel was the first to hold him, as they sewed Daniella up after the C-section, and Joel has been there for Ben every day since. Liesel called five years after Idzia was born. She announced Idzia's existence and at the same time denied him any right to participate in that existence. She might as well have called and said, "Here's this creature. I made her. She's entirely made of my influence and ideas, but you pay for her, you horrible man."

"When you break that bond," Joel once said to Daniella but then shook his head. He couldn't put words to it. Maybe there should be something there, but there wasn't. He'd had sex with Liesel, OK. No denying that. But he hadn't made a child with her. She hadn't let him make a child with her.

OUTSIDE BOSTON, the skyline eventually emerges from the gray haze. Joel has plenty of friends in the area from his med school days, but he won't call them on this trip. He doesn't want to chat about what's going on. The

Fourth of July party was bad enough. His plan is to stay the night at the Charles Hotel then drive out to Logan in the morning.

Once he checks in, he finds a lounge-type bar. It is not the sort of place he tends to like, with its gray barrel chairs, low lights, and piano playing softly in the background—too much enforced relaxation—but it is more or less empty, and the other restaurants he checks out are too fancy, too much of an occasion. He wants a quick meal and a chance to concentrate on the *New York Times*.

He feels dispirited, thinks of calling Daniella. He looks about the lounge, then begins to turn his attention to the paper when he realizes that he has been here before. In med school, before he met Liesel. Some jazz singer was performing that night. He can see her now: blond, heavy, dressed in a too-sexy outfit and ending each song with a belt-it shriek that always drew applause, though it just sounded showy and unpleasant to Joel. He'd been here on a blind date; embarrassingly, he was doing classified ads in the back of the *Phoenix* in those days. He only managed three meetings with strangers before he gave the idea up. He can't remember now how his date that night had described herself, only that she was friendly, pretty with a delicate face and shiny brown hair, but also heavy. She had the kind of fat that hadn't gone to her face but still made her seem like a hardy German butcher. It was she who had suggested the performance.

Joel didn't appeal to women. Not back then. There wasn't a woman in Joel's medical-school class who'd deign to look at him, as best as he could tell. The cliché was that doctors received no shortage of attention from nurses, but that had not proven to be Joel's experience. For some reason, everything changed after Liesel left. He dated several women and was used to nervous "Call me?" requests at the end of evenings. And all these women were nice, too. Attractive. It was all so easy. It was surreal. "I should have gotten divorced when I was seventeen," he told buddies. "Maybe then I'd have had a date for the prom."

"You've grown into your face," his sister said, as if that explained his good luck. "The nerdy Jewish look and cheese . . . you know, they both need a little aging to achieve their full potential."

As much as he liked the women he dated—he found himself giving advice to the ones in their twenties and registering the ticking biological clock of those in their thirties—he knew Daniella was the one the moment he met her.

Joel is glad now that he has not booked two rooms for tomorrow night. Yesterday, he had thought perhaps Idzia would like to see Boston, but he does not want to spend another night here. He will stick with his original plan, which was to drive straight back to Maine from Logan. There is only so much of his past he wants to confront in one week. Or perhaps that's not what he's feeling. Perhaps it's that proximity to the places where he once felt like such a failure will be transmogrifying. He'll be back to who he once was. A man unlucky in love.

WHEN JOEL CALLS from the airport to say he has Idzia, and is on his way home, Daniella says, "So, what's she—"

"*You* know," Joel says.

"Can't talk right now?"

"That's right but . . ." his voice lowers. Daniella senses his turning away from the girl, leaning his chin down and pressing his lips to the cell phone.

"Yes?"

"I don't know," he says, voice hushed into near inaudibility. "You'll just have to see."

Oh, Daniella is a child of her generation, as who is not? Ever ready with a therapeutic pop lyric to help her understand the events of the moment, then ready to critique her own shallowness. Is there nothing more going on in her head than the Rolling Stones? Apparently not, for while she waits for Joel to return with the girl, she sings (in her head, her inner voice perfect, her outer reliably out of tune), "You can't always get what you wa-aaant. You can't always get what you wa-aant." The drive north will help, she is sure: a chance for them to make an initial stab at getting to know each other.

"HI," JOEL CALLS from the side door. "We're here."

Daniella heads to the kitchen, with Ben close behind her. She isn't expecting to be shocked; she specializes in inner calm. But she can't help but be taken aback.

Liesel may be crazy, but she hasn't lied. Idzia is a little monster. She has four fangs, which stick out over her lower lip, and she looks a bit like a teddy bear, sans fur. Her skin is a bright green, and there are three small nubs—like minute goat horns—on the sides and back of her head. It's definitely a shock, yet Idzia looks oddly familiar. Daniella smiles, then hits on it. The girl looks like one of Ben's Ugli dolls, big-eyed and smiley, despite the unlikely color and decided misshapenness of her form. For a monster, in other words, she's awfully cute.

"Well, hello there. We're so glad you are here," Daniella offers.

Idzia says nothing, but waddles in. Her feet seem attached to her torso penguin-style, without the benefit of legs.

Though they have had the talk that the therapist recommended, Ben darts out from behind his mother and embraces Idzia. "My sister!" he cries and pats the green dome of her head, as if he has just been presented with the best stuffed animal ever.

Idzia puts her short arms around Ben and growls.

"Turns out her English is a little rough," Joel says.

Daniella wakes on these words—"little rough"—takes some time to realize she's had a ridiculous dream. That she who for so long has wanted another child has been gifted with a monster child. *Well, thanks, subconscious!* she thinks. *Always ready to upset!* She's alone in her bed. Joel's in Boston, probably driving to Logan now to pick up Idzia.

DESPITE HIS RESISTANCE to the idea, Joel has made a sign that says "Idzia." Around the large Magic Markered letters he'd printed on a shirt cardboard from the cleaners, Ben has drawn small stick figures. They are climbing up the letters of her name and rendered in pencil, so not dark enough to obscure the basic intent of the message: *Idzia, come over here.* Still, Joel is vaguely hoping he won't have to use his sign as he waits for Idzia in baggage claim, that it will be apparent who she is. He misses the old days, when you could actually go to the gate and see people disembark. Then, it was easier to sort out who was who. To the degree he has imagined their greeting, Joel has pictured Idzia coming up to him at the baggage claim and shyly saying, "Dad?" and then the two of them embracing, before she goes to grab a large bag from the carousel, and he waves her away: *No, no, I will take care of that.*

But when Joel gets to the airport the next day, he realizes that his fantasy is entirely unrealistic. It's an international flight, after all. As such, he must wait behind a hip-high gate in front of a white wall with a single door, through which will come people who have passed through customs, weary from having submitted themselves for approval, ready for relief but emerging, slack-faced, into the clamorous terminal. The hassles of a taxicab and Boston traffic still await them. "No entry," the sign above the exit reads, as if the foreign country isn't across the ocean, but behind the door.

There are perhaps thirty people already massed at the gate when Joel arrives. He has no idea if they are waiting for people from the same plane or from different international flights. He overhears British accents, then French. He catches a few words of Hebrew, sees a few women in headscarves. Slowly everyone seems to find his or her parties and depart until he is one of only four people standing by the exit. No one else emerges. Has he made a mistake? Arrived on the wrong day? But he knows he hasn't. Idzia was to fly from Heathrow to Toronto, then Toronto to Boston.

Joel goes upstairs to the Air Canada counter.

"Hmm," the clerk says, pressing her lips tightly together, as if in regret, "I'm just not seeing that name here." Joel insists she must be wrong, but she shakes her head no. Joel tries Lufthansa, the airline for the first leg of Idzia's flight, but the news there is the same.

Joel pulls his cell phone out and looks at it as if it will tell him what to do.

He wants to call England, but his cell plan won't cover that. And even if he could, Liesel wouldn't be able to reach Idzia. She has no cell phone, as Liesel informed Joel last week, when making the arrangements for today. Still he'd given Liesel *his* number to give to Idzia. If there was a mix-up, Idzia could always go to a pay phone and call collect. So why hasn't Idzia called?

He guesses the next step is to call Liesel and see what she knows, but he doesn't have her number. Why would he? It's true he might have thought ahead to Idzia's return flight, when he would have to reach his ex, but of course he wouldn't need Liesel's number then. Idzia would know it.

Instead he phones home and says, "Small problem here." He know that Daniella can't just check their phone to get Idzia's number: "Unknown caller," after all. And with these new digital plans, the bills no longer list every number called, as in the old days. But maybe there's a way to do this through their carrier.

"I'll try," Daniella says. "Maybe they won't give us the number but will ring through anyway."

"OK," he says hesitantly. He doesn't imagine the phone company can or will do this.

"And maybe there's a White Pages for London. I'll call and see what I can find out and call you back."

"Well, we're *hoping* it's London. I mean . . ." *Jesus,* he breathes. He doesn't even know where Liesel lives. He has assumed she was in London, because she lived there once and because that's where the flight is from. Well, that, and because when he asked Liesel if Idzia spoke English, she'd said, "Of course. What do you think?" What he thought was that having been born in France, Idzia might only speak French. And then where would he be? Only able to speak in tourist phrases to his own daughter. "She's a British citizen," Liesel said, and Joel wondered how she'd pulled that off. Had Liesel married a Brit?

"How would I know what she can and cannot speak?" Joel had said. "You've never actually let me talk to her, remember?" He was yelling, but he didn't care.

Joel looks for a place to sit. There is a dearth of benches in this terminal, a giant space in which no one is encouraged to linger. What can he do? He can't leave, for what will Idzia do if she arrives and no one is here? Perhaps she is just on the next flight? His cell rings. It is Daniella, but she is only calling to say that the phone company says they have no way of locating the number. "They can put a trace on the phone. But that's if she calls again. Then we press star fifty-seven. The police have to trace it three times before they can—"

"What does this have to do with our present situation, may I ask?"

"Well, nothing, I guess," Daniella says. "It's just they told me—"

"Nothing of any use," Joel says, finishing her sentence. He is older than Daniella by ten years, and at times like this he feels the difference in their ages. Isn't it obvious that putting a trace on phone calls in the future isn't going to do anything for them now?

Daniella is silent.

"OK, OK," he says. "Well, I have no fucking idea what I'm going to do. I guess I'll just stick around here waiting for a bright idea."

Joel hangs up and goes back to Lufthansa and Air Canada to see if Idzia might be on a different flight. He has already asked this, but he finds a different clerk at each counter and asks again. *If the data doesn't fit the theory, the data must be changed!* he and his med school roommate used to joke in lab. Now that's the phrase that goes through his head: *The data must be changed!* But the new clerks refuse to change the data.

Then it occurs to him: she might have come in on a different airline. He goes to the Delta counter to see if they have any record of Idzia. Perhaps she is flying through Zurich?

Nothing.

Joel walks back to the customs door and waits till travelers start to spill through. Then he starts. There she is! A young woman with brown hair tied into a ponytail. Droop-shouldered, which didn't show in the photo, and sad-faced, she comes through the door, rolling a small suitcase behind her. But then a man rushes toward her and folds her in his arms, and Joel sees that she is no teenager but a woman in her thirties.

And thus begins his frantic period, but it is a frantic period in which he does nothing but wait, an activity that requires patience, the very trait he does not have. He can't leave the airport, for what if she arrives? But there is no evidence that she will show up. There are two more flights from Toronto today. She is not booked on either. Ditto the flights through Zurich. But maybe she is traveling under another name? He finds a bench to sit on but returns to the door each time people start to stream through. There is a whirligig Rube Goldberg–type machine in a large glass case by the arrivals door, and its bells and twangs have gone from charming—something Joel would enjoy showing Ben—to irritating. He starts to write this episode in his head, as if he is a character in his own novel. *He stands hopefully by the door,* he recites to himself, but he is not hopeful. He is bewildered, panicked. If there had been a plane crash, wouldn't he know, even though there are no TV monitors in the terminal? Where might she be? But then his panic starts to give way to a strong suspicion. Could Liesel have done this just to mess with him?

It is his turn, he imagines, for furious, untimely phone calls. If only he had Liesel's number. But he doesn't, so the call that he makes is to the Charles Hotel. He'd like a room for another night.

He comes back in the morning. But Idzia doesn't arrive the next day, and he sees he has no choice but to go home.

THAT SUNDAY EVENING, he stands in the kitchen, looks out through the back window past the fields. To the right, Daniella and he have a small stand of apple trees. The fields themselves end in woods, where there are trails that lead back into the water district. How Liesel hated this when she was here. "Too much white," she'd complained, and of course the winter could wear on anyone, even someone like him who loves to cross-country ski, who sees the white as an excuse to get out and explore, rather than a terrible trap.

What could be going on in Liesel's head? Why is she doing this to him? Has she completely snapped? Sometimes he tries to figure her out from a clinical perspective. He's always told Daniella that Liesel has a personality disorder, but he doesn't really know if that explains her. She's not quite a sociopath, but she's got that peculiar mix of charm (for she did have that, back in the day) and self-serving behavior. But even as he wonders what she could be thinking, he feels furious. He shouldn't have to deal with her anymore. She is a mistake, a nineteen-year-old mistake, and she should move on with things. He has.

MORE AND MORE, JOEL BELIEVES that Liesel's planned it, that she's planned it all—their anxiety, Daniella's newly acquired insomnia, all of it sprung from the botched visit from Idzia. But Daniella doesn't agree. She doesn't think women work quite that way, that they have nefarious motives. More like emotions they can't conquer. ("That is ridiculous," Joel says when she tells him this.) Still it is true that Daniella wakes often at night now, and not to the ringing phone but to her own bad dreams or nattering thoughts. The nightmares are garden-variety anxiety—she needs to return to college, for she is four credits short for graduation; her son has eaten a walnut-laden coffee cake, though he is allergic to nuts—and her hectoring thoughts are almost always about a project at work, a mistake she has made. But once fully awake, Daniella's mind drifts away from the concern that woke her and over to Liesel and Idzia.

In the days after Joel's trip, Daniella pictured Idzia wandering about the international terminal at Logan, unable to escape. For some reason, Daniella imagines the terminal as being like the Boston subway, where you supposedly once had to pay a toll upon leaving. Idzia, with no American currency, no way to pay, never finds a way out of the airport. Actually Daniella doesn't know if the subway ever really had an exit fare, but still she finds herself humming "Charlie on the M.T.A.," a tune about a man unable to get off the subway because he doesn't have the required nickel. Daniella doesn't mean to sing the song, of course. It's more like the song gets into her head the way Ben's do. She can spend half her day drafting while "Birdhouse in Your Soul," a song she once liked, plays nonstop, the melody seeming only to signal the very emptiness of her own brain. Daniella sings the Charlie ditty, but with the pronouns changed for Idzia: "Did she ever return? No, she never returned, and her fate is still unlearn'd." It bothers Daniella when she catches these lyrics in her head. It's not a joke, after all.

It's not a joke.

But it is the truth. All the more the truth because Daniella and Joel never hear from Liesel and Idzia again. It's not just that the days pass from July into August, with no Idzia arriving. It's that the phone calls stop. They stop altogether.

ALL THIS HAPPENED in the summer of 2005, when Ben was six.

He turns seven, then eight. The years pass: 2006, 2007. Time moves forward, and still no Idzia. Liesel doesn't call to yell. She doesn't demand money. Joel thinks of trying to track her down through her bank account, only his bank no longer deposits money in Liesel's account. Not since Idzia turned eighteen. Through the years, it has been a small amount—just $300 a month—a figure that surprised Daniella when she learned of it. Not more? It was so very little to contribute to one's child. Joel had shaken his head, irritated, when she first broached the matter. *Not more.* Not more without visits.

Back in 2005, Daniella made Joel try with the banks nonetheless. But he got nowhere. Couldn't the bank just contact the owner of the account for them Joel had asked? Not give them the contact information, but just send a message to the account owner? It was a matter of great urgency. But no, the bank insisted. No, they could not. And then the bank finally admitted that they had no such account active. Well, was it closed out? Joel had asked, but the bank wouldn't answer. A clue, Daniella thought, but to what?

Joel remembers that when he received the picture of Idzia, he dragged the photo onto his desktop, then deleted the email. He hadn't thought he'd need it later, that he'd become an obsessive cybersleuth, Googling "Liesel Pearlman" and "Idzia Pearlman" at intervals throughout the years, always finding nothing. Who has no digital thumbprint, in this day and age? Only people who don't exist. But Liesel, he knows, is all too real.

2008, 2009, 2010, 2011.

Then in fall 2011, the phone rings in the middle of the night. "Yes?" Daniella says, worried.

"Grandma," the female voice says on the other end. "I'm in a lot of trouble. I'm in Canada, and I got arrested. I had some . . .," the voice hesitates, "drugs, but it was just marijuana, and they say they'll let me off, but I have to give them five hundred bucks—"

"Hello," Joel says, having gone downstairs and picked up the other line. "Liesel?" Joel says. "Idzia?" The voice continues. "The policeman says he'll explain." Then a male voice joins the conversation, reassuring, saying, "It's OK. It's OK. Your granddaughter won't have a record, but we do need to get that five hundred dollars wired here . . ."

"Who is this?" Joel says, angry.

"It's me, Grandpa," the voice says, and Joel says to Daniella, "Hang up, Daniella. It's a scam."

"What?" she says through the phone, but he has already hung up downstairs and is now calling up the stairs to her, his voice harsh: "Put the phone down, put the phone down." It is a con, he explains. He actually knows someone at work with adult grandchildren who fell for it.

"Maybe . . ." Daniella begins, but realizes she is being ridiculous. Idzia would not call Daniella Grandma. She would not call her own father Grandpa. She feels relieved. There was something, she sees now, in the slur of the voice that suggested not the stepchild Daniella would have liked but a petty crook, someone you couldn't leave alone in the house because she'd slip bills out of wallets, loot the jewelry box. The voice on the end of the line portended bad experiences ahead.

2012. And still no word.

Daniella will never tell Joel, but Idzia has come to seem to her like all those children she never had during the years she was miscarrying. She got the child she wanted when she had Ben, so that first miscarriage no longer pained her, but the ones after Ben *did* still hurt, especially the baby who was a girl, whose heart Daniella had heard beating through the stethoscope. This was the pregnancy that wasn't just a "blighted ovum," as they called a fetus that failed to develop. With a blighted ovum, you didn't really lose a child but a hope. But with the girl whose heart she had heard beating, there had been an actual small being, who had then died. (Daniella still can't figure out why the nurse chose to tell her the sex of the child after it was gone.) At the time, Daniella had been so violently ill with morning sickness that when she realized her pregnancy wasn't going to continue, she'd felt momentarily relieved. No more vomiting. But later she kept remembering that heartbeat. It is that possibility of a girl, at any rate, that Daniella thinks of late at night, when she wonders, *Where is she? Where is Idzia?*

2

LITTLE WORLD

IDZIA PRESSES ONE of the tiny desks onto the small stage then turns for a toothpick to remove the glue leaking from under a desk leg. "Shall I just get us the chicken-lentil from Marks & Spencer then?" she asks her mother.

Liesel makes a gacking sound.

"What?" Idzia asks. "I thought you liked that one."

"Ack," her mother says and drops a tiny office worker onto the dining room table. The worker joins eight other miniature men, all waiting to have their wee bums affixed to wee chairs.

"What about the red curry? That's not too many calories." Not that Idzia thinks her mother should give a fuck about calories. She's enormous all right, but it's not from eating. It's from steroids. Yesterday's breakfast, lunch, and dinner consisted of a single container of yogurt. It's a brilliant idea for world hunger. You don't eat, and you just get bigger.

Liesel accidentally brushes the man she has dropped to the floor.

"Hey," Idzia says as she stands to go into the bedroom. "Careful."

The miniature office workers are for Idzia's toy theater. Ditto the small desks. It never occurred to Idzia to make a toy theater till her friend Katie told her about a contest being run by "The Ministers of Mini-Marvels."

"The mini-who?" Idzia had said when Katie first mentioned it, and Katie had shrugged. Who cared who they were? The rest was what mattered. Grant Gallery. Juried exhibition. Toy theaters. Dimensions: 40 × 60 centimeters. Deadline: July 6.

"Big time," Idzia said. The Grant Gallery was in the East End.

Later, Katie leaned over Idzia, her breasts brushing Idzia's back, as the two did an Internet search to figure out a few things. The Ministers were a guerrilla art group, responsible for happenings all over the city. Their motto? "We're not truly marvelous but then neither are you."

"Sod off," Katie said when she read that out loud. She didn't like that sort of attitude. Roundabout snooty. They might not be marvelous, the Ministers, but they had connections. It would be amazing to have something shown at the Grant.

Normally, Katie needs to fill Idzia in on things, but when Katie, who is from Copenhagen, started to explain, in her funny Danish accent, the whole toy theater concept—how the theaters were just like real theaters in miniature, and how people like Jane Austen and Robert Louis Stevenson used to play with them—Idzia said, "Actually, I know. I know all about them."

Idzia had first seen *petites théâtres* in Paris. Her mother had pointed them out at the Musée d'Orsay, but Idzia had also seen one at her mother's friend's apartment. It was picnic basket–sized with sets and little figures that slid on and off the stage with wires.

Even though Katie's not from here, she's ferreted out London's oddball pleasures in her one year as a student better than Idzia's managed in the twelve years she and her mother have been here. Or have been here most of the time. There was that weird trip to Morocco, a stint in Geneva.

Idzia goes into her bedroom to get the nine one-inch computers that she assembled yesterday. It's not *actually* her bedroom, since Idzia and her mother are in Bertie's apartment, where they both have been staying since Liesel had to quit her job as house manager at the Fletcher. "*This* theater will do," Liesel had said earlier in the day, when Idzia asked when she'd last been by the Fletcher. It's a little strange now, sharing a bedroom with her mom, but they've been in close quarters most of their lives. Plus, it might not last long. Katie has a roommate who is thinking of moving out, and if she does, Idzia can move in. It's the life raft Idzia has been swimming to for years. Her own place, university.

Katie's making a toy theater, too. Hers isn't a stage set for a "real" play. Katie thinks that's what most contest participants will make. Mini *Macbeth.*

Itty bitty *Iolanthe*. Petite *Pygmalion*. Instead Katie's making a stage occupied by a large wishing pool with pretend coins. Katie's going to attach her computer to the theater and play audio of different people saying what they wish for: "I wish I could stop thinking about him"; "I wish you saw me for who I really am"; "I wish people wouldn't kill each other"; "I wish it was over"; "I wish I didn't hate everything that came out of my mouth"; "I wish we could go dancing"; "I wish I could slam my laptop down on top of his head." (These are really things that Katie has recorded!)

It seems so imaginative. Everything Katie does seems so imaginative, but for once Idzia likes her own idea better. She's making an office with nine desks, a 3 × 3 grid, and on each desk she's putting a computer, and on each chair there'll be a worker, and each worker is going to be diving headfirst into his computer screen.

"Because that's what we all are," she'd explained to Katie. "You know, being sucked headfirst into the stupid things."

Idzia feels this way. She can spend hours surfing the Web. She checks email constantly. What is she hoping for? Love, probably. Approval. *I saw your painting. It's fantastic!* This even though what paintings she has are stored underneath the bed she's sharing with her mother. Ditto her laptop, when it's not turned on.

Idzia finds a shoebox in the bottom of the bedroom closet and puts the mini-computers in it, slides the door closed. The outside of the door is a giant mirror, so Idzia can't help but confront herself—the blue bra sticking out from under her sleeveless T-shirt, the pants she's barely managed to button shut, all the red spots from where she's picked at her face. Disgusting. She lands one hard punch in her stomach, scrunches her face, and says, "You are so fucking fat." The worst of it is she's got her period, and all she wants to do is eat. Half the afternoon she's been having a debate with herself. Bag of salt-and-vinegar crisps: yes or no?

Walking into the hall that leads back to the dining room, Idzia calls, "We could split a red curry. If you don't want a whole one."

Liesel coughs again, campily, as if she's vomiting up a Marks & Spencer meal.

"OK already," says Idzia, as she rounds the corner into the living room, "we don't need to . . ." *To eat,* she is going to say, but her mother is *not* coughing campily. She isn't even coughing. She is making a strangling noise and slipping off her chair and onto the floor.

"Mum?"

Liesel's chair slides toward the wall. Her bottom hits the ground, and she lands on her back, wig several inches above her head like some renegade hat. Idzia sees all this, but she can't absorb it. A petulant child has tossed the doll of her mother across the room, and this is how she has landed, facing the ceiling, bereft of hair, with a puddle—a puddle?—forming on the floor below her.

"Mum!" Idzia cries. What is happening?

Her mother does not answer. Is she dead? But she can't be dead. She is moving, after all. She is shaking from side to side, as if someone is rattling the maraca of her body.

"999," Idzia says out loud. Then "999" again, as if she is in danger of forgetting the numbers if she doesn't repeat them as she runs for the phone. She presses the buttons hard, 9-9-9. *This is an emergency,* she thinks. *We are having an emergency.* Liesel's eyes open briefly, but only the whites show. Not doll, not maraca, but zombie. "Mum!" Idzia screams again and just then someone answers the line. "I need an ambulance," Idzia calls into the phone. "My mother is having a seizure." It is only when she says the word that Idzia knows, for sure, what is happening.

"What's going on?" her mother says, all of a sudden. She doesn't sound like herself. She's facing the ceiling, but her eyes are moving around in a way that suggests she's not seeing anything but scanning her body to figure out where it is and what it wants. She says in a monotone, "Call Bertie."

But Idzia is still on with emergency services. She is giving directions. "It's off Camden High Street. It's . . . God. God. What's the number here?"

"146," her mother says. "Call Bertie."

"146," she says and hangs up. "They're coming." *OK. OK,* she tells herself. She pats the air, as if it to say, *OK, everyone. I've got this under control.*

Her mother points at the dining room table. She does not appear able to get up. Idzia understands that the puddle underneath her mother is urine. "Her work number's there . . ."

"I called the ambulance," Idzia says. She has taken care of this, she means. She has done the right thing. Her mother does not need to turn to a "real" adult. Idzia *is* a real adult.

But her mother keeps saying "Bertie," so Idzia finds the number—it's on the inside of a date book her mother keeps in her purse—and calls. She tells the woman who answers that she needs to speak to Bertie Russell right away. It's an emergency.

It takes forever for Bertie to come to the phone. And as she waits, Idzia wonders things that she might have (but hasn't) wondered before. Like: Bertie Russell. As in Bertrand Russell. He was someone famous, but who? Not a Christian, that's all Idzia can remember. Some important person who wasn't a Christian. Didn't they think of that, Bertie's parents, when naming her? But then they wouldn't have named her Bertrand, of course, they would have named her Roberta, they would have named her . . .

"Hello?" Bertie's voice comes over the line, and Idzia explains, as best she can, what is happening.

"OK, Idzia," Bertie says evenly. "You did the right thing. When the paramedics get there, let them know to go to UCLH. If they want to take her to Royal Free, just explain that her doctors are here, and I'm here. Do you hear me?"

"I hear you." Though Idzia doesn't quite, not in a way that will allow her to retain the information. She finds a pen and writes "Royal Free" with an unhappy face and "UCLH" with a happy face.

It's not clear to Idzia how she and her mother get to the next step, how they get through the unimaginably long minutes of waiting for the ambulance. Do they talk? Do they worry out loud? Does Idzia chant *Don't die, Don't die, Don't die* in her head? Idzia has a strange brand of aphasia. In the very moment that the present slips into the past she forgets it. Disaster has turned her into a Buddhist. *For fuck's sake, I'm in the moment; I'm in the moment already. Will you leave my mother alone?* Whom is she addressing? God? The Buddha? Allah? She has not a clue. Eventually, the doorbell rings and Idzia buzzes in a man and a woman from the London Ambulance Service. The woman squats down to Liesel, takes a pulse, asks questions. "I've got cancer," her mother tells them. Then she starts to shake, though not in the way she was shaking before. Liesel is crying, or maybe she is only trying not to cry. And she is trying not to cry, Idzia understands, because Idzia is here. *Mum! You can cry!* But Idzia can't say that, she knows. If she says that, it will make things worse.

"I have cancer," her mother repeats. Idzia can't think of a time before today when her mother has actually said those words.

"But you're in remission," the male ambulance worker tells her, as if he can't bear to hear the bad news without something to leaven it.

"No," her mother says, and Idzia hates the man for making her mother announce the unhappy fact, for the way even *he* wants her to cheer him up about her diagnosis. *It's cancer. Spot of bother, not to worry.*

Idzia interrupts to say authoritatively, "It started as breast cancer, but now it's in her brain. They've done radiation." She means on the brain. "And chemo before." She feels something like pleasure at her no-nonsense recital of the facts. Isn't she a brave little match girl, so young and with a mother so ill? But it can't be that she would really think such a thing. Now, of all times.

Outside the apartment building, strangers turn and stare as her mother is carried out on a stretcher. Across the street, there's a man with a cello in a body bag. That can't be right—"body bag"—but Idzia can't think of the correct word. The man must be going to his lessons. There's a folk music school across the street from Bertie's place. How can he be going to his lessons? No one should go to lessons at a time like this. Pretty music? No, that will just have to be excised from the world for awhile. A dumbfounded girl in purple tights stands waiting for Liesel's stretcher to pass. Why doesn't she just walk around them? Why does the girl have to *stare* as if her mother is the traffic accident du jour?

There are two ambulances outside. Why would they have sent *two?* The way the paramedics slide Liesel into one of them makes Idzia think of a drawer at a morgue. *Oh, Mummy.* "Do I go in front?" Idzia asks the female paramedic, but for reasons that Idzia doesn't understand, the woman says that Idzia cannot accompany her mother but can sit in the back of the ambulance that *isn't* carrying Liesel. Idzia dutifully climbs in and takes a small seat that faces out the back of the ambulance. The worker puts her hand up, a salute of a good-bye, and closes the door. The sirens begin, and the ambulance lurches into the street.

As they bump along, Idzia starts to feel a bit carsick and then *really* carsick. She's never been good at riding backward, always makes sure she doesn't when she's on the Tube. She flushes with heat, puts her head down by her knees to stop the dizziness, but that only makes it worse. *Make it stop,* she thinks and then starts to cry. How can she be feeling for her own discomfort when who knows what is happening in the other ambulance?

At the hospital, orderlies take Liesel out of the ambulance and whisk her into Casualty, and then Bertie is there in her nurse's jacket and pants, walking toward Idzia in those spongy white shoes, her arms open for an embrace.

"Baby," Bertie says and hugs her tight, doesn't let go. She has cool skin, the very thing that you might suppose that a big, red-haired woman covered in freckles wouldn't have.

"I thought she was going to die," Idzia starts to sob. "I thought she was going to die."

"It's OK," Bertie says and pats her head. "It's OK."

THEY DON'T MAKE IDZIA sit in the waiting room but bring her right into the small Casualty bay where they have wheeled her mother. The doctor starts mentioning tests. There will be a CAT scan, and there will be something else. Idzia has no idea what he is talking about. Bertie nods and asks questions that also don't make sense. Will there be a something-something or a something-something? They've already got an IV going, and where the needle enters the back of her mother's hand, there is a trickle of blood that no one has bothered to wipe away. Liesel appears to be in a shallow sleep, so there is nothing for Idzia to do but stand next to the high bed with the railing and watch her doze.

Liesel's bald, but not completely. There are tufts of brownish hair that cling to parts of her head like patches of dirty chicken fluff. When she wasn't sick, Liesel had a thick curly mane that she tossed from shoulder to shoulder when she laughed. It was light brown with a hint of red, not Bertie's deep auburn. Idzia's own hair is thin and straight, mousy. Her mom's hair is an opera. Her own is a pointless haiku. Liesel hated the way she lost her hair. If she was going to have to lose it, she wanted to look as smooth and elegant as Patrick Stewart. She had seen him in *The Master Builder,* and when the chemo started, she announced her plans to be his understudy, pretending not to know that the show had already completed its run.

Liesel's eyes flutter open. "You go home now," she says.

"Are you crazy? Mum, I'm not going home."

"Do you know what she's doing?" Liesel starts to tell a nurse who is hanging a clipboard on the end of her bed. "She's entering a competition for . . ." but then she seems too exhausted to finish the thought. She reaches over, pats Idzia's hand, and whispers, "My good girl."

"My excellent mum," Idzia says back.

"Little monster," Liesel says, her eyes shutting.

"Horror show," Idzia responds. It's a joke going back who knows how far, the compliment followed by the affectionate putdown.

"I think they're going to give you a little something to help you rest," Bertie says, and as if on cue, a nurse comes in and sticks a needle into the tube that leads to the IV bag.

Bertie waves Idzia out and says, "She's right. You go. I'll be here."

"I don't want to go," Idzia says, hearing the slight whine in her voice. They are treating her like a child, but she is seventeen. She's not an idiot. She can handle this. And even if she couldn't handle this, how could things possibly be improved by returning home alone?

"I do need to go to the loo though," she allows. It is only as she says this that she realizes how badly she wants to pee. "They won't move her, will they?" She means before she gets back.

"No," Bertie says, and Idzia appreciates how together she always is. Her green eye makeup and lipstick never smudged, her hair twisted up and pinned behind her head, even her plump flesh feels sensible. She's big but shapely. She isn't spilling beyond her borders, as Idzia feels she is. She has packed her flesh efficiently into its container. "We'll be here awhile."

WHEN IDZIA PULLS her pants down in the bathroom, there is blood everywhere. Blood has soaked through her underwear. Blood coats the insides of her legs. Not just smeared up by her groin, but trickling down toward her anklebone. Like an idiot, she has forgotten to change her tampon. She has forgotten that she even has her period, and in the drama of the afternoon she has managed not to feel herself leaking. She takes off her pants—tan, of course, though most days she wears black—and there is a big stain on the behind.

"OK," she says aloud as she looks at the mess, though she doesn't know exactly what she's assenting to. She starts to weep. Somehow the blood feels like it belongs to her mother.

Idzia wets globs of toilet paper and starts to wash up. It feels like it takes forever, the blood swirling into the toilet bowl water, like some vampire version of the milk that her mother likes to watch swirl in her iced coffee. When she's done, she washes her face, puts her dirty pants back on, sticks her head out the bathroom door, waits for a nurse to walk by, and calls, "Pardon? Pardon?" She explains the situation and asks the nurse for some scrubs. A decent human being would get them for her, but this nurse just tells her to go up to the third floor and ask there. So out Idzia goes, damp bloodstain on her arse, and as she does, she passes a man carrying two plastic bags of blood in his arms, as if they're just these grisly schoolbooks he has to study later. Blood! It's all the rage here! The idea is to keep that stuff *inside,* she wants to remind the man. *In*side, not out. She feels her rising hysteria. *I think you've forgotten something!*

Idzia takes the lift to a third-floor ward, where she finds more nurses. She waits for them to look up from their work to receive her question, but they do not. They are aggressive in their failure to look up. They do not seem to be busy. One jots something in a notebook, another thumbs through papers, a third forks a piece of birthday cake into her mouth, and then finally, because there is really no delaying it any longer, a plump Indian woman lifts her head and says, "Yes?"

She fields Idzia's question without any generosity and sends her to the fourth floor. (Idzia pictures the career fair, twenty years in the past, one of these middle-aged women, still in her teens, walking by a table, fingering a pamphlet and thinking, "Well, I'm a bitch. Why don't I give nursing a go?")

On the fourth floor, a nurse (moderately pleasant, what's the deal?) directs Idzia down a long corridor. "The supply room's at the end," she says pointing. "See that open doorway down there?"

Idzia nods and heads toward it, passing under a sign that reads "Manseau Wing." To the right of the entry, a black guard with closely cropped hair sits behind a small desk.

"You can't come in here," the guard says in a lilting voice. He sounds Jamaican or maybe Bajan. Lively up yourself and all that. Only he has the serious manner of someone who has never lively upped anything.

"Is that where the supply room is?" Idzia asks.

"Yes, but you can't go there." He is friendly enough as he says this. Friendly yet aware of the rules.

"Are there scrubs in there?"

"There might be, but you can't go there." She heads down the corridor anyway. "I said you can't go there," he repeats, but Idzia keeps walking. No-bloody-body is going to tell her what to do. She hears the scrape of the guard's chair, as he stands, presumably to follow her, dangerous criminal that she is. The evidence being, of course, the stain on her bottom. She has been murdering people by sitting on their heads.

"Ma'am," he calls. "Ma'am."

Idzia picks up her pace, but he quickly catches up. Idzia senses him just behind her, resisting an urge to physically restrain her. At the end of the hall, the open door reveals a treasure trove—shelves of toilet paper, neatly stacked boxes of tissues, towers of paper cups. It almost makes her feel safe, the clean plenitude. Why not opt out of Bertie's altogether and make this her bedroom?

"Ma'am . . ."

"You leave me alone," she says to the guard without even turning her head. "My mother is dying. You don't tell me what to do."

"I'm sorry your mother is dying, but you still can't go there."

"I've got a problem," she says to a young, bespectacled, balding man standing just inside the entry to the supply room.

She cannot believe she has just said that her mother is dying. Her mother *isn't* dying. Her mother *can't* be dying. But she feels the power of the words. *My mother is dying, so I can do anything I want.* The guard starts to say something, but Idzia talks over him and says, "The nurse downstairs said you'd give me some scrubs. I've got blood all over me, and I need some scrubs." Perhaps she sounds psychotic. There is clearly not blood *all over her,* but the supply room man somehow seems to grasp the situation. He holds up his hand to the guard, says, "It's OK, man. Let it be," and the guard nods, appeased, and heads back down the hall.

"Thank you," Idzia says as the man hands her the scrubs, packed in plastic. "Thank you. Really." Just because she has been rude to the guard doesn't mean she is a rude girl.

In a bathroom by the supply room, Idzia changes and feels a momentary shame at her pleasure in the scrubs, their light cleanliness, the loose pants after her own dirty, too tight ones. All week long her clothes have been a punishment. She checks her watch. How long has she been gone from Casualty? She throws her stained pants in the trash and adds her sweaty shirt. She never wants to see the clothes that belong to this day again.

When she walks back past the guard on her way to the lift, she tries not to look at him. She hates him for whatever he thinks about her. Bitchy little white girl. She hates him for whatever racist thoughts he believes she holds. *I'm not a racist,* she wants to spit. *You jerk.* So she doesn't catch his eye when she goes by, but then when the door to the lift opens, she turns back to him. He is staring at her, just as Idzia suspected, so she says, "My mother is dying!" He looks almost like he is again going to say he is sorry to hear that, but before he has a chance to be kind in any small way, and even though it makes no sense, she says, "My mother is dying, and it's your fault."

WHY DOES SHE KEEP EATING? That's what she wonders when she's back home. It's late, and she has a bag of crisps that she bought at the store, and she's eating the whole thing. She is doing this while sitting on the bed, facing the closets with their wall of mirrors. Not that there is anywhere else to face. The room isn't much bigger than the bed. She sits in her bra and panties, watching herself chew while warm tears make their way down her face. People always tell her she isn't fat, but they haven't seen her dumpy stomach. She grabs a handful of flab, shakes it at herself like a big flapping tongue. "You big fat idiot," she says out loud to the girl in the mirror.

Katie is a runner. Katie runs every day, and she seems entirely uninterested in food. Idzia can't turn off her interest. Even now.

She crumples the bag and then hears the front door open, Bertie coming in. Tomorrow, Idzia promises herself, she will skip breakfast and lunch. She'll eat dinner but only after her shift at the restaurant. Maybe her mum will be home by then.

When Idzia comes out, she finds Bertie sitting at the dining room table, key still in hand, bag still slung over her shoulder.

"Oh, luv," Bertie says.

"What's happening?"

"Well," Bertie breathes heavily. "Your mother is throwing blood clots. That's why she had the seizure. They have to see what they can do to stop that. And there's more cancer. In the back of her mouth. Probably her stomach. That's probably why she's been having so much trouble eating."

"So we can start another round of chemo," Idzia begins, because this is how things have been. Not long after Liesel and Idzia moved into the apartment, Bertie showed Idzia an article in the paper about long-term cancer patients, how they never go into full remission, but they survive; they're treated over time. Idzia knows her mum's cancer is stage 4, but she refuses to flip to the back of the breast-cancer book her mum has bought and consider the numbers there. Who cares what they say? What do percentages matter, when what happens to her mother, whatever that is, will happen 100 percent? Bertie came to the restaurant one night, had a burger with a friend, and then told Idzia, "We're going to get your mother better. Don't you worry."

Now, though, when Idzia starts to talk about more chemo, Bertie says, "No. No more chemo. Her body can't take any more."

"But then she'll just . . ." But Idzia doesn't finish her sentence. She hasn't realized, not really, not yet—despite the fact that anyone else would realize, despite the fact that there was *another* day when Bertie came to the restaurant and said, "I'm going to take care of you. You know that? We've set it up with a lawyer"—that her mother is going to die.

Idzia smiles, just because Bertie is looking at her, and she can't figure out what else to do with her mouth. *How does a person even do it?* Dying, that big accomplishment? She doesn't even know how it is that cancer kills you exactly. She knows it *does*, of course, but what happens? It doesn't grow into the heart and stop the heart from beating. It doesn't choke off the air supply, unless it's a different kind of cancer. Soon enough, she supposes, she will have an answer to her question. "Well," she says to Bertie. "OK." By this she doesn't mean that it *is* OK. Only that she's heard. She gets it. She's still got the bunched-up crisp bag in her hand. She will throw it out. That's the next thing she has to do. That's a clear action, and it needs to be taken. After that, she has no clue.

IN THE MORNING, over the phone, Liesel is insistent. No visitors, though Bertie has offered to call friends from the theater and let them know where Liesel is. "I don't want them to see me like this," Liesel says, and Idzia doesn't get it. Her mother loves having people around her. If Idzia was sick, she would definitely want all her friends in her hospital room saying, "We love you. We love you." She'd want a crowd. Evidence that she mattered.

Liesel doesn't mind if Bertie visits, though. Or Idzia, of course.

On her mother's instructions, Idzia waits to visit till the afternoon, but she can't go too late. She's got her shift at Hache starting at 4:00 p.m. "Why a vegetarian wants to work at a hamburger restaurant, I don't know," her mother had once said, when a few of Bertie's friends were over.

"To earn money," Idzia had said spitefully. "I'm working on that stable income thing." Now she feels bad she said it. Her mother managed a pretty long stretch as Fletcher's house manager.

At the hospital, Idzia finds Liesel dozing. "Mom," Idzia says quietly.

"Oh." Her mother starts as if from an approaching attacker, then wakes. She works her mouth around. She seems to be trying to rid herself of some unpleasant taste. "Well," she says, her tone gravelly and exhausted, "I've got a surprise for you."

"You had a surprise for me yesterday," Idzia says. "And I didn't like it."

"No, no, a good surprise," Liesel says, offering a weak smile. Idzia has the feeling she always does before her mother does something that she thinks is fabulous and that Idzia hates. "You, my dear, are going on a trip. You're going to America."

"No, I'm not," Idzia says.

"Yes, you are. I already got you a ticket."

"That's because the travel services are so good here," Idzia says and then feels a little sick. The travel services *are* probably good here, and where everyone is traveling to is the grave.

"Well, Bertie got them for me. She's got a computer in her office or the nurse's bay or wherever it is. Anyway, the flight leaves this Friday, and you're going to meet your father!" Liesel says this as if she has just offered the best of treats to a very young child. Ta-da! A bicycle on Christmas. Disneyland Paris for the school holiday.

"What are you talking about?"

"Where are they?" Liesel tries, unsuccessfully, to turn toward the nightstand, then taps the table they've rolled over her bed. "They're here somewhere. It's time you met him. So I talked to him this morning . . .

"You *talked* to him?" The idea that her mother would have her father's phone number is remarkable to Idzia.

"Stranger things have happened. And he's all ready to meet you. He's got a little boy, so you've got a half brother."

"Mom," Idzia says, "I am not going to America. I don't want to meet my father. Why would I want to meet him?"

"I've already bought the ticket," Liesel says, as if this decides the matter. She adds details. Idzia will fly into Boston. Her father will pick her up. Bertie will scan a picture into the hospital computer and send it to him so he will know what she looks like. The return tickets are in August, before university starts.

Idzia says, "Mom, I don't know what you are thinking, but this isn't happening." Liesel closes her eyes, then opens them and says dramatically, "Listen, honey. I'm very, *very* sick."

"I know that!" Idzia snaps. Her mother says this as if it is new news, as if she has been kindly shielding Idzia from the horrible truth of her cancer for years now.

Her mother keeps her eyes closed, says, "We'll talk about it later."

But the next day they have a different disagreement. Liesel is weak, asleep for most of the day. When she briefly wakes, she seems too uncomfortable for talk, but she tells Idzia that she doesn't want her to visit, that she wants her to go home and finish her toy theater. When Idzia protests that she has no plan to do anything but go to work and come to the hospital, Liesel says, "You're making it worse. If you don't take care of yourself, you're making it worse." Then she closes her eyes, and Idzia can tell she's once again trying not to cry.

Tears well in Idzia's eyes. This is the worst sort of reprimand.

"OK, Mom," she says softly. She stands, kisses her mother's cheek, and says, "I'll go." But then she can't stand the solemnity of the moment, so she says, as if she's some action hero, "That's right, baby. I'm going but I'll be back." Only her mother doesn't laugh. She has already fallen back to sleep.

Idzia goes home and works on the theater, though her enthusiasm for the project is gone. She is beyond tired. Still she is obedient. As excruciating as it is, she stays away from her mother's bedside for the rest of the day and promises to stay home on Wednesday. She'll count on Bertie to look in, to give her the updates.

KATIE RINGS TO SAY she wants to look at Idzia's theater. "You're done, right?"

"Not quite," Idzia admits. She is hand-sewing a curtain for the stage, though of course she could just ditch this last task. She doesn't *have* to have a curtain. Only she has had the idea to stitch the words "Web Design" on the curtains, and she's hoping people will get it, the idea that computers are a web we've woven for ourselves. It seemed clever when Idzia first thought of it, but now, as she attaches the felt letters to the maroon velvet, it seems stupid and over-obvious.

"I have to see it," Katie says. "Can I come over?"

"Yeah," Idzia says.

It takes about an hour but finally the doorbell rings.

"My girl," Katie says, hugging Idzia at the door. Katie's pixie haircut has been ruffled by the wind, and she's wearing a green army jacket and jeans, plus a black T-shirt that says "Humanoid." "Wow," she says, as she comes into the apartment and sees the toy theater on the dining room table. "It's the winner. I know it."

"Come on."

"Really," Katie says. She turns to Idzia, who has taken a seat at the table, and kisses the top of her head. "You all right?" Idzia has already emailed Katie the salient details about her mother.

"I guess so."

Katie is gay, which is only complicated because Idzia has a crush on her. It's a girl-crush, a nonsexual crush, but it's all-consuming. If Idzia is somewhere and Katie's there, she's always aware of where Katie is. When Idzia is alone, she always wants to talk to Katie but she measures out her phone calls. She's afraid of pestering her or being too often the caller, instead of the called. Does Katie like her, or suffer her? Each time Katie instigates an exchange, Idzia feels relieved. She holds onto the sense of Katie wanting to be her friend for three maybe four days, and then her fears kick in again. If their friendship is a game of tag, Idzia is the one who tags first. Katie responds, but that's not quite the same thing as being the one to reach out in the first place.

Once when Idzia was at Katie's flat, Katie and Gillian, her girlfriend at the time, were in the bed in the living room—all the rooms had beds; it was how they were able to afford the place—and Katie had flapped the blanket open and said, "Idzia darling, just come on in." Then she'd asked, as if genuinely puzzled, "Why haven't we ever all done it?"

Gillian didn't seem to be paying attention. (Idzia can't imagine a world in which she'd just not hear her partner suggest a threesome.) Idzia had laughed at Katie but felt a wave of sensation rise from her feet up her back. *Why not?* But the answer came to her in the same moment, *Because I would never.*

THE THEATER HAS TO BE at the gallery by day's end Wednesday. At 3:00 p.m., Idzia puts the final stitch in the *n* of "Web Design." She goes into

Bertie's cellar storage to fetch a box to transport the theater. As she's coming up from the cellar, she hears the phone ring in Bertie's apartment. She manages to get to it before the answering machine comes on. "Idzia," Bertie says, "your mother wants you to come."

"What's happened?"

"Just come. She can't talk. Her tongue is all swollen. But she wants to see you."

"What do you mean—" Idzia starts to ask, and Bertie says, "I'll see you" and hangs up.

When Idzia gets to the hospital, her mother is awake and frantic, her eyes wild. She opens her mouth and says, "I ought oo."

Idzia looks at a nurse who is bustling with a bag below the mattress, one that seems to be collecting urine. When did that get added to the list of things attached to her mother?

Her mother looks terrified. Not a look Idzia has ever seen on her mother's face before. Liesel points to her mouth and shakes her head.

"Her tongue," the nurse says. Idzia's mother opens wide, as if at a dentist's. Idzia starts. Her mother's tongue is like a giant red baseball in her mouth. "Mummy. Oh, Mummy."

"I ought oo . . ." she repeats.

"What? What?"

"Here," the nurse says and hands her a pad of paper. "Have her write it down."

"I thought you were in America," Liesel scrawls, but her handwriting is so unlike her normal script that Idzia almost screams. "Hello, earthling," Idzia used to say to her mother when she was eleven, and Liesel would look at her and smile, and Idzia would amend, "I mean 'Mum.'" Then she'd make her eyes go up and to the right, and she'd say, "Nothing suspicious. Nothing suspicious." But now it feels like there really *is* an alien here. Liesel would *never* print words like that.

"Mum, I was never going to America."

"At ay is it?" Liesel says.

Idzia looks at the nurse.

"Wednesday," the nurse says.

"Can't you make that go away?" Idzia says, pointing at her mother's tongue, but the nurse looks confused. "Her tongue, I mean. Not *her*." And then it is as if she's said some horrible magic words, and the talking fish from the sea is going to hold her to her foolishness and actually make her mother go away rather than just stop her tongue from looking so red and painful.

Of all things to go wrong. Her mother, her mother. Her mother who can't shut up. Finally shut up.

"We'll up the morphine," the nurse says.

Her mother waves her hand, irritated.

"You don't want more morphine?" the nurse asks.

Liesel shakes her head angrily. That isn't apparently what she meant.

She picks up the pencil, writes, "Go away," and holds it up to the nurse. Then she tears off the sheet of paper and writes "Friday. Ticket."

Idzia has no idea what this is supposed to mean. "The ticket's for Friday?" she tries.

Liesel closes her eyes and nods.

Idzia doesn't have the heart to say that it doesn't matter what day the ticket is for; she's not going. Her father is just someone who once slept with her mother. Whoever he is, he's never done anything for Idzia, and she definitely doesn't want to meet him now.

Her mother doesn't open her eyes, but Idzia can hear her breathing heavily.

A minute ticks by. Then another. Has she fallen asleep?

Idzia sits down in the hospital room's chair. Thirty minutes go by, and her mother's eyes are still closed, her breath still labored. Should Idzia get a blanket and just stay the night? She could. There's nothing stopping her— no shift tonight. Only she wants so badly to sleep, and she knows she won't be able to in the hard wooden chair. Idzia stands to ask the nurse if she can stay, when she feels a blob of blood plop onto her underwear. She turns for the bathroom, and sure enough, she is leaking again. Her period is only supposed to last seven days. This one has gone on for ten.

The blood somehow decides things. She will go home, wash up, come back first thing in the morning. Her mother can't miss her while she's sleeping.

BACK AT BERTIE'S, there's a note on the dining room table: "Katie called."

Bertie, Idzia guesses, is asleep for the night. Or reading a novel. She likes all things cultural—books, plays, films, and art exhibits. It's part of the reason she and Liesel first took to one another. Once Idzia asked her why she'd become a nurse when she was such a lover of the arts, and Bertie had smiled, as if at an unappreciative parent, and said, "I find it rewarding to look after people in hospitals."

Idzia calls Katie back. "Hey," Katie says. "Where's your theater? I thought you were going to bring it."

"I had to go see my mum."

"Oh." This seems to throw Katie for a moment, then she says, "Right, well, I asked, and they said if you can get it to the gallery by 9:00 tomorrow morning, you can still be in the competition."

"I don't know," Idzia says, though she is aware that she wants Katie to convince her. She wants her theater to be in the contest. She wants to win. She wants to win and to be able to visit her mom and say, "Guess what?" Though, of course, by the time the winners are announced, she wants her mum to be out of the hospital. Out of the hospital because *home,* she adds, in her head and for the Fates, who might be thinking—she knows they are thinking—out of the hospital because *dead.*

Idzia chats a little more with Katie, but she's as tired as if it were midnight. After she says good-night, she packs her theater as carefully as she can into the box, then crawls into bed. She sets the alarm for 7:30 a.m., then thinks through her plan. She will rise, shower, dress, get on the Tube, switch at Moorgate and get off at Aldgate. If she drops the theater off at 9:00 a.m., she will be back to her mother by . . . what time? She can't quite figure it. She recalculates the length of the ride and the walks to and from the gallery and to the hospital, but before she is through, she is asleep.

WHEN SHE WAKES, five minutes before the alarm, she is a mess. There's blood all over her sheets, and this though she put in a super plus tampon at bedtime, got up once in the night to change it. The diaper of the sanitary napkin . . . *that* she refuses to employ, though the evidence is that she should get over this particular disinclination. She strips the bed—the sheets, the mattress pad—washes out the blood in the sink, then throws the mess in the washer, hopes Bertie wasn't planning to do her own load.

She checks her watch. It is the worst possible time to cram into a subway with her theater, but what can she do? She picks up the box and heads out. She's not even reached the corner when she has to balance the box on a gate and give her arms a rest. It's not the weight but the awkwardness of the box that is a strain. She heaves the box up again and makes it all the way to the Pizza Express, where she rests the theater on someone's bike. After that, she gets all the way to the corner and finds another bike, right by the Cash Point.

"Big issue, big issue," she hears the homeless man outside the Tube repeating. He is sitting on the pavement, and there's a small dog with a little red jacket perched between his knees. The man's got a small boom box, and he's rocking out, swinging the dog's lead as he hawks magazines. *Misery, sure,* Idzia thinks, to some private interlocutor, *but with a beat.*

As if he knows she's having a thought about him, the man glances up and says, "Well, luv," he nods at her box, "looks like you're having a time."

What does he mean by this? "Right," she says.

"Good for you, luv. Good for you."

Inside the Tube stop, Idzia has to balance her load on her right thigh and then swing it up over the turnstile. She's well into this maneuver when a guard opens a gate, and says, "Just go ahead."

"Thank you," she says, though she wonders why she's so grateful. Shouldn't everyone be this kind?

When her train comes, it's as bad as she feared. Completely packed, but she just pushes on. On any other day, she'd say, "Pardon. Pardon," and wince apologetically, but today she thinks she can take up her space in the world, her space and her theater's space, and people will just have to get used to it. She doesn't move too far into the car. Around her there is a too-thin, androgynous black women, chewing gum, and wearing a hat with earflaps, though it's already July. Another woman in a burqa; her blue-framed glasses, cheap purse, and sneakers giving some sense of her personality. A man in black jeans is bopping back and forth to whatever's on his iPod, and when Idzia has a second look at him, she notices he's reading *The Holy Bible,* that grooviest of texts. Well, that's one to share with Katie. Idzia is aware of doing this, of saving up her perceptions to share with Katie. And Katie never disappoints in her reactions, like the time Idzia felt panicked when she was going up the escalator at Holborn when all these people were coming down, and she wondered, "What if I stop moving?" Which had felt profound when she thought it, but when she said something to Bertie, Bertie had just looked at her blankly. But Katie had said, "I know, I know. I've thought that, too. It's all going so fast and what if you are like 'No. I refuse. Stop'? Only you can't stop, because there is this societal agreement. Move forward. Move forward."

At Moorgate, Idzia gets off for the Circle line. It's 8:40 a.m., so she still might reach the gallery by 9:00 a.m.. She knows what Bertie was trying to say when she came to the restaurant all those months ago and said that Liesel and she had gone to a lawyer. Bertie was saying that she would be Idzia's guardian if her mother died. And with Idzia nearing eighteen at the time, what Bertie really meant was that she would help her out, that Idzia wouldn't be alone. The bad thought has come to Idzia that if her mother dies, she will have the bedroom to herself, that she won't have to worry anymore about what is going to happen to her mother, because what is going to happen to her mother will have already happened. Katie has said, "Just because you think bad thoughts doesn't mean you really feel that way. It's just your brain has to test things out. It's like your brain cells are saying, 'I'm just going to visit this thought for a moment,' and then you say, 'OK. Had my visit. Not going there again.'"

Idzia can't believe how lucky she is, having Katie as a friend.

Also, Katie doesn't nod her head in mindless agreement when someone talks about how important your attitude is when it comes to cancer. After a girl said as much to Idzia one night at a party, Katie said to the girl, "Right. Known carcinogen, crankiness. Also stupidity, but *you* seem to be doing all right."

The train to Aldgate comes. It's packed, and hardly anyone gets off, but Idzia and others manage to press on. Someone offers Idzia a seat, but she can't take it, because with the theater, she needs two seats. Instead, she balances the box against the pole and digs her feet into the ground to steady herself. There is a man violently jiggling his leg across from her. From the far end of the train, she hears someone saying, over and over, "*You* know what I'm saying. *You* know what I'm saying." A mother sits at the edge of a seat near her; a baby with snot covering his upper lip hangs in a carrier at her back. She's got another one in a carrier in front of her. A little girl by her side is chanting, "I *want* it. I *want* it."

Idzia tries to see her watch. When will she get to her mother? Almost 8:50 a.m., and the gallery isn't supposed to be far from the Tube, so maybe . . . She hasn't quite finished figuring when there is a white flash and the car is violently jarred. Idzia trips, loses hold of her box, hears the theater break as it falls to the floor. She hasn't fully formed a curse of regret—*Oh, fuck!*—when she understands that the theater isn't what she needs to worry about. She hears glass shattering and falls backward, as other people fall toward and then on top of her. The entire car seems to be tipping over. A single scream, then more screams. Smoke. She feels something wet on her calf. Her period? Again? A velvety darkness sweeps up from the ground, a shadow version of what Idzia felt when Katie suggested she get into the bed with her and Gillian, a wave of feeling that doesn't excite sensation so much as close it down, starting at her ankles and rising through her back until everything disappears. But just before that happens, some tiny and invisible part of Idzia detaches itself and dives headfirst into one of the tiny computers in her toy theater; it travels through an imaginary wireless network and arrives at Liesel's bedside, where Liesel is waiting for her daughter so she can take her last breath. "It's OK," the mini-Idzia says, when she finds herself pressed into a mattress, stroking her mother's arm. "It's OK."

IT IS JULY 7, 2005, and it is not her own blood that Idzia feels. Initial reports will speak of a power outage on the line, but soon that will change. The BBC will get the story. CNN, ABC, CBS. They'll tell what really has happened. They'll put it all together. Four coordinated attacks, bombs in rucksacks. Fifty-six people dead.

Like Idzia, the Circle line bomber still lives with his mother. Like Idzia, he works at a restaurant. (In his case, a fish-and-chip shop.) Like Idzia, he is not showing up for work tonight.

3

WHAT YOU HAVE

BERTIE HAD BEEN LIVING in London for three months when she first touched a dead body. It happened on her Thursday afternoon shift. She went into room 210 to check on Dr. Jan Liss, a neurologist who was dying in the very hospital where he once (and Bertie now) worked. "He sent me my first patients, back when I started out," she heard a male voice say. On the other side of the ceiling-track curtain, a short man in blue scrubs was sitting at the foot of Dr. Liss's bed. He shook his head, clearly broken up. The surgeon, if that was what he was, was talking to an older woman. Liss's wife. Bertie couldn't remember her name. Pamela? Prudence? P-something. The wife nodded, as if in agreement with his words, then said evenly, as if it were an ordinary enough response, "I think Jan just stopped breathing." A second, younger woman, sitting at a table in the room's corner—the daughter probably—looked up from the book in her lap. The wife said, more amazement than upset in her voice, "Jan just died."

"I'm so sorry," Bertie said and left the room.

"Dr. Liss is dead," Bertie told Kathleen, the ward supervisor, a broad blond woman with a face reddened and roughened by old acne scars. "I . . . what do I do?" Bertie had been told at some point in her training, of course, but she'd lost that file in the hard drive of her brain, just when she needed it most. *To lose one parent, Mr. Worthing, may be regarded as a misfortune; to lose both looks like carelessness.* Of all things to flash through her brain. Nursing school lessons were gone, not so Oscar Wilde. What was the matter with her?

47

"OK," Kathleen said and went to hug everyone in room 210. Bertie hovered tentatively behind her. Kathleen said softly, and not to anyone in particular, "I'm just going to put the back of the bed down." Bertie remembered then that it was important to make a dead person lie flat, so his body wouldn't stiffen in the wrong position. Already Dr. Liss was dusky, his mouth hanging open. Kathleen put a towel under his chin. "We'll let you be for now," Kathleen said to the family, and Bertie followed her out.

When Dr. Liss's family left, Kathleen removed a drip and catheter and sent Bertie for clean towels and linens. When she came back, they set to washing Dr. Liss. His body was heavy, heavier than when he'd been alive. "Look out," Kathleen said, when they turned him. Bertie grabbed a dangling arm. She hadn't counted on him being so floppy. Kathleen told Bertie to close Dr. Liss's eyelids, but they didn't stay shut, so Kathleen told her to get cotton balls and wet them and place them on his eyes. Kathleen whispered as they worked. She didn't have to, the family long gone, but Bertie understood that this was the ritual.

When Dr. Liss was clean and his hair brushed and all his old dressing and dirty linens stuffed in a rubbish bag, they had to put absorbent material in the orifices that would be draining. Bertie remembered that now from school: packing the body. Still she'd never done it. She went to get forceps and cotton wool. "When I was in India—" Kathleen said, when she returned.

"When were you in India?" Bertie said, not fully aware she was interrupting until after she'd spoken.

"After school. It was important for me to get away." This hint at a life beyond, of possible emotional turmoil, was rare for Kathleen. She was kind but private, always sat alone with a book at lunch rather than joining the gabbling in the cafeteria. It made Bertie like her, even if it meant she couldn't turn that fondness to friendship. "Anyway," Kathleen continued, "bodies decompose quickly down there. The heat. You can't wait to pack them. I was at a field hospital, and there was no cotton wool, so the women shredded their saris." Kathleen extended a hand for the forceps. "I'll do it this time," she said. Bertie nodded her head in thanks.

When the orderly arrived, Kathleen gestured toward Bertie and said, "She's not yet been down to the morgue." The orderly smiled, as if this were good news. He waited while Kathleen called two other nurses to help with the body bag. When they were through, Kathleen placed a clean sheet over Dr. Liss, picked a flower from the assortment in his room, and laid it on his chest.

Bertie followed the orderly. Once they were alone with the body in the lift, the orderly jiggled the stretcher, laughed a monster laugh, and said, "It's alive! It's alive!"

Creep, Bertie thought.

Even so, she was shaken.

AT HOME THAT EVENING, Bertie lay in bed with a cold washcloth folded on her forehead, something her mother used to do when she had a headache. Once the washcloth was warm from the heat of her face, Bertie got up to see to dinner. She couldn't get over the feel of Dr. Liss, the way the image of her fingerprints had stayed on his skin rather than filling up with blood.

Her roommate, Gloria—a relentless Eeyore, her puckered face like oatmeal just before it boiled—was in the living room, flipping through the scrapbook on the coffee table. It held assorted things from Bertie's childhood, her time at university and then nursing school. Maybe it was because she was coming from a dark room into light, but everything felt strange to Bertie, as if air molecules were breaking up. On the Tube ride home, she imagined the dusky death that all the riders had under their skin. The flat weight of their unanimated bodies. It was so important. It was so important, a life. Until it wasn't. Then you were just a thing to be disposed of.

"Bertie," Gloria said. "This is wild."

"What?"

"This," Gloria said, pointing to the scrapbook, and Bertie saw that she'd come to the clippings about *As You Like It*.

In the summer after she received her nursing degree and before her job in London began, Bertie had been persuaded by acting friends to try out for a play—a real play, not just amateur theatricals. Bertie had always been shy, but she'd also always been obsessed with the theater and during nursing school had even fallen in with a crowd of actors from Old Vic, the drama school Laurence Olivier founded. She regularly ran lines with Louise Lizzimore, her closest actor friend. The auditioning was just a lark—Bertie never expected anything to come of her efforts; how could it, given her lack of real experience?—but one unlikely event followed another. She got the lead, good reviews, and then a slew of write-ups, reporters exploiting the human-interest tidbit, the unusual story: a nursing student who tried out on a dare and had so thoroughly mastered the gender-switching role despite her demonstrably female figure. ("Big boobs," you could almost hear the newspapers trying not to write.)

"Roberta Russell . . . We Like It!"

"Newcomer Shines as Rosalind"

"All the World's a Stage for Bristol Nurse"

And it wasn't just the local papers. There was a squib in *Time Out*. The *Times* ran something. "We'll get the *Guardian*," the director enthused, though he was wrong about that. The BBC called to do a radio piece. Once it aired, Bertie's parents rang daily to report on some old friend or another who had heard the broadcast.

"I didn't know you were an actress," Gloria said. She hadn't learned much about Bertie's life because she was usually too busy complaining about her own. Also, they worked more or less opposing shifts.

"Well, sort of and sort of not, as you can see." Bertie gestured toward the scrapbook.

"I didn't know you were famous."

"Well, I wouldn't say I was famous," Bertie laughed.

But she had been, in a way. Last summer she'd been getting a takeaway supper for herself, and someone walked up to her in the shop and asked, "Are you Bertie Russell?" When she said she was, he had her sign his napkin.

WAS IT GLORIA'S QUESTIONS or the dead man that made her walk over to the Fletcher Theatre the next day to ask if they used volunteer ushers?

The woman in the box office handed Bertie an application form, and Bertie felt a flutter of hope. London had been lonely so far. She'd arrived last fall, happy for her first job, but she hadn't found anything like the friends she'd had while in nursing school.

Within a week, Bertie got a call, instructing her to meet the house manager, Liesel Pearlman, on Saturday morning in the Fletcher lobby.

"Bertie!" a medium-sized woman cried out in welcome, when Bertie arrived at the appointed time. "Yes?" Bertie said, confused. The woman acted as if they already knew one another. "It's me. Liesel Pearlman."

"Oh, yes, of course."

The woman looked to be around forty, older than Bertie at any rate, probably by ten years. She had a round, bland face, uninspiring as a pancake, offset with dramatic, long curly hair. "Come," she said, holding her arm out. "We'll talk in the restaurant." Separated by a glass wall from the theater, the restaurant was sleek, with a long metal bar and photographs hung salonstyle on the walls. It wasn't open at this hour, but Liesel had a key. After Bertie waved off Liesel's offer of tea or coffee, they sat in the corner. "So," Liesel began, wiping crumbs off the tabletop as she sat. "I am *so* excited to meet you." There was something of the jolly nursery school teacher about her. Or maybe it was only that she was wearing a black jumper and black-and-white striped tights, which put Bertie in mind of a Dr. Seuss character. "I have to tell you," Liesel said. "I heard all about you on the BBC, and then I saw your application in the pile, and I thought, 'Yep! Here's one I want to meet!'" Liesel's accent was hard to place. At first she sounded liltingly French, then as if she'd grown up speaking the Queen's English, and finally flatly American. Yep.

"But you aren't acting anymore," Liesel said, looking at Bertie's application. "How could you give it up? I mean with your success."

Others had wondered the same. "It's just . . . I love the theater. But it wasn't for me." The truth was acting had made her too anxious. She'd sometimes felt like her body was full of bees, all buzzing in their effort to get out. The success was heady, no denying that, but the six-week run of the show had been one of the hardest stretches of her life. She threw up before she went onstage. She dry-heaved after the curtain went down. Once she'd even vomited between acts.

"Well, yes," Liesel said, after a few more questions. "We'd love to have you usher. It might be a while before I can get you on the schedule."

"Oh, wonderful!"

Liesel smiled. "Something about you reminds me of me when I first started working in theaters."

This didn't seem possible. Liesel was broader-mannered, friendlier than Bertie knew herself to be. Still she was pleased by what she took as a compliment. Liesel took both Bertie's hands when they parted, as if their connection, along with the volunteer opportunity, was now assured.

BUT BERTIE DIDN'T HEAR from Liesel. Weeks went by, and her loneliness grew more oppressive. Bertie had had friends, of course. Back in nursing school, and then when she'd done the play, but that felt like a long time ago now. Finally, one night, Bertie was invited to a hen party for a ward nurse who was getting married. They played pin the tail on the donkey, only they placed a giant silhouette of a man on the wall and the idea was to affix his member between his legs. After, everyone was supposed to go around the room and offer a sex tip. Were these the sort of people with whom she would now have to spend her time? It seemed so. (And, also, what sex tip could she offer? Her romantic résumé listed only one boyfriend, and this back in nursing school. He'd been kind but lazy, too exhausted by the idea of a long-distance relationship to maintain the attachment once Bertie moved to London. In the years after university and before she'd started nursing school, she'd had some . . . things. But you wouldn't call them relationships. You wouldn't, Bertie thought, want to confess anything about them to another human being.)

Bertie departed early from the party, coming home to a message on her answering machine. Liesel wondered if she was available to usher for a Thursday-night performance.

WHEN THE DAY CAME, Bertie was excited, already imagining the friendships she might establish with other ushers, the coffee she'd take with Liesel. But Liesel was too busy for chat on Bertie's first night, and the other ushers were tight-lipped older women who seemed drawn to volunteering less for the chance to see plays for free than for the fun of not letting latecomers through the door.

Perhaps theater was not going to come to her aid, as it had throughout her life, the enthusiasm such a reliable comfort. Even now, she read plays instead of novels. She regularly bought tickets—the West End when she could afford it—though she attended alone, the pain of this sometimes blooming around her as she took her seat. *It hurts,* she remembered a child on a psych ward saying as he rocked in his bed, subject to nothing crueler than the torments of his own brain. *It hurts.*

Yes.

Even so, she kept with the volunteering. Though the other ushers remained aloof, Liesel and she talked animatedly whenever they saw one another. *How are you? How are you?* Liesel would cry. *What have you seen lately?* (Answer: *Abigail's Party, The Syringa Tree.*) Liesel was a big hugger, laugher, and interrogator. *What's it like, being a nurse? How do you handle it if someone dies?* ("Badly," Bertie allowed.) Sometimes Liesel would bring Bertie into the green room and introduce her all around, then say, "Oh, God, I have to check on the concessions!" and Bertie, having no real business in the room, would give an embarrassed wave to all those people she'd genuinely like to meet . . . and depart.

"I'm having a health scare," Liesel said once, when she saw Bertie in the bathroom after a Sunday matinee. "I should ask you about it sometime."

"Yes, please!" Bertie said, but then Liesel looked down at her watch and said, "Shit! I'm going to be late. I've got to fetch my daughter."

"You have a daughter?" Bertie was poised to say, but Liesel was already out the door.

A SATURDAY NIGHT in April found Bertie, post-performance, in the Fletcher lobby, killing time so as not to arrive too early to meet a few nurses at the Electric Ballroom. She hated the Electric Ballroom, with its loud noise, punk scene, drinking—the place had *four* bars—and drugs. You could have a man there, of course, but you didn't want whom you could have. Once a stranger came up and licked her from her clavicle up to her cheek. One long repulsive, purposeful stroke. Just thinking about it, Bertie wanted to take a shower. Still, she didn't want to have no plans for the evening, so when the nurses asked, she'd said yes.

She pulled a copy of Tom Stoppard's *Arcadia* out of her bag and started to read. After a moment, a young man sat on the bench next to her and said, "What'd you think of it?"

She looked up, startled. Was he talking to *her?*

With his long nose and pointed chin, he looked slightly elfin or bemused, but in a slacker way. He was wearing a leather jacket over a pink T-shirt with red lettering that said, "I'm the mommy. That's why."

"So?" he said, slightly impatient. Apparently he *was* talking to her.

"I like it," Bertie said. "I'm not far in, but there's this very precocious girl who . . ."

"Not that," the man said, waving his hand at the book. "*That.*" He cocked his head in the direction of the performance space.

"Oh, God," Bertie said, just realizing whom she was talking to. "I didn't recognize you." The theater was just then doing Dylan Thomas's *Under Milkwood,* and this was Geoffrey Walker, who played the "First Narrator." He looked a lot older onstage.

"I like it," she said, now meaning the performance. "And you . . . you're great,"

He sniffed and said, "Maudlin production" in such an authoritative and dismissive way that she didn't feel like she could respond. "And my performance is pretty crappy, too."

"No," she began, but he held up his hand to stop her. Perhaps he was too used to compliments. He was the biggest celebrity in the cast, with three West End credits to his name. "Listen, Liesel tells me you're incredibly well-versed in theater."

Bertie didn't say anything.

"Liesel? The house manager. You know her, right?"

"Yes, a bit, but . . . She did?"

"Yeah, she said you've seen a lot and that you've read even more."

"Well," Bertie said, holding up her book. "It's kind of a passion."

He nodded and said, "So I'm trying to plan out a future project, and I've got this possible space in my mind, and I have this idea about directing." He sniffed, again as if in dismissal. Then, in a manner simultaneously sheepish and sarcastic, he said, "Would you 'take a business lunch' with me?" He hooked his fingers in the air to indicate the quote.

"Yeah, sure." She laughed. She wasn't entirely sure what he was asking for. What did he mean by "possible space in my mind"?

"I'm thinking you might know some plays I haven't heard of. I can tell you the sort of thing I'm thinking of doing."

"OK. I don't see why not."

"What's your number then? I'll give you mine." He took a piece of paper from his wallet and wrote his name and number, though of course she knew his name.

She ripped out a corner of the back page of her book and gave him hers.

"Thanks, Ms. Russell," he said.

"Oh, call me Bertie." It was strange for a young man to assume such formality, and it sounded weirdly insulting, as if he'd done it because she, not he, required this sort of deference.

"Right," he said, waved a good-bye, and walked up the stairs to the green room.

She turned over the paper. It was a receipt from Oddbins, which was, Bertie knew, a liquor store on Kentish Town Road. She folded the paper back into her hand, held it tight: her reason to skip the Electric Ballroom.

BUT HE DIDN'T CALL. A week passed, then a second. *Just call him yourself, why don't you?* If she weren't so frightened of this sort of effort, she'd be a lot less lonely.

But she couldn't.

Then, after her second dead body, she felt emboldened. That same sense of the disposability of one's passions, fears, and concerns. This was her only life; she'd better not waste it.

Or maybe her reasons weren't so noble. Maybe it was simply because she ran into Liesel, who said, "Did you and Geoffrey Walker ever get to talk? He was so keen on meeting."

So she called.

A woman answered. Bertie hadn't thought Geoffrey was asking her on a date—he'd clearly said "business lunch"—but she was surprised. Something about his manner—though what?—had suggested he was unattached.

"Hello," she said. "This is Bertie Russell. Is Geoffrey there?"

The woman was silent, and Bertie assumed she'd made a terrible gaffe, that Geoffrey was some lothario, and here she was accidentally calling the long-suffering girlfriend, who would no doubt suspect the worst. But then the woman said slowly, as if in recognition, "Ber-tie?"

"Yes?" Bertie said, confused.

"It's me. It's Louise."

Bertie looked down at the piece of paper in her hand. Had she accidentally called Louise, the old acting friend who'd first told Bertie to try out for *As You Like It,* and with whom she had often run lines. "It'll be a hoot," Louise had said back in Bristol. "We'll both try out!"

"Oh, I . . .," Bertie said now. "Louise?"

"Yes. I'm in London. I wasn't going to tell anyone."

"You? Oh, oh, OK." Bertie couldn't get her bearings in this conversation. Even so, she felt hurt. Surely she wasn't just anyone? How could Louise come to town without calling?

There'd always been this slight slippage in the friendship. When Bertie had asked the *As You Like It* director what part Louise had in the play, he'd said, "I didn't cast any Louise." Later, Louise said she'd never actually tried out for the show. But hadn't she said she *would?* Wasn't that *the point?* Doing it together?

"Why are you calling Geoffrey?"

Bertie felt accused.

"He gave me his phone number. I mean . . . he wanted to talk about plays . . ."

Last fall, Louise had married Edward, one of Old Vic's visiting acting instructors, and they'd moved to Birmingham for his new teaching job. It had been a complete surprise. Louise seemed so clearly headed for London and the opportunities there. She'd even asked about sharing Bertie's flat. When

Louise called to invite Bertie to the wedding, Bertie had blurted, "You're not pregnant, are you?"

"God, no," Louise had snorted.

Now Louise cleared her throat, somewhat wearily, and said, "Well, like I said, I wasn't going to tell anyone, but since you know, why don't you come for dinner?"

"That's OK," Bertie began.

"I need to make dinner anyway. Geoffrey's been eating digestive biscuits for all his meals, so someone's got to put things in order here."

"Right," Bertie said, still confused. How did Louise know Geoffrey?

"I might as well tell you that I've left Edward."

"You . . . you what?" Bertie felt as shocked as when Louise said she planned to marry him.

"I couldn't stand it anymore. Geoffrey did a guest class at Birmingham—on acting for film versus acting for theater—and he really saved me. He convinced me to come down here to be with him. I don't know what I'd have done otherwise."

"I thought you were happy with Edward."

"Happy? Whatever gave you that idea?"

Bertie was quiet for a beat and then said, "I guess it was that getting married thing."

THREE NIGHTS LATER, Bertie followed Louise's directions to the dismal council flats where Geoffrey was staying. Bertie didn't normally get nervous walking alone in London, but she felt a prick of fear as she turned on to Geoffrey's empty road. She'd brought a bottle of wine, as she'd learned to do when still in Bristol—a liquid ticket to the evening's festivities—and if someone had an urge to emerge from an alley to clutch her throat, she could smash it over his head. There were rails on the upper floor of Geoffrey's building. Some sort of balcony probably, but from the pavement the suggestion was of barbed wire, a prison encampment. Yet the building was hardly secure, the front door propped open by a stone, receiving the damp of the evening. Inside, the foyer was dim, all but one overhead bulb burnt out. Bertie took the stairs then followed a long hall redolent of curry to #29. She knocked. Once. No answer. And then again. After what seemed a long time she heard Louise's voice, as if from a great distance, cry, "Come in." Bertie opened the door onto a cramped room with a twin bed and small desk on which sat an old-fashioned manual typewriter. There were books everywhere. On the desk, but also strewn about the floor, as if someone hadn't been reading but tossing them. "I'm in here," Louise called from deeper in the apartment, and Bertie walked into the next room, which had a broken-down couch with a sheet thrown over it. Beyond, Bertie found Louise in a kitchen, dark with brown cabinetry and yellow linoleum. The room, despite its feel of poverty, was clean, and Louise wore an incongruously glamorous outfit, a black tweed skirt and short-sleeved black turtleneck, black tights and pumps, her blond hair elegantly twisted and pinned to the back of her head. There were plates and cloth napkins set on the floor next to a small table piled high with newspapers and books.

"Here," Bertie said and presented the bottle of wine.

"You shouldn't have," Louise said.

Bertie shrugged and smiled. "I remembered you liked this one."

"No, I mean you really shouldn't have. Geoffrey's got a little problem with alcohol. He's trying to quit."

"Oh, I'm sorry. Well, we don't need to drink it."

"No," Louise said decisively, and she turned for a drawer and ferreted out a corkscrew. "*He's* the one with a problem. It's his responsibility to learn how to deal with it. Not ours." She opened the bottle and put it on the floor.

There was a sound from behind a door at the far end of the kitchen. Bertie raised her eyebrows, and Louise shook her head. *Not now. Later,* she seemed to be saying. Geoffrey walked in from a bedroom with a mattress on the floor and clothes strewn about, as if the place had been ransacked.

"Hey," Geoffrey mumbled, looking down.

"He's not feeling so great," Louise explained.

"I'm sorry," Bertie said. Then: "I don't need to stay. If this is a bad time . . ."

"No, you're here already. Might as well," Louise said.

Not exactly the words you'd hope for from a host. Bertie decided she'd eat and make a quick exit.

Geoffrey and Bertie sat cross-legged on the floor while Louise put chicken, potatoes, and green beans on each plate.

"Are you sick?" Bertie asked Geoffrey.

"I'm fine," he said tightly.

"Right," Bertie said. "So you two met in Birmingham?"

"Thank God," Louise said. "I don't know what I'd have done if Geoffrey hadn't taught that guest class. It was a dinner together afterward that really saved me."

"That guy was an asshole," Geoffrey said, meaning, of course, Edward.

Bertie didn't think she could say that that had never been her opinion and that she rather liked Edward. "I thought you all thought he was a great teacher, back in . . ." She cocked her head to the left, as if west to Bristol.

Louise rolled her neck, looked up at the ceiling, and said, as if Bertie were hopelessly naïve, "What can I tell you? Those that can, do; those that can't, teach."

For whatever reason, this seemed to irritate Geoffrey, and he said, "Be right back." He got up for the bathroom.

When he was gone, Louise put her hand on Bertie's and said, "I'm trying to learn what is required of me here. It's different. I know I need to drop some of my need to . . . I don't know . . . take a sort of care."

Bertie waved at his full glass of red wine. "He's not drinking, so that's good."

"Actually, he's got a bottle of something in the bathtub. That's why he's in there now. He thinks I don't know."

Bertie wrinkled her nose. "Maybe I'd better go," she said.

Louise looked toward the bathroom. "Maybe," she agreed.

In their student days, there would have been a follow-up phone call the next day—to analyze the situation, to set a date for another get-together—but London was a new world, and Bertie didn't hear anything.

ONE NIGHT, after a particularly trying performance at the Fletcher—an audience member vomited during the first act—Liesel came up to Bertie and said, "Hey! Geoffrey was just talking about you. He wants to see you, but he's afraid to call."

"What?" Bertie said. This seemed impossible.

"Shall I be your fixer then?" Liesel said, in what Bertie thought of as her British voice; her accents shifted and were sometimes hard to place. "I'll tell him to ring you."

"Yes, do," Bertie said, and within a week she and Geoffrey were at a table at World's End, a historic pub next to the Camden Town Tube stop.

"I have this idea," Geoffrey said, "of writing a play, and it would sort of be like *Anne Frank* but Anne Frank in Bosnia. Same story line, just change the names and places. Do you think that would work?"

"I guess," Bertie said. "I suppose it would all depend on how you did it."

He turned his head to the center of the room like a petulant boy annoyed by his mother. "When I was a girl," she began, mostly to have something to say, "fourteen maybe, I had a crush on someone at school. It was my first crush. On a real person, instead of a movie star. He was in the school play." She stopped for a second. "They were doing *Anne Frank* and he had the part of Mr. Frank. But the week before the show he died in his sleep."

"A fourteen-year-old kid?"

"He was a little older. Sixteen maybe. A brain aneurysm, people said. My father was convinced it was drugs. After that, the tragedy of the play and the tragedy of his death were always linked in my mind, as if the play couldn't help but kill people."

Geoffrey reached across the table to take Bertie's hand, but she shook him away.

"That's OK," she said. "I'm not trying to be . . ." She mimed a person playing the violin.

"Christ, it's not like I'm sliming all over you," Geoffrey said angrily.

"Oh, I know that," Bertie said quickly. "Of course I didn't think that." She looked away, embarrassed, could feel herself flush.

Geoffrey cleared his throat, changed his tone. He said, "All this week people have been telling me about tragedies or accidents. It's like you always learn of these things in clusters. Even Louise finally told me about her motorcycle accident."

"Louise had an accident?" Bertie said, panicked.

"Not now. What could she get up to while she's at her mum's?"

"She's at her mum's?"

"It was when she was in drama school. Didn't you know?"

Bertie laughed. "When she fell off the Vespa? And skinned her knee? I'd hardly call *that* a motorcycle accident."

"Well, she made it seem . . ."

"She likes a good story," Bertie said. Which was true. Part of Louise's actress self. If hyperbole made a story better, then hyperbole was required. Still, lying about the Vespa spill irritated Bertie. If Louise wanted to know what a vehicle-accident victim looked like, Bertie could take her to Casualty any day. Even the lucky ones never got off with a skinned knee.

LOUISE CALLED, many months later, to say she was back in London, having come to check Geoffrey into "the madhouse."

"What?"

"Yes," she said wearily, as if she was often charged with such tasks. "He went on a terrible bender, dropped out of the play he's supposed to be doing, kept pacing the apartment and saying, 'I can't do it, I can't do it,' so his agent gave me the name of a posh psychiatric hospital in Marylebone, and I deposited him at the door."

"Oh, no," Bertie said.

"Actually I hung around. I was a little nicer than all that, and I tell you, if you want to flip out, this would definitely be the place to do it. You'd never guess it was a hospital. Fitness room, café, bathrobes. They don't seem to be worried about people hanging themselves with terrycloth belts."

This, again, with a tough nonchalance, as if she were long used to suicidal threats and stunts, a roll of the eye in her manner. God, so much *theater* in *theater people!*

Geoffrey had been in the hospital for two weeks, she added, and was getting rather buff from lifting weights in the fitness room.

"So . . . ," Bertie said. "Can I do something to help?"

"He doesn't want visitors."

"Right," Bertie said. "And you?"

"Well, that's why I called. I thought I better get the name of a psychiatrist for him to see. Once he gets out."

"Right," Bertie said. She offered a few names she knew from the hospital.

"Aren't you a luv?" Louise said in the voice of an old biddy.

"Yes," Bertie said. "I am a luv. That's exactly what I am."

Louise laughed.

"Shall we get together?" Bertie started to say, but her question crossed Louise's "Bye-bye then," and the sound of the dial tone.

THAT SAME WEEK, Liesel asked Bertie to lunch, and within minutes of sitting down, confided that she had a lump in her breast, definitely malignant. She couldn't decide between lumpectomy and radiation or mastectomy and chemotherapy. It wasn't *clear* she needed the latter. "Cancer 'lite,'" she said by way of explanation. "Glad I got it that way instead of fully caffeinated." She smiled. "I don't know what to do." Then she added in a little-girl voice, "*Tell* me what to do." It was a joke—the voice and the asking for directions—but not really.

"I'm sorry," Bertie said. "That's a hard decision."

"I think I should just do the lumpectomy, and screen really, *really* carefully after."

"That makes sense," Bertie said. But she'd have said the same if Liesel had come to the opposite decision. Good advice sometimes came down to intuiting what a person most wanted.

Liesel nodded, as if in agreement.

"Schedule it on a Friday if you can. I don't work Fridays. I can come with you," Bertie offered.

Liesel grabbed her hand; her eyes teared. "No, no, but could I ask you to stay with Idzia? I don't want her to be all alone and worrying."

Idzia, Bertie had by now learned, was Liesel's daughter, a precocious teen who sometimes sat in the green room during performances.

Only Liesel never did call Bertie to monitor Idzia, and Louise never did follow up with the psychiatrists Bertie recommended, though Louise did find him a different doctor at Bertie's hospital.

Oh, well, Bertie thought, an inner shrug telling her to pay no mind, you couldn't tell why people chose what they chose, though part of her wondered why someone would ask for aid and then not take it. *I want what you have. But wait! I forgot. What you have is no good.*

BERTIE NEXT HEARD from Louise in the autumn. Geoffrey was out of hospital, and Louise seemed cheery about his progress. The two women arranged to meet for tea and then a walk from Primrose Hill to the south side of Regent's Park. Bertie had been in London for over a year now, and she had her favorite spots and routes. As they walked, Bertie told Louise how she longed to find a new roommate: Gloria had a way of making the world seem so bleak, as if they were already dowagers with no prospects in the world. "Which I do feel at times," Bertie admitted, then wished she hadn't said anything.

"Do you think Geoffrey's violent?" Louise said suddenly. She stopped by the entrance to the zoo.

"No, why?" Bertie made a little waving motion, so they'd move away from the animal stink and toward the park's central thoroughfare.

"We had a fight last night. You know he's got a new apartment now. I helped him move out of that horrible place he had. So we were in bed, doing it, you know, and when we were through, he put his hand up under my head and made a ponytail of my hair and then pulled my head back and said, 'OK.' Like things were all better. So I was thinking, 'What a relief. Back to normal.' And then he pulls hard and says, 'I still don't know what to do about the fact that I want to sleep with Bertie Russell.'"

"That's ridiculous! He's not interested in me. He only said that to hurt you."

Louise said, "Well, it worked."

"What a horrible thing to say."

"I can't tell you how hard he pulled. No one's ever done anything like that to me before."

"Louise," Bertie began, ready to deliver a speech about how she should have nothing to do with Geoffrey if he was abusive.

But Louise interrupted and said, philosophically, as if she'd decided not to let the matter bother her after all, "I guess he's got his problems."

"Yes, but . . ."

"I'm going to California, you know. I've got a part in a Hollywood movie, if you can believe it. Not the lead, but it's a good part."

"I didn't know, but that's good. Good for you. I'll miss you. I so like having you in London."

Louise smiled vaguely and said, "Oh, that's so nice to hear."

AT THE THEATER, Liesel waved her lively hellos, seemed always too busy to talk, but then grabbed Bertie's fingers one night and said, "Dinner! How is it that I've never had you over? Can you come? Monday? It's the only night I can do anything social."

"Of course, love to," Bertie said.

Liesel lived in Kensington, a tony address. The house had spectacular art, giant gilt mirrors, posh midcentury-modern furniture, one lamp like a giant glass globe over the dining room, another like an elegant, upside-down umbrella in the center of the living room. "This place is amazing," Bertie said when she arrived. Liesel had always given off the air of the bohemian single mother who was making life work with odd compromises and barters. Every time Bertie complimented her on a sweater or dress, it turned out it was something she'd found at a consignment shop.

"It *is* amazing," Liesel agreed, leading Bertie back into a broad white kitchen. Idzia sat at a table at the far end of the room, doing what Bertie assumed was her homework. It turned out the place was just a housesit owned by a Swiss couple who only used it in the summer. Liesel and Idzia stayed for free during the school year. "We're nomads once June comes," Liesel said, explaining that they crashed with friends, lived in hostels. Once they even spent the night at a homeless shelter, which Liesel seemed to find amusing.

Bertie was appalled. "Don't let that happen again. Come stay with me. I've got a room. I finally got rid of my terrible roommate."

"Are you serious?" Idzia looked up from her work, eager.

As if Idzia were an over-exuberant dog, Liesel said, "Down, girl, down."

"Of course I am serious," Bertie said. "If you ever need a place, especially with all of this." She waved her hand in the direction of Liesel's breasts.

Liesel put her hand to her chest and said, "Oh, I'm fine. This is all fine."

"Really?" Bertie said. Liesel had offered no follow-up reports on her condition, had only once said that the radiation was making her feel fagged out.

"Yes," Liesel said, and then in a more emphatic way, eyes traveling pointedly to Idzia and back. "*Yes.*"

"Like I say, I've got an extra room. If you need it, it is yours."

"Are you serious?" Idzia repeated.

"I do feed her, you know," Liesel said, clearly embarrassed by Idzia's manner. "I fed you once this week, didn't I, sweetheart?"

When Bertie left that night, she hugged Liesel good-bye and whispered, just because the dinner had made her uneasy, "You *are* all right, then?"

Liesel cocked her head. "Actually, not so great. If you know what I mean."

A wave of dread knocked Bertie to the beach of herself. *Oh, my God,* she thought. *I gave her the wrong advice.* "Yes," she managed. "I know what you mean."

When Bertie next saw Liesel, she was clearly wearing a wig, but when Bertie tried to ask about what was going on, Liesel said in a silly voice, like that of a prim schoolteacher—she even held one finger up and wagged it with her final words—"Yes, yes, my medical friend. You think you must know everything, but you must not!"

Whatever was this supposed to mean? That Bertie should mind her own business?

NOT THAT NIGHT, but soon after, Geoffrey—who she thought had drifted entirely out of her life—called to say he was a patient in the psych ward at Bertie's hospital. Could she, he wanted to know, go to his flat and get him a script? "If you wouldn't mind. I mean, I hate to ask, but since you've got to come to work in any case."

"OK," Bertie said. "What . . . ?" She was going to ask Geoffrey what was going on, but instead she said, "You all right?"

"Not really," he said. "I sort of thought I better check myself in. You know. You can imagine." There was something in his voice that made her back off further questioning. No, she couldn't imagine. She'd always been better with the clear-cut lines of physical suffering.

"I'm sorry it's been a bad time," she said. He gave her the name of a neighbor who could let her into his flat.

She found him at the hospital the next afternoon. He looked terrible, slumped into himself and exhausted. "It's scary in here," he said, his voice a whisper.

Indeed, Bertie thought. He wasn't in the luxury-liner psych ward anymore.

"People here are crazy."

He seemed to think he wasn't in that category. Bertie thought he wasn't either. She still had the idea of his mental troubles as being part of his actor persona, but then she went and read his chart. His girlfriend—not Louise but someone named Meredith Brookner, according to the charts—had broken up with him, and he'd tried to hang himself.

"So, Geoffrey," Bertie said slowly, not giving away what she now knew. "I'll stop by tomorrow after work. That OK?"

"Yeah. That would be good." But after work the next day, Bertie found Geoffrey's bed vacant. He'd been transferred out. His parents lived in Sheffield, and they wanted him closer to home.

AS FOR LOUISE, she next rotated back into Bertie's life in August. She emailed from wherever she was to say hello and let Bertie know that she'd be at the Fletcher in the fall. She'd been cast in the Yazmina Reza play *God of Carnage*. "So see you soon!" she enthused.

But when the time came, something was wrong. "Oh," Louise said vaguely when Bertie stopped by after an early rehearsal to say hello. Louise stood to hug her, then gestured to the stage to indicate it wasn't a good time for a break. "We'll have to get together."

"Yes," Bertie said, but instead of pulling her datebook from her bag, Louise waggled her fingers good-bye and whispered, "Later."

A week into the run, Liesel found Bertie after a show and said, "Let's go into the restaurant. I've got to tell you something."

Bertie's heart clenched. Had the cancer spread?

They settled at the bar.

"So," Bertie said. "Are you all right?"

"Yes, yes. I'm trying not to worry about it. You can only go so crazy, right?" When Liesel talked like this, she seemed so much more like an American than a Brit, and it occurred to Bertie that she'd never heard her whole story. Something had put her off asking about Idzia's father, though she wondered what the facts were, if he'd ever been in the picture.

"You know Marie Helene?" Liesel said.

Marie Helene was one of the four actors in *God of Carnage*. Bertie said, "I've seen the show, but I don't know her."

"I was talking with her and saying how excited I was that Louise Lizzimore was here, since I saw her in *Why Not?*" This was the movie Louise had done in America. "And Marie Helene said, 'I don't know. I don't trust Louise.' So I asked why, of course, and then Marie Helene told me that she and Louise were talking about *you*."

"About me?" Bertie said.

"Yes. At some point I told Marie Helene about your acting stint in Bristol, which she thought was very cool, and Marie Helene was telling Louise that she wanted to meet you. But Louise cut her off and said, 'You have to stay away from Bertie Russell. She's evil.'"

"What?"

"She said you were evil."

Evil? What could that mean? She knew her friendship with Louise had changed, but why would she say *that*?

"And then Marie Helene said that the very next day she saw Louise hugging you at the opening-night party. So Marie Helene said she didn't trust Louise. After seeing that."

Bertie remembered the hug. How could Louise have called her—have called anyone—evil?

"Who is evil?" Bertie said. "Hitler. Stalin. I mean . . . *evil*."

"Yeah." Liesel laughed. "You kind of have to take that as a negative."

Bertie was silent.

"I didn't want to upset you. Just warn you." She added, "I think she was thinking more of evil as in witch evil. Not so much genocidal maniac." When Bertie didn't laugh, Liesel said, "You know, she's always seemed kind of full of herself to me. I mean, actors are, but even more so. I'd try to let it go if you can. I only told you because I wanted you to know you can't trust her."

"Right," Bertie said. Only she couldn't let it go. She took the word on her walk home, then to bed and to work the next day. The word rode with her on the Tube. Evil! Evil! She was a nurse! Her whole life was devoted to helping people. That was *her role*. Hadn't she visited Geoffrey in the hospital? Hadn't she offered Liesel and Idzia her apartment, if they were ever stuck without a place? She worried about other people all the time. How could *she* be evil?

From then on, Bertie avoided Louise on the nights she ushered. Finally, though, because she could not let it rest, she called Louise. When Bertie repeated what she had been told, Louise said, "That's not true. If Liesel Pearlman said that, it's not true." Why would Louise, while denying it, name the person who had, in fact, said it? "And anyway, people tell me that you call me a liar."

"I've never called you a liar. I've said that you tend to hyperbole. You do, but I . . ."

"Oh, let's forget all this. Come over, and I'll make you dinner. Come tonight."

"I can't," Bertie said. "I'm busy."

"Well, soon then, we'll get together soon."

But they didn't. Bertie told Liesel she'd rather not usher till the show finished its run.

AND THAT WAS THAT. Louise didn't call when she left town, and that was fine. That was behind her. It was over! Bertie was promoted at the hospital. Her life became fuller, in the way lives eventually do. Things were changing now, she thought, in all the best ways. It occurred to her that she'd existed, for a long time, as if she was a side act. Others were in the main ring. But she couldn't keep that up. When her time to die came, she didn't want the camera to be out in the hall with the nurses. She wanted it to be right in the room with her. She only had this one life. She had to stay right here with it. She had not to be distracted away.

"WEREN'T YOU FRIENDS with that actor?" a voice said one night on the wards. Bertie looked up to see Kathleen, the ward supervisor she'd been paired with back in 2002, when she'd first touched someone who had died. Kathleen had moved to a hematology floor, but sometimes she visited when a patient was transferred to Bertie's unit. Kathleen was peering at a computer screen. "Louise Lizzimore, you mean?" Bertie said. She had no memory of ever talking about Louise to Kathleen.

"No, Geoffrey Walker."

"Yes," Bertie said.

"He's dead." Kathleen pointed her chin to the screen.

"Oh!" Bertie gasped, then said, automatically, "Was it suicide?" Kathleen nodded.

Bertie took one step closer and saw the headline, "Actor Dead at 33," then turned away.

Bertie couldn't absorb the facts in a way that made sense. He'd hanged himself in a hotel room, the news report said. He'd secured his wrists with duct tape, so he couldn't, at the last minute, change his mind.

"Oh, God," Bertie said. She'd heard stories of suicides through the years, the way one does, but never a detail like that.

A few days later, Liesel sent an email: "I recall you came to know him well, isn't that right? I didn't even know him much—I can only remember having a few conversations with him, during the run of that show—and *I'm* having trouble getting my head around it. I gather he suffered from depression. Still, it's hard to square it. His life looked so charmed. Speaking of charmed—ha, ha, ha—remember when you said Idzia and I could come stay with you if we needed to? Well, I hate to say this, but we need to."

THE RECEPTION AFTER the funeral was held in a wood-paneled club in Kensington. Attendees were directed up the elaborate central staircase to the second floor. As Bertie passed through the foyer, she saw Louise on the landing midway up. She was talking—but it seemed more like performing—to a group of men clustered around her. She wasn't a well-known actress at this point, but she was poised on her real fame. In the future, there would be starring roles and an Oscar. There would be photo shoots in *Vogue* and articles in which Louise's earnest goodness was singled out for praise. There would be interviewers who would say she didn't seem to have a mean bone in her body. But Bertie didn't know any of this yet. Bertie didn't know how much these characterizations would smart through the years.

"Bertie," Louise said slowly, as she turned and took Bertie in. "Good to see you." Louise came down a few steps to hug her with one arm.

"Good to see you, too," Bertie said, leaning halfheartedly forward.

It was clear that Louise hated her.

Bertie hated Louise, too.

The men looked on, but without interest. Bertie was not pretty. She was not someone they were supposed to know. Bertie smiled at them and kept walking.

Louise returned to the men. She actually stood a step above them on the stairs, and they all turned their heads up toward her, as if to the queen.

In the reception room, not yet filled with guests, Bertie flashed on a drive she and Louise had taken one day in Bristol. They had some workaday errand to do; she vaguely remembered it had to do with getting new tires. While they were driving, Louise turned to Bertie and asked how much she weighed.

"Oh, I don't want to say," Bertie said. She was embarrassed by her weight, always had been.

"No, tell me," Louise said encouragingly.

"I know it's stupid," Bertie said. "I just can't. I really don't want to."

But Louise kept insisting, and Bertie felt more and more embarrassed, because why not just offer up the number? It wasn't a big deal. But she couldn't. She couldn't. Bertie was aware of why Louise was asking. She wanted to comfort herself with her lower weight. She knew she was better than Bertie. But she didn't know how much.

4

DOCUMENTS

JOEL PUTS THE FILE on the kitchen table. "Come," he says, his arm beckoning. "Have a seat."

At the sink, slicing a lemon for iced tea, Daniella says, "Remember, we don't have to do this."

"Yes," Joel says. "We do."

Just then a car honks in the driveway.

"Saved by the bell." Daniella smiles. She turns, and Joel rises for the door.

It is Amy, Joel's sister, all good cheer and bluster, her car trunk full of supplies "Wine," she calls from behind her car. She is already unloading. "1992. Kosher. It's the best," she says. "Which just means it doesn't taste like Kool-Aid." Amy doesn't even drink, but she's quick to judge. Also to enthuse. She compliments herself a lot. Evaluates others. At first, Daniella read this as a fault. Now it seems like appealing frankness. It helps that Daniella's on the receiving end of Amy's compliments, but even if she weren't, Daniella would like Amy's other qualities, her no-nonsense spirituality and ethical sense. Amy's almost the only person Daniella knows who believes in God, though Daniella's not clear on what that belief means to Amy. Still, Daniella has an almost superstitious sense of Amy as knowing things, of having sussed out how things truly *are.*

Certainly she's picked the right moment to interrupt Daniella and Joel.

"I see you've got some ginger ale and Coke in there," Joel says, peering into Amy's trunk. "I hope you got a good year."

"You can sniff the bouquet later," Amy says.

Joel sneezes majestically in response. Something blooming in the fields around the house has everyone sniffling. The upcoming nuptials: "I"-snort-"I do." Joel thinks they should offer Benadryl as a party favor.

"Don't help," Amy says to Joel as he reaches in for a box. "I need the exercise."

"You?" Joel says.

"Yes, and soon as I drop this, I'm going."

"Where?"

"The gym. Where else? "

Amy is a serious weightlifter. She is stout but sturdy—"I'm fat!" she'll say, no complaint, simply a declaration of fact—and Daniella always wonders what the gym rats make of her, a bossy Jewish woman with winged bangs and dark hair feathered to her shoulder. ("What do they make of me? They *love* me," Daniella can almost imagine Amy saying, but of course, Daniella hasn't asked.) "Feel my arm," Amy has demanded, and Daniella has. She is as hard as, what else?, a rock. "Don't mess with me," Amy says.

"God, I won't," Daniella says.

"OK," Amy says when all the boxes are in the mudroom. Aside from the wine, she's bought platters, linens, dishes, and cutlery. Her husband's the manager for a high-end caterer in Boston. These items will save on the cost of the post-ceremony lunch to be held in a barn—an elegant one, outfitted for such occasions—a few miles down the road. Amy turns her full attention to Daniella. "You're so thin!" she cries, a compliment she repeats every time they meet. Often also how pretty. "It's because you're an architect," Amy muses now. "Have you ever met a fat architect? No, you have not, and that is because *they do not exist!* What I'm trying to tell you is that I'm not fat because I eat too much but because I picked the wrong major in college. Now someone give me a doughnut. It took a lot of effort to say all that, and I need some nourishment."

"We don't have doughnuts," Daniella says, "but I can go get some."

"I'm joking, darling," Amy says. "OK." She clap-wipes her hands off, then says, "I'm out of your hair. I'll see you later."

"So," Joel says when Amy is gone, "avoidance is no longer possible." He pretend-cackles and waggles his fingers like a witch, then he gestures to the folder on the kitchen table. Daniella slides into a chair. Joel takes the seat to her left and says, more seriously, "I want you to know the true story. I want you to know everything."

As Daniella has already told Joel, partial knowledge suits her fine. Still, Joel insists. It's a rite of passage, like the giving of the ring and the sending of the invitations. The second wife's task: the reading of the divorce file. Joel wants to work through his past, page by page. "I don't want you to go into this blind," he says.

"I've got a pretty good idea of what I am doing," she says. He is forty-one to her thirty-one; of course, he has more of a history than she.

"Humor me."

"Don't I always?" She reaches for his hand, offers a squeeze.

There's something so theatrical about picking a certain moment to "do" his first marriage. Or maybe there's only something theatrical about the moment he has picked: a few days before their own wedding, everything already planned and paid for, reversing course no longer a true option for the drama-averse. Still, it's no big deal. She's happy enough to do what he wants. They sit down at the table, open the fat file, start at the first page. She will read; he will explain. She will merge what he tells her into what she already knows. They will begin.

The Commonwealth of Massachusetts
Department of Public Health
Registry of Vital Records and Statistics
Certificate of Marriage

FULL NAME GROOM   FULL NAME BRIDE
Joel Ethan Pearlman   Liesel Rosenthal

I HEREBY CERTIFY that I joined the above-named persons in marriage at No. 656 East Street, Dedham, on November 9, 1985.

Henry Isaacs, Official Station Rabbi

HE'D LOVED LIESEL, thought she was charming and fun, when he first met her on vacation. He lived in Boston at the time, she in London. Their relationship moved fast. Too fast, his parents said, but then allowed how it was nice to see him with someone. He'd never had a girlfriend before, not even in college. (This wisdom from Amy, she of the quick confidence and blunt pronouncement.)

Liesel left England four months after she met Joel. It was time to come back to the States anyway, she said. She didn't want to go back to Schenectady, where she was from, where she still had family. ("God, no!") She was too late to enroll for a final semester of college. (She only needed four more classes for her B.A.) Joel gave her a state to come home to. ("What a gift!" she mugged, over the phone, when they discussed the logistics. "A direction in life. It's what I've always wanted!")

She was rash, anyone could see that, but not so rash as to move in with Joel right away. She found a dispiriting apartment in Brighton. Also a roommate, later to be maid of honor. Within a few months, though, she was spending all her nights at Joel's, and soon enough she had officially moved in. (The roommate, Allison Day, a frequent dinner guest. Paella or grilled chicken as apology for Liesel's failure to come through with her half of the rent.) Joel was ready to marry Liesel then, but he had the idea he needed to be financially secure before he asked for her hand. He had that old-fashioned sense of responsibility. (Or sexism, Amy had once said to Daniella. Liesel couldn't find a job on her own? The answer seemed to be she couldn't. It fell to Joel to set her up with a brief-lived position at a Boston hospital.) But after Joel and Liesel had been together for nine months, Maine Medical Center in Portland made Joel an offer, and he was ready for everything: a marriage, a home. Kids soon enough, he hoped. And anyway, he didn't think he could ask Liesel to follow him to Maine if he didn't make a commitment.

(Wry Amy: "She'd have followed him anywhere. Bird on a rhinoceros's back. She didn't have a life exactly. She attached herself to other lives. She was a. . . . What's the word I'm looking for? What's the word?" "Flea?" Daniella hazarded, and Amy coughed out a "Ha!" Said, "That's about the truth.")

Joel moved to Maine, got an apartment near the hospital, bought a farmhouse soon after, his life's major pieces falling into place with surprising alacrity.

He invited Liesel to visit one weekend so he could show her the farmhouse. (It was his, but he couldn't take occupancy till late fall, when the sellers moved to Arizona.) After he toured Liesel through the property, Joel took her for a hike at a nearby state park. All the way up the mountain, Liesel yammered about the chickens she might like to keep in the yard, the back barn she'd like to do over as a painting studio. Her favorite part of the house was the tire swing, which hung from a branch of the giant maple in the side yard. She hoped the original owners wouldn't take it with them.

The state-park path rose gently, then emerged from the trees onto a broad boulder with a dramatic view. The Atlantic in one direction. The White Mountains in the other. Joel got down on one knee and handed Liesel the box with the ring. She opened it. "Oh, Joel! Oh, Joel!" she said and pulled him up for an embrace. She kept sputtering, "Oh, Joel!" exuberantly, as if she couldn't be more surprised. Hadn't she just moments ago been planning how she would occupy his home? Finally he had to say, "So is that a yes?"

"Oh, of course, honey. Yes, it's a yes. Yes!" She hugged him. A big, triumphant, the-lovers-find-each-other-at-last hug.

IN THE COURT OF COMMON PLEAS, CUMBERLAND COUNTY, ME
Domestic Relations Division   CASE #: 65-DIV-945

JOEL ETHAN PEARLMAN Plaintiff	
vs.	**JUDGMENT ENTRY** **DECREE OF DIVORCE**
LIESEL ROSENTHAL PEARLMAN Defendant	
	January 12, 1987

HE WAS BLINDSIDED when she left him, five-and-a-half months into the marriage, though she had been behaving oddly in the weeks before she departed. One day Joel came home to find her on the front parlor couch, sobbing hysterically. He was terrified.

"What happened? What's going on?"

She shook her head. "Nothing, nothing happened."

"So what's the matter?" She couldn't even catch her breath to answer him. "What is it? What is it?" he'd continued, even dropped melodramatically to his knees by the side of the couch to hold her head, which was pressed into the brightly colored cushions she'd enthusiastically sewn a few months earlier. The room was cold. She hadn't turned up the heat in the front rooms or built a fire in the kitchen's woodstove. Had she done *anything* all day? "I can't help you if you won't tell me," he said softly. But she wouldn't tell him what was wrong, just kept snuffling, "I can't. I can't," as if she'd come to the absolute end of everything. He didn't get the sense that she was saying, "I can't tell you," but "I can't go on."

AND EVEN IF SHE HAD TOLD HIM, would he have been able to help? The truth was she didn't always appreciate his help. He'd do the laundry, and she'd take it as an insult. "You think I can't do anything," she'd say.

"No, I just wanted some clean underwear."

"Don't make fun."

"I'm not making fun. I'm serious. Everything was dirty, so I did it."

In Boston she liked just wandering around, seemed to have a talent for cheering up the strangers she met on the T or in parks and coffee shops. Her goodwill extended farther than he thought safe or advisable. She once let a homeless man come to the apartment so he could take a shower.

In Maine it was another matter, because she didn't drive. There was no shortage of places to go for solitary walks, but only one place to find people in a convivial mood: a country diner about half a mile up the road. Liesel started to go there most mornings, and that seemed to her cheer her.

One night when Liesel was kneading bread for a challah, something she'd taken to making as part of her preparation for converting to Judaism, she said she'd met someone with a pickup who was going to help her clear the junk that the previous owners had left in the back barn. "I need to start thinking about painting again," she said. She'd been serious about art in college, and handy with crafts all her life (witness the pillows), but she hadn't done anything since she'd come back to America. Didn't he think it was time for her to get back to it?

Liesel wanted to plow the road to the back barn, so her new friend's pickup could drive in and haul out the barn's assorted trash: rotting lumber, warped screen windows, and decrepit wicker furniture. So far, Joel had just let the snow build up on the road. Now it was probably too packed to plow.

"Why don't you wait till spring?" Joel said, tapping on an adding machine. He was organizing bills in preparation for doing the year's taxes while she braided the dough. It was dark as midnight, though only 6:00 p.m., and Joel had that feeling he sometimes had of their house as the lone source of heat and warmth in the universe, though in fact a five-minute drive would land him at a convenience store with cheap beer and freshly cooked, if reliably lousy, pizza.

"You won't help me? I bet there's something in there I could refinish."

"Of course I'll help you," Joel said, standing to clear her dough bowl, then thinking twice of the effort. Ordinary politeness or rude one-upsmanship? You had to be careful when it came to a dirty dish. "Call a snowplow. Do whatever you want."

"It'll be good. I can finally support myself," she said of the painting.

"Even people who have gone to grad school and have had gallery shows don't exactly make a living on their work," Joel said.

"Why do you think I can't sell my art?"

"That's not what I meant," Joel said and refrained from pointing out that she hadn't yet made any artwork to sell. "Just that the art world is very difficult."

Painting wasn't the only thing she wanted to do. One night, she said she was going to become a nutritionist. Another, that she'd like to work at Portland's rape crisis center.

"OK," Joel said to all this. Her eating habits were peculiar. Her frequent stomachaches led her to wacky elimination diets. She couldn't eat onions, dairy, and mushrooms. Then dairy was OK but nightshades were bad. Fat, in general, was a no-no. As for the rape crisis center: She tended to over-sympathize with those in pain. Perhaps it would be too much for her? He didn't offer this, though. Instead he ventured, "Why don't you talk to someone about that? Maybe do an informational interview?"

Even this suggestion angered her. "Why can't you just accept that this is what I want to do?" she would say, though, of course, what she wanted to do seemed to change on a daily basis.

"So, good. It's what you want to do. Fine."

"Don't get angry."

"I'm not angry. My not agreeing with you 100 percent isn't me getting angry."

Sometimes when they had these conversations, Joel would think of a day during their honeymoon in Italy. They'd woken early in Padua, and Joel was thinking they'd go see the Arena Chapel, which had the famous Giotto frescoes. After, he figured, they'd try a nearby student cafeteria that, he'd read in a guidebook, offered good, cheap food, and a sense of university life in Italy. But Liesel blew up when he suggested this itinerary. Why did everything have to be so planned out? Couldn't they just go? Couldn't they just *be*?

"Fine. We'll *be*," he said. "OK, begin." He gestured out to the streets. *Lead the way.* In the end, they got lost in an uncharming section of town and rather than find a nice or interesting place to eat, Liesel had an abrupt drop in blood sugar that forced them to the nearest spot for food: a dark, dirty café. When Joel went to the bathroom, he found it covered in blood. He raced out to tell the waiter. The waiter looked irritated as Joel tried to stumble out an explanation in Italian. Once he caught on, the waiter hurried into the bathroom to see for himself. He came rushing out, screaming something in Italian. Others ran in and came out screaming. It was surreal, easily the worst day of their trip.

A MONTH AFTER JOEL CAME HOME to find Liesel crying on the sofa, he found her sobbing with the same choking hysteria at a negative sign on a pregnancy stick. She'd only just gone off the pill. It wasn't likely they'd be pregnant yet. He'd been surprised that she'd even purchased the test on one of their visits to the pharmacy. But she cried as if this was it, the final round of IVF for which they'd emptied their bank accounts. Now they'd never have a child.

"What's the matter with you? We only just started trying."

"There's nothing the matter with me," she snarled. "You are always putting me down."

He raised his hands in the OK-I'm-backing-off posture. What the hell was she talking about? He *never* put her down.

Two weeks later she left. Who is desperately sad that she isn't pregnant one day then ready to leave her husband two weeks later?

Liesel Rosenthal Pearlman, it turned out.

HER DEPARTURE WAS AS STRANGE as the end of their time together. Sometime after she was gone, she called and said, "Hi, how are you?" as if he was just an old buddy with whom she'd fallen out of touch.

He waited for her to say more. He assumed she was calling about the summons and complaint for divorce. She'd have that by now.

"So, just wondering how you are. Whether, I don't know, you are dating anyone?"

Was this a joke?

"No, Lie-sel," he said tightly. "I'm not *dating* anyone."

"Why do you have to be like this?" Liesel said. "Can't we be friends?"

He had no idea where she was calling from.

None of Joel and Liesel's mutual friends seemed to know what Liesel was up to either. Or even to be in touch with her. As far as Joel could tell, he was doing all the announcing of the separation and impending divorce, to everyone's complete surprise. That got a little hard to take. How shocked everyone was. Well, yeah, who is married for only five months? Movie stars on a bender, not people who have dated for almost a year before they marry, not people who have had a chance to figure each other out.

Sometimes Daniella wonders why Joel was so unwilling to stay friends. It can't have hurt to be on good terms with Liesel, but when Daniella asked, Joel said, "I didn't want to be her friend. I wanted to be her husband."

"Fair enough," Daniella had said.

SIX MONTHS AFTER LIESEL LEFT, Joel got a phone call from Allison Day, Liesel's maid of honor. "Hey, Joel," Allison said. "It's been so long since we've talked. I'm thinking of coming up to Maine for Labor Day weekend and wanted to see you guys."

"Me?" Joel had said, puzzled.

"Well, both of you, of course. If you are going to be in town," Allison said.

"You do know Liesel and I split up, don't you? We broke up six months ago."

"What are you talking about?"

When Joel tells the story about Allison's phone call to Daniella, he almost yells. "I couldn't believe she didn't even tell Allison! Allison was her best friend! Her maid of honor! She didn't just drop me. She dropped everyone when she left."

This being Liesel's pattern, Joel had come to realize, too late to protect himself. Liesel abruptly took on enthusiasms; she was smitten. Until she wasn't. It never occurred to Joel that he would be one of these enthusiasms.

And once she was gone, she was completely gone.

He didn't even know where to send the separation agreement. He finally mailed it to her mother in Schenectady. Liesel had said, when she'd left, weeping and apologizing, that she didn't want to be a bad person, that he deserved someone else, that she didn't want anything from him, no money, nothing. She just had to go.

Of course it wasn't as easy as that. Their bank accounts were linked. (There was so much he'd done for her: sorting out her school loans, paying down her credit-card debt, legalizing a name change she'd made—but never officially—when she was younger.) And he couldn't leave her with nothing; he'd been more or less supporting her since she came to America. So they split what was in the bank. He didn't give her any of the house. Or part of his practice, which he knew (from an older doctor) she could have asked for if they'd been married longer. Once it was clear that this wasn't a matter of belated cold feet, that she was really going, he never wanted to see her again.

WHEN THE SEPARATION PAPERS CAME BACK, the postmark was from Paris.

Paris. *What the fuck?* he thought. Some new lover whisked her away? Or she just went there because she had dual citizenship through her father? "I'm so continental," he remembered her joking once, then walking around the house saying "Mon dieu" and "C'est incroyable!" and "Goddamnit, I need a croissant." Then she'd nuzzled his neck, said, "Don't I remind you a little of Brigitte Bardot?"

"My wife! French as a French fry, I always say."

Her father had been born in Marseilles, which was hard to believe, because he didn't sound European at all. Not from what Liesel said. She made him seem like a stereotypical right-wing, born-again Christian, down to the canned lines attributing his business success to his faith. He had a terrible relationship with Liesel. She hadn't even wanted to invite him to the wedding. She only wanted her stepfather, and that simply to make her mother happy, but Joel had convinced her she'd regret it later if she didn't invite him, that there was no way to make up that sort of slight.

And then not a one of them had come.

They were frightened of long drives, Liesel said, making excuses. "I wonder if they are agoraphobic," she added. "We never went anywhere when I was a kid." But after that she had little to do with her family. "I've got you now," she said with apparent relief. Joel never met Liesel's father and only her mother and stepfather once, when he and Liesel were returning from a trip to Saratoga Springs, where they'd gone to visit Joel's college roommate. They arranged to gather at a bar at an Albany Radisson hotel, a dismal place with gray green carpet and walls. (The location seemed odd. Why not just go to their house? Who visited their parents by hitting the bar?) Liesel's overweight mother and truly obese stepfather weren't good at making conversation, though her mother was kind enough. Mostly their eyes drifted vacuously to the TV on the wall. They seemed entirely uninterested in meeting Joel, in seeing Liesel. After, Joel was relieved that Liesel wasn't more attached, even happy they hadn't come to the wedding. He didn't want to have to spend time with them. They were stupid. They were racist. (Of her own curly hair, Liesel's mother had said, "I know, I know! It's a mess! I look just like a nigger." Joel didn't think he'd actually heard a person utter the word till it came out of Liesel's mother's mouth.) On the drive home, Liesel told him that when she was a girl, one of her uncles had mailed his brother shit.

"What?"

"I know! Lovely, right?" Liesel said. "He was mad at him, so he mailed him shit."

"Jesus," Joel said. Human or dog, he thought to ask, as if it mattered. Rabbit? Perhaps that wouldn't be so gross?

"That's my bloodline," she said campily. "Gosh! I wonder what our kids will be like!"

"Let's just adopt a gerbil," Joel said.

"*Now* you get why I don't like them?" Liesel said, for he had goaded her all along to be more in touch. He was so close to his own family that it was hard for him to understand her minimal attachment.

As for the Paris postmark on the separation papers, once Joel digested the fact, he let it go. But not Amy. She was oddly obsessed by the detail. "Paris? Paris?" she kept saying. "Don't you want to find out what took her there?"

"No," he said.

But Amy did.

"If I were stupid rich . . ." Amy once said to Daniella. "You get what I'm saying? Not just rich, but *stupid* rich. I'd have hired a private detective. Not to get her back. Who'd want her back? But just to know. I kept on wondering what happened to her. I didn't like her, after what she put Joel through. But I was curious. I mean, what happened? Where'd she go? *Why'd* she go? He was taking such good care of her. Who *was* she? I mean, really, in the end, who was Liesel Pearlman?"

November 2, 1992

MOTION TO MODIFY
Circumstances have changed substantially since the Court's Judgment of
Order in this Case. The changes concern the following issues:

___ Parental Rights and Responsibilities
___ Primary Physical Residence of the Minor Child
___ Rights of Contact or Visitation with the Minor Child
_X_ Child Support
___ Spousal Support (Alimony)
___ Other

The change in circumstances are as following:

I ask the Court to review the Judgment or Order and make the following
changes

Back child support for five years and six months for his daughter, Idzia
Pearlman. Ongoing child support for his child till the age of 18.

AMY GOT AN ANSWER. Eventually. Well, part of an answer. Liesel disappeared for five years and then reappeared with her hand out. So much for
saying she didn't want anything from Joel. He had a child, she thought it
was time to mention. At first, Joel didn't believe her. He'd seen that negative
pregnancy test before she left, and it hadn't been like they'd been amorous in
the final weeks. She wouldn't kiss him. She flinched when he drew his hand
across her hip. But she wouldn't tell him why she didn't want him. They'd
had a good sex life before. "Liesel," he said, sharply one night, after she'd
recoiled from his effort to hold her. Just to hold her! She'd always said she
liked sleeping nestled in his arms.

"I'm sorry," she said. "I know. I know. It's just I need you to be more like a
roommate right now."

"Even roommates talk to each other," Joel said. "You need to tell me what is going on."

"Would you mind sleeping in the guest room tonight? I just need some space. I can't explain it."

"OK," he said, defeated. It was freezing in the guest room. There were no heat vents on the second floor. The temperature wasn't so bad in the master bedroom, which was closer to the kitchen with its woodstove, but it was impossible in the guest room, which was largely closed off from the rest of the house. Within an hour he was back in his own bedroom. "This is my bed," he said to Liesel, his anger having bubbled up during his frozen sojourn to the front of the house. "I bought it, and I'm going to sleep in it."

And just then, she turned to him and said, "I know, I know, I'm sorry, I'm sorry. I love you. I do. I don't know what's the matter with me. It's like I can't think straight about anything anymore. Please forgive me. You're right. I need to go to therapy."

"Of course," he said. "It doesn't matter." And he meant it. They made love then. Their last time, as it turned out. It had been long enough since they'd done it that Joel came within minutes, and so he followed her apologies with his own.

It was too brief, he knew.

Too brief, but it did the trick.

There was nothing ambiguous about the paternity test on which he'd insisted. Idzia Pearlman was his. She even had his name. (Amy: "Why would Liesel keep Joel's *name?*") Idzia had been out there for five years, and he'd never even known of her!

To: Liesel Rosenthal Pearlman
From: Joel Pearlman
Re: Visitation request
Dated: March 17, 1993

As per the ORDER IN MOTIONS, Docket No. 23-DV-919 of March 10, 1993, I am hereby notifying you that I would like to exercise my right to visitation with Idzia Pearlman from the period of July 5–July 19, 1993. Please be prepared to transport Idzia to and from Charles de Gaulle Airport in Paris. Please have her clothes packed and passport ready for a trip to the United States.

Please confirm whether or not these plans are acceptable in writing at the earliest possible time.

Thank you.

Joel Pearlman

JOEL *DID* PAY what the U.S. courts said he owed. Not that he had any choice, the government garnished $300 a month from his hospital paycheck. The sum was wired into her bank account. But Joel *didn't* pay the back support, once he realized Liesel had no intention of letting him see Idzia.

Sanford Harriman
Attorney At Law

April 17, 1995

Re: Pearlman vs. Pearlman

Dear Jerome Wex:

Enclosed please find a cashier's check payable to your client, Joel Pearlman, for $8,000 as per Judge Kingsley's Order on Motions dated October 17, 1994.

Very truly yours,
Sanford Hallowell

cc: Liesel Pearlman

April 25, 1995

The Law Offices of Jerome Wex

re: Pearlman vs. Pearlman

Dear Mr. Pearlman:

Enclosed please find a personal money order drawn from the escrow account in the amount of $8,000.00. This represents the sanction for the refusal of Ms. Pearlman to contact you regarding your registered mail R026905795. I understand that she accepted the registered mail, but did not respond to your request for visitation.

Thank you for your attention to this matter.

Very truly yours,
Jerome Wex

cc: Liesel Pearlman

BRIEFLY, LIESEL TOOK IDZIA to Morocco to live. Joel only knew this because a registered letter was returned to him unopened. Simply put in another envelope and mailed off. No return address, but a postmark from Fes, Morocco. Fes? Morocco? Joel recognized Liesel's handwriting on the envelope. Long, looping letters. Elegant, though hard to read. *Retour à l'envoyeur. Return to sender* in French, not Arabic or Berber. Perhaps this meant Liesel was not planning to stay very long. Learning the language of the new country seemed like just the sort of enthusiasm that she'd take up, then drop when the verb conjugations proved too difficult.

What kind of life was his daughter being subjected to? Joel couldn't guess. He had no associations with Morocco beyond rugs and mint tea. Still, Morocco provided something like a break. While Liesel was there, Joel's lawyer found a loophole that allowed Joel to make his back child support contingent on visits. More than once, Joel's lawyer had explained that typically custody and child support were separate decisions. This baffled Joel. How to enforce compliance, if not with money? If the Liesel now was anything like the Liesel he once knew, she needed more than the $300 a month she was getting from him. She'd never held a job for an extended period of time and had no head for anything financial.

Morocco was not a signatory to the Hague Convention on Civil Aspects of International Childhood Abduction. As such, Joel's lawyer was able to arrange things so that Joel paid the back child support the U.S. courts said he owed (plus interest) into a registry. Liesel could have that money if she allowed visits. But if she didn't, she couldn't.

What was the point of the money piling up if no one was going to withdraw it? The action addressed this eventuality as well. A sum was returned to Joel on a quarterly basis, by way of a fine. Not the whole lot, of course, but a portion. Letters were now sent to Liesel's and Joel's lawyers, noting the amount of the check drawn on the escrow account. It was this that sent Liesel over the edge. She started calling Joel regularly, always at night, at a time designed to wake him, and with increasing anger about his selfishness, his greed. How, *how*, she wanted to know, could he steal money from his daughter? His own daughter?

"She can have the money if I can become her father. You just have to let me see her," Joel said.

"So you can brainwash her against me?" Liesel said. "I don't think so."

November 14, 1995

Department of State Bureau of Consular Affairs
Office of Children's Affairs

Dear Mr. Pearlman:

I am writing to update you on recent activity in your case and the actions that have been taken to help you resolve it. We have spoken of these actions, but I hope the summary provided will be helpful to you.

The U.S. Embassy staff in London contacted the taking parent in writing to request a welfare and whereabouts visit. The taking parent verbally declined the visit and would not cooperate further. Therefore, due to concerns for the American citizen minor's welfare, and our role in monitoring the welfare of children at the request of a parent, we will enlist the assistance of a local private or public social agency which may provide assistance to determine the child's current condition. As soon as we have a report, I will contact you.

Sincerely,

Carla A. Jones

December 20, 1995

Department of State
Bureau of Consular Affairs
Office of Children's Issues

Dear Mr. Pearlman:

I am writing to update you on recent activity in your case and the actions that have been taken to help you resolve it.

In response to our request for a welfare and whereabouts visit of your daughter Idzia Pearlman: We are pleased to inform that we have received a response from the U.S. Embassy in London.

A visit was conducted by Ms. Allesandra Jobson of the Court of Justice London in accordance with article 5 of the Vienna Convention. They reported that Idzia was in satisfactory condition and have provided a letter that we attach that confirms this. We hope this provides some reassurance and are pleased to have been of assistance.

Sincerely,

Carla A. Jones

THERE ARE PAGES of documents that just repeat every few months. The language is always the same; only the dates change. The same "Motion to Modify" with Liesel's handwritten complaints: "Stop the FINES! In contempt of international court." The same (ignored) requests for visits from Joel.

Then the attempts to figure out if Idzia is OK. First Idzia is visited by welfare workers in London. (London is where the two seem to go after Morocco. But Joel doesn't really know where they are, just tracks where the lawyers send their letters.) In the file is a letter to Joel from the federal Abduction Prevention Unit. (Daniella has a bad feeling. Hasn't Joel gone too far here? Accusing Liesel of abduction? "I just got information," he says. "I didn't pursue anything." He points to a paper from the Children's Passport Issuance Alert Program. "I didn't do this either.")

Daniella feels weary of this file. She tells Joel, "This is enough. I get it."

"No, not all of it," he says. "Not everything."

"It's OK," she says.

WHAT IS DRIVING THIS? Daniella already *knows* this story. Of course, a point of shame for Joel is how she found out about Liesel. A late-night call. Joel picking up the phone, going into the other room, and talking in hushed but angry tones.

"Who was that?" Daniella said when Joel came back to bed. At first, she had thought it was the hospital.

"My ex-wife."

"You were married?"

They had been dating for a few months at that point. Daniella felt that slight tightening of the skin that comes with alarm. Was her boyfriend not who he appeared to be? It didn't seem possible. He had too many friends, too much of an open manner, too wide and social a life to have a secret existence.

"I was. For five months in 1986. I'm not in touch with her anymore," Joel said. "She, however, is in touch with me. Whenever she's on the rag, as best as I can tell."

Daniella didn't like this, blaming a woman's hormones for her emotions, but she didn't say anything.

"Periodically, she likes to call and tell me what a bad man I am. Then she asks for money. Not a very effective strategy."

"But if she complimented you?"

He laughed. "She only has to do one thing to get money from me: Let me see my daughter."

"You have a daughter?" Daniella said, a little sick. This seemed an awfully big fact to have failed to share. "Why doesn't she let you see her?"

"Because she's an angry, crazy bitch," Joel said.

"Right," Daniella said, and because he was clearly angry, she added, "Maybe you can tell me about it later."

THE WEDDING NEXT WEEK is going to be simple: immediate family at the synagogue, a slightly larger crowd invited back to the barn for a catered dinner. Joel doesn't have the taste for a big blowout, given he's already had one and look where that landed him. Daniella once overheard Amy saying, "It's not Daniella's fault he's been married before." Meaning, Daniella guesses, that she shouldn't be denied the pouf and drama of a wedding just because Joel has a disastrous marriage in his past. But Daniella doesn't care. She's never understood the to-do around weddings. She just likes the idea of having an excuse to fly her college girlfriends into town.

September 20, 1996

Jerome Wex
Attorney At Law

Re: Joel Pearlman vs. Liesel Pearlman

Dear Ms. Pearlman:

Mr. Pearlman's attorney has proposed that we settle this case. Mr. Pearlman would get half the money currently held in escrow. You would get the other half. Mr. Pearlman would sign off his rights to visit Idzia, and he would not pay any more child support. He would forever give up the right to contact her. She would retain the right to inherit from him. If you remarry, Idzia could be adopted by your new husband.

I think this is a good solution. If you continue to refuse to let Mr. Pearlman to see Idzia, you will spend all the money that is in my trust account in fines, penalties, and lawyer's fees. This is not a good result for you. I strongly urge you to consider accepting this offer of settlement. This will bring the whole matter to a final end.

Meanwhile, if you continue to interfere with Idzia's contact with her father, the court will continue to fine you through the trust. You can avoid bad results by letting Idzia speak with Mr. Pearlman on the telephone.

Very truly yours,

Jerome Wex

THIS IS THE SHAMEFUL HEART of the file, but it is also something Daniella already knows, for it happened one year into her relationship with Joel: He signed off on his rights as parent. He tried to end all of it. The drama, the legal fees, the calls. He wanted it to be over. He wanted to change his number to stop Liesel from calling him. If it meant losing a chance at a relationship with his daughter, so be it.

They were in Boston, visiting Amy, when Joel told her his decision about his daughter. He didn't consult her, just announced it as a done deal. Daniella was surprised. "Maybe you shouldn't," she started to say, but he held up his hand and said, "Decision made. It's over." After, in the kitchen, while Daniella and Amy were doing dishes, Amy made her pronouncements: "It's good he finally did it. It was jeopardizing his work, his relationship with you, his peace."

"It never jeopardized his relationship with me," Daniella said, though that wasn't quite true. In the beginning, after it was divulged, it made things a little shaky. She put her hand out for a dish to dry.

"Of course it jeopardized things with you!" Amy insisted. "And it jeopardized things with Idzia. And, please, can we talk about what a crazy name that is? Idzia! Joel knows Liesel says terrible things about him to her. He knows from the phone calls. What kind of relationship can he have with a girl whose head has been crammed full of lies about him?"

"I guess," Daniella had said, unsure. Idzia was still his daughter.

"I'm telling you. He can't! It's *not possible*. After a point with a crazy person, you just have to step away. Or you become completely *mishegah* too. What will happen to that girl is that she will find her way or she won't." Amy brushed her thick hair back with a soapy hand, looked up at the foam stuck to her head, and said, "My horn. Jews do have them, it turns out." Then she wiped the foam away and said, "And you know what, she *will* find her way. And you know why? Because half of her genes belong to my brother."

Joel's lawyer has offered up a version of this same thinking: "Kids of divorce, when they become teenagers and try to individuate, butt heads with the parents they are living with. They get curious about the other parent. They have a fantasy of having something better than where they are right now. It's when you'll have your chance. Your daughter needs to know that you are trying. That's all. I predict she will come around and try to contact you eventually."

And what if the daughter sees a copy of this letter? Daniella wonders. Would she want to contact him after *that*?

Perhaps not. Here is where Joel has made his real mistake, but Daniella didn't say it back when he made the decision, and she doesn't say it now.

"So, that's that."

"That's that," he says, and picks up the thick file, hugs it to his chest. "I can put this in the basement now." He means this literally (the basement of the house, where old files are stored) but also presumably figuratively. But the way he hugs the file, Daniella knows it is not going into any figurative basement. It's staying right upstairs, on the main floor.

If there were documents for her relationship with Joel, what would it contain? Nothing really. A simple story: *Joel and Daniella. They got along.*

And just like that, Daniella feels concerned. Is there a problem here?

Is she not interesting enough?

She's the good wife. (Well, soon-to-be-wife.) She knows that. She knows that!

Is she also the dull one?

Has she failed, in her placidity, to be compelling? She is not ever, she knows, the topic of conversation, as Liesel is. It's never bothered her before, but suddenly it does.

I told you I didn't want to know everything, she thinks as Joel leaves the room for the basement. Her inner voice surprises her with its bitterness. *Didn't I tell you that?*

And just then, Amy, her timing again impeccable, clomps back in, all sweaty from her workout. "Hey," she says, letting her gym satchel thunk to the floor. "How you guys doing?"

5

TWO BLESSINGS

"IT'S GOOD TO BE HERE," Raymond says, and he slips his hand into Liesel's.

"Yes," Liesel lies. "I'm having a sort of spiritual feeling, you know?"

Raymond doesn't laugh. Ray-mon. No "d" when he pronounces it, the name so much more elegant in French. He doesn't even seem aware she has made a joke.

They are in St. Peter's Basilica with ten thousand other people—give or take a thousand—and they are waiting for the Pope. They have been waiting— they have all been waiting—since 9:00 a.m. "See the Pope? You want?" a tour guide said to them yesterday at the Colosseum. Liesel hadn't assented, had only offered that same stunned look of incomprehension she offered everyone when she was traveling. Unfazed, the tour guide had pushed two tickets into her hand. "You must go," he insisted. "Or I give to someone else!" Liesel had bobbed her head obligingly. And anyway, what else was there to do? Mention her last name? Pearlman? Not your first choice for a Vatican hoedown, though she is only "almost" Jewish. Stalled in the process of con- verting is how she likes to think of it. "Actually, go ahead, give to someone else," Liesel wanted to say this morning, when she and Raymond joined the crowds in St. Peter's Square, this before the Basilica's doors opened. It was like being on a stalled subway, everyone pressed against her. Only no one smelled of urine. No one was trying to feel her up. The religious had a few things going for them. Still, the numbers made her nervous. She couldn't quite see to the edge of the crowd, to how far she'd have to walk to be in the open. "It's OK if we don't stay," she had told Raymond, as if it were her wishes that were being catered to all along. But Raymond, brought up Roman Catholic—though Liesel has not been particularly impressed by his piousness in the year they have been together—insisted on staying.

"It's like we've been chosen," he said. "Why did the guide give them to us? He could have given them to anyone."

True.

Though Liesel has an answer. She thinks the guide caught her at the moment, overwhelmed by the horrific debauchery of the past, all those human parts as lion snacks, that she made for the Colosseum bench. The guide must have thought that Liesel was a good and kind person, deserving of a ticket. But it wasn't the past that occasioned Liesel's lightheadedness. It was the very present-tense situation of her stomach. She's had digestive trouble for most of her life, though back in New York, when she complained to doctors, they thought she was exaggerating. She eats more, eats less, low fiber, high fiber; whatever she puts in, her body protests.

Yesterday, dehydration likely made her tip into Raymond on the ascent up the Colosseum stairs. "I better sit down. Maybe get some water." He paused over her solicitously. An American woman offered a canteen, and despite its warmth and aluminum taste, she started to feel better. Her eyes filled. Crying—why?—at the simple kindness of others.

It's not dehydration that is getting to her now that she is actually in St. Peter's Basilica, seated in a chair, and waiting. Now that she's had over an hour to marvel at the tile below, the vaulted ceilings above, the gigantic gilt-framed paintings at the altars to the left and right, the famous (the famous!) Michelangelo Pietà behind her and to the right. (It's behind plastic, and Liesel wonders if this is because it is *too* famous, if people have tried to touch it in the pre-plastic past.) The problem right now is that Liesel needs to go to the bathroom. Everything may be soaring upward in this space, but she is, as ever, hopelessly rooted to the earthly.

"I'm sorry. I'm so sorry," she says finally, knowing her admission will not be welcome. "But I've got to go to the bathroom." (Oh, the legions of men who grimace at the apologizing woman. "What are *you* sorry for?" they bark.

The question so rude and impolite that it contains its own answer. *Sorry because you are going to turn this into a fault of mine, so I thought I'd beat you to it.* Self-deprecation as self-defense. Or weapon, depending on your point of view.) The vacation idea had not been for a tour of Italian restrooms, though it feels, at times, like that is what it has devolved into. And what a revolting variety of bathrooms the Italians have! Why not turn the ingenuity that made the impossible-to-believe dome above her head into, say, a toilet seat? Or an actual toilet, since she has twice been directed to a restroom that is merely a hole in the floor, around which there are muddy footprints.

Raymond looks around, as if he might find, what? A porta-potty in one of the apses? Do the French even know about porta-potties? His face scrunches in irritation. "Can't you *wait?*"

If she had more character, she'd wait. That's the implication.

Liesel gives the apologetic and hurried answer of someone who's spent a lot of her life asking people to just hold on so she can run to the bathroom. "I know, I know. It's a pain." She waves downward. It looks like she'd indicating her crotch. "I mean, no. I'm sorry. I'll be right back," she says. "We've got time."

The service, she means, is still thirty minutes off.

THOUGH EVERY SEAT in the Basilica is taken, the aisles are clear. Liesel hears the click, click, click of her shoes on the beautiful marble. Candle flames by the altars seem to flicker in her wake. At the side entrance she stumbles through a request for directions, but the guard—a white-blond man, pale to the point of disappearing—holds up a hand to stop her. "I speak English," he says, pointing outside to where she needs to go.

She makes one wrong turn but then finds the bathroom, recognizable from the substantial line that snakes out the door. Liesel can almost feel Raymond's impatience from inside the cathedral. *What is taking her so long?* He has told her St. Peter's is technically not a cathedral, but she still doesn't understand why. It *looks* like a cathedral. Not that she's an expert, but she's been in Notre Dame and definitely sees the family resemblance.

Inside, the bathroom consists of a large windowless space with stalls running along one wall and sinks opposite. In the middle of the room, there is a long table, on one side of which sit four nuns, each in front of a stack of the sort of cheap napkins her mother used to buy for weekday dinners. This, it seems, is the toilet paper, and judging from the other women's transactions, it must be purchased. Liesel flushes. She doesn't have any money with her. Raymond has everything. She moves forward when it is her turn, indicates her pockets, holds up her empty hands, and shrugs. The nun turns her head left to right. A no. Can this be a woman of God? Liesel puts her hands together, prayer-style. Inside the "cathedral" people will be praying for the end of war and for cripples to walk again. She just wants some toilet paper. The nun lifts two tissuey napkins and hands them over to her.

You have *got* to be kidding, Liesel thinks. I am my own cholera epidemic. This will not do. She doesn't have the Italian to ask for more, so she simply gestures and says "por favori," as she mimes the nun adding more to her napkin pile. The woman passes over one more niggardly napkin. Bitch, Liesel thinks. She cannot help herself. Doesn't the nun have a body, or is it all like the cathedral, transcendence and air?

Liesel wouldn't mind floating away.

What comes next is as violent and disgusting as Liesel supposed it would be, with the napkins not sufficing, her not knowing what her next move should be, then creeping out of the stall, gesturing to the nun again, *Please, more.* And the woman handing over one more napkin, and Liesel again putting her hand up in prayer, again saying *Por favori.* She offers up a winning, oh-silly-me sort of smile. The nun hands another napkin over, but when Liesel indicates that she needs a whole stack, the nun shakes her head. A curt no.

Liesel imagines herself telling this story later, as a joke. "So then I belted her one," she will say. But in the moment, it is not funny. Her eyes tear. She reaches over and just takes what she needs. The nun makes a guttural sound of protest, and a woman still in line calls out what must be a reprimand.

I hate you, Liesel thinks as she reoccupies her stall. *I hate you all.*

BUT WHY STOP AT NUNS and women (fellow travelers!) who themselves only want to pee? There is next the guard at the Basilica door. Not the pale one from before, but a new man. Short cropped hair, short meaty body.

He will not let her back into the nave. Again, her impossible attempt at Italian: "Mi mario," she says, no need to explain that Raymond is boyfriend not husband, that they only started living together a few months ago, though they have been involved for over a year. But this new guard refuses. He has power. Why not exercise it? Eventually the pale guard returns, and Liesel explains the situation to him. "Ah," he says in apparent understanding, but then as Liesel steps forward, he extends his arm to block her movement. "Stay here," he says. "Trust me. This is where you want to be."

"My husband," Liesel begins, and just then there is a commotion outside. She turns to see a procession of men in white with red capes and skirts pressing past her. A man all in white, with a large gold cross in his hand, turns to her. He hands the cross off to someone at his side and reaches his arms toward her. She starts back, then belatedly realizes who it is. "I," she stutters as Pope John Paul II, with his floury white face, his cartoon beneficent smile, lowers his hands to her head. *My God,* she thinks. Appropriately? She feels each of his ten fingertips as a separate message on her head. His eyes—a blueberry blue, like an infant's—lock on to hers, and he says something. In Polish? In Latin? In Italian? There is no time to process what the language might be, much less understand his words, before he moves past, reaching next for a baby a mother has thrust into the aisle.

Did you see what just happened? Liesel wants to cry to someone—anyone!—at her side. But she is, despite the people surrounding her, all alone in the moment.

Behind her the English-speaking guard says, "I told you this was where you would want to be. You can go in now."

She hurries to her seat, which is (blessedly?) at the end of the row. She doesn't need to cross in front of people in order to rejoin Raymond.

"What took you so long?" he says.

"Did you see *that?*" she whispers. "At the door?"

Raymond shakes his head.

"The Pope just blessed me!"

Raymond turns and looks back at the door, as if the event will replay itself now that he's paying attention.

"It was like . . . It was like . . ." But she doesn't know what it was like.

"Ah," Raymond says. "I'm not the only one who knows you are special." He gives her a kiss on the cheek.

She smiles at him, reaches her hand to his. The ineffable. Could they be capable of sharing it together?

He looks cool and stylish with his tan suit and the blond hair that he habitually flicks out of his face, tossing his head even when it isn't in his eyes.

"I love you," she says. She knows she doesn't mean it. The great love of her life is in her past. But she wants to mean it. And she does love *things* about him. ("Like his apartment!" she thinks, for a joke, and then her inner self admonishes her inner self. Mostly because she *does* love his apartment.)

"Right," he says and leans to give her another kiss as the mass begins, the low murmur of men's voices rising from the front of the nave. "Love you, too."

THE SUIT HAD MADE HIM seem worldly from the start, when she just knew him because he stopped in for a coffee and a croissant every morning at Boulangerie Manon. It was he who made her appreciate the bakery. She'd only been there a week when she met him. At the time, she had thought that only she would land in a French bakery that had all the style of a Baskin Robbins, what with its tacky wall decorations and long glass counter, underneath which sat the (admittedly beautiful) *macarons, glacés,* and *pains au chocolate.* He ordered, took in her American accent, and smiled. "So Manon doesn't just have the best croissants in Paris, now it has the prettiest woman," he said in English. Her young boss, Marianne, stepped from the back room, where she was unloading a morning delivery, and said, "Raymond Dupré. Meet Liesel Pearlman." Marianne brushed her palms on her apron and made an espresso, part of Raymond's regular order, then said, "Raymond lives across the way." Marianne pointed to a vibrant blue metal door that sat in a larger (and older) wooden gate. Even then, Liesel sensed that the door opened, like others on the street, onto a complex courtyard off of which there would be apartments she'd like to explore. At one time, these buildings were the homes of princes and dukes. Now, the well-to-do of this century had carved the *maisons* into small, oddly shaped flats.

"I don't think so," Liesel had said, turning down Raymond's compliment, but not at the correct moment, so it sounded like she was saying that the croissants weren't special. Or that Raymond didn't live where he in fact lived.

"But it's true!" Marianne laughed.

Liesel likes her employer. She is a gentle, heavy woman, shy but always eager to please, always warmhearted. She wears her long shiny hair cinched in a ponytail, and its thickness, cleanliness, and gleam seem an extension of her own good sense and sturdiness. There's something of the wise peasant woman about Marianne, though Liesel doesn't think she is out of her twenties. She has always worked in the bakery, but owns it only because a stroke killed her mother a handful of years ago.

As Raymond and Liesel were talking, Marianne had pulled out a notebook from under the counter. It was full of clippings declaring Manon to be among the best places in Paris for a croissant.

"Oh, no." Liesel started to clarify what she'd meant, but then just said, "I am so sorry. Never mind." Her French was pretty good, but sometimes she still missed things.

THE BAKERY JOB HAD COME at something like a crisis point, three years into Liesel's stay in France. When she'd first come to France, pregnant and alone, she'd worked (and lived) at L'Atelier Bleu, a residential program for developmentally disabled adults. It was a beautiful place in Provence, run according to the teachings of Rudolf Steiner. Liesel doesn't know how long she might have done this—tolerated a marginal salary because it came with room and board and childcare for Idzia—when suddenly L'Atelier Bleu closed down due to some scandal at the higher levels. Within a week the residents were shipped back to their families, and the staff dispersed too.

Liesel didn't know what she'd do. She didn't have savings, couldn't put together even a single month's rent. But at the last minute she found a housesit in the Marais, signed up for a childcare subsidy, and learned about the bakery job.

THEIR FIRST DINNER OUT, Raymond had taken Liesel to a café just down the street from the bakery. It was small and always full. Liesel knew this from walking by. "Oh, you'll love it," Marianne said when Liesel told her she was going there. She named a French film star—Liesel didn't know him—who frequented the place. This, and Raymond's manners—formal to the point of foolishness—made the evening feel slightly unreal.

"So what do you do for a living?" Liesel finally asked. Her own problems with employment made her newly obsessed with how people put a life together. She'd missed that step where you educate yourself into a living. She had just educated herself into knowledge, she thought ruefully. Well, some knowledge. A little bit. She'd been a straight-A student, though she left college before she got her degree.

In response to her question, Raymond said, "Here's where you decide you don't like me after all." He was getting a step ahead of himself. She hadn't yet told him she liked him. She'd just agreed to dinner. Only she *did* like him. He was elegant and gracious, always waving female customers ahead of him in the bakery line. She liked the kind attention he paid to babies in carriages.

"I'm in funerary services," he said.

"Ah," she said, and he held up his hand.

"What you don't get, what most people don't get, until they've lost a loved one, is what a service I provide. People think it's creepy and about dead bodies. That's not what it is about. It is about providing a service. You are doing something for a family that needs to be done, that they don't want to do. I come home at the end of the day, and what I think about is the living, what I've done to help *them*. And just in case you are wondering, no, I don't touch dead people. I'm a funeral advisor. In line to be the funeral director."

This meant, he gave her to understand, that he was the person who did all the arranging—coffin selection, funeral details, burial service. As Raymond and she dated, over the course of many months, Liesel came to picture him with one hand on a widow's back, the other arm extended to a limousine. "It's OK," she imagined him saying, as he helped the woman maneuver into the backseat, so she could go bury her husband. "It's OK." She saw the quick way he'd provide a tissue and bend to a confused child and offer a peppermint.

People always said, "It's OK." Instead of "Holy fucking shit, this is hideous, and it's going to keep on being hideous and painful for a long, long time. Probably you'll never get over it."

But of course when you were suffering, you didn't want to be told that the pain would continue. You wanted to make it stop. Perhaps "It's OK," though plainly a lie, was the kindest and most generous thing one human being could say to another. And Raymond had made it his profession to say it.

A good man, then. Raymond was a good man.

One night, when Liesel was worrying over her housing options—her yearlong housesit was up; she couldn't afford anything decent on her bakery salary—Raymond said, "You could move in with me?" They had dated for ten months, mostly Friday and Saturday dinners out and a rushed hour of making love before Liesel went home to Idzia. On Sundays, they typically had some sort of outing focused on Idzia—Bois de Boulogne or Parc de la Villette. Liesel couldn't think of anything to say to Raymond's suggestion but yes.

AND THAT IS HOW SHE COMES to be in Rome. Raymond and she have decided to take a honeymoon of sorts to celebrate their first three months of living together. It is the first time that Liesel has spent a night away from Idzia. Marianne is babysitting for the weekend. Liesel came to Italy five years ago on a real honeymoon, but that had not been a good time. She remembers sneaking out of her hotel bedroom one night to cry; she'd been so worn out by her husband's, Joel's, irritation at her, especially when he blew up after she got them lost in the streets of Padua. What did it matter? It was their honeymoon! Of all times to chew your wife out. Now she can really appreciate the country, and what a thrill to see all the art she'd previously only seen on a screen in her "Introduction to Art History" classroom. But there is the problem with her gut. And then the ache of missing Idzia. "All those years I thought I wanted a man," Liesel used to joke with friends about her early twenties. She didn't mind confessing how much she liked falling asleep with her child in her arms, how well she enjoyed being the object of her daughter's affection. "I didn't want a man. I wanted a three-year-old."

Other times, trying to get the same laugh, she'd say, "Adulation?! I'll take it!"

In St. Peter's, as the men at the altar murmur on, she thinks she will accept the Pope's blessing, then give it to Idzia. Can a blessing be transferred? One of the things that she liked about Judaism, which she studied in the months before she married, a gift she thought she'd give her Jewish husband, was that there was a specific prayer in which the parents held their hands over their children's heads (arranging their fingers in a "Live Long and Prosper" Star Trek configuration) and blessed them. (Actually, it turned out Spock took the hand thing from the Jews.) In the synagogue, you could see how the adults, and even the crankiest of children, loved this one moment of connection, the priestly blessing. The parents held out their hands and said, essentially, "I love you, I care for you, I want good things for you."

Maybe Liesel's parents had kind and peaceful hopes for her, too, but they'd certainly never said so.

Whatever mistakes Liesel is going to make as she parents Idzia—and she knows there will be plenty, sometimes she feels her failures even as she's in the midst of erring—she isn't going to make *that* mistake. She's never gone a day without telling Idzia that she loves her.

Next to Liesel, Raymond looks at his watch. The mass, he has already told her, will not be long: an hour at the most. She wonders if he is really paying attention to the words or if, like her, he uses the time as an occasion to drift deeply into his own thoughts. Maybe that's a kind of prayer?

"I need some money," she whispers. "I have to go to the bathroom again." He routinely carries all their money and then hands it to her with a flourish, practically pushing it on her, as she demurs: *No, he mustn't. No, he needn't.*

In fact, she isn't in a position to refuse what he hands her; her bakery wages go only so far.

Now, he bristles in frank irritation. Do all men chafe at the small adjustments one needs to make in order to be with another person? Or is it just the particular men she happens to sleep with?

The fact is the "honeymoon" has been taking a toll. Too much time alone with one another. Even in the last three months, when they have been living together, Raymond and Liesel aren't long in each other's presence, what with their respective work hours. Raymond is often gone—out "on a call," as he puts it, for the funeral home. Or he is with friends. He has even taken to working a few shifts at a noisy restaurant on the Rue de la Bucherie, though this completely puzzles Liesel, since he makes a good salary. It doesn't quite fit her image of him. His tastes are almost haughty, and the restaurant is in such a crowded, noisy, touristy part of the city. But he says he likes it, that he has friends from his school days who are working there. The restaurant sits on a site where "damaged meat," whatever that means, was once salted and boiled to feed the poor. He gives her this detail about the Middle Ages as an offering. He knows she likes an oddball fact.

She should mind about the restaurant job, about the hours it keeps Raymond away, but she doesn't. She likes best when she is alone with Idzia in the apartment or when it is just Idzia and she headed out on an errand.

In a way, Raymond and Liesel are no closer as live-in lovers than they were as boyfriend and girlfriend with separate domiciles. Raymond is kind to Idzia, but a little stiff, as if he can't quite remember that he, too, was once a child. "What's the matter with her?" he'd once asked as Idzia was stubbornly refusing to put on a raincoat.

"There's nothing wrong with *her,*" Liesel had snapped. "She's a child. There's something wrong with *you,* because you don't know that."

It was the only time Liesel had been rude to Raymond. It is so important to Liesel not to descend into the bickering she has had with other men. If she does, she can't think *they* were the problem. She will have to admit that *she* is the problem. To his credit, Raymond responded to her reprimand with silence.

Now in the Basilica, she says of her need for the bathroom, "I can't help it."

"I know that," Raymond says. "It's just it won't be much longer." He passes her some coins.

Liesel would like to wait. She doesn't want to go back to that bathroom. She tries to focus on all the air above her, how it seems ready to lift something essential in her up to the ceiling. "All religions are really one religion," Joel's sister, Amy, had said, when Liesel approached her with the idea of converting to Judaism. "Christians, Muslims, Hindus. Everyone's going the same place. They're just taking different paths to get there." Amy was a Hebrew school teacher, and Liesel had thought she'd say, "Great. Come on over to our side." Instead she seemed to be saying, "Actually, honey, stay where you are."

THERE IS SOME DISTURBANCE in the front of the nave, and Liesel realizes that Raymond is right. The service is over. She can't leave now, even if she wants to, because the men in white robes—bishops? some garden-variety religious muckety-mucks?—are starting to process back down the aisle, gold crosses in hands. She sees Pope John Paul II among them and re-experiences the earlier moment, the way it felt to look in his eyes. She really had that clichéd sense of great depths beyond. Almost as if she could have looked through the Pope's pupils and found God on the other side. But then she isn't just reexperiencing the earlier gaze. The Pope has come up to her again! He puts his hands to her head, looks deep into her eyes, and mutters some words. She is, if anything, more shocked than she was before. As soon as he is past, Liesel feels hands at her back and then on her arms. At first she wonders why people are pushing to get out of the row so quickly, but then she realizes they aren't pushing her forward; they are trying to touch her. She hears a woman's voice, then a man's, their words apparently addressed to her. Raymond puts his lips to her ear and says, "They are asking what he said to you." But Liesel doesn't know what he said to her. A woman pulls at Raymond's jacket sleeve and says in French, "It's extraordinary! He came to her twice! It's extraordinary!"

A different woman says, also in French, "It must be because she looks Polish."

I look Polish? Liesel thinks. *What could that mean?*

She doesn't need to be one of the fervent Roman Catholics who surround her to realize something important has happened. Two blessings. Who gets two? Perhaps the Pope knew she had transferred her earlier blessing to her daughter, so he has come back to re-bestow his grace. "I love you, I care for you, I wish good things for you, too."

A MONTH LATER, Liesel finds the gun. It is in a small box on the high shelf of Raymond's apartment's hall closet. She gives a little yelp when she sees it, as if it is not just lying but aimed at her. She closes the lid, shoves the box back onto the shelf. "What?" she says out loud, as if someone will burst through the wall—in the manner of a smiling, outsized Kool-Aid pitcher—and explain this surprise to her. Gingerly, she reaches in and opens the lid again.

The gun is still there.

The box in which it lies looks exactly like the box she *is* looking for—the one that holds the warranties and instructions for the apartment's appliances. She is on a search for manuals because she has managed, in preheating the oven, to lock the door. Her day's plan involved surprising Idzia with cookies after school. Not fancy French cookies—no shortage of *macarons* in their life—but peanut butter cookies with Hershey's kisses, a treat from Liesel's own childhood. She has found the chocolate kisses and peanut butter at a store that has turned American food—Spam, instant macaroni and cheese, Frosted Flakes—into something like a delicacy. It is not the first time that Liesel has accidentally locked the oven door, but in the past, Raymond has always been home to fix it.

Why would he have a gun?

In case the people he deals with aren't really dead, and he needs, before he inters them, to put them out of their misery?

It is not right to make jokes. It is right to focus on the matter at hand. And the matter at hand is that Liesel has never known anyone who owns a gun, and she doesn't intend to start now.

She steps off the stool she's been on and slumps into the chair by the phone. She will call Raymond at Pompes Funèbres Lavallée, she decides. She has to. It is true that this is something Raymond has expressly asked her never to do. Jacques Lavallée does not like his employees to take personal calls, and given the nature of the business, Raymond feels Jacques has a point. You can't be in the midst of talking to the bereaved and say the French equivalent of "Just a sec. Hold that thought, will ya?"

But this is an emergency. Lavallée will have to understand. Liesel dials, and the phone rings once, twice. Perhaps Lavallée wouldn't count a woman sick with anxiety as an emergency, but that is his problem. Liesel develops a profound hatred for him as she listens to the third ring then the fourth. What an intolerant bastard! How can he proscribe calls altogether? An answering machine clicks on. "Bonjour. You've reached Pompes Funèbres Lavallée. Will you leave a message so we can assist you?"

Liesel isn't expecting a machine, hasn't composed a message in her head, so she hangs up.

He must not have a gun. She cannot live in a house with a gun.

She checks her watch, but there is no time to take the Métro to Lavallée's to find Raymond, and anyway what if she got there only to discover that he is out at some cemetery she can't get to without a car? Only she must act. She cannot wait till he comes home to talk, since Idzia will be in the apartment. Nor can she spend a whole evening in his company without speaking up.

"What are you talking about?" Idzia insists whenever Liesel lowers her voice to speak privately to Raymond. On script, Liesel will say, "Nothing," but Idzia is a smart girl, and this doesn't satisfy. This irritates. "Tell me," she will insist, and there will be no end of fussing until Liesel comes up with a plausible lie. Liesel can't get away with a "Just how much I love you, Little Muffin" or "Something on the news that was strange."

"*What? What* on the news that was strange?"

"Angry people doing angry things." *God* doing angry things, she sometimes wants to add.

"*What* angry things?"

Jihadists blowing up trucks, Mike Tyson being sent to prison for rape, five hundred killed in an earthquake in Turkey. The public tragedies that shake Liesel up so much that she can't think straight. She hopes her daughter will grow up to be less porous to the unhappiness in the world. Then again, she hopes her daughter won't grow up to be a jerk. Not two wishes that exactly dovetail.

Liesel waits five minutes, then calls Pompes Funèbres Lavallée again. When the answering machine clicks on she is prepared. She clears her throat and says in a polite, sweet voice, "Bonjour. This is Liesel Pearlman, calling for Raymond Dupré. Would you ask him to call me at his very earliest convenience?" She sits tightly in her chair for five minutes, feeling the heat of the gun in the closet as if it has been recently discharged, as if it is still smoking. Do guns actually smoke? She doesn't know and doesn't want to know. She just wants the thing out of the apartment. Her hands reach for the phone. She shouldn't, but she can't stop herself. She leaves another message. "Would you let Raymond know I need to hear from him immediately?" She does this one more time—"Please let me know if Raymond is out, and if so, is there another way I might reach him?"—and then goes down the stairs and across the street to the bakery. Perhaps Marianne will be able to calm her?

But when she gets to the street, she remembers it is Monday. The bakery is closed. Indeed, that is why she isn't working, is why she planned to spend the day making cookies. And maybe confiding wouldn't be such a good idea. What would Marianne think of Raymond, if she knew?

Liesel goes back upstairs. Her stomach is cramped—her stomach is always cramped—but it is worse now that she is upset. She leaves yet another message on the answering machine. "I am sorry to be a bother—I know this is so very forward of me—but it is very important that I hear from Raymond."

Don't the French have strict gun laws? Isn't this one of the virtues of the country? Baguettes, relaxed attitudes about sex, and strict gun laws?

With the oven locked, Liesel has to abandon her baking project. She puts the flour and sugar back in the pantry, returns a mixing bowl to the cabinet. After that she can't make herself do anything more productive than fret. She peers out the window. She has always wondered about the elegant woman who lives across the courtyard. Now there seem to be half a dozen men in her living room, all milling about in their handsome suits. What can they be doing? Legislating something important for the history of France? The windows are open, and she hears the light tinkling of music, also the cries of children. There is a woman who watches toddlers the next courtyard over, and one of them is always wailing.

Finally, Raymond calls.

"Bella," he says. He started calling her this in Rome, and the name has stuck. "How are you?"

"How am I? Did you get my messages?"

"No," he says. "What messages? When did you call?"

"I've been calling and calling," she says.

"You know I can't take calls at work."

"I know, I know. I'm sorry. I just had to."

"Well, I'm here now. You sound upset."

"I'm very upset. I was looking for the oven manual. You know, in the closet by the front door. And I found a gun."

"Yes?"

"You have a gun?"

"Yes, yes," he says mildly. "I like to go to shooting ranges."

"You like to go to shooting ranges?" she repeats. It is as if he has said he likes to dress up as a purple bunny and hop around the living room.

"Yes. I'll take you sometime."

"I'm all set, thank you," she says, sarcastic, but he doesn't seem to read her tone. There are pistol ranges in France? She clears her throat, takes a deep breath through her nose, and says, "Raymond, I can't live in a place where there is a gun. I can't, and my daughter can't. You are going to have to get rid of it."

He laughs. "That's not for you to tell me, Bella. It's my apartment."

This is, of course, true. "Well, you have to. For me. I just can't do it."

"I'm sorry," he says, perfectly polite, "but I am not going to agree to that."

She doesn't know what she can possibly say to this. "Please?" she tries.

"No, Liesel. But now listen, the reason I am calling is there's a chance to do a shift tonight at the restaurant, and I said I'd take it."

"Is that where you are calling from?" She processes belatedly that she has been hearing, all along, noise in the background. Only it is too early for him to be at the restaurant, the regular workday not yet over. Liesel puts her hand to her forehead. This feels painfully familiar: a conversation in which she is going to try to get a man to do something he does not want to do. "I really wish you would come home." She sniffs. She checks her watch. She has to get off the phone. She has to go get Idzia.

"I'll come home," he says soothingly. "Just a little later than I was planning."

"OK," she says reluctantly. "But, wait, why do you need a gun?"

"I just told you. For the shooting range."

"But can't you, like, rent one there? They must have some."

"No, no," he laughs, as if at her darling foolishness. "I want my own. I will see you later tonight. Don't you worry about a thing."

"At least . . . remind me how to unlock the oven door?"

LIESEL HAS NEVER BEEN GOOD at letting something go, once it begins to agitate her. Still, she tries to imagine that a gun, kept in a closed box high on a shelf, is not a problem. She fetches Idzia at school, and they bake the cookies together, which actually is more pleasurable than if Liesel just did it herself. It is sweet to see how carefully Idzia rolls the balls of dough in sugar then carefully presses a chocolate kiss into each ball. Idzia wonders if they can sell the cookies at the bakery—she has a doll she'd like to buy with the profits—but instead they make up small foil packets to deliver to her teachers in the morning.

Sometime after 1:00 a.m., Liesel feels Raymond's body thud down next to hers, but she is mostly asleep and can't force herself up and out of slumber, though she senses the absolute need for wakefulness. She makes efforts to speak, but she is dreaming, and no sounds come out of her mouth. Raymond has bathed off the smell of the restaurant; and in her dream, he is somehow not Raymond but Joel in a white doctor's coat. His hair is damp, and he exudes a soapy sweetness.

She is up before Raymond in the morning. She takes Idzia to school, and by the time she returns Raymond is gone, and she must go to work. Because Raymond has a *planned* shift at the restaurant tonight, she calls the funeral home again. She knows he will not like this, but she cannot wait till tomorrow to revisit the matter of the gun. She sits at the small table next to the wall phone where Marianne typically takes orders.

This time, after she dials, a woman answers. "Pompes Funèbres Lavallée. May I help?" When Liesel asks for Raymond, the woman says, "Pardon?"

Liesel repeats herself.

"Ah . . ." There is a sound as if the woman is putting her hand over the receiver in order to talk to someone else, then she says, "One moment."

A minute passes. Liesel wonders if the woman has forgotten about her.

She is about to hang up and call again when a man's voice comes on the line. It is plainly that of an older man.

"Madame," he says. "I take it you are looking for Raymond Dupré?"

"I am."

"And do you mind if I ask who you are?"

"I . . ." she starts. "Forgive me. I know he isn't supposed to receive calls at work. It was just . . . it is very important."

"Yes," he says. "Perhaps you are the same woman who called yesterday?"

"Yes. I'm sorry!"

"No, no," he says, in a soothing tone. "That's no matter. But can you tell me your name?"

"Yes, yes, I am sorry. Didn't I say? I am Liesel Pearlman. I am Raymond's girlfriend."

"And how long have you been his girlfriend, if I may ask?" Liesel blinks, confused. "Well, no you may not," she wants to say, but then the man says, "The reason I am is asking is that Raymond Dupré hasn't been in our employ for six months. We had to let him go."

Liesel is silent, and then she says, "I don't understand." When the man doesn't respond, she says, "And who are you? Who am I talking to?"

"My name is Jacques Lavallée. I am the owner."

"So you would know," Liesel says quietly. "If he wasn't working there."

"Yes," he says. "I would."

Where is Raymond right now, if he isn't at work? "And why did you fire him?"

"That," he says, "is confidential."

"Oh, of course," Liesel says, hurriedly, apologetic, *what are you sorry for?,* and then because she cannot think of anything else to do, she adds, "I have to hang up the phone now."

LIESEL PRESSES HER FINGERS to her forehead. What is going on? Why would he pretend to be going to a job he doesn't have? This, at least, explains the restaurant shifts, but not why he dresses for work every morning, Monday through Friday, and leaves the house at the same time as always. It also doesn't explain why he still hands her a big stack of bills on Friday evenings and says, "For whatever you need to buy." The money is for the groceries, but it is always more than she needs. When she tells him so, he says, "Buy yourself something nice then. A dress maybe? A necklace." This makes her squirm. She has never been overly attached to things. She's moved too much in her life for that. She likes design and fashion, but not the sort of clothes he would have her wear. She doesn't like elegant garments. She likes what you might find in a vintage shop: quirky tops, surprising colors, something with a sense of humor. She scrolls back through the weeks. If he lost his job and was just waiting tables, how did they afford the trip to Rome? How does he afford the apartment? Rents in this neighborhood are among the highest in the city.

"What has happened?" Marianne says when she sees Liesel, hand to head. As Liesel starts to tell her story, she begins to shiver. Is she overreacting? She can't tell. Marianne pats her back. "It is OK. It is OK. I am sure there is some explanation. You know men. Their pride. He just didn't want to tell you. No man likes to admit he has lost his job. Men are men."

This seems so French. Is it also wise? Liesel has no idea. "What shall I say to him? When he comes home?"

"Just tell him you know he is no longer at the job, and he shouldn't have worried about telling you. You want to share in what is going on in his life. You . . ." Marianne makes a rolling motion with her hand. And so on, and so on. The two laugh.

"You are a good friend," Liesel says. "I don't deserve such a good person."

"Where'd you get that idea?" Marianne says. "You are like my sister." She gives her a hug and a double-sided kiss. Then she brings her apron up to her own eyes and dabs. "I am lucky for you and lucky for little Idzia." It is true that Marianne, who is not yet married, dotes on Idzia. She has even bought a small apron, so Idzia can play pretend at the bakery. "Now go. It will be OK. You will see."

These words take Liesel all the way through the rest of the afternoon till she picks Idzia up at 4:00 p.m. from *l'ecole maternelle.* Then the sense of unease returns, in increasing intensity. It will be, she knows, hard for her to focus on Idzia. Nonetheless, she takes Idzia to the Place des Vosges, where they play "chase," a game that exhausts Liesel, but which she engages with to the best of her ability. The idea is to pursue Idzia through the linden trees and almost catch her or catch her but then let her wriggle out of her grasp so they can take another few laps around the park. Liesel is generally winded within five minutes.

Idzia, though demanding when she senses adults trying to hide something from her, is a pliant child. Liesel tries not to announce too soon her readiness to move on. On her own, Idzia will never ask to leave the park, but if Liesel says it is time to go, she will follow without a word of protest. Even when Idzia plays dolls with herself, there is none of the conflict Liesel remembers in her own childhood pretending. "Let's go!" one doll will brightly say to another. "I'm coming!" the other will announce cheerily. And then Idzia, the narrator, will say, "Mom! They're going to the zoo!" Life, it seems, is all celebration.

"I think we need to go," Liesel finally says to Idzia. She needs to use the bathroom. Her stomach is a mess.

By the time they get home, Liesel is overwhelmed by the desire to call Raymond at the restaurant and just get through the discussion they must have. If she were a different mother, she'd give Idzia cough syrup, knock her out, so she could get on the phone. But no.

THAT NIGHT, with Idzia asleep and Raymond home from the restaurant, Liesel beckons him outside the apartment door. Finally. "Let's sit," she says. They crowd on the top step of the stairs that curve down to the ground floor, and Liesel confronts him with her discovery. Raymond laughs lightly. "I didn't want to worry you," he says. "I still have a job." He laughs again. "Jacques said he fired me! That is just like him. I quit! I had enough of him, always finding fault. My shoes weren't shiny enough! He told me that once. Are my shoes ever not shiny?"

Liesel had to admit that they were always shiny.

"I work for Pompes Funèbres du 10ème. We can call them right now. I work in the monuments office. It's good to try a little something different. Today a man came in, and he said he wants a gravestone for his brother that says, 'This is the worst thing that ever happened to me.'"

Liesel laughs. "Not really," she says.

"Really. Could I make something like that up?" Probably not, Liesel admits to herself. He isn't a particularly funny person. In that he is different from her previous partners, all of whom had a good sense of humor.

"Come," Raymond says and waves her back into the apartment. There he hands her the phone, then recites a number.

"But no one will pick up now," she says

"You'll get the answering machine. That will be some proof, and you can call again in the morning. Talk to Geneviève then."

"Genevieve?"

"Yes, the secretary."

"It's not that I don't trust you." But of course she doesn't exactly, so she sits and dials the numbers that he recites.

Sure enough, a machine answers and says, "You have reached Pompes Funèbres. We are unavailable at the moment, but please leave a message. We will return your message shortly."

She hangs up.

"But why wouldn't you tell me?"

"I just didn't want to worry you," he says, taking a seat at the kitchen table and toying with the stem of his dinner wine glass, still half-full from the meal they finished hours ago. "It's not quite the same as Lavallée. Not as good a reputation, so maybe I *was* embarrassed." He takes a sip, as if considering the words that are to come. "A step down, if you see what I mean, but a much nicer place to work. And it's true I prefer to be the funeral advisor to selling stones. It's an adjustment."

"I see," she says. It's not like she is aware of where on the reputation ladder one funeral home exists against another, but she can see that the change in position might be a demotion.

She feels satisfied for the moment. His explanation mollifies, but then in the morning she thinks, *No, something still doesn't make sense.*

ON HER NEXT DAY OFF, Liesel searches the house. Though the apartment is small, it has an abundance of closets. There is the large downstairs closet, where the gun is, and where there are napkins, liquor bottles, light bulbs, and stamps. There is another downstairs closet with brooms and mops. A spiral staircase leads to an upstairs balcony that is lined with closets. One has sheets and towels, one blankets, one Idzia's clothes and another Idzia's toys. In the bedroom—there is only one; Idzia sleeps in a nook on the balcony—there are three closets, each with built-in drawers. One has Liesel's clothes, another has Raymond's, and the third amounts to a junk pile— old coats, hammers, sunglasses, books. On the very top shelf, one above the gun that seems to pulsate in its box, Liesel—on the stool again and on tiptoe so as to be able to peer over the edge—finds a box of about thirty small keys, much like the one that she and Raymond use for their mailbox. Behind the keys is carton of manila files. She pulls it toward her, then slides its weight into her arms, and steps awkwardly down. She sits on the bed and starts sifting through the contents. Each file is rubber-stamped with the words "Pompes Funèbres Lavallée." Ah, work files! She opens one. It contains several forms: *Certificat de décès, Acte de décès, Permis d'inhumer.* All for Jean Luc Petit. She looks through the other folders. The same forms but with other names: Pascal Antin, Armaund Larose, Claude Marotte. They, she presumes, are among the people for whom Raymond has arranged funerals. But why wouldn't he have returned them when he left the job? And why store them here, instead of on some table, so he would remember to bring them back?

She has to do something with this discovery, but what? Liesel calls Raymond at work—no proscription on calls at his new place of employ—but the answering machine picks up.

She calls fifteen minutes later, but again the machine.

Nota bene: If you are a funeral home and want to help the grieving, have someone pick up the phone at all hours.

The agitation she feels as she continues to flip through the folders increases. Nothing makes sense.

OK, she thinks at length. She will do Raymond a favor. She will return these files. That way he doesn't need to deal with his old employer. Will he consider this a favor? Perhaps not. Certainly not. She is being willfully naïve. She knows that. But if Liesel does this, something will happen. She feels that flutter of panic and excitement that comes with the suspicion that you are putting something into motion. Whatever happens, she will know more than she knows now. It might not be much more, but it will be more. She must not give the files to the secretary, though. She must insist on handing them directly to Jacques Lavallée. *I am sorry. It is very important that* . . . She writes the moment in her head, convinced it must play out the way she imagines it, if she is to learn anything. Something in Lavallée's bearing will let her know whether he is lying about Raymond being fired or whether Raymond is lying about quitting. And with this knowledge, Liesel will . . . Liesel will . . . She can't finish the thought. She is not entirely sure what she will do with this knowledge and why she needs it. She only knows that she does.

Liesel takes the Metro over to the 15th, where the funeral home is. Liesel has never gone there before. Is this odd? That she never went to where Raymond worked? But then why would she?

She feels she's failed at some basic attention one is supposed to pay to one's lover, a solicitous interest that she does not (she knows) have. Raymond is her boyfriend, but he is not the man for her. She has known that from the start. You don't get to choose the man for you—a fact that movies, French and American alike, ignore. What you get to do is to pick the best from what is available, that oft-disappointing lot, and hope you both manage a form of affection.

Is this true, or just what she is thinking because her own mood is so dark? She doesn't know.

When Liesel arrives at the address—so late in the day she is afraid the office will be closed—she sees that Pompes Funèbres Lavallée is not the gloomy sort of place she has imagined but a storefront whose façade has been thickly painted a glossy forest green. It looks like a travel agency. A landscape painting in one window and a model sailboat in the other add to the impression that the journeys offered within are all pleasant ones. Thankfully, a woman behind the glass is still working at a desk. Liesel puts the files on the ground to free a hand so she can try the door. It is locked, so she knocks lightly. The woman looks up, startled, then hurries to the door. "Are you closed?"

"Ah, no," the woman says wryly. "Like the cemetery, we are always open for business."

Gathering up the files, Liesel steps through the door into what is clearly a waiting room, though it is a disorienting space, more like an architect's office than a funeral home's. There are white canvas chairs, bonsai, and low shelves with photography, fashion, and design books.

When Liesel gives her name and asks for Jacques Lavallée, the secretary says, "Oh, yes. I remember." She places a call and then an older man emerges from a hall to the right, his arm extended for a handshake or because he is walking an invisible dog. Liesel fumbles with the folders pressed to her chest so she can extend her own arm. Lavallée is a slim man, his shoulders curved, his chest almost concave, but in his fine suit he projects a certain gravitas. His features are angular, his hair the brownish-gray of a squirrel. He looks like the director of an art museum. "Hello," she says. "We talked on the phone the other day?"

"Yes, yes. Please come back to my office."

"I was just cleaning house," she says as she follows him down the hall, noting a bald spot on the back of his head in the shape of a light bulb. "I realized Raymond had some of your files, so I thought I had better return them. He has a new job, you see, and I didn't think he'd have time to get over here."

"Very kind of you," Lavallée says as he gestures toward a chair. Her sense of this business keeps changing. Unlike the waiting room, Lavallée's office is windowless, and despite the Danish modern furniture and a lone watercolor print of Claes Oldenburg's *The Eraser* (of all things), it feels gloomy. But not in the way an American funeral home would be: because it reminded you of death. This office feels gloomy, because it reminds you of how miserably colorless life can be.

"Did you really fire him?" Liesel says abruptly, as they both sit. "He says he quit. I guess I am a little surprised. I know he works so hard, and he certainly cares about his work." When Lavallée doesn't respond, Liesel says, "Don't mistake me. I'm not trying to get his job back. Like I say, he has an excellent situation right now." Of course she has no idea if his current situation is good or bad. "Only I was trying to sort things out. Not for him. For myself."

She smiles.

He smiles back.

"You see," she says helplessly.

"I am just being quiet because I am thinking," he says. He flattens his tie with the palm of his hand, then falls silent again. Liesel doesn't keep talking, though it is her way to fill an awkward silence with words. "I am deciding what to say," he continues at last. "And what I want to tell you is that I cannot divulge anything about hiring and firing decisions. But perhaps I can let you know that we do not let our funeral assistants take folders home. Even *I* don't take folders home. There is a lot of private information in those folders."

Liesel remains silent. Lavallée says, "You're young."

"Not so young. I just turned thirty-three."

"I have a thirty-three-year-old daughter." He sighs. "What would I do if you were my daughter?"

Buy me an ice cream? Liesel wants to say, as a joke.

"I'd tell you to break up with your boyfriend. That's what I'd say, but what daughter ever listened to her father?"

"What do you mean?"

He holds up his hands in a stop-gesture. "I've said too much." He stands, so she stands, too.

"But . . ." she starts.

He shakes his head "no," then makes an "after you" gesture with his arm, so she will walk ahead of him to the waiting room. He follows her all the way to the sidewalk. "Try," he says, once they are outside, and as if he is indeed her father, "to take care of yourself."

BY THE TIME SHE IS BACK at the bakery, sitting at the table by the wall phone and confiding in Marianne, she is a mess. What could be going on? She can't even guess. She has been advised to get away from Raymond, but why? She starts to weep. She wouldn't even mind leaving him. Her feelings for Raymond have always been lukewarm. She just can't work out the logistics in her head. Where will she go? How will she live?

Marianne reaches across the table to pat her hand and says, "I have an idea. OK? But I have to ask something of somebody. I can't explain, but I will tell you in the morning, I think."

"OK," Liesel says, agreeing, since what else can she do?

"Just don't say anything to Raymond. Don't let him know you went to Lavallée's."

"What's your idea?"

Marianne shakes her head, unwilling to explain. "If this doesn't work, then we will figure something else out."

"It's like you are speaking Chinese. I don't know what you mean. Figure out what?"

Marianne gives her a hug. "Sometimes when you are upset, it's like that. Nothing makes sense. Just keep quiet for now."

"Jesus Christ," Liesel says, looking at her watch. It is time to get Idzia. During her pregnancy, when she was so upset by all that had happened in America, her biggest fear was that she'd be a depressed mother. Since then, she's heard people say it's not so bad if children see you emotional; they need to know grownups cry, too. But that's not true, Liesel knows. Not the way she cries, racked with sobs, despairing. That's not good for any child. Now she wipes her face.

"I look OK?" she asks Marianne.

"Not your best, I will admit. But you're fine."

"OK. I'll see you."

IN SOME WAYS, Liesel is very good at keeping a secret. In other ways, not at all. She is good at secrets that concern her. Her ex-husband, Joel, never figured her out. Joel doesn't even know about Idzia, though Liesel can see him clearly in the shape of Idzia's face and in her coloring. She doesn't *want* Joel to know about Idzia. He will want to share her. Worse, he will want to *have* her. He will come up with all sorts of arguments against how Liesel is raising Idzia. She can see him using the money he has to try to wrest full custody from her. Not that he's a bad man. Actually he's a good man in his way. He's just convinced he's right about everything and that Liesel is wrong. "You put me down constantly," she once told him. "You're always disagreeing with me. You're always telling me everything I do is wrong."

"What are you talking about?" he'd said. "I've never put you down. Ever!"

"That," she said, "is just another example of you telling me my thoughts are wrong. You just did it. Just now."

"Jesus Christ, Liesel. What kind of logic is that? You're a lunatic."

"Thank you," she'd said. "Thanks a lot."

She is not going to share her daughter with someone like that.

Liesel is also good at keeping other people's secrets. But not if they don't make a point of letting her know something is to be kept under wrap: she loves to analyze people and can be loquacious about them. Once asked, though, she will keep a secret forever.

But it is almost impossible for Liesel to keep a confidence when telling will assuage a fear. It is almost impossible to keep a secret when she needs *help*.

That evening, with Raymond home in his reading chair, flipping through the newspaper, and Idzia awake, she can barely keep still. She wants to drag the phone into the bathroom and call Marianne to hear her say again what she has already said. She has had no time to shop during the day, so she makes a simple omelet and salad for dinner. Idzia takes a few bites then heads to the floor of the living room to play with her blocks and dolls. Raymond sips his wine and says, "Good. Too many late nights for me."

"I know," Liesel smiles. "But you still like it? The restaurant?"

"Yes, yes. It's good for me. I am in a cage all day. It is good for me to get out. That is the sort of animal I am."

She flushes. This embarrasses her. After one of their early dates, he had announced his intention to sleep with her by saying, "What would you say if I told you I wanted to make love to you?" He said this in a dramatic way, as if she might be shocked.

"Oh," she had said, as if taken aback, though in her head she'd thought, "I'd say, 'Why aren't you just asking me if I'd like to fuck?'"

"And let me know about you," he says now, taking her wrist and rubbing his thumb over the back of her hand in a way she finds creepy. "I've been the absent lover. How was your day? What did you do?"

"Work, then Idzia and cleaning. I actually found some of your old files from Lavallée. Up there." She points to the ceiling, since the bedroom with its closet is directly above where they sit. "So I just took them back, thought I'd get that done for you."

His thumb stills, though he keeps his hand in hers.

Why has she said the very thing Marianne told her not to? *What is the matter with her?*

"I was thinking what with the day job and the restaurant, when are you going to ever get there, and I thought it would be nice." She knows it wouldn't be nice, of course. What she wants is for him to tell her what is going on, for him to confess, to make plain that he was angry at his boss, so he kept the material to mess up the man's filing system or his licensing or something. If he can be honest about his dishonesty, then everything will be OK.

"Maybe I wish you hadn't done that," he says and stands to clear his plate. At the sink, he rubs his hand through his floppy hair and says, "Best to let me take care of my own business."

"Oh, yes, of course. I'm sorry. I thought it would be welcome." A lie to prod the truth out of him, but the truth doesn't come.

"Not welcome this time, I'm afraid," he says, not turning around, his arms tight, his hands pressed firmly against the lip of the sink.

"Because? I mean I won't do it again. Well, if the opportunity arose, but why wouldn't it be welcome?"

"Liesel," he says tightly. "I don't want to talk about it just now. I'm going to head out for a walk."

"Oh, we'll come," she says and gestures to Idzia, though it is late, and her daughter is plainly sleepy, has not attended, in the way she normally would, to this conversation.

"No, no. I'll be back."

He leaves, and when he returns, he just says that he is exhausted and must go to bed.

The next day he does something unheard of: He calls *her* at work.

"Bella," he says, when her sticky hands pick up the bakery's phone. "Bad news. I have to go on a job for a while. I'm thinking it might make sense for Idzia and you to find someplace else to live."

"What?"

"I'm just going away for awhile. A trip for work. I'll call you when I get back. The rent's paid through the month, but you might think about finding a new place."

"Raymond . . ."

"I'm in a little trouble right now, Liesel," he hisses. "Just in a little over my head, and I'm going to ask you to please, please, *please* not let anyone know I called you. Can you promise me that?"

"Yes," she says. "Of course."

"You kind of screwed me over here, Bella. Not angry at you. You didn't know. But you kind of put me in a bad position."

"I'm sorry," she says. "I'm so sorry. Where are you? Work?"

"No, not at work." He sighs.

"Are you home then? Just come down and we can . . ." The bell at the front door of the bakery rings. Someone is at the counter and needs her.

"No, not at home. Kind of mad at you," he says, but in a nice voice.

"I'm sorry," she says again.

"Bye, Bella," he says, and then, as if he's dropped something on his foot, "Merde." He breathes in deeply and says, "Au revoir."

The woman at the counter buys *une figue,* a ball of chocolate and fig paste wrapped in marzipan.

"Enjoy," Liesel says as she hands it to the woman and then, since the habit of blurting is with her, "It's my favorite sweet in the store."

SHE IS ALONE IN THE BAKERY, and she wants nothing more than to run across the street and check the apartment, for she has a suspicion. It is not a busy time of day. Still she can't just leave. What if someone stops in? Finally, though, she can't stand it any longer, and she dashes across the street, through the blue door, across the courtyard, down the far staircase (pushing the button on the wall that only lights up for a minute, so people can find their way without there being a waste of electricity), up the concrete and brick stairs, and into the house. The box on the shelf is still there, but the gun is gone. Ditto the box with keys. Liesel races back to the bakery. There are two customers there. She apologizes then serves them hurriedly.

She calls Marianne at home.

"I have something to tell you," Marianne says. "I was just about to call you. I went to my brother-in-law. He's in the police for our district. I asked for his thoughts. You know I had an idea, yes? Because I like crime novels. You know this about me."

"What?" Liesel cries. "Just tell me."

"Well, when you told me about the files and the keys, it sounded to me like, maybe, mail fraud. Like maybe Raymond was not reporting people's deaths, so he could take their CNIS and maybe apply for credit cards, or I don't know what else. To get money in some way. He's always seemed to have a lot of money, you know? For what he does for a living. Funeral assistant? It's not a rich man's job."

The CNIS is the national identity card, la Carte nationale d'identité sécurisée. Liesel uses hers all the time, mostly to write checks, but also back when she first opened her bank account and more recently when she applied for a credit card. She used her CNIS when Raymond and she went to Italy. Not that she intended to, but she forgot her passport, and the officer at the train station said the CNIS would do, so long as she didn't intend to leave Europe.

The bakery's bell tinkles again. "Oh, Marianne," Liesel says into the phone, because this makes too much sense. If Raymond applied for a credit card under an assumed name, he could then collect the card at a mailbox he rented under an assumed name. Thus the keys. "Hold on. I will be right back." She sells a baguette. She is ready to turn back for the phone when a mother comes in for an ice cream for her child. The girl dithers over the decision. Liesel makes increasingly urgent suggestions. "Chocolate? Everyone likes chocolate. No? Vanilla. That's my favorite." Liesel is so impatient as the mother slowly counts change out of her purse that she finally says, "Madame. Never mind. It is my gift to you." She retreats to the back room before the mother even has a chance to respond.

"I'm back," Liesel says to Marianne, then licks her hand, still wet from scooping pistachio ice cream.

"So I explained the situation to my brother-in-law and asked what he thought. I didn't mention your name. Or Raymond's. I just said, is this possible? And he said not only was it possible, but that the Bureau of Postal Investigation had just that day started watching someone in the Marais because of this very thing. Stolen files."

This must be Raymond, Liesel knows. They have started to watch Raymond, because Liesel returned the files, because Lavallée somehow knew what he was up to. Or perhaps he always knew (and that was why he fired him), but never had any evidence until Liesel walked in.

It explains his words to her. It explains everything.

    ·

AND SO SHE LEAVES PARIS.

She leaves Paris because she can't be sure—not entirely—that it is safe to stay. Might Raymond return with thoughts of revenge? She can't imagine Raymond violent, but then she can't imagine him as a crook. She can't imagine him with a gun. The one friend who might take her in is Marianne. But she can hardly move in with Marianne. That is just where Raymond would look for her, if he had a mind to look for her.

So she must go.

But before she leaves, she has something to do, because she is not going to be able to do this on her own, not in the way she has been living to date, not with Idzia to care for. She is going to need a destination and money to get there. She is going to need a way to pay for rent and food.

She is going to need Joel.

She doesn't want to need him. He will ask things of her. He will make his demands. But she needs his money.

In Rome, after she left St. Peter's Basilica, she had felt insubstantial, as if her skin were dissolving. But not in a creepy way. In a magical way. Like she was somehow becoming part of everything. She was doubly blessed. Of all things. No one was doubly blessed (the woman in the nave had said so). But she was. She with her Polish-looking visage. Only as she picks up the phone to call Joel—she has never forgotten his home number, not in all the six years they have lived apart—she understands that she isn't doubly blessed. Not at all. She is a homeless woman with a little girl. She is doubly in need of blessing.

6

THE FOX

"THE THING ABOUT RAISING CHICKENS..." Joel begins.

"Yes?" Liesel says, already annoyed. They are lying in bed in their chilly room on a cold December night. She has an urge to turn over, hug her hot water bottle, and cluck.

Instead she says, "Go on. The thing about raising chickens is . . ."

"The fox! That is the thing! How are you going to feel when you get up in the morning and instead of picking up a nice warm egg, you have to pick up chicken parts strewn across the lawn?"

"Do you have to be so negative?" Liesel says. "Buck-buck-buck," she adds. "Buck-buck." It's her version of a chicken noise, though she sounds more like a car that won't turn over. She would not like to pick up chicken parts. She's always been squeamish.

"I'm not being negative. I'm being realistic," Joel says. He leans over and kisses her on the shoulder, then starts to rub his warm hand over her stomach and up to her chest. "Somehow I get the idea that I'm the one who's going to be responsible for that chore. The amassing of strewn chicken parts."

He means for her to laugh, so she does, but in a "Ha ha ha" way that says, "I am not amused."

Chickens have been on Liesel's mind for some time—ever since Joel first showed her the property he'd bought in Maine. This many months earlier, on the same day he proposed. *Marry me, and, oh, PS, here's the house I bought. Hope you like it?* She *did* like it: a cute white farmhouse with green shutters. She pictured chickens pecking in the backyard. She pictured a trim garden. She pictured herself sweeping the front porch and inviting neighbors in for lemonade.

Not that she'd ever gardened before. Or knew anything about chickens. Or even liked lemonade. Still, the property felt ready for her attentions. It had a small red barn with a sagging asphalt-shingle roof. Apparently once a brooder hen house, it is now full of junk. Old windows and boards, broken wicker chairs. Mouse turds arrayed like chocolate sprinkles over everything. Still, there is evidence of its former life: long metal troughs that Liesel imagines once held feed; an odd spindle-shaped top that might have been instrumental in dispersing water.

"If you don't want to drive me," Liesel says, "I'll walk." Though twenty-six, she doesn't know how to drive. Not exactly. She had a license, back in New York, but she lost it somewhere in her travels. She never used it anyway, save as ID.

"Don't be ridiculous," Joel says, kissing her neck, but in a comforting way, not a sexual way. "Of course I'll take you." He has finally caught on that her mood is not a friendly one. "I'd love to take you." Then he gets all campy: "Oh, let me take you, please!"

They are talking about an evening seminar on raising chickens. Liesel saw the class advertised in the "Community Bulletin" of the local paper and had an "A-ha!" moment. She has longed for chickens, and here is her chance. Now Joel wonders why there is a need for such a seminar in the middle of winter. Liesel doesn't think the timing is *that* odd. You keep them year-round, after all. And in any case, if now is when they are dispensing knowledge, now is when she's going to the dispensary.

The public library, where the class is being held, is exactly 3.3 miles away, down a narrow but well-trafficked road. These days, snowbanks narrow it even further. In daylight, Liesel treads its shoulderless edge because she can't stand being shut up in the house all day, but Joel and she both know it would be foolish for her to walk after dark.

"Honestly." Joel kisses Liesel again, more of a "Good-night for now" kiss. "If it's something you want, then I want it, too."

"OK," she says, snuggling into him. "I'm not mad at you anymore."

THERE ARE ABOUT TEN OTHER PEOPLE in the library's seminar room when Liesel arrives. "Hey," she says on entry, but no one so much as mumbles a hello in return. People have told Liesel that Mainers are nice, but this has not been her experience in her single month as resident. Only one couple came to introduce themselves when she and Joel moved in. On her walks around the neighborhood, she has wondered if she might meet someone, but people are rarely out. In Boston, if she saw a neighbor out in the evening, she'd say, "Come over. Let's have a glass of wine." She'd tried that trick here, to her great embarrassment. Just a week ago, when she was finishing her daily walk—later than normal and with a flashlight, since it was dark—she saw a neighbor collecting her mail and newspaper. Liesel got brave and headed over to introduce herself.

"Oh, you're who moved into the Petersons' house," the woman said, knowingly. The Petersons weren't the previous owners, but the ones before that.

The neighbor was thin, wearing earmuffs and a dowdy down coat. People didn't much care about personal appearance in Maine. Liesel supposed it was so cold that fashion was a liability. The neighbor's gray-blond hair was feathered in a way that Liesel associated with high school girls in the '70s. The two exchanged basic facts. The woman had five grandchildren, all in the area. She watched them half the week, and their other grandmother watched them the other half. At one point in their chat, the neighbor shook her paper and sighed, "Nothing I want to read in here." This turned them to the gruesome news story the local paper had been covering ever since Liesel and Joel moved in. It was about a man who had locked his stepdaughter in his oven and cooked her, because he thought she was Satan. The woman and Liesel both admitted to trying to turn off their brains to forget the details. The girl had called, "Daddy, let me out. Let me out," until she'd stopped calling. "Oh, let's not even talk about it now!" Liesel cried. It made her sick. She was furious at herself for having read the article. The local newspaper was just a catalogue of horrors. "You're right, dear," the neighbor said. They turned to a discussion of the cold, and then Liesel said, because things seemed to be going well, "Would you like to come over? Have a glass of wine?" The woman said, "No, oh, no," as if the idea was vaguely repulsive.

And that was the end of the conversation. Liesel has seen the woman once since. She was out in the yard with some children, building a lopsided snowman. Though Liesel waved, she sensed a stop for another chat would not be welcome. She had the idea that the woman took her for an alcoholic. She should have suggested tea.

In the library, Liesel feels a low fury at the others for not talking. Isn't it a basic kindness to say hello to others? Everyone in the room looks to be in his or her fifties or sixties, not quite elderly but old enough to look defeated. They all wear jeans and bulky sweaters, rendering them as shapeless as russet potatoes. They seem sunk into a cranky gloom. The one man who appears younger—later thirties or early forties is Liesel's stab at it—is wiry and mountain-man-bearded in a green and blue flannel shirt, jeans, L. L. Bean boots, and a baseball cap. *Original,* Liesel thinks, sourly. In college she read a book on the meaning of clothes that argued you liked people whose *style* you liked. Now that she lives in the land of down parkas and fleece vests, she seems doomed to friendlessness. Sometimes in the supermarket she'll try to spot someone she can imagine being a friend, but there is never a soul. There's never even someone her own age. In Boston, it was just the opposite. Everyone seemed interesting, and the city was full of young people. Each day felt like a glorious adventure.

Eventually, an obese woman with white hair and a cheerful, knowing face comes in and says, "Hello, everybody. I am a chicken activist. Bet that's the first time you ever heard that!"

No one smiles, so Liesel laughs noisily in a way meant to express appreciation. "First time, for sure!" she pipes up cheerfully. *God,* she thinks, *these people.*

The chicken activist passes out flyers about jumbo Cornish Rock Cross broilers and Black Sex Link pullets ("I'll black sex pullet you," Liesel imagines saying to Joel later that night), then spends the hour describing how to buy a chicken, how to build a coop, how to mix feed, and how to butcher. Cutting up her future pets is not something Liesel has considered. She is in it for the eggs. (She likes when the flyer about the "automatic egg turner" makes the rounds.) She is in it because she wants something to love, and because she has already imagined the Christmas card she will send out next year. It will feature Joel wearing a Santa cap with a hen in his lap. Not that she has ever sent out Christmas cards, but the prospect of the photo makes her want to do it. Joel is Jewish, and Liesel is hoping to convert to Judaism, but no matter. It'll be more of a general holiday card. She can sew a blue Santa hat instead of a red. He'll be a Chanukah helper! It'll be a hoot! When the hour is up, the teacher announces that they will talk about brooding chicks next Thursday night. Already Liesel can imagine the chicks' fluffy softness in her palm.

THE SEMINAR IS JUST ONE PART of Liesel's three-part effort to like Maine. She is also taking driving lessons, something she should have mastered back in high school. As it is, driving scares her, and all the more so as she's convinced that an accident involving a poorly plowed road is in her future. Joel tells her she is crazy when she confesses this. (Joel tells her she is crazy a lot.) But you can't really drop your fears just because someone thinks they are irrational. You can just fail to express them. Part three of the effort involves breakfast. A few days a week she eats at Little Mike's, a greasy spoon that's one mile down the road, in the opposite direction of the library. Liesel doesn't generally like greasy spoons. Her digestive system is so relentlessly touchy. A breakfast of eggs, bacon, hash browns, and toast can mean trouble for days. But she has always liked hanging out in coffee shops. She likes looking at other people and guessing at their lives.

On the morning after the chicken seminar, Liesel sits at the counter by Little Mike's register, toying with the menu, though she knows what she wants. Today, the waitress is wearing a headband with reindeer antlers. "The usual?" she says when she sees Liesel.

Liesel smiles. "Yes, thank you."

The woman is a type for whom Liesel feels real sympathy. She must have once been sexy. Now her breasts have fallen and her stomach rounded out, though she still has long, muscular legs. Her skin is wrinkled, permanently tan, a look Liesel associates with a hard-knock life. The waitress moves quickly, seriously, but always brightens at a customer's teasing. She brings Liesel hot tea and oatmeal with a side of browning fruit. Liesel eats as she considers the morning paper. There is a little section on "Volunteer Opportunities," which she mulls over. They need someone to run a crafts class at the Maine Center for the Blind, someone to watch abused children at Parents Anonymous meetings, and someone to drive the elderly to and from clinic appointments at the Portland Health Center. If she could get there, she'd be good at the crafts class, she knows. Or with the children. But of course all this will have to wait until she has her license, and at the rate she's going, that isn't going to be anytime soon.

Just last week, the driving instructor took Liesel for her written test, and to Liesel's great embarrassment, she'd failed. "I thought you were supposed to be smart," the instructor had said when Liesel announced the results outside the DMV. The instructor knew Liesel was married to a doctor, and perhaps that was why she'd come to this assessment of Liesel's IQ.

What could Liesel say to this? "No, no, actually I am *supposed* to be stupid, so this really is in keeping with expectations"?

Now she hears the waitress ask someone, "What's she getting for Christmas?"

A male voice says, "I'm thinking about a college education."

Liesel looks up and sees a flannel-shirted man. He is wearing a Carhartt coat and has a petite toddler with blond hair and a perfect smile sitting in the crook of his left arm. A coffee cup is in his right hand.

"That's all she wants?" the waitress says.

The girl looks around in a sweet manner. Liesel has the idea she's never fussed a day in her life.

"No," the man says. "She also wants bubble wrap and ribbons."

The waitress laughs.

Then the man turns to Liesel and cocks his head in something like recognition.

"Yes?" she says. After a beat, she realizes who he is. "I know you," she offers. "You're the man from the chicken class." It has taken her a while to place him because he has shaved off his ludicrous, untrimmed beard. He is younger than she first thought. Not in his forties, maybe not even in his thirties.

"That's right," he says, smiling. "And you're the laughing woman."

"I am?"

"It was nice, your laughing. That group was a little dead the other night."
His affect is flat, or maybe it's just shy, but his words are clearly friendly.

"I know. Dead and buried."

"Peter Kitely," he says and puts down his coffee cup so as to extend his
hand.

"Liesel Pearlman."

They chat a little about the class. He asks if she lives around here, and
she points down the road. He lives in Portland, he says, but works for a hard-
wood-flooring place just across the road.

He lifts the arm on which his daughter still sits peaceably, observing
everything with apparent good humor. She is wearing white tights and a
pinafore dress over a turtleneck. Liesel thinks she has perhaps never seen
such a beautiful little girl in her life. "The nanny has a cold, so it's take-your-
daughter-to-work day. Or take-your-daughter-to-work week."

"Where's Mom?" Liesel says. She knows it is nosy, but it is the obvious
question.

"Mom's at the law office. They're not as flexible over there."

Liesel bobs her head as if to say, "I get it."

"So, I'll see you next week?" Peter says, as he retrieves his cup.

"No, I'm afraid. I ... uh ... don't drive, and my ride ... well, my husband
has a meeting that night, so I can't get there." It still feels funny, and a little
thrilling, to say "my husband."

"If you want to go, I'll take you."

"Oh, no," she starts to protest reflexively, though in fact she wants to
say yes.

"It's hardly like it's a problem," he says. "I'm going myself."

"Oh, OK. Yeah, that would be great."

HE ARRIVES IN AN OLD PICKUP. He must be coming straight from
work, since he smells faintly of sawdust, and he is wearing a beat-up pair
of jeans with holes through which one can see the waffle weave of his long
underwear. He's not got his coat on, the heat in the cab is on full blast, and

though he is slight, she feels uncomfortably aware of the musculature of his chest, apparent under his blue pullover.

"Freezing," he says when she hops in. He rubs his arms.

"I know," she says, a visible puff of air coming from her mouth.

When he puts his hand back on the wheel, she notices that half of the second finger of his left hand is missing.

They arrive at the library only to be told they have come too early. The session is from 7:00 p.m. to 9:00 p.m., not 5:00 p.m. to 7:00 p.m..

"Since when?" Peter asks. There are others who have shown up too early too, all of them standing in little puddles left from the snow they've tracked in.

"We posted it." The librarian points to a flyer above a coffee urn at the entrance.

Peter shrugs. Why would they have the notion that people were going to come to the library in advance of the seminar and study the wall above the coffee pot? He turns to Liesel and says, "What do you want to do?"

"I'd like to come back, but if you don't want to hang around . . ."

"Um . . . we could get dinner?" he says. "Then come back?" He talks to her as if she is older, as if he needs to defer, a trick Liesel notices mostly because it is something *she* does. She always wants the other person to be the grown-up in the room.

"Um, yeah, dinner," she says. "Dinner would be great."

They drive to a restaurant in the next town over, which Peter says is a basic all-around place. "It's not great," Peter adds as they get out of the truck, a shrug of an apology. "There's better in town," he says, clearly meaning Portland.

Inside, it's fairly crowded. A record is playing a little too loudly: Tina Turner's "We Don't Need Another Hero." They sit in a booth in the corner. He gets a beer, she a wine. The menu is long, and all the dishes have stupid names. "Lighthouse Linguini," the "L. L. Betcha Love It" for a surf-and-turf dish. She can see ordering is going to be hard for her. Hamburgers, French fries, pasta, lobster stew. If she doesn't eat a salad or vegetables, she'll be cramped up in the bathroom all night.

When he wraps his hands around his glass, she notices his finger again, stubby and lewd.

"Is it dangerous? Your work. In the mill, I mean."

"Not so much. I don't actually mill the wood. I lay the floors. I'm usually out and about during the day. Different houses."

"Oh." She nods.

"And you. What do you do?"

What can she say? "I'm kind of between things."

Peter has left his thin wool hat on, and his hair curls out from under it. His skin looks chapped, as if he's spent too much time in the cold. She notices a few small freckles across his nose and cheeks. They give him a little-boy look, not apparent when he had the crazy-man beard. He's actually, she realizes, quite handsome in that young-man-carpenter way. Her eyes dart to his fingers—all, save the injured one, slender, almost girlish—and then to his arms. His sleeves are rolled up and on the forearms are tattoos, an elaborate art nouveau woman on each side, curling crimson tresses that suggest a wrought-iron gate.

"How long have you worked there?" Liesel gestures at the door, as if the mill is just outside.

He laughs. "Not too long. It's my day job. I'm actually an actor. Karen took the job here." Liesel assumes Karen is his wife. "And I'm trying to make the best of it. The good thing is they're really flexible about the hours, let me take off when I need to. I've got almost nothing now. Acting-wise. Just a book for the blind—I do a bunch of those tapes. And I do workshops for kids at Portland Stage. But I've got something this summer in the Berkshires. Still, you know, I'm a snob. I miss New York."

"Wow," Liesel says. "I've never met an actor before. I've always wanted to."

"As you can imagine, we're a shy, selfless bunch."

Liesel smiles. "What's your favorite role? I mean what was the best part you ever played?"

"That's a great question. Normally people ask if I've been in anything they've seen. Sometimes people even ask if I'm famous, if you can believe that."

"Are you?"

"In my own mind. Very famous. Star of the play of my life, that's for sure."

Liesel smiles again. "So, favorite part?"

"Just before we moved I did *The Mystery of Irma Vep*. It's completely silly, but I like hamming it up. It's two actors, but we played eight different characters between us, and changed costumes thirty-five times. A real workout. It was in the Village. I should say Chekhov or something, I suppose."

"I like silly," she says.

"Irma Vep is an anagram for vampire. It's about vampires and werewolves, but still pretty funny."

She likes silly. Not so much vampires.

He says, "Why didn't you ever learn to drive?"

"I guess . . . well, I learned a little, but basically my father wouldn't teach me."

"Why not?"

"Controlling. Very. And then I asked my college boyfriend to help me get better, but he didn't want to, and after that I lived in cities, so I didn't really need a car."

"And now?"

"I'm taking lessons. It's just . . . with the ice . . . I'm kind of scared to drive."

"I getcha. It's kind of an extreme sport, this time of year."

"Right!" Liesel laughs, pleased to have been taken seriously.

They talk on, running through their basic biographies, talking about what their spouses do. At some point, when Liesel confesses the chickens are because she's feeling at loose ends in her house, he says, "They need someone at the box office at Portland Stage. Then you could meet all the actors you want. Well, if you went poking into the green room for doughnuts."

"God!" Liesel says. "I'd love to do that! That would be so great! Only the car thing. If the hours didn't work around Joel's schedule . . ."

"Why don't you just take a cab?"

"I don't know." And she doesn't. As soon as he says it, it seems so obvious. It's not like Joel wouldn't give her the money. "I guess it never occurred to me. I sort of think of cabs as going with cities."

"You can't stand in the road and hail one, but you can call one. Seems like a cab is a pretty simple solution."

"Yeah, you're right."

In the background, she hears Prince singing "I Would Die 4 U." When she moved to Boston, after living in London, she remembers being at a party with some of Joel's friends, and when she said she didn't know who Prince was—she didn't, and had barely heard of Bruce Springsteen—they were all shocked. She'd felt obscurely proud. She liked not being so plugged into American culture. She liked that she never went to the kind of restaurant she is sitting in right now.

"What's it like going in and out of people's houses all day?"

"Lonely housewife? The handyman? You can imagine how that plays out," he says, joking, but still it catches her off guard.

"How *does* that play out?"

"The video store down the road." He points outside. "They've got a room in the back, under-eighteen not admitted. The grim truth is all there. Mostly, though, I like *The Muppets Take Manhattan*."

"Haven't seen it," Liesel says, relieved by the Muppets reference.

"You'll see it," he says, "trust me—as soon as you have kids. But I'm not answering your question. When I'm in someone's house, it's usually unfinished, so I'm not really visiting a place where there are people yet. So it's not interesting exactly, but it is peaceful. And I always take a break and go for a long walk. It's a ritual I got into."

"I love to walk. I walk all the time." She's no athlete, but she loves to wear herself out physically. She has the idea it helps with her stomach.

They miss the chicken seminar. Not intentionally. It's just when they finally look down to their wrists, it's 7:30

"We can still catch the end?" Liesel says. It is a two-part seminar. There won't be more lessons after tonight.

"Nah," Peter says. "Unless you want to. This is better."

She smiles, flattered, then confesses that she has felt some dimming in her enthusiasm about chicken rearing in the past week. The chicken activist told them that chickens attack their injured brethren: "If one gets cut, they'll all peck at the wound."

"Not very friendly," Liesel says now.

"Good point," Peter says. "If you are looking for companionship, I'm going to encourage you off chickens and onto puppies."

"Puppies!" she says, as if it is the most outlandish thing she's ever heard.

"Camel?" Peter tries, and Liesel laughs.

On their honeymoon Liesel had complained to Joel that they didn't ever talk, that they didn't really "talk" talk. Even now, Joel listens to what she has to say, but he doesn't quite respond to it. He doesn't engage with it, save in the form of resistance: *She is so silly. She is so ridiculous. Where did she ever get that idea?* On the honeymoon, he had said, "Of course we talk. We're talking right now."

"That's not what I mean. I'm talking about building a conversation, where one idea leads to another and you construct something together."

"I'm just being myself," he said.

"God, you," she growled, frustrated. Why couldn't she make herself understood?

"What do you want, Liesel?" Joel had finally said, in exasperation. "What do you want?"

"This," she thinks, as she sits in the restaurant with Peter. "*This* is what I want." Such a First World need, she knows. Communication. Not the basics—food, shelter—and yet it feels like sustenance.

By the time Liesel gets home, she is so turned on—turned on by everything: the chat, the mild flirtation, the job possibility—that she calls Joel at the hospital and asks when he will be home.

"Soon," he says. "Why?"

"I've been out flirting with a man from my chicken class, and I need you to come home and make love to me."

He laughs and says, "I'm on my way."

A WEEK AFTER HER DINNER with Peter, she takes a cab to Portland Stage. There, Peter introduces her to Elizabeth, the box office manager. "I'll come get you after the interview," he offers, and Liesel nods yes. It isn't an interview, though, more of an explanation of what she will have to do. Elizabeth is a fast-talking, cheerful young woman. (Potential friend, Liesel notes, right away.) She shows Liesel how the tickets are organized with a different wooden box for each performance of each show. She instructs Liesel on how to file reserved tickets. She pulls out a seating chart, enclosed in sticky plastic, then takes her into the theater and walks her around, explaining which seats have the best view, which are off at an angle. "You have to let people know if they get a ticket here or here," she says, pointing at the walls. "Just so they don't complain later."

Elizabeth used to work at a theater in an old barn in Westport, Connecticut. She says, "You had to tell people the view was 'partially obstructed,' when it was behind a post. People would ask what 'partially obstructed' meant, and you were supposed to answer, 'Partially obstructed.' But when the box office manager wasn't there, we'd say, 'You can't see a damn thing.'"

"I love it," Liesel laughs.

"But it's not like that here," Elizabeth says. "All the seats are basically good. Takes the pressure off when you know you're not screwing anyone over."

This is a relief. She could not work at a job that required her to be, even in this small way, immoral.

"So, easy enough?" Elizabeth asks and taps Liesel's arm with the rolled-up seating chart.

"Yes," Liesel says. It doesn't seem too complicated.

"I like you. You're hired."

"Really?"

"Ab-sa-toot-lute-ly. Can you start next week? We need someone 12:30 to 7:30 p.m., Tuesday, Thursday, and Friday."

"That would be fantastic!" Does she seem overeager? Perhaps someone so pleased about answering phones and dispensing tickets will strike Elizabeth as off-balance. No matter. The offer has been extended.

"We'll do the W-2 on the first day," Elizabeth says.

They shake hands and Liesel goes outside. She realizes she hasn't asked about pay. She figures she will find out on the first day. There is no amount, no matter how low, that she would refuse. At this point, if they charged her for the opportunity to work, she'd probably agree.

"I can't thank you enough," Liesel calls to Peter, who is crossing the street toward the theater just as Liesel steps onto the sidewalk. "This is amazing. This is going to turn everything around."

"Happy to help. Lunch?" he says, as if this were the agreed-upon plan all along.

"Let's!" she enthuses.

"I know a place." They drive a handful of blocks to a Japanese restaurant in the Old Port. She loves the décor: the bamboo wood and rice-paper screens, the simplicity of everything. This is only her second time in a Japanese restaurant, and she hasn't quite made up her mind if she likes, or is repulsed by, sushi. Still, it's good. It's all good.

Over the meal, they talk about what they have not yet talked about: their marriages. Or he does, anyway. She finds the idea of confiding in a man about Joel—or really to anyone about Joel—disloyal. It's not like gossiping about a boyfriend, when you talk as a matter of weighing whether you should proceed with the relationship. With Joel, the decision has been made. She has married him. He is her husband. That she wept on her honeymoon, worn down by Joel's annoyance with her, is not something she wants to confess.

But this doesn't mean she's not curious about other people and their marriages. There is nothing more interesting to her than the private lives of others.

Once, when Joel and she were on the T in Boston, she saw a hefty, middle-aged black man who had dreadlocks piled into a giant doorknob at the top of his head. He was wearing a leather jacket that had a map of Africa over the left breast and the name of some basketball team over the right. At a stop, a heavy young woman got on, and they hugged and started talking animatedly.

"Don't you wonder what they are talking about?" Liesel said, gesturing with her chin to indicate whom she meant. "Or how they know each other?"

"No," Joel said, disparagingly, as if it were a stupid thing to wonder about. They'd had a huge row about it when they got off the subway.

He was apologetic later, and still later, back on the subway, they saw a woman with powder caked all over her face. "Check it out," he said, when the woman started to apply mascara in the bumping and heaving car. "An Olympic feat," he remarked.

"Thank you," she said, getting that he was observing this by way of further apology.

Now, Peter tells her that he married young, right out of college. "Should have waited," he admits. He has two children: the girl Liesel has seen and an older boy of six. Peter says that he and Karen squabble a lot, and they might not have stayed together if not for the kids. Neither of them likes the idea of the children being made to commute between households. Neither of them likes the idea of spending half the week away from the children. "We just love them too much," Peter says.

Liesel nods. "That sounds hard," she allows. "Are you going to just . . . is that the rest of your life then?"

"Well," he shrugs. "She's had some . . . things. A guy at her office, for a little while. I suspect someone else. I did, too, a few years back, when I did a play in Rhode Island. And I had one other girlfriend, before that, for many years. And now, actually, my wife's dad died, and she—my wife, I mean—gained a lot of weight. Sort of in response. And it's kind of made her feel frozen, when it comes to . . . well, touching, anything related to the body. She says things will be different when she loses the weight. I tell her I don't need that. I'm not super-thrilled, you know, but it would be OK. I mean, I'm not going to *weigh* her before I kiss her."

"Seems like, I don't know, not the best way to conduct a marriage."

"Everyone has affairs," he says, seeming both resigned and defensive.

Do they? Liesel wonders. She doesn't know *anyone* who's ever had an affair, save for public figures. Not, she supposes, that people would be chatting about it, if they did.

"I'm sorry," Liesel says. "Sounds kind of bleak."

"I suppose," he says, so dispiritedly that she says, in a campy sort of way, "God, I'd like to help. I could come sit in your lap?" She means it as a joke, isn't at all thinking of it as a come-on, but he looks startled. He waits a beat, as if considering, then says, "That gives me a hard-on."

Oh." Liesel looks down, panicked. *Why* has she said that? *What a thing to say!* Of course he wouldn't take it as a joke. It doesn't sound like a joke at all. Her skin feels so sensitive that the air suddenly seems like too much. She tightens her groin. She is embarrassed and, she is disturbed to realize, completely turned on. She looks back up. "I . . . You know." She shakes her head to the left and right. *No.*

"I didn't mean," he starts.

"Oh, no, no. I didn't think you meant . . . I mean, yes, I know that." She looks down again then up.

She picks up her chopsticks and pokes at a little piece of orange fish before her, then sets them back down again. *I was swimming in the sea, now I'm sitting on a plate,* she thinks, a little ditty for the invisible child at the table.

"I'm sorry," he says.

"No, I am. I started it."

He coughs.

Though they are clearly both uncomfortable, they make it through lunch. He tells her who's nice at the theater, who's a little harder to deal with. She tells him what her life was like in Boston. Not long after she'd moved to Brookline, Joel had found her a job at a doctor's office. It was for some smoking study, and she helped run lab tests. She learned how to spin blood, which was a little weird. The subjects didn't get paid for participating, but they got free cigarettes, which was clearly worth it to them. At some point Joel figured out that a cigarette manufacturer was funding the study, so she'd quit the job. With his blessing, thank goodness. She moved in with him then, and he pretty much covered her expenses after that. She would go for her walks during the day, all around the city, then come home and make something special for Joel for dinner.

"I really got into cooking then," she says. "And I've always kind of been into crafts. I used to paint in college."

"Carpentry's been good for me," he says. "Balances out the intensity of the acting. Nice to use a different part of the brain."

"I better call a cab," she says eventually.

"I can take you. I mean . . . I've got to go back out anyway. I've got to pick up some lumber for a morning job."

"Right," she says. "Yeah, then, yes, that'd be great, if you don't mind."

"Liesel," he says seriously, almost in reprimand. "Obviously I don't mind."

She is about to start apologizing, but instead she says, "I know." She feels, for no reason, like weeping.

When they get to her house, she turns to thank him. He leans toward her and says, "Kiss me," so she does.

IN THE MORNING, she flutters about the house nervously. Anxiety, regret, and longing so braided together that she can't disentangle them, can't distinguish anything beyond the *intensity* of her feeling. (Though when does she not feel intensely? "You always get so upset," she hears Joel chide.) She doesn't go to Little Mike's, doesn't want to bump into Peter, but then when he doesn't call that day—she hasn't given him her number, but he could look it up easily enough—she registers her disappointment. It is not really true that she doesn't want to see him. She *wants* to see him. Only she doesn't want to . . . No, she stops herself mid-thought, disavows her own effort to be moral.

She *definitely* wants to see him.

She just wants him to want to see her first.

But she's not sure anything has actually happened—that what has registered for her as a big event has registered for him as the same. And why should it? Some kissing in a car. A few errant minutes. Only she was so swept away. When she thinks about it, music swells and refuses to crash, just pulls her helplessly in, and the mixed metaphor works for her, because she can feel herself being smashed on the shore by this. Before she knew Joel, back in London, she'd been a nanny, and once the kids went to bed, she'd retreat to her room and listen to heartbreak music, too much Patsy Cline. The music made her crazy with longing and loss, but still she listened. The songs cracked her open, got to the dead center of what she wanted and didn't have. Kissing Peter felt like having it, like finally, *finally* having it. Only possession was elusive. She could feel the moment going even as she experienced it. "That was fun," he said when they parted, and she felt the sting of the word. Fun?

Liesel is not an adulteress. She would never cheat on Joel. She would never cheat on anybody. She is not that kind of person. She doesn't even feel attracted to Peter in anything like the conventional sense. While he had his hands on her cheeks, and she had her hands on his arms, she didn't feel sexual exactly. She just felt her deep desire to be doing precisely what she was doing. The kissing was like an extension of the talking. *What do you want, Liesel? What do you want?*

This.

She has a cheap sewing machine, and earlier in the month she bought fabric for curtains and pillows. She's pinned everything but not sewn, perhaps because what will she do once the chore is through? But now that she has a job, there's a reason to finish things up. She gets the cloth and machine out. What could she possibly say to Peter if he called? She doesn't know. She rehearses some possibilities, writes dialogue in her head, dismisses the lines she gives to herself, to him. *Stupid.* When she lived in Boston, sometimes she would walk by a woman—it was always a woman for some reason—and see by her facial movements that she was having an impassioned conversation in her head. Often it seemed to be an argument, but sometimes it looked like a fantasy of love.

She tries to upend her own thoughts, to write a conversation in her head with Joel. But it doesn't work. She can't even daydream herself into satisfaction. What a horrible mistake. She has married a man with whom she doesn't like talking. It's not till she formulates it this way for herself that she realizes it is true.

She stills the sewing machine, puts her forehead on the table where she is working, and cries.

THAT WEEKEND, Joel and she spend Saturday doing errands and Sunday with the *New York Times.* She likes that Joel reads the *Times,* that he's smart enough for the puzzle. He is lying on the couch, and she is on the rocking chair reading, when he says, "This clue . . . this reminds me of something." He tells her a story about a patient he met when he was on the urology rotation that would make him decide on his specialty. No one could figure out what was wrong with this woman. She had blood in her urine, severe pain in her lower back, and general weakness. But her kidneys, her urethra, and her bladder all looked fine. They'd done CT scans, ultrasounds, cystoscopy, and kidney biopsy. "All of which," Joel says, "you wouldn't really sign up for, if you could avoid it." A cystoscopy, he explains, involves the insertion of a small tube with a light on the end through the urethra.

"Ugh," Liesel flinches. "You do this procedure?"

"Yes, Liesel," he says, as if she is a simpleton. "I'm a doctor."

The kidney biopsy involved needles through the back. The woman had fainted when she'd stood up from the procedure and complained of severe pain in her back. Then she'd started vomiting. They ended up admitting her.

"God," Liesel says.

"So, wait, though. Here's the story." Joel registered that the woman had a Band-Aid on her forefinger. "That," he says, "was my first clue." He asked for a urine sample and insisted that a nurse be in the bathroom with the patient. The woman made a big deal about it. She was embarrassed, needed her privacy, couldn't pee with someone else in the room. But Joel insisted. The sample came back clean. Ditto a subsequent one. Then they let her go to the bathroom without supervision. When she came out, Joel noticed she had her third finger tucked into her palm. "What's this?" he said. "Oh, nothing, I cut myself," she said.

On purpose it turned out. Joel's guess was right. She'd been putting blood in her own urine to contaminate the sample.

"What?" Liesel says.

"She had Munchausen's syndrome. It's a mental disorder, where people fake symptoms. Sometimes they even hurt themselves or, as with this woman, manage to falsify their lab results."

"Why?"

"Oh, you know, they want to be paid attention to. They want their kids to call them." Joel rolls his eyes.

"Wild."

Liesel loves when Joel tells stories like this. It isn't true that she and Joel can't talk. Here they are, on a Sunday morning, talking. It was unfair of her to think otherwise. *She* is unfair.

Later, though, when they go out to the supermarket to do the week's shopping, Liesel looks at his car and says, "Your left front tire looks low, don't you think?"

"It isn't low," he snaps. "Why do you always think something is going wrong?"

"I . . ." She can't stand this about him, his short fuse directed toward her. Her voice gets wobbly. "I just said it looked a little low."

"What are you getting all upset about?"

"Nothing," she says and wipes her mitten across the bottom of her nose. Do they ever go a full day without this friction? Is this the way she must live from now until forever?

ON MONDAY, when Liesel goes to Little Mike's, Peter does not come in, and she assumes he is purposefully avoiding her. Then she reprimands herself for the narcissistic thought. She is likely not even on his mind enough for such calculation. She debates whether to go again on Tuesday. She can already sense how deflated she will feel when he is not there. Why set herself up for disappointment? But she goes anyway. The sun is up, the ice thawing, so she walks down the road more briskly than usual, and this is a pleasure. The longer she walks, the better her mood. This has always been the case. As she hops over the muddy portions of the shoulder, she plans what she will wear for her first day of work. She'll be hidden in the box office, largely taking calls, until the half hour just before the show, when people will come in for their tickets. Even so, she wants to look nice. It's not for other people as much as herself that she pays attention to her clothes. Mostly it's to prove to herself that she hasn't given up. At Little Mike's, she takes her seat at the counter and wills herself not to look up hopefully every time the door clangs open and shut.

Finally, Peter does come in. "Hey," he says offhandedly in her direction. "Hi, Liesel."

"Oh," she says, "hi," already hurt by his manner.

He turns to talk with the waitress, and he is so affable and flirty with her that Liesel flushes. He just has this manner with everybody! Hadn't he been super-flirty with the waitress that night of their first dinner? And, too, at the Japanese restaurant? Why did she think it had anything to do with *her*? But then he sits down next to her and says, "Walking home?"

She nods yes.

"I'll drive you," he says. Not a question.

When he parks in her driveway, they sit silently for a moment, and then finally he says, "So?"

But she cannot be the one who determines what will come next. Eventually she says, "This is Joel's house. I didn't even pay a dollar for it."

"OK?" he says, giving an "And why are you telling me this?" lift to the word.

"Just explaining why I'm not inviting you in."

"I know," he says. "You shouldn't invite me in. I've got to get to work anyway. I'll call you?"

"Yes," she says. "Call me."

She goes into the house and sits alone for a long time without doing anything.

PETER DOESN'T CALL. Instead he comes to the box office on Thursday night, just when it is closing.

"I had to sign a contract to teach more workshops," he says, explaining his presence, though it is 7:30 p.m., and the administrative offices are closed. He asks how her first two days have gone.

"Pretty slow," she admits. "Except for the brief stretch before the show."

"Come," he says, and she turns off the box office lights and locks the door. "I'll show you where we do the kids' classes." They walk up one flight of stairs, then another. They are quiet, because the performance is under way. On the third floor, he opens a door onto a cold room with mirrors on two walls and a barre on another. It looks like a dance studio. "We keep a little costume room here," he says and walks her into a side room that is stuffed with boxes out of which stick random bits of things: pink sequined fabric, a long white glove, and a jester's hat. She'd love to be a seamstress for a costume shop. She wonders how you get such a job.

He puts his hand on her back, as they move forward into the room.

"Stay here?" he asks. She turns back to him, not quite sure she's heard correctly, and they start to kiss. It is silent, save for the noise of their lips. "No one's touched me in a long time," he says, then breaks away and laughs. "Well, not counting my kids, of course."

"I'll touch you," she says, as if it is just a favor, a benevolent act, because she is a kind person. She puts her hands under his shirt. His chest is hairy, animal peltish, and she knows it would put her off if she weren't so otherwise drawn to him.

It is time for her to go home, but she doesn't want to. She likes how luxuriant this kissing feels. It doesn't feel like kissing that must lead to something. Has that ever been the case with a man before? With her London boyfriend, Liesel used to make out a long time, only because he came so fast that it seemed the only way to make the event last more than thirty seconds. Still, it was clear that they were just postponing till they got to the part he really cared about.

"I can't remember when I last had sex," Peter admits, and she whispers, wondering if she is trying too hard to sound sexy, "Then I better give you a blow job."

He is already hard as she drops to her knees and undoes his belt, unzips his pants. He stays standing, his fingertips in her hair, as if for balance, and then he steps back from her mouth, takes himself in his hand, and comes, groaning in that way men do. He says her name as he comes, two syllables, Lie-sel, and it sounds pretty to her, which it rarely does; mostly it feels like what it is, fake and strange, not really her at all. He has come all over his fingers. He laughs, looks around for a scrap of fabric to wipe his hand, and laughs again. "God," he says and takes her hands to pull her up to his side and hug her. "God."

They stay like that for what feels like a long time, before he says into her hair, "I've got to get home. Everyone's probably waiting."

"Right," she says, feeling odd. "Home."

On the return cab ride—Joel not able to pick her up because he's had a last-minute call into the hospital—she feels almost blank, a blankness she associates with a surfeit of emotion. She knows guilt is in there and worry and confusion and pleasure, but none of these dominates. She has an idea of what she's supposed to be feeling. She's seen movies. She's read *Madame Bovary*. (In French, no less. French was always one of her best subjects at school.) But she doesn't feel any of the things she sees depicted in movies or reads in books. She knows the idea of hurting Joel makes her sick. The idea of hurting anyone makes her sick. She thinks of Karen, dealing with her father's death by comforting herself with food. How sad. Who would want to add to the burden of a woman like that?

Not Liesel.

SHE PUTS OFF SEEING PETER AGAIN. She dillydallies. She gives up Little Mike's, which is fine, because the place always seemed like it was long overdue for a visit from the health inspector. Peter doesn't seem particularly eager to arrange a meeting again himself. Whatever is going on, they are at least on the same page.

Only she talks to Peter, almost daily, by phone. She loves talking to him. He tells her about his troubled, drug-addicted brother, about a girlfriend who broke up with him when he left town for a week to go to his mother's funeral. He tells her about standing over his father's bed and giving him an extra dose of morphine, just because he hoped it would help him finally die, then crying, "Oh, Daddy!" because he was holding his father's hand and felt the actual moment when his pulse stopped. He tells her what it was like to hold each of his children for the first time. About a time when he was fighting with his wife and almost backed his car into a small child. Aside from mentioning this fight, he avoids the topic of his wife entirely, and Liesel doesn't ask. She doesn't want to be able to picture her too clearly. As for Liesel, she talks about some things—part of what happened in London, but not all; a lot about how tough it was growing up in Schenectady. She confesses that she used to read the files of patients when she worked in a doctor's office in college. "The stories were so good," she says. It's not something she's even told Joel, who would be appalled at the snooping. But Peter is not appalled that she would be curious. He says, "Do you remember them?"

"Sort of," Liesel says.

"Tell me one."

But she can't think of one. Not in all its particulars. Instead she tells about the Munchausen's patient and then a story Joel has told on himself, any number of times. It is about when he was an intern, and a woman came into the emergency room with a boy named Leroy, who'd stuck a marble up his nose.

Joel was down on his knees and working with forceps to get the marble out, but every time he seemed to get the marble in his grasp, it slipped and moved farther up the boy's nose. A trickle of blood came streaming out of his nostril, and he started to cry. Joel grew tenser and tenser as he seemed to be upsetting the boy more and more.

So there was Joel, frustrated, his knees starting to groan, rooting around in the weeping boy's bleeding nose . . . when a big black man came into the emergency room. Everything about his manner said that he was Leroy's father, and Joel felt sure the man was going to deck him. This is the part of the story that Liesel doesn't quite like to tell. It's a little racist. Why would a big black man be any more likely than any father to swing at a doctor making his son bleed? The big man said, "Leroy, you stick a marble up your nose?" The boy bobbed his head up and down. "Give it here, Leroy," the man said, and Leroy blew the marble out of his nose.

Peter laughs with pleasure. People always do with this anecdote.

Should she be using Joel's story to entertain Peter? Once, when she was saying how devoted Joel was to his patients, Peter said, "Sounds like a great guy," and Liesel had nodded, even though she was talking on the phone, and said, "He is."

ONE MONDAY AFTERNOON, Peter ends their phone conversation by saying, "Workday tomorrow?"

"Yes."

"Well, maybe we can find each other." He says this a lot. It doesn't quite mean, "Let's get together." It just doesn't rule out the possibility that they will get together, at some point in the future.

"Maybe," she says, hoping, but not committing either. She can't say she wants to see him. She can't forswear seeing him. She cannot shipwreck herself on the shoals of this marriage. There has to be a line out, a possibility that this life she has made is not the life that she must live.

One morning, Peter takes her to a beach house just south of Portland, where he is laying floor. The house is closed for the season, but the heat has been turned up so he can do the job. It is a gray-white day, snowing just

lightly. Peter fishes here in summer, says he'll have to bring her back sometime, and they can walk on the beach, but they both know that this will never
happen. He gives her a tour, starts to kiss her when they get to the master
bedroom.

The beds aren't made up. It seems pretty disrespectful to make love on
someone's mattress pad, and Liesel says so, but Peter kisses her, leans her
back on the bed, says, "Don't you worry about that."

If the kissing has been perfect, the making love isn't. She feels self-
conscious about being naked in the bright light of the room. He clearly is
uncomfortable, too, and at first he can't get a hard-on—"I'm shy," he says,
cocking the tip of his penis as if it is a comical puppet, uninclined for the
stage—and there is the usual fumbling apology and reassurances: "I'm kind
of tired," "It doesn't matter to me; I just like being with you." But then he
does get a hard-on, and they do have halfhearted sex, which is lovely and
close but maybe not as sexy as he might have wanted? She wonders a lot
about what he wants. If he is basically abstinent these days, it should be
good, shouldn't it? As for *her* wants, she's always been confused. She suspects she isn't able to lose herself the way other women do. Either that, or
the whole world is just lying about how terrific sex is. But she has always
loved being held afterward. It is the point, as far as she is concerned. And as
if he knows this, Peter pulls her close after he comes. The two of them fall
asleep, legs and arms tangled together.

And for the rest of the month, she wakes up with this wish: not to make
love to Peter, but to lie with her head on his chest.

Is this an affair? Liesel doesn't think of it like that. After all, they have
only made love that one time. She would never go to a hotel with Peter. Or
she doesn't think she would. She feels more sympathy than judgment about
Peter's difficult marriage, and anyway, it's clear Peter loves his wife, whatever their troubles. She doesn't think she'd be able to care for *him,* if he
didn't care for his wife. The mistress who wants her lover to leave his wife . . .
that's a stock character whom Liesel doesn't understand. How mean! How
sick! Though she knows most people would argue that the actual infidelity
is what's mean and sick. Once, standing on the sidewalk in front of the Portland Stage, she has what must be a panic attack, as she imagines Peter's wife

finding out about her and Peter. For a moment, she is so overcome with anxiety that she can't move, can only put her palm to her chest and think, "OK," as if to steady the beating there. She has dreams where she calls Peter, and Karen picks up and says, "Why do you keep calling my husband?"

So she should stop talking to him, she knows.

But she loves him.

He doesn't love her. She knows that. Or she thinks she does. She suspects that the physical part of the relationship is more important to him than it is to her. (After all, Joel wants her. Her previous boyfriends always wanted her. She hasn't been denied touch.) She doesn't need sex from him in the way Peter needs it from her, even if he is getting it from her in this minimal form.

She wonders if she's giving it up in the way a high school girl will. "I've got to do it so he'll still like me. So he'll still like me *that way*."

Christ.

Only she wants to make love with him. She wants to kiss him more than anything she has ever wanted in her life.

Sex has its hazards, though. Physical intimacy builds in distance. You can only be so close to someone who you want to want you. As soon as you desire, you lose all power.

So January goes, then February. Out for coffee one morning he says something about his "friends" in the past, not using the word "lover," and dislike for him flashes through her. Would any one of them be happy to be so minimized? Perhaps she doesn't like him at all, a serial adulterer, a guy who can't stop cheating, who has convinced both himself and others of his narrative: husband ignored by wife he loves but still loyal (if not faithful), despite all she denies him. Liesel notes once again that flirty is his automatic manner with all women, but that doesn't stop her from being charmed by him, from wanting his attention and approval. And when he says he just wants affection in his life, she thinks, "Well, sure, of course. Who doesn't?" and her sympathies are with him again. (And also who is she to judge? Look at what she is doing.) In March, they make love in a different house where he is putting in a floor. "I love you," she says when they are through, though she can feel the words are a mistake even as they leave her mouth.

But instead of saying, "Love . . . there's that," as a long-ago boyfriend of hers once said, he says, "I love you, too, Liesel. Why didn't you say so before?"

"Why didn't you?"

"Waiting for you," he says. He kisses the tip of her nose and says, "I should have. We could have been saying it all along."

She kisses him back. Thinks (oddly): *Thank you.*

It is a Friday morning, before her shift at the box office, when they have this conversation. They don't talk over the weekend. They never do, since Peter can't call, of course, when Joel is at home. There's a terrible snowstorm, and Liesel stays in, making soup and muffins, while Joel works clearing the drive, raking snow from the roof. On Sunday there is rain in the morning, which freezes in the afternoon. Joel goes out to break up the ice with a shovel. Liesel watches Joel work as she rehearses and re-rehearses the conversation she had with Peter, as if it will reveal new meaning once she has sufficiently examined it. You can know you are foolish, but still not stop yourself from *being* foolish. At one point, she sees Joel slip and fall in the driveway.

"Jesus," she says as she goes running out. "Are you all right?"

"I'm fine. I'm fine," he says.

"Let's hire someone to do that. I don't want you to do that."

"Liesel, I said I'm fine. That means I'm fine." He is so angry! Is this going to be her life? Living with his small rages? Thinking about Peter? Isn't it normal, reacting to his fall? Wouldn't she be a jerk if she didn't express concern? (You are a jerk anyway, she reminds herself. You slept with another man yesterday.)

Liesel doesn't hear from Peter on Monday, Tuesday, or Wednesday. She never calls him, since where would she call? His house? Obviously not. His job? That wouldn't work either. What an idiot she was to say "I love you." Now he doesn't want to talk to her, she realizes. He hadn't wanted to respond in kind. Isn't that a truism of male-female relationships: nothing pushes a man away like a declaration of love? It's true even in friendships. You can't be overeager. It messes things up. And then she feels angry at Peter. Jerk. What a jerk for not calling.

But if you look at it from another point of view, he would be a jerk *for* calling. A bigger jerk. A cheating-on-his-wife creep. She knows that. It doesn't take the edge off her sense of loss, though. She feels brokenhearted and miserable.

"What's the matter?" Joel asks mid-week. "You seem all . . ." He seesaws his palm in the air to suggest disturbance.

"I'm not sure," she says. "Probably just getting a cold."

SHE OPENS THE BOX OFFICE herself on Thursday morning. It is her first shift of the week. She feels bereft, is still accommodating herself to the fact that Peter has not called, that perhaps he is never going to call. This is the downside of the thrill of hearing from him, feeling so crushed when she doesn't. It's cold in the box office; someone must have turned the heat down the previous night. A stack of old newspapers is on the side desk, also old coffee cups. Why hasn't anyone cleaned up? She has always hated a mess. She throws the trash away, and then, because the Mountain Dew bottles and partially emptied coffee cups still make the room feel filthy, she goes out back to empty the can in the dumpster. She comes back and checks the answering machine to see if there are any messages. But no. She positions herself on her stool at the window. There is nothing to do till someone calls, so she pages through the newspaper to see what's there, even though it is last Monday's paper.

She is just skimming till she gets to the "Local/State" section.

ICY ROADS CLAIM LIVES OF THREE MAINE RESIDENTS

Three people were killed in two separate car crashes blamed on freezing rain that swept the state on Sunday.

Harry and Deborah Jones, 56 and 57, of Cumberland were killed when their car hit a tree after veering off Blackstrap Road in North Yarmouth. Their daughter, Nancy Paulson of Westbrook, reports they were returning home from church at the time of the accident. Harry Jones was killed at the scene. His wife died later that evening after being transported to Maine Medical. In a separate incident, Peter Kitely, 29, of Portland was partially ejected when his pickup truck skidded out of control on an entrance ramp to I-295, running into a barrier and dropping onto the road below. He was pronounced dead at the scene.

"No no no no no!" Liesel screams, a jackhammering stutter of a refusal. She drops the paper.

"Oh, God." She breathes once, heavily, then grabs the paper, rereads, as if the letters will scramble and reorder themselves, as if they will offer something different on a second read. "Oh, God. No."

WHEN JOEL COMES HOME THAT NIGHT, Liesel is on the couch curled up into a ball, crying hysterically.

Her coat and her pocketbook are in a pile on the floor. "What's the matter?" he says, and then with growing alarm, "What's happened? Has something happened?"

But she can't say anything. She would have to stop crying first. "I can't," she finally says. "I can't."

"You can't what?" he says. "Let me know, Liesel. I can't help you if I don't know what is going on."

She isn't quite sure how she even got home. She knows that when she was still at the theater, she called the cab company, and before she even announced her name or location, she said, "You need to come back." (As if talking to Peter himself: *You need to come back.*)

But then when it was time to say her name and where she was located, she was unable to speak.

"Who is this?" the man on the other end had said, annoyed, as if at a prank call.

"I . . . I . . .," Liesel tried and finally said, "You were just here."

"OK," the man said, slowly. He was only the dispatcher, of course, didn't know what she was talking about.

"I just need you to come back," she said and started to sob—*Oh, his children!*—and she hasn't stopped since.

Now Joel holds her, and she leans into his chest. He pats her back, but this just makes her cry harder. They stay like this for a long time with Joel whispering, "It's OK. It's OK. I love you. It's OK." At some point, Liesel must have arranged for someone to cover her shift in the box office, but how she managed this Herculean feat, she isn't sure. Time moves forward, time in which Liesel tries, unsuccessfully, not to imagine Peter's last moments, time in which she tries not to imagine the various ways in which his head might have cracked open, his body might have smashed. He is all, all gone. There is no break in her tears. Finally, Joel says, very gently, "I think you have to stop crying. You are going to have to stop crying. You are going to make yourself sick."

He holds her tighter and then says, very softly, "Liesel, honey. Liesel. I'm going to bring you to the hospital. I think they need to give you something to calm you down. I can't write you a prescription myself."

"OK," she says, small-voiced. She wants to be sedated. She wants to go to sleep for as long as it will take for this to go away. But of course it won't ever go away.

They drive to Maine Med. Right away they take her into an emergency-room bay. Is this because it is a slow night or because Joel pulls strings? He leaves her side, presumably to go talk to someone. A man comes back in his stead and says, "I'm Doctor Myers." He rubs her forearm. "Having a rough time, eh?"

She nods.

"I'd like to have someone come down from our psychiatry department. Would that be OK with you?"

"No," she says and starts to cry harder. "No, I can't do that."

"Well, OK," he says, lifting his hand. "We don't have to do that. Why don't I just give you something to calm down, and we can go from there?"

He gives her a shot, and she thinks she has never been more grateful for anything in her life. She starts to fall asleep, but even as she is dropping off, she knows she can't sleep forever. She will wake up, and Peter will still be dead.

FOR A MONTH, she tries to live with Joel. Or she tries insofar as she is capable of trying anything. Mostly she works very hard at not weeping. She misses a period, and she thinks perhaps if she has a child, she will find a way to move forward. But when she takes a pregnancy test and learns she isn't pregnant, she breaks down in tears again. She knows it isn't going to work. She knows she will never be able to explain anything to Joel. She can't tell the truth. How could she? She just needs to leave. Joel and she make love one night, and after, Liesel starts to sob uncontrollably.

"You need to talk to someone," Joel says. "You can't go on like this. You need help. *I* need help."

"OK," she snuffles, but she knows she is not going to see a therapist. She knows what she must do, though she doesn't yet know how. The next day she tells Joel that she has to move out. She cannot function in this marriage without Peter, a calculus that she thinks most people only make in middle age, but she is not middle-aged, thank God. She is not too old to get out. She tries to let him know as kindly as she can, but he is furious and unbelieving. "What are you saying? What are you saying? Are you crazy? We just got married! We made love twelve hours ago!"

BECAUSE SHE HAS barely any resources, at first she goes only as far as the West End of Portland. It's a neighborhood of mansions, all of them beautiful, and most built in a time when a wealthy family would have had live-in servants. There's an elderly donor to the theater who has unused servants' quarters in her home, and she lends the small rooms to Liesel. The woman—Marika—is French, and at some point Liesel mentions that she has always wanted to go to France, that she has French citizenship through her paternal grandmother. "Ah!" Marika says. "Then I have an idea for you." Marika puts in a few calls, then sits Liesel down and says, "I can get you a job in France, if you want a job in France."

"Yes," Liesel says. "Please." Marika knows Liesel is heartbroken, but Liesel hasn't told her why, has just said she's in a bad place right now.

The position will be at L'Atelier Bleu, a residential program for developmentally disabled adults that Marika's friends run. It's in a gorgeous building, on beautiful land, Marika says, but the work may be dirty: cleaning rooms and toilets, bathing residents who can't take care of themselves, men and women alike. Marika will give her the money for a plane ticket.

"I don't mind," Liesel says of the work.

"How good is your French?" Marika asks.

"It's OK," Liesel says. College French, but she can always learn more. She wants to be in France. She wants to be so far away that she doesn't have to offer up any explanations for her tears, for her abrupt departure from her marriage.

When she leaves, she doesn't know she is pregnant. That last time with Joel, it turns out.

All she knows is a fox has come into her henhouse and destroyed everything.

7

GOVERNESS

SHE WAS A GOVERNESS, he supposed. At least she was in the employ of a family from London. Only it didn't quite make sense that they had the means for a governess, let alone one who could fly with them to Barbados for a week's holiday. They were staying in the same rundown hotel that Joel was. He hadn't expected fancy; even so, the place's beleaguered air disappointed. It's what he got for doing this trip on the cheap. Not that he had an option. He had no money to spare. He'd be a doctor soon enough, but that didn't mean instant riches the way it did in the old days. It didn't matter that he was training at one of the best hospitals in America. There was a glut on the market. Even the newspapers were aware of the problem, everyone speculating about what it meant that the supply of doctors exceeded the demand.

Joel's roommate, George, had found the hotel with the help of a Coolidge Corner travel agent. It looked like a deal when they were still in Boston, slipping on ice as they walked past the Longwood subway stop up to the hospitals. Ticket and five nights at a hotel, breakfast included, kitchenette ditto, for $495. But then Joel arrived—alone, George's ninety-two-year-old father having chosen an inconvenient time to finally abandon life—to find a roach (also dearly departed) in one of the coffee mugs, another by the bed's nightstand. Otherwise the room was clean. A little threadbare in its appointments, the old sheets and the fraying wicker chair by the sliding glass doors, the shallow balcony with the cheap plastic chairs. The balcony itself looked out over a modest pool and an open-air hut with four stools drawn up to a bar, though no one ever seemed to go there for a drink. And why would they? There didn't seem to be a bartender.

It was from the balcony on his second night that he'd seen her, walking with a couple and two children, clearly headed for the beach, their arms laden with towels, snorkels, and flippers. He heard her laugh, saw her toss her thick, curly hair from one shoulder to the next. He guessed she was an older sister to the children, but then reconsidered. She looked too old for that, closer to his twenty-eight than the teen she'd likely be if she was a sister.

The strand was another disappointment. The hotel wasn't beachside, but across the busy road that seemed to circle the island. You dodged traffic, walked between two homes—it felt like trespassing, so much so that Joel suspected the hotel didn't even have right of access—to reach an expanse of sand, which had the advantage of being largely empty. As far as Joel could tell, it was used mostly by locals. Which meant that on his first long and pointless day in the sun, he was the single white person on the beach. "So no one's trying to braid your hair with beads," his sister, Amy, said when he gave her a call, late that second day. The phone rates were ludicrously expensive, but he was lonely, needed to talk.

"Actually, I got approached three times," Joel said.

"Right," Amy said.

Joel had been balding since college and wore what hair he did have cropped close to his head.

But whatever. He could cross a road; he didn't need stacks of pillows on his bed. In one way, he was glad George wasn't here. George would have made a stink, insisted that things be as he'd imagined them. He had a general fastidiousness that struck Joel as prissy. He used a Sharpie to mark his towels with a "G" in one corner, so he wouldn't accidentally use Joel's towel. George used one side of his bath towel for his face, the other for his body. He hung his towel on a hanger, so the two sides wouldn't touch. Joel couldn't even remember how he discovered this. (A late-night drunken conversation that he'd blocked out: "How do you feel about your towel?" "I'm good with my towel. You good with your towel?" "Well, wish it was a little fluffier. Like a little fluff, but OK. I'm happy. Can't complain.") Of course, once Joel did learn about the towel labeling, he gave George grief. Then Amy dropped by the apartment. Joel started into George, and Amy said, "He doesn't want to rub his ass all over his face. What's wrong with that?" Then she paused, looked at her brother, and said, "Oops. I forgot who I was talking to."

JOEL WAS IN BARBADOS because he was looking for a woman. He hadn't quite admitted that to himself. But why else would a single person head for the Caribbean? He didn't fish, thought his asthma was incompatible with scuba diving. "Good-night, honey," George joked on one of the rare occasions when they were both in the apartment around bedtime. Normally one of them was doing a night at the hospital. "I like you, bud," Joel said. "But you're not exactly what I had in mind."

"We decided we need sun," Joel told everyone on his rotation. It had been a long winter, overcast for days. "I think George has rickets. I'm ready to make that diagnosis." Joel had convinced himself it was the chance to swim and read a book on the beach that he was after. But you could only tread water for so many hours. After that, the day would loom large. More so without George's companionship. Joel could be aggressive in seeking out experience when he was with a friend. Not so alone. He needed the toehold of another person to take the rental car and head north to look at the green monkeys or go into town to see the historic synagogue. He didn't think he'd manage to pull off a restaurant dinner alone, though he was curious to try flying fish. Back in Boston, he imagined the kitchenette was an unnecessary extra, but on the evening of his first night on the island, he found a poorly stocked supermarket and bought carrots, broccoli, and chicken and had the same stir-fry he ate most nights in Boston. A Banks beer from a rum shop—an afterthought on his way home from the market—made him feel like he was, in some small way, experiencing island culture. "Only I forgot," he said to Amy over the phone, "I hate beer."

He sat on the balcony that second night, letting the wind brush his face. The air was sweet and light. On the drive from the airport, he'd noticed a gaudy red flower blooming. He couldn't identify it, was grateful simply to see a flower in January. Now, he could hear the waves' metronome beat and sucking retreat—splash, never mind, splash, never mind. He was nearing thirty and had never had a long-term relationship. And not for lack of trying. He was horny and earnest. That should have gotten him somewhere. But it hadn't. Still, he thought, tears springing to his eyes, he hoped he'd die before his wife. He didn't want to be this lonely in old age. Not even thirty-six hours in the country, a woman as yet unacquired, and the verdict was in. He'd be a mess of a widower.

AS BEST AS JOEL COULD TELL, there were three employees at the hotel: two women, who worked the office, and Basil, who seemed to be the fetch-it boy. It was Basil who had brought Joel a stack of towels his first night, when the room proved to have none. As for guests, Joel had counted twenty as he sat, ignoring his beer, on the balcony. But when he came down for breakfast in the morning, there were only three tables occupied, two by the family he'd already observed, another by a short Asian woman with a hat and a darker-skinned college girl who might have been her daughter, only she looked to be Indian or Pakistani. No one seemed to have been served yet.

The breakfast room was really an extension of the lobby, but the staff tried to make it festive by putting flowers on the tables. Joel picked a table near the family. He'd whacked off last night to the thought of the woman with the laugh, the glimpse he'd had of her breasts. She'd had a gauzy brown beach dress thrown over the halter top of her bathing suit. Today, she had a bikini top and a towel wrapped around her waist.

As Joel slid into a seat, Basil emerged from the office with a pot of coffee. "Hello, everybody," he sang out. "Where we all from?"

The Asian woman kept her head down, apparently discomfited by the idea that she was supposed to talk to the room at large. But like a dog sensing terror, Basil turned to her first. "Ireland," she allowed.

"Oh, OK. Ireland. Good. Good," Basil said, and Joel wondered if someone might actually offer an unacceptable response. The Asian woman's answer seemed, at the very least, wrong. Or at least like it needed some explanation. How would an Asian woman with a Pakistani daughter end up in Ireland?

The father of the family, more game, said, "We're from London." The woman Joel had noticed yesterday smiled and nodded. "I like to say I'm from London by way of Zurich," she said, though her accent sounded American. She might have been American. She had a round, somewhat flattened face, as if her features felt uninclined to intrude too forcefully on the world.

"I'm from the States. From Boston," Joel said. He'd read somewhere that foreigners hated when you said you were from America; it sounded arrogant, as if you somehow imagined the Americas comprised not two whole continents, but just one bloated country.

"An international gathering, right then," Basil said. "Well, what I have for you dis morning is a nice bowl of fruit, eh? And some rolls, right?"

People nodded noncommittally. They could hardly disagree.

Joel wanted to say something—"Where in London?" maybe or "How long have you lived in Ireland?"—but the Asian woman and her companion fell back to talking softly between themselves, and the family turned their attention to the little girl, who started to protest that she didn't like fruit. Joel straightened in his chair, as if to suggest he was ready for the business of being alone. He had brought a *Newsweek* with him to the table, and he pretended to read while he eavesdropped on the family.

THE CHILDREN WERE UNPLEASANT. Joel liked children—for a while, he had toyed with the idea of pediatrics—but the girl (she must have been about seven) was whiny, the fruit being only the first of her complaints. She was bored; there was nothing to do. Why couldn't there be a TV in the room? Her brother, a thick-chested boy perhaps three years her senior, had long curly hair and a shirt printed with the name of what Joel presumed was a rock band. He seemed very much the kind of kid who would in half a decade be dealing drugs at high school, sneering at those who, like Joel, would demur. But the parents seemed all right. Soft-voiced as they said that there were things better here than TV, plus shells to collect on the beach and warm water to swim in and later they might find a place for an ice cream. After a while, Joel figured out that the young woman's name was Liesel. When the whining girl returned to her disappointment about the entertainment options, Liesel told her that she'd grown up without a TV. The girl was aghast. "But what did you do for fun?"

"Lots of things," Liesel said brightly. "Like I had a pet llama."

"You did not," the girl said. The boy had plugged himself into a Walkman and was bobbing his head to whatever music he found there.

"I certainly did," Liesel said. "I fed her Captain Crunch. Her name was Aunt Lucy."

"No way."

Joel didn't think he was so obviously looking at her, but Liesel caught Joel's eye and smiled. "*You* believe me, don't you? About the llama?"

"Absolutely," Joel said. "I had a pet goldfish when I was a kid. I fed her Lucky Charms."

The boy looked at him as if there was nothing stupider than an adult trying to be funny.

"It was a picky goldfish. He only ate the marshmallow pieces."

Liesel laughed, a big, delighted laugh, and Joel was pleased until the laugh went on a beat too long. The hilarity was a little creepy. Was there something wrong with her? He flushed, felt the heat moving across his face to his ears, then turned his attention back to his magazine.

So much for that.

HE'D BROUGHT JOHN IRVING'S *The Hotel New Hampshire* with him, and he spent his day poolside reading. He picked a shady spot, but even so pinkened at the brow. It was a quiet day, restful—he had the pool area to himself—but he appreciated none of this. He ached with loneliness, wondered if there might be a bookstore in town. Over the course of the day, he managed to finish off the Irving. Liked it. Would have liked it better if there were someone to talk to about it.

The next morning, Joel hesitated at the door of the breakfast room. The same tables were occupied by the same people. He wasn't sure where he should sit, but then Liesel looked up and said, "Hello, Boston. Just keeping abreast of the news." She turned a newspaper toward him.

"Cannabis," she added.

"I'm sorry?"

"Paul and Linda McCartney. Arrested on possession of cannabis. Right here in Barbados."

He couldn't quite gauge her tone. Amused?

"What's cannabis?" the boy asked.

"Nothing," the father said flatly. A command to the boy not to press further.

"Why won't you tell me?" the boy said, clearly sensing he was on to something potentially interesting. "You never tell me anything!"

"They had to cut their vacation short," Liesel said, in what Joel now realized was mock sympathy. Oh, the travails of the rich and famous!

"Could you just . . ." the father said and widened his eyes, made a sharp gesture with his head toward his son.

"Oh, right," Liesel said. "Sorry." Then she passed the paper to Joel.

"Rock stars like drugs. This is news?" the mother said.

The father stared at the mother, as if she'd just made the final connection that would turn their thick-chested boy into a junkie. Rock stars and drugs!

"So what are *you* going to do today, Boston?" Liesel said in a pointed way that suggested this was the distraction she had to offer for the family already wishing they'd scrapped the Barbados vacation for a down payment on a future detox stay.

Joel didn't have a good answer—"Haven't yet decided" was what he came up with.

"When are you going to decide?" Liesel said, in a way that seemed coquettish. "Life is a boat in the river. It moves forward. You can take this tributary or not. A failure to decide is in itself a decision."

"What?" he said, unclear on how to respond given that the family was listening.

She laughed—again the laugh that went on a beat too long. So it was a joke. She blinked and said, "I took a philosophy class in college."

"Oh," said Joel. This seemed to require a response, but instead of sharing what tributary he'd picked for today (reading, jogging, masturbating; he might shake things up with a chocolate bar), he said, "I took a lot of biology."

This seemed to be just what they all needed to start talking. Biology?

Biology where? Biology why? Doctor? What kind of doctor? Joel recognized the way in which a stranger was a relief to a family. Thank God. Someone with new stories.

THE FATHER WAS A LAWYER. The mother a stay-at-home mom, but she was toying with pursuing interior design when the kids were old enough. As for Liesel—Liesel Rosenthal, she said, and Joel instantly wondered if he could ask *her* if she'd like to check out the island's synagogue—she was getting her master's degree in London. She was studying Virginia Woolf. She'd done all her coursework in Zurich, then decided to move to England to take advantage of papers at the British Library. "In between helping out with these little devils," she said and scrunched up her nose at the little girl, who looked at her blankly, then said, "Can we go outside?"

"Yes," the mother said. "Both of you go." She tapped her son's arm and made a waving, run-along-now motion with her hand. He lumbered after his sister toward the pool.

"You've read Virginia Woolf?"

"Oh, of course," Joel nodded. Being assigned the book was the same as reading it, he decided. In truth, he'd never managed to get through *To the Lighthouse* in college. She seemed to greet this admission of his knowing Virginia Woolf with less delight than boredom, as if the very last thing she'd like to do was talk about the novel. Which was a relief, since even if he had read the book, there was no chance he'd know something that she didn't. Finally the husband stood and said, "We'll get the kids ready for the beach." He waved Joel toward his seat. "You guys keep visiting. It's Liesel's day off."

"No, that's tomorrow," she said.

"Let's change it to today," the father said.

He winked at Joel, who appreciated the opportunity, less so the wink, the fraternal "Go for it."

"All right then," Liesel said, clearly a little disoriented by this change in plans. She gathered her hair in one hand and twisted it, as if to make it more manageable, before she let it drop down again on her back. She yanked at the strings of her bikini top, tightened up the whole arrangement. God.

"So, I don't know if you are up for this . . ." Then he smiled—he felt like a jerk, there was no way not to when you were making an overture to a woman—"but I was thinking of going to see the synagogue in town. Apparently it's been disused for years, but they just started restoring it."

"Synagogue?" she said, confused.

"I thought, since we're both Jewish."

"Oh, I'm not Jewish."

"You're not Jewish? Liesel *Rosenthal?*" he asked, as if she might have forgotten her own last name.

"It's a long story. I'm actually . . . um . . . Anglican. I mean . . ." She stopped, as if she knew she was about to be caught in an unconvincing lie. "Yeah, Anglican." She seemed to be deciding on a faith only at that moment.

"Of course! All those Anglicans in Switzerland. What was I thinking?"

She didn't laugh. "I'm not Swiss."

"Oh, I thought . . . since you . . ." He stopped, confused. How had he happened on this notion? He tried to rewind the conversation. Because? Because what? Because she said she'd moved to England from Zurich. *Hadn't* she said that?

"Like I said. Long story." She waved her hand to make clear that it was a long story she didn't want to tell.

"Right," he said, willing to abandon the matter. He felt momentarily undone by desire, flashed on . . . things he shouldn't have flashed on.

They fell silent for an embarrassing moment. Having been derailed from the conversation about doing something together, Joel felt like he couldn't reextend the invitation to the synagogue.

"But I'm interested in other religions," she finally allowed. "Where is the synagogue?"

"In Bridgetown. On the far side from here." He'd looked at a map yesterday.

"That's great! I've been wanting to go into town."

THEY BUSTLED UP to their respective rooms and then down to the lot behind the hotel, where he'd parked the alarmingly small car he'd rented at the airport. She had changed into jeans and a sleeveless white T-shirt, which was almost sexier than the bikini top, something about having more left to the imagination. But the car wouldn't start. "No worries," he said. "I'll call the company." He didn't get out of the car, though, because he couldn't think of a nonawkward way to suggest going back to his room, which was the next step if he was going to use a phone.

"Let's just walk there," she said.

"Walk?" On the trip in from the airport and then again when he'd found the supermarket, the road into Bridgetown with its narrow shoulder hadn't seemed all that walkable.

"It'll give us a real feel for things."

"OK. But I've got an idea we can't walk all the way to the synagogue. I'm pretty sure it's too far."

"We could hitchhike."

He laughed, then saw that she wasn't joking, that she was someone who thought hitchhiking was a lark, rather than an opportunity to have one's mangled body dropped in a roadside ditch. "Sorry," he said. "I'm the cautious type."

"You can meet some pretty interesting people when you hitchhike."

He shrugged, a hitch of his shoulders that meant, *Even so, I'm not doing it.*

"I know," she said and tapped the dashboard, her voice growing more animated. "I heard there's an amazing beach on the north edge of the island. Instead of the synagogue, why don't we do that? Basil told me. He said you can take the bus there." She pointed out the window, in the apparent direction of the bus station.

"Basil?"

"Who brought us breakfast yesterday?"

"That's right," Joel said. Today it had been one of the two front-desk women who'd brought the rolls and fruit.

"We've been hanging out a bit, and he told me."

This was unwelcome news. Joel could not imagine that someone who was spending time with Basil—a man who looked like he was only biding his time here in Barbados till someone swooped in from America to put him in a high-fashion underwear ad—would cotton to his own pale body. It was reasonable enough, he supposed, in American terms, even if he already had a soft mound of flesh forming above the belt.

"You're a doctor!" Amy would cry when she saw him snacking. "Stop eating chips."

"Almost a doctor. Not yet," he said. "Also, I don't eat chips so much as I support Maine potato farmers."

"I'll give you a little health tip, in case those MDs at Harvard haven't finished their study on the matter. *Doughnuts aren't good for you.*" She was a rather big consumer of doughnuts herself. She had a lot of advice for others, none of which she herself took.

Basil probably was a doughnut eater, if they even had stuff like that down here. But he'd be one of those sweets-eating, beer-drinking, womanizing, lazy lunks who still had muscles on his muscles, who was perfectly built. During their own brief interaction, as Joel had tipped Basil at his hotel room's door (this outside, all the rooms let onto an open walkway with stairs to the ground), a drip of air-conditioner condensation had landed on Basil's shoulder, and there was something in the way the man had reached up to brush it away that made Joel think he was just happy for a chance to caress his own shoulders. *My sweet embraceable you.*

You couldn't have been a single man for as long as Joel had and not have an interest in self-caressing, but Joel liked to do it in private.

"If you're spending time with Basil, maybe you don't want to ..."

"Oh, God, no, not like *spending time.* He's married. His wife just had twins. Actually, he might not be married, but the woman he is with just had twins." She paused. "And they're his," she added, as if Joel might not have put her meaning together.

"You're kidding?"

"Not at all. We were having a beer two nights ago, after I put the kids to bed ..."

Joel wanted to interrupt and say this sounded very much like "spending time," but he kept his mouth shut.

"... and, get this, he told me he had twins, and I said, 'How old?' and he said, 'Five hours,' and I said, 'What? What are you doing here then?' and he said, 'Talking to a pretty lady,' so maybe he's got some idea, but trust me, I don't, so I said, 'You hooligan. Let's go see them,' and we did. They're the cutest little things."

"You went to the hospital?" Joel said.

"Yeah. They were still there."

This surprised Joel. There was such a clear line between tourists and locals here. It seemed uncrossable. In this country, you were either white and being served or black and doing the serving. It was uncomfortable, but it was also the economy. Some people would say that Boston wasn't so different. "It's not my fault," Joel wanted to say when the city's race divide seemed most in evidence, as when the black orderlies or cafeteria workers at the hospital greeted him with surly indifference.

"Monica's amazing. That's her name," Liesel went on. "I guess you'd have to be if you had Basil as a husband."

Joel wasn't sure what this meant: that the wife was beautiful? That she was long-suffering? He supposed if your husband showed up in the maternity ward with a pretty white woman, hours after you'd given birth, you were *something,* but maybe "long-suffering" wasn't the word. Maybe "fucked over" was more like it.

"I know!" She tapped him lightly on the forearm. "Let's skip the beach. Do you have a kitchen in your room?" He nodded. "Let's make Monica cookies."

Joel was about to say that perhaps Basil's wife wouldn't appreciate this offering when Liesel said, "She'll need the help. She's supposed to bring snacks to her art opening, and I said I'd help out. I was going to do it tomorrow. At least I was when I thought tomorrow was my day off."

"Art opening? I'm not following. Let's—" he said and gestured to suggest they get out of the hot car.

"Yeah, of course, sorry," she said as she elbowed her door open. "Sometimes I forget people aren't in my brain with me. So let's see." They started walking back through an alley to the small courtyard where the pool was. "I guess what happened is that Monica had the babies early. She's a painter. She has an older son, but I can't quite tell if Basil is the father . . ." She drifted off on this thought then seemed to find her place and said, "Anyway, she has an art opening tomorrow night. At first she thought she'd miss it, but then they discharged her. I guess she couldn't go if she had the babies with her, but the hospital is going to keep them for awhile. They're small, so they need to"—she waved her hand—"I don't know . . . hatch." She laughed (that laugh). "I know that's not the word, but you know all about this medical stuff, right?"

He nodded. They were standing at the base of the stairs that led to his room. "I'm not an obstetrician, but, more or less." He had only once delivered a baby, a boy so slippery that Joel had almost dropped him. He counted it among his life's most terrifying moments.

"Anyway, she thought she wasn't going to make her own opening, but now she can. I told you she was amazing."

Joel nodded again, though he wasn't quite sure what part of this story struck her as amazing.

"I swear—the women here. It's just like they are in some rocky northern European potato field, and they squat down to give birth then stand up so they can keep picking potatoes. I'd be in the hospital begging for drugs and asking never to be discharged."

"Digging," he said.

"What?"

"You don't pick potatoes. You dig them."

"Right. You get the idea."

"Just saying, but I mean, cookies, sure," he said. "That'd be a really nice gesture. I bet she'd appreciate that. Hot to bake, though. Maybe we can sit out on the balcony while they cook? I can get us some Cokes or something?"

"Oh, I don't need anything." She smiled. "Just the pleasure of your company. I wonder if they'll give me tomorrow night off, now that they've said today is my day off. I don't really want to bring the kids to the opening." She grimaced at the presumed horribleness of the idea, then laughed, and the laugh no longer struck him as off-putting but as generous, something she did to make things festive.

He laughed, too, thinking, *No, don't take them. Take me.*

THE COOKIES SHE WANTED TO MAKE were called Peanut Blossoms.

"I know that cookie," he said, when she described her plans. "That is a cookie I have real feelings for."

They moved through the supermarket, looking for the required ingredients—peanut butter, Hershey's kisses, and other exotica. The store was clean, but so old and lit with such bright fluorescents that it felt dirty.

"I'm not kidding," he said. And he wasn't. To make the cookies, you rolled balls of peanut-butter dough in sugar, then pressed a Hershey's kiss into the dough till the ball cracked. Years ago, Amy had won a bake sale contest with the cookies, and because she had (at that point) never won anything in her life, the prize made a big impression on her. She made the cookies often, reliving her glory, as it were, so he knew the cookies in their every detail: how they tasted just out of the oven, how they crunched later in the day, how the dough under the chocolate kiss stayed extra moist, what it felt like if you scraped the pointy top of the kiss off with your teeth. Once, Amy had made the cookies, put them in the oven, taken them out and put them on plates, not realizing that the pilot light had blown out. The cookies were still raw. "They're pretty good this way, too," he remembered saying, his teenage mouth crammed full of uncooked dough.

"We had a name for them," Joel said, after he'd given Liesel his history with the cookie. "We called them 'Instant Diabetes Cookies.'"

The laugh. Then, "Nothing I love more than a man who names his food."

"Nothing?" he said, eyes arched, mock lascivious.

"Not a thing," she said and smiled flirtatiously, as they put the items from their grocery basket in front of the store clerk.

That sort of took the "mock" out of "mock lascivious."

EVEN WITH HER MANNER as encouragement, he was nervous. Joel knew he wasn't the best-looking guy. Sizable nose, receding chin. But what could he do? He was Jewish and looked it. "The ladies like the nose," Joel joked to George. "They know a big nose means a big . . ."

"Mouth," George interrupted to say. "They know you've got a big mouth, even when you shut up. But you don't shut up."

"Also a big attraction for the ladies," Joel opined. "Chitchat. The ladies *love* the chitchat."

Joel and Liesel went back to his room and fell to talking, as they pulled items out of the bag and started to search the kitchenette with its insubstantial-looking oven for the necessary equipment. In the end, they had to make do with a soup spoon and a salad bowl for mixing the dough. As they worked, he learned a little about her past: a childhood not in Zurich, as he had thought, but in upstate New York, a father who was a born-again Christian, a sister who couldn't stay out of trouble, a mother who was kind and hardworking but codependent. She sometimes worked Liesel's sister's shift at Arby's when her daughter was too messed up to go herself. Once Liesel's mother called in sick to her own job so she could work her daughter's. And she got caught! Her boss came in for a sandwich. Also Liesel wasn't really studying Virginia Woolf. She'd just come up with that for her employers when she first met them. Now, sometimes, she'd tell them she was going to study at the British Library, but she'd really just walk around or go to a movie. Basically she was caring for the children and trying to figure out what was next. She loved London. In college she had liked art, and she still liked to paint.

"So maybe art school?" he said, as if scripting her life was now up to him.

"If some money drops out of the sky and falls on my head. That'd be an idea. Once I recover from the concussion."

He smiled at the joke but had the desire to pony up the tuition. Not really. He didn't know her. Still, the thought occurred to him. He was old-school, believed a man should be a provider, not that he'd be so stupid as to say it out loud, in this day and age. Though probably as recently as ten years ago, it wouldn't have been so shameful to admit. He was liberal, but didn't always like how liberalism had turned basic male responsibility into a sin.

Liesel was clearly impressed that he was going to be a doctor, said more than once, as he offered up his own thumbnail history, "You must be so smart," as if intelligence was a skill she hadn't managed to pick up herself. He shared the basic facts of his life: grew up in suburbs of Boston, away for college (Skidmore, biology major), back for medical school at Tufts, now finishing up his internship in urology at Beth Israel. He loved his mentor, thought he was brilliant, was scared about what was next, wasn't willing to go to rural Alabama or some other horrible place to find work, so it was sort of a stressful time.

"We both don't know where we'll be in a year," she said, wise-womanish.

He nodded, though in fact he had some applications in. He had no guarantees, but he had an idea of the possibilities.

"You know," she said, when they were putting the second batch of cookies in the oven, "I better check in with the Linvilles."

"Who? Oh, yeah."

"Just to see when they are expecting me back and all."

"Right," he said, waved a baby bye-bye.

By the time she returned, he'd burned batch number two.

"Sorry," he said when he opened the door at her knock. He held out the charcoal cookies, arranged in a flower pattern on the plate, pointlessly neat, given he was about to dump the whole arrangement in the trash.

"Don't worry," she said. "Gives the room a nice outdoor barbecue smell." She closed the door behind her. "I've got to go." She grimaced, as if in apology. "They were fine about the day out, but they want to go to some restaurant tonight. The good news is that I can have tomorrow night off for the show." She smiled. "Can you come?" She was so bubbly and cheerful, he couldn't tell if she was asking him to be her buddy or if this would be something more charged. Not that he imagined a date. The '60s and '70s had blown apart the notion of a date. No one he knew had ever actually gone on a date. They just spent times with their friends, and then things had an edge, or they didn't. An impossibly murky way to propagate the species, he'd once said to his roommate George.

"I'd love to go," he said.

"It's at 7:00 p.m., but we don't want to get there too early." She looked at her watch, as if for scheduling advice. "Leave here at 7:15 p.m.?"

"Sure," he said.

"Perfect," she said and leaned toward him. He thought she was going for his cheek, but instead her mouth landed squarely on his lips and lingered for a second. He reached for her, and just like that they were making out, kissing deeply and passionately. He wrapped his arms around her back; she pulled his hips toward hers. He thought they would stop, but they didn't. They went on and on.

"Hey," he said, pushing back for a moment, embarrassed, trying to catch his breath.

"Right," she said, and they started kissing again. She maneuvered him around so his back was against the door, then put her hand on the front of his pants, the stiffness there. *Well,* he thought, then put his hand under her shirt.

"I said I'd come right back. They are really going to wonder where I am," she said in a voice that suggested not her eagerness to go, but how sexy misbehavior could be.

"Well, if you have to go . . ." he said, his hand pushing further up under the cup of her bra. He felt a bit like he was pawing her, but she seemed into it.

"I do," she said, flirty, dirty-voiced. "I've *got* to get out of here." She undid his pants, dropped to her knees, her hand slightly chilled as it wrapped around his cock. "I just have to do a little something first."

THE FAMILY WASN'T AT BREAKFAST when he came down, so he didn't see her again till she knocked on his door that night at 7:15 p.m.

"Hello, you," she said as she slipped into the door. She was wearing a green skirt and a brown top with thick pink thread embroidered at the edge, the sort of clothes, he imagined, that she'd found at a vintage shop or that an artist friend had made. They didn't seem like something you could just go to the store and buy.

"Hello, you," he said, and just like that they were making out again, acting as if they were going to leave, even as they undressed each other.

"We'll be late," she said as she unhooked her bra.

"We don't have to go," he said, as he pulled her underwear down.

"No, no." She put out her hand to stop him for a moment. "I *want* to go," she said, completely serious. "We *have* to go. Art is really important to me." Then dirty-voiced again, back collapsing on the mattress, legs parted to receive him, "I just need you to do a little something first."

TOO QUICKLY, they were back in their clothes. He suppressed the urge to ask some variant of the "Was it good for you?" question. It had been, at the least, good for him. "You," he said when he'd come, and this had made her kiss him harder, as if the very thing she'd been waiting for for the last twenty-plus years was the chance to get a virtual stranger off on a Caribbean island. He'd never been with a woman who talked dirty during sex before. Granted, he hadn't been with that many women, maybe they were all raunchy truck drivers, and he was the only one not in on the secret. He couldn't say he didn't like the talk—or her general enthusiasm—but once he came, he was super-sensitive. He had to take her hands away from him and put them to her sides. "Tickles," he said, by way of explanation.

Once they were in the car—a new and slightly bigger one; he'd made an exchange with the rental company—she pulled a mimeographed sheet of paper from her small purse. It was the invitation to the art opening. On the back, she'd scribbled directions to a place called Pelican Village, where the gallery was located. "OK," she said, as he unrolled the window. The evening was pleasant, just a bit of the day's heat lingering to make things comfortable. She leaned over, whispered, "Handsome. Off we are." Then she straightened her back, added in a voice she might share with anyone: "Be forewarned. I'm not so good with a map."

And indeed she wasn't. They went this way, then that way. He almost plowed into a car. Driving on the opposite side of the road unnerved him. Even the straight shot he'd already made a few times to the supermarket had shaken him up, but this was more complicated. "Just tell me before we get to the intersection, please," he said.

"Right, OK. Sorry," she said.

But they arrived, intact, at a parking lot by the sea. ("Car park," she called it, a Britishism she'd adopted as her own, and Joel thought of how Amy had done a college semester in London and returned with a boatload of affectations and a hate for all things American.)

PELICAN VILLAGE WAS A MAZE of huts with tall, pyramidal-shaped thatch roofs. Each hut had a garage-sized door that swung open to reveal pottery, baskets, straw hats, and the like. "Let's look," Liesel said. They walked into one shop with miniature versions of chattel houses. Liesel picked one up. Joel had already read a tourist brochure about the houses. Back in the day, plantation workers could own their homes, but not the land on which they were built, so they built small, colorful chattel houses, which could be moved as needed. He told Liesel, "You can tell which ones are the real chattel houses by looking at the foundation. The ones with rubble stone are the real ones. The cement aren't." She put down the figure, then said, "I could see having a business here."

This seemed unlikely. "What would you make?" Joel asked, nonetheless.

"Dresses maybe. I'm pretty good at sewing. I made this," she said, indicating her outfit.

"That's amazing."

"Yeah, I've always been the handy sort." She shrugged.

They passed a restaurant—The Pelican—on their way to the gallery. There were diners outside under umbrellas, which seemed a little silly now that it was dusk. Liesel said, "Basil says this is where the politicians come to eat. Maybe we'll see the prime minister."

"No doubt."

"I'm serious. He comes here to eat with the other ministers of government. And the press, too. They have great discussions."

She seemed almost childishly pleased as she parroted back what Basil must have told her—the Algonquin Round Table, Barbados-style, and here she, a foreigner, knew about it! Joel felt compelled to point out that she wouldn't recognize the prime minister, even if she happened to see him.

"I guess so," she agreed. By then they had entered the crowds surrounding the gallery. Joel's experience with art openings was limited. He'd once gone to a dilapidated Boston office building where each office space had been taken over by an artist. He'd wandered with Amy from room to room, checking out the work, grabbing snacks. Amy always said, "Thanks, really nice," or something similar, when they ducked out of a room.

When they were out of earshot, Joel would say, "You liked *that?*"

"God, no," Amy would answer.

"Then why'd you say you did?"

"To be nice."

Joel was plenty nice, but that wasn't something he'd do. He wasn't a bull-shitter. He wanted his words to have weight. If he said, "You're more likely to die of old age than of this prostate cancer," he meant, "You're more likely to die of old age than of this prostate cancer."

Liesel had packed the Peanut Blossoms into a sauce pan—there wasn't anything else in the kitchenette—and moved with purpose through the gallery, which was L-shaped and open on two sides. Liesel found a table on which people had put cheese sandwiches, grapes, and food that interested Joel simply because he couldn't identify it. There were gallon jars of something at one end of the table. Rum punch, he supposed. "What's this?" Liesel said, pointing to a fried, unfamiliar item.

"Fish cake," a man by her side said. "You never have fish cake?"

Liesel admitted that she hadn't, and he said, "Then you missing out," and he took a cake, put it on a napkin, and handed it to her.

Joel had to go to the bathroom, so he tapped Liesel's shoulder and said, "I'll be right back." By the time he returned, Liesel had made some friends. At least, she was standing in a crowd of young black people and some older whites, chatting animatedly. "Come meet!" Liesel cried when he neared the circle. She introduced him around. First to an Israeli, who'd come to advise the government on farming practices. Then to an artist, who lived near Monica and worked as a meter reader for the waterworks. "He walks the whole island," Liesel says. "No car. He covers the whole island on foot." There were others: an artist who taught at a local school, a collector who had a particular interest in Monica's work, a wife of someone with the British high commission, and a man who worked for the Arts Council. How Liesel had managed to figure this all out in the time it took him to pee, he didn't know. Schmaltzy calypso music played over the loudspeaker. Liesel seemed to like it, though. She asked for the name of the artist, and the man from the Arts Council said, "Why, that's Red Plastic Bag!" then added that he'd been the calypso monarch many times. When Joel and Liesel allowed that they didn't know what this meant, a slump-shouldered black woman wearing a black cloth headdress, white blouse, and long black skirt explained that the best calypso singer of the year was the monarch. "Monarch" as in "king." (Joel had been thinking "monarch" as in "butterfly.") Red Plastic

Bag had won the title last year, but there had been no monarch named in 1983 because the contest had been rained out. This got everyone discussing weather: What a relief it was to be through hurricane season. Liesel said to everyone in the circle, "We're going to check out Monica's work."

"Monica," the slump-shouldered woman said before they could get away, "she a strong woman. She had those babies. Six hours later, she is in the car, going home, but she stops at Cave Shepherd to buy her Troy—that's her boy—a present." Strong, but perhaps a little stupid, Joel thought.

Liesel turned to look at the paintings, planting herself in front of a stylized image of boys kneeling in a river. Joel walked up to the neighboring painting, which showed people gathered outside some tropical hospital for immunizations. Tables were arranged under palm trees, and people were extending their arms, and occasionally revealing their bare butts, for shots.

Joel turned to say something to Liesel, but he saw she had edged next to a handsome young black man—white shirt hanging loosely over black pants, braided hair pulled back into a stubby ponytail.

"Like it?" she said to the man.

Did everyone have to be her friend? he thought jealously.

"Oh, yeah, he is one of the most talented artists we have," the young man said.

"This isn't Monica's?"

"No, she's over there." He pointed to the other side of the gallery, where there were smaller pieces—watercolors, it turned out, when Liesel and Joel made their way over. The watercolors were of typical island scenes: a view of the hills with palm trees and chattel houses, the beach at dusk, and an old woman walking along the roadside with a red parasol. They were pretty paintings, the colors deeply saturated, the view of life bucolic without being sentimental. Joel liked them, but had an idea he shouldn't tell Liesel this, that her own tastes might be too hip for art that was "merely" pretty.

"What do you think?" Liesel asked. Luckily Joel didn't have to answer, because Liesel cried out, "Oh, here she is," then turned to a woman with a ragged Afro and big red plastic earrings. Monica, apparently. She was wearing a black T-shirt that had been cut at the front to widen the neck and a red gauzy skirt that fell to her ankles. There was a gap between her front teeth, and her eyes seemed somehow off—perhaps because they weren't quite symmetrical, the left sitting slightly higher than the right. But she had a round happy face and an easy smile. "Welcome, my friend," she said, then touched the wall as if to steady herself. "I'm a little . . .," she waved her hand as if to indicate they knew what she was going to say, and then asked, "Where are the babies?"

"The babies?" Liesel said. "In the hospital, right?"

"I need the babies."

Liesel looked at Joel for a moment, as if he could find the sense in this, then said, concerned, "Are you all right?"

"I'm fine," she said. "Just stood up too fast, I think." She smiled again and then collapsed forward into Joel's arms. He thought of the clumsy weight of a futon, when one tries to roll it up and move it.

"Monica?" Liesel said.

"I'm fine," she said and started to struggle out of Joel's arms, but he held on.

"I don't think so," Joel said. People started to turn with concerned expressions.

"There's nothing the matter," Monica said. "I've got to ask you," she said to Joel in a warning tone he took as angry feminist, "not to touch me." She pushed back abruptly then fell again, her head barely missing the edge of a table. People turned to reach for her. "Really. Don't worry," she said, steadying herself. But she slumped to the floor again. Only then, on her hands and knees, did she say, reluctantly, "Maybe I'm a little dizzy."

"OK," Joel said and knelt next to her. "I'm a doctor, and I need you to lie down now." He took her hand—it was clammy—then pressed the back of his hand to her forehead. She was burning up. "Call an ambulance," he said to Liesel. "Get someone to call an ambulance." She disappeared, presumably to obey, and he started ordering others around. "Get some of that melted ice water on some cloths for me." "Get me that pillow." He pointed to a foam cushion on a square seat. "Prop up her feet with that."

"Can you tell me your name?" he said.

"Monica Braithwaite."

He took her hand and felt for her pulse. It was too rapid.

"And where are we, right now? Can you tell me?"

"Right," she said, and put her hand to her head, but didn't answer.

"And today's date? Can you tell me what day it is?"

"That's what she said. One smart dead at two smart door."

"I'm sorry?"

"Like I said about the babies."

Was she delirious?

He felt her stomach and wondered how long it would take the paramedics to arrive. "There's a hospital five minutes from here," he heard someone say. "Neville already called."

He held her hand until the ambulance arrived. It parked by the gallery door and two men alighted. "She needs to be admitted right away," Joel told them.

"We can do our job now," the taller of the two paramedics said, irritated, gesturing to say he wanted Joel to go away now.

Joel stayed put. "Her pulse is high. Also a fever. Definitely disoriented. Possible heart attack or stroke, but she's recently delivered two babies—twins—so my guess is puerperal fever." One of the paramedics looked at him blankly. "Maybe you call it childbirth fever down here," Joel went on. "I'm going to need you to get her on an IV and give her antibiotics right away."

"We've got this now," the same paramedic said.

"Yeah, you may be right," the other paramedic said, clearly addressing Joel. "Eighty over sixty."

Monica had her fingers to her temple, as if to stop the spinning of her head.

"We better come with you," Joel said. Someone was going to have to give the woman's most recent medical history. Basil, if he had been at the opening at one point, didn't appear to be there now.

The paramedic shrugged, less in agreement than resignation. "No, I'll go," said a woman in the crowd. "Monica's my best friend."

Joel didn't know what to do, but he stepped back and said, "As long as there's someone who knows her history."

THE CROWD DISBANDED when the ambulance left, people heading for the car park, murmuring in that chastened way people talk after an emergency. "You're a good man," someone said and gave him a soft thump on the back. Liesel, subdued in manner but her eyes alight, said, "Let's not go back just yet. Let's go walk on the beach." They crossed the road to the water, then walked north and away from Pelican Village. "This used to be a separate island," she said. "And it had a lot of pelicans. They kept people with leprosy on the land. But when they made the harbor, it got joined to Barbados. That's why it's Pelican Village." He wondered how she'd learned this but was already sensing she was a collector of peculiar facts, an enthusiast for poignant miscellanea. The beach grew darker as they walked, the island's lights receding. "Let's sit," she said, and they sat. She took off her sandals and buried her feet in the sand. "I've never seen anything like that," she said of his performance in the gallery.

"It's what any doctor would have done."

"You saved her life!"

He laughed. "Not really." In fact, he felt some unease. *Should* he have followed the woman to the hospital? He had thought he shouldn't tussle with the rescue workers about it, that he should just let them go. Now he wondered.

"She's not going to be OK?"

"Oh, no. She'll be fine. I'm sure of that." In fact, sepsis, if that was what she had, could be fatal. She *could* die, but at a good hospital, they'd get an IV going, get her temperature down, some antibiotics in, and she'd be fine.

"Thank God you were there. It's obvious you're an amazing doctor."

"Thank you," he said, less in agreement than to stop the conversation. It hardly felt like a major medical achievement. Still, he liked the compliment. He knew some of his friends didn't think urology was ambitious enough. He had chosen the specialty because neurology was too depressing, general surgery too competitive, and orthopedics too boring. Urology seemed interesting, and it was close to general surgery (stomach, pelvis) without *being* general surgery.

"So few people know how to take care. I mean really *take care*," Liesel said. "It's like I've been looking for it my whole life. Basic kindness. You'd think it wouldn't be so hard to find. Women have it. Not that I'm trying to be prejudiced against men or anything, but women do have it. Men don't."

"I don't know about that," he said.

"The men I know don't have it. My father doesn't have it. He sort of abandoned ship a long time ago. And my boyfriends . . . they've all been a little selfish, you know?"

He nodded his head, though he didn't know. How would he know?

"You're not selfish."

"I'm not," he said, for though he had the normal array of faults, he didn't think selfishness was one of them.

"So you're him!" she said, jokey. "The man I've been looking for my whole life."

He smiled and said, without thinking, "I hope I'm him." But then he realized he meant it, warmed to the idea that here they were, these two people separated by a continent, whose paths had managed to cross on a Caribbean island. There had to be a moment—didn't there?—when you found the woman of your dreams. What if this was it?

"True love," she said and leaned over and kissed him. Ridiculous, he knew. They didn't know each other, but even so he had this odd sense of his being opening up to wrap itself around her. Why not?

"Maybe we'll get married," she said, and he could tell she was half-serious. The palm fronds rustled in the breeze. He scooped sand into his hand and let it fall through his fingers.

"Just a plane flight to Las Vegas and the Elvis chapel, and we'd be on our way," he allowed.

She hit him with the back of her hand. "No way! If we do it, we're going to do it right. We're going to do everything right." She was just flirting, but still. She kissed him again. "We'll be perfect."

And he had this sense, strong as anything he'd ever felt, that she was right, that they *would* be perfect. That it would actually happen and once it happened, it would all work out, and it would work out because Joel knew on some level what to do for a woman. Not sexually—there was a lot to be learned there, he supposed. And not practically, he imagined. Who didn't need to be schooled on the correct Tampax box color to purchase? But in a larger sense he knew. He knew the important things. You weren't like Basil. You didn't fail to show up for a woman. You were there when she needed you. You were there when she fell.

8

SWISS COTTAGE

HOW QUEER THAT SUBWAY PASSENGERS never look you in the eye. That's what Sara Wilson is thinking as she exits the Tube. *Man's inhumanity to man. Nameless faces in the crowd. Oh, cruel life.* And just like that, her eyes meet the eyes of a man at the station's entrance. Fancy that. The universe reacting to her inner thoughts. What are the chances?

At first, Sara thinks it is an accidental meeting of the eyes. But the man appears to be looking at her quite pointedly. She returns his gaze. He glances away and glances back. Well, two can play that game. *She* glances away and glances back. He is middle-aged, with a short haircut that emphasizes the rectangle of his forehead. It's terribly hot, so he's taken off his suit jacket—light gray, lightweight, good choice for the impossible weather—and thrown it over his forearm. His look is one of expectation, "Yes?" he might be asking. He shyly lifts a small sign that reads, "Liesel Rosenthal." He raises his eyebrows. "Are you . . . ?"

Liesel Rosenthal. What kind of name is that? Swiss-Jewish. Sara has the horrible image of the Swiss Miss girl, the one from the cocoa mix, clawing concrete inside a gas chamber. It's something Sara learned about in high school—the claw marks inside the gas chambers, that is—and she's worked for most of the years since then to get the image out of her head.

Unsuccessfully, obviously.

Today is one of the worst days of Sara's life. It seems only right that such a ghastly vision should come for a visit.

She would like to be Liesel Rosenthal actually. Well, she'd like the Swiss part, the ringing cowbells and chocolate shops, not the death camp part. *Liesel*. Why not?

UNFORTUNATELY, she is Sara Wilson. Not Swiss or Jewish or English even. She hails from Schenectady, New York. Oh, drear city. She's the daughter of a salesman. Of what? She doesn't know. How could she not know? Because it changes, because it is vague. Spray-cleaner nozzles? Test tubes? He has peddled these things. Pre-fab containers for your spring seedlings? That, too. He sells things for which you need no store. He gets in the car and goes out and makes deals. He seems to have a gift for persuasion. Only he's found God recently and won't settle for hawking his wares; he wants souls to convert.

It pisses his employer off. And who is his employer? This, too, seems to change. Sara doesn't know and doesn't care. She doesn't want to see him. And he, presumably, doesn't want to see her. It's been years. He's never been much interested in his children. So why did he even have them? That is another thing Sara does not know.

And her father is only part of the reason she is glad to be in London, thank you. She is in London and miserable, but she is at a Tube stop and not in the parking lot of a mall. There appear to be takeaway shops across the road, and—surprise!—an ugly faux Swiss chalet at her back. A Swiss Cottage, she realizes. Thus the name of the Tube stop at which she has chosen to alight: Swiss Cottage. Aha. A place outside which you might expect to find a Liesel. Part of the reason she travels on the Underground and gets off at random places is to learn new things. The day's errand is not in vain. She has learned a new thing.

Maybe it's not a chalet. It doesn't suggest skiing or snowy heights. It is yellow-brown, with an Alpine balcony on which hangs a banner that reads "Traditional Sunday Lunch, Served 12–4." A few tables with green umbrellas are scattered outside, though why would anyone want to dine al fresco on such a busy street? Side of exhaust with your fish and chips? The words "Ye Olde Swiss Cottage" are painted on the façade of the building, just under the roof. A pub, plainly. A pub where (Sara doesn't need to enter to ascertain this) the glasses are dirty and the food miserable. A pub where they put a high premium on stupidity, a low one on fresh vegetables.

Grubby, Sara thinks harshly. Still, what does she care? It is London. It is Europe, and Sara wants to drop to the pavement, throw her arm around a trash can (no, rubbish bin, that's what they call them here), and say, "Please. Please let me stay."

IT IS TIME FOR SARA WILSON to go back. Go back to the United States. ("Helloooo!" she wants to call to the man at the Tube stop, the one who thinks she might be Liesel, as if he might be capable of preventing her departure.) If anything announces the necessity of return, it is the day's events, but Sara can't imagine going home. Or she can imagine it all too well: her mom and that fat man she's married parked in front of the TV set, the small vase of flowers her mom will put on the guest room dresser if Sara returns. (Nice touch! Nice touch!) The ancestral home is long gone; the ancestral home was a crappy split-level in Cohoes, traded for a different but equally crappy split-level in Schenectady. All split-levels are crappy. Why else would they come so often onto the real estate market? And her mother is ever ready with a checkbook. No disappointment apparent. She'll take it. She doesn't need beauty in her life, because she has drama. She has Justine.

Justine is Sara's older sister.

Gladys is Sara's mother.

Someone has to be named Gladys, someone has to buy crappy split-levels, and that someone is Sara's mother.

And just because it seems there's no point in being fucked up if you aren't also fucking someone else up, there is another character who must be noted. There is Camille. Justine's daughter. Poor Camille.

IT HAS NOT BEEN a typical week. Not for Sara, Justine, Gladys, or (presumably) Camille. If it *were* a typical week, Sara would not be at the Underground station at all. She would be doing what she originally planned to do today, which was go to a funeral. (It speaks volumes, of course, that funeral attendance is today's happy alternative.) She would not be considering the man who is looking at her, wondering if she should approach him. She would be in another part of the city entirely, and she would be saying, "I am so sorry for your loss."

But say it *was* a typical week. Say that everything had gone as it always does.

If that were the case, then back in Schenectady, Camille would be running about Gladys's split-level. And if Camille was not actually running around Gladys's split-level, Gladys would be heading out to get Camille at daycare, so she could come home and run around the split-level. It is to Camille's credit that she wants to run around. What Sara would do, if she were at said split-level, is collapse in a depressive heap until someone rounded her up and took her out to dinner at some place like Red Lobster, where she would have two glasses of lousy white wine and come home and collapse into a depressive heap.

Justine and Gladys can't afford daycare, but they've managed to tuck Camille into someone else's care for enough of the day that they both can maintain their (crappy) forty-hour-a-week jobs.

If this was a typical week, then eventually Justine would come over to Gladys's place. She'd arrive looking long-suffering and exasperated, though why Justine should be exasperated when *she* is the exasperating one is anyone's guess. She would be wearing the uniform for whatever crappy job she has at the moment: Arby's or Dunkin Donuts. ("Crappy" is the operating adjective in Sara's family.) Camille's father is missing in action. He actually might be in prison. (Justine has done a stint there, too. In the past, she supplemented her Arby's pay with some sex-for-reimbursement. That afforded her a five-day vacation in jail. Since then, she's had an even longer stay, this time in the pen.) The plain fact is Justine's not 100 percent sure she knows who Camille's father is. Why not insist on a paternity test? Sara has said. That might land Justine some cash. She already has the herpes. Why not get *everything* she can out of the bargain?

But this is just Sara's take on the matter. She doesn't like her sister. She doesn't like the way she treats her daughter. Not long before Sara moved to

London, she had taken Camille to a school picnic because Justine couldn't get off her shift in time. When Justine finally arrived, she didn't even walk onto the playground where hotdogs were being dispensed and the kids were chasing each other. "I want to stay," Camille had raced up to the playground gate to say. It wasn't an obnoxious insistence on her desires; it was more a gleeful announcement. She was having fun! That day, her wavy hair was long and pretty, like a hippie girl's, and she'd actually woven a flower garland— well, a weed garland; they were dandelions—for her hair. Justine had whispered to Sara, "I hate all these people. They're fucking her over in school. They're just blowing her off."

The teachers had actually seemed quite nice so far. Earlier, one of them had enthused, "You have sunbursts in your hair," and leaned down and given Camille a little hug.

"Come on," Justine said, tossing her head in the direction of the car, and Camille had left, not throwing the tantrum that another kid might.

What runs in the family appears to be not giving a shit about your offspring. Or caring but being so busy taking care of the fuck-ups that once you've picked the wildflowers in the backyard, you need a break; you need to watch some TV.

No.

Sara cannot go back to that. She'll kill herself before she goes back to that.

And she means that literally. She'll slit her wrists. In the bathtub. She's already promised herself this.

And what is Sara doing, as she thinks about her horrible family? She is looking at the man with the sign and trying to figure out his lips. It's amazing the number of things you can think about at once. She's trying to figure out why his lips look so weird. They're too red. They're too soft for a man's, but he's plainly a man. He has the expensive look of a banker, someone recently moved from air conditioning to the hot press of the day. The requisite circles of sweat under his armpits. The day's tie loosened but not removed.

The radios and TVs are going on about the heat wave. This morning, when Sara was still in the apartment—she likes calling it "a flat," as they do here— she ran a washcloth in cold water and wore it as a hat, while she tidied up.

"Are you Liesel Rosenthal?" the man finally asks, hopefully.

In the twenty-four years that Sara has been alive, she has not often been in airports, but when she has been, and when she's seen people in baggage claim holding up signs with people's names, she has had the fantasy of going up and saying, "Hi. I'm here."

"Are you Liesel Rosenthal?" the man repeats.

"Yes," she says, and she feels cold with fear at what she is about to do. "I am."

The man looks at his watch. "You're early," he says.

Sara looks at her own watch. It is 5:45 p.m. She doesn't know how she has managed to make it this far into the day.

"Well," Sara says, and in the Rolodex of possible manners for this interchange, she picks "chirpy." "I *like* to be early."

"Me, too," the man says. "So we're off to a good start."

"Right," Sara says. She is supposed to be at the funeral in fifteen minutes. Her boyfriend, Michael, must have figured out that she's not coming back to the apartment. Maybe he'll go without her. More likely, without having anyone to goad him into attending, he'll stay home. "It's not like I really knew the guy," he's said more than once over the course of the week. "He's your *land*lord," Sara has been replying, as if Michael might forget his relationship to the man if Sara didn't fill him in. Michael is the kind of guy who will skip a funeral, but once there happily serve as pallbearer. Actually if you say to Michael, "Will you come over and take this pile of rocks, load it onto a truck, drive it across town, and then unload it? And after that, will you reload the truck and bring the rocks back here?" Michael will say, "Sure. OK." But if there were a rock in the path leading up to his building, he'd never think to move it. Someone has to *ask* him to do the favor. It isn't like he needs the gratitude either. The man has no ego. He just needs someone to give him the idea to act.

"I thought you'd be younger," the man with red lips says.

"Oh," Sara says. "How old did you think I'd be?"

"Twenty-two. That's what the agency said."

She feels a flutter of fear. What is "the agency?" A matchmaking service? Or . . . not a sex thing, surely? You wouldn't just hold up a sign if you were expecting a hooker? Would you? Tootsie Hendries? Blowsalot Smith?

"Almost right. I'm twenty-four," Sara says. She might as well tell the truth about something.

"I guess we should go somewhere to talk."

"That sounds good to me."

"Maybe you should suggest a place." He smiles. Ingratiatingly, Sara thinks. He appears to be trying to win *her* approval. Perhaps the agency is a job agency, and she is, of all things, interviewing *him* for a job. But how likely is that? A twenty-something interviewing a forty-something? "I don't know this neighborhood," he adds.

"I don't really either," she says.

"The agency said you were from here," the man says.

"Did they?" She coughs. "I am. I mean, I was . . . a long time ago. Things have changed."

"I thought you grew up in Lucerne."

"Yes," Sara agrees unhelpfully, leaving him to resolve the discrepancy.

Behind the man, she notices a blond girl, probably twenty-two, her hair parted neatly on the side and pulled back into a ponytail. The strap of a schoolgirl-type bag crosses her chest. She appears to be waiting for someone. The real Liesel Rosenthal, no doubt.

"Oh, I remember," she says quickly. "Over there. There's a place we can get some tea." She points down the road, away from the Swiss Cottage. "It's called . . . it's called"—she starts to walk, and the man follows. "I'll know it when I see it," she says, picking up her pace, she hopes imperceptibly. He seems unfazed by her brisk trot, and he matches her stride, happy apparently to begin whatever it is that they are about to begin. Sara walks a block, then another, all the while saying things like "I remember it as being here, but it might have been . . . Oops, no sorry, I guess a bit farther." But she doesn't see anything promising. There's a low-rent electronics shop, a bank, a laundry, a filthy-looking nail salon. Stores with their grates pulled down. "I guess it's gone," she says. "Things turn over so quickly in this neighborhood." She has no idea if this is true.

"Let's try one more block," the man says, and just then, they come to a narrow Indian restaurant.

"Maybe here?" Sara suggests.

"Sure. Why not?"

They step inside.

"Two," the man says to the waiter, though this hardly seems necessary. They are obviously two people, and just as obviously, the restaurant is empty. They don't need help finding a seat. Perhaps the food is terrible. People always say that the only good food in London is Indian. Sara has repeated this wisdom herself, though actually Indian food gives her phenomenal gas. It doesn't quite seem cosmopolitan to own up to this, though, even to herself.

The waiter hands over large menus, but the man says, "We'll just be having something to drink."

So this is not a date for a super-early dinner. "I'm going to have a beer," he tells Sara. When the waiter comes back, Sara asks for some tea, smooths the skirt of her black dress over her thighs. Michael always says she looks sexy in this dress. "But not too sexy?" Sara asks the part of her brain now reserved for Michael's opinions. "Right?" Why inquire, though? Like Michael, her inner voice is rarely sympathetic.

"What shall I call you?" Sara says. She is hoping the question will make sense, that he has one of those names that has two versions. Don't most men? Michael or Mike? Lawrence or Larry? Higgledy Piggledy Pop or just Pop?

"David. David, I should have said. If you called me 'Mr. Burke,' I'd go looking for my father. And Martha, when you meet her, she goes by Mattie. Mattie Burke. She took my name. I know some women don't these days, but she did."

"I'm looking forward to meeting her," Sara says automatically. Is this the right thing to say?

"Yes, we'll get there. Right now I want to ask a few questions. I mean, I have your character references." He reaches into his suit pocket and pulls out a fat white envelope. "You have quite the fan club." He unfolds the pages within the envelope, makes some mumbling sounds as he scans what's there. "And Mattie called the . . . let's see . . ." He is holding what looks, from Sara's side of the table, like an application form, ". . . the Nikelsons for a chat."

He smiles at her. He still seems to be trying to win her over, though why would he be doing that, if *he* is interviewing *her?*

"Well, they adore you, as you must know."

"Yes," Sara agrees, warming to the idea of a fan club. There is something fat and satisfied in his face, she decides, though he is not fat, and his eyes are curious, in a way that makes him seem kind.

Oh, what is the matter with her? There's nothing fat and satisfied in his face! She's looking for flaws. It's purely self-preservation, this fault-finding. She's trying to make herself feel better about herself.

"And the letters on file are very complimentary as well. The bag game: that's a clever idea."

"Right," Sara says. What could this possibly mean?

"Our kids are just about the same age as the Nikelsons'. At least when you started with them." He reaches into his back pocket and pulls out his wallet, flips it open for a picture of a beefy little boy with a wide smile and a girl with dark-brown hair. The two of them hold opposite ends of a kite, and the boy's fingers spread into a peace sign above the girl's head. "Alfred's eleven." David points. "And Penelope's seven. Penelope's the one we really have to worry about. She's very attached to her mother."

"I love children," Sara says, because the nature of this interview is finally dawning on her. "I always have. Even as a little girl, you know, I'd play mommy with my dolls. Not that . . . you know I want to *be* a mother yet. It's good just helping out with other people's kids."

"Now I know you have your studies . . ."

Sara doesn't say anything. What studies could she possibly have? One of Michael's friends is a reporter, and he once told her that he kept quiet when people finished answering a question because eventually they started talking again. Even when they didn't want to. Silence prodded them on. That's how he got his best information.

"So the trick will be to balance your studies with Mattie's schedule. Thank God you don't have the coursework, but I assume you'll go to the library."

"Yes."

"I almost did a dissertation," David says. "In philosophy, though, not English."

"Oh?"

"I gave it up, thank goodness. I'm not quite cut out for the penurious life of the mind."

"Oh." She gives a little laugh. "I'm thinking of giving mine up, too."

David looks a little startled.

"Perhaps the agency didn't mention?"

"No."

"I guess they can't tell you everything." Sara smiles.

"No."

Sara keeps quiet. He seems disappointed.

"Well, more time for the kiddos then."

"Exactly," Sara says. "That's *exactly* what I was thinking."

He starts in on his questions. What would she do with the kids on a rainy day? On a sunny day? Does she mind doing a little cooking and laundry? What would she do if the children wouldn't go to sleep?

Sara eagerly lists off activities. (Museums, gardens, playgrounds, games, crafts, puppet shows. What else were you to say?) Then she says she loves to clean. (True. It helps when she's anxious.) And that she doesn't mind sitting in a room till a child falls asleep. (Also true.)

David seems inordinately delighted by her answers. What did others tell him? Sara pictures a stout woman with thick ankles and the beginnings of a gray mustache saying, "A few hours in front of the telly ain't a bad thing. Helps keep 'em inside. Away from the nutters, don't you know? Mind you, a bit of grime never hurt nobody. More important things in life than washing up the dishes, I always say."

Sara smiles at David and says, "I remember my childhood so well. I remember what I wanted to do—the things that were important—and that helps me. You know. When I'm with children, I know what they want. And often I want it too. I guess I'm a kid at heart."

Is this too much? "Kid at heart." Yeesh.

David says, "I can't tell you how good this is to hear." He takes a sip of his beer, then clears his throat. "So before we head over to meet them, I wanted to talk pay and also let you know about the apartment. It's in the basement, but it still gets good light. It has its own bathroom, but not a kitchen. We'll be expecting you to join us for meals on your days on. But we're thinking Mondays and Tuesdays for days off. The girl we had before went to visit her aunt on those days, but you're perfectly welcome to stay, and we aren't the sort of people who mind you having visitors. We'd prefer no overnight guests, if you know what I mean, but we don't want you to feel like a maid. We want you to feel like part of the family. We offer five hundred pounds for the month. You're to help yourself to anything in the kitchen, and anything you need for the apartment is on us. If there's something you want at the market, we'll pick it up. The last girl wanted everything off the books, so we paid her in cash, but we'll do it any way you want, of course."

Sara tries not to smile. She would most definitely like everything in cash and off the books.

"How does that sound?"

And since there is no point in lying about this, Sara says, "That sounds great."

"Mattie has the final say, of course. We'll need to see you with the kids, but I have a good feeling about this," David says.

SARA'S WEEK HAD STARTED BADLY. On Sunday, the phone rang at Michael's, and when he said, "It's for you," she was stumped. As far as she knew no one had her number at Michael's—or no one who wouldn't want to chat with Michael first. She hadn't given the number out.

"Who is it?" she said, extending her arm.

Michael shrugged. "Friend of yours, I guess." He was on his way out to meet his own friend at a pub.

But it wasn't a friend. It was her mother.

"Hi, honey. How are you?"

"I'm OK." Something always tightened in her chest when she heard from her mother. She felt guilty for not wanting to talk to her.

"I hate to bother you, but we've got a situation here."

Instantly, Sara knew something was up with Justine. "What's happened?"

"Well, Justine had a little run-in with the law."

Oh, crap, Sara thought. So far, Justine had been relatively lucky in her run-ins with the law. Three years ago, she'd had the bad taste to put a gun to a man's head. Criminal threatening with a firearm! ("It was a drug thing," Justine had whispered to Sara, in the same way she might have said, "It's a women's thing" to a man wondering why she always brought her pocketbook with her when she went to the bathroom.) "And anyway," Justine told Sara, "It wasn't like the gun was loaded." *She was just trying to be persuasive!* The location of the bullets hardly seemed to matter to Sara, but it did to the courts, thank goodness. They disregarded the firearm attachment to the charge. So Justine got eight months at York Correctional Institution for a misdemeanor.

Gladys cleared her throat and began, "So first there were some break-ins in the neighborhood."

"Jesus."

"And then someone stole our TV."

"Oh!" Sara said relieved. She had thought her mother was implying that Justine was responsible for the break-ins.

"Yeah, she took the TV," Sara's mother said flatly.

"*She* stole the TV?"

Her mother didn't answer. Instead she started into a different story, and it took a moment for Sara to catch on that her mother was telling a story about Justine's car being pulled over by the police.

"Actually, the light was out—you know that whatchacallit—the headlight. Jesus Christ, I can't remember a thing. The headlight was out. A padiddle."

Sara's family used to play a game where you were supposed to call out "Padiddle" if you saw a car with only one headlight. It wasn't all bad, her childhood. She needed to remember that. Her mom had tried to make things fun.

"So the cops pulled her over just to let her know, and she was three sheets to the wind, so they had her step out of the car, and she was a little . . . belligerent, I guess you'd say. One thing leads to another. They search the car, thinking drugs, but instead they find half the neighborhood's stereos in the trunk."

Sara's mother took a breath and added, "But that's not why I'm calling."

"It's not?"

"No, I've actually got some bad news."

Her mother's voice was grave. Hadn't she just delivered bad news?

"Justine's got breast cancer. She's going to have to have a mastectomy."

"She what?"

"She's got breast cancer. She called me last night and told me. I guess she just found out."

Sara couldn't process what her mother was saying, so she said, stupidly, "She's twenty-eight."

"You'd think I'd know that."

"No one gets breast cancer at twenty-eight."

"Well, she did." *How precocious!* Sara thought, panic already starting to take her over. Justine: bad at reading, bad at math, below grade level in every way, but not, it turned out, behind in the way you'd most hope to be. Her mother went on, "She was taking a shower. Felt a big lump in her armpit. Says she went into the clinic and they let her know what it was."

"What clinic?"

"I don't know. She's got to schedule the surgery." *Oh, God.* Sara felt cold. As her mother continued to talk, Sara snaked the phone over to the bookcase. She had a copy of *Our Bodies, Ourselves*—she'd brought it all the way from New York—and she slipped it out, started flipping the pages. So far, she'd only really perused the "emotional well-being" section. She knew she had some problems in that arena.

"There's another problem."

"What are you talking about?" There can't be *another* problem. She had done something bad, and something bad had been done to her. Didn't that about cover the range of possibilities?

"So you know when the cops pulled Justine over, she didn't have her license."

"No?"

"It was suspended. After the DWI."

"Jesus," Sara said. She hadn't known about a DWI, but why not? Why not throw that in? A DWI in a community where it was impossible to get around without a car?

"So when they asked for her name, she didn't want to give it, because she knew they'd look up her record. She was telling them the car belonged to Bill, and she didn't know about what was in the trunk." Sara presumed Bill was a boyfriend. Not a name she'd heard in connection with Justine before.

"What'd she do?"

"She gave the police your name."

Like the news about the cancer, this didn't register with Sara for a moment.

"They ran you and that was a relief. You know, that you have a valid license and all."

Sara was actually afraid of driving and rarely did it, but she had her license, though it was going to lapse in a month. She'd have to retake all the tests since she wouldn't be back in New York to renew it. "They bought that? Why didn't they fingerprint her or something?"

"Why would they fingerprint her? It checked out. And then I came to bail her out, and we have the same last name, so nothing struck them as fishy."

Sara didn't say anything.

"We're in a tricky situation," her mother said and then noisily chewed on something. Was she eating *nuts? Popcorn?* Something a little salty to accompany the movie of her life? She cleared her throat. "While we wait for the trial, I mean. You know, because she's going to get some serious time; what with the previous arrests and the DWI, she's not really looking like an upstanding citizen."

Sara was only half-listening now. Wouldn't having breast cancer be enough? Couldn't her sister argue that that should be her punishment? How do you even *do* prison with cancer? she wondered. Years earlier, Sara had been in an emergency room after a snowblower cut off a piece of a friend's finger. (He'd been trying to dislodge a twig from the fan-blade.) Sara had gone with the friend to the hospital, then lingered while a doctor stitched him up. In the waiting room, she noticed a thin, delicate Asian man in an orange jumpsuit. He had hair down to his waist and a pencil line of a mustache. Sara had been looking at him for a long time before she realized he was handcuffed to his chair. What could he have possibly done? Such a slight person? And why was he in the ER? Everyone who wasn't already on a stretcher seemed to be vomiting or bleeding, but he was still, not looking at the TV or (obviously) flipping through tired magazines. Just sitting in the chair and thinking.

Would they take Justine to an operating room, remove her breast, then slip her into an orange jumpsuit and send her back to a cell? Sara remembers a friend's mother who was always taking out her prosthetic boob and putting it in her pocket or accidentally sending it through the washing machine. Would they even give Justine a prosthetic? Or let her have reconstruction? Justine didn't have health insurance. Who would pay for the necessary treatment? Sara's heart was racing. Oh, Justine! She did so many things wrong, but she didn't deserve this! Though no one really "deserved" cancer. Not that the idea of matching that particular misfortune with criminal behavior didn't make a kind of sense. Murder? That'll get you pancreatic, my friend. Robbery? OK, we'll let you have uterine, no spread. Shoplifting some licorice? You're golden, but we'll give you a little basal cell carcinoma to scare you off any future bad behavior.

As Sara was thinking all this, Gladys said, "Justine just feels she can't *do* prison with cancer." It was as if she were talking about college course options. *Justine just doesn't feel she can do physics and organic chemistry. It would be a little too hard.* "Anyway," Gladys breathed, "that's the whole point of my call. Wanted to know if you could help out."

"Help?" Sara said but then realized what her mother was asking. She wanted Sara to confirm her sister's lie, to pretend that *she'd* been the drunk girl with a bootful of loot and the sudden desire to mouth off to a cop.

"I . . . OK," she said. "But, no, I . . ." She stopped. Lying would make her a criminal too, and surely no judicial system would fall for such a ruse. "I guess I don't want to do that, Mom." And then, because this seemed so disloyal, she added, "I mean if it would honestly help Justine, I would. But I don't think it would work, and it would just kind of get me in trouble."

"You don't need to decide today," her mother said pleasantly, as if she hadn't heard Sara's words. "The case is pending trial. But we'll need to know before too long. I didn't want to ask you. I know your sister is doing a terrible thing here. I'm just—" And here her mother stopped, and Sara realized she was crying. "Just frightened for her. You know?" Her voice had grown small, little-girlish.

"Oh, Mom. I'm sorry. I'm *sorry*." She started to cry, too. "Should I come home?"

"No, no. What would coming home do? Let's talk in a day or two, though. We'll figure it out then. I mean what the best thing to do is. I don't know."

Sara had hung up and dried her own eyes. She finally reached the breast cancer section of *Our Bodies, Ourselves*. There, on the upper left corner of the page, was a woman, apparently outdoors, her arms jubilantly thrown asunder—*Oh, how I celebrate myself!*—and she had a chest with one full breast and one zipper. Or that's what the scar looked like to Sara. Sara did what she thought you should do when you looked at such a thing. She screamed. Then she slumped onto the couch and sobbed. She couldn't believe this was going to happen to her sister.

The rest of the week Sara flip-flopped between confusion and tears. It was impossible to know if she should do what her mom was asking. Michael was no help. He offered an initial ten minutes of concern then made it clear that Sara's weeping irritated him. "Come on now," he'd say. "Come on." Translation: Shut up.

MICHAEL AND SARA HAD MET through an art professor, back in New York. One day the professor had told Sara, "You should meet Michael. You're both talented."

"Oh?" Sara said.

She had seen Michael in the studio. His British accent interested her, but she wasn't attracted, exactly. His too-round face with its boyish haircut—parted on the side and neatly combed against his scalp—made him look a little dopey. But she'd liked the compliment—her professor thought she was talented!—so when the professor had an end-of-semester gathering, Sara sought Michael out. He was from London, it turned out, just in Albany for the spring semester. Sara didn't last long at the party; the professor had cats, and she was wildly allergic. But when she left, Michael came. She wasn't even sure she wanted him to.

But then that was that.

Sara followed Michael back to London. He had an apartment rent-free in a building off Clapham High Street. In return, he served as the building's janitor, replacing light bulbs, trimming hedges, and minding the rubbish bins. Otherwise, Michael didn't have a job, just some dwindling funds from a school loan. Eventually Sara found herself standing over the classifieds, saying, "What about this? What about this?" while he rejected every alternative.

She didn't have a work permit. What were they going to live on?

Finally, Sara dragged Michael to a job interview. The restaurant down the road was looking for a baker. It was a place that specialized in cinnamon buns the size of a baby's head. Also something called a Bunty Cake: made of croissant dough, shaped into a biscuit round, and drizzled with orange syrup.

So now that was Michael's job. Making pastries. You couldn't get him to do anything, but once he had an assignment, he kept at it until someone told him to stop. He was an object at rest until someone forced him to be an object in motion. Then, once he had the motion thing going, he stuck with that. It made him, in his own way, dependable. Sara appreciated that. Or she tried to.

WHILE MICHAEL WORKED, Sara made economical meals and took over the janitorial chores. The hominess of the setup appealed to her. Still, eventually Michael and she started bickering. Sara guessed they should break up, but she didn't want to go back to New York. Months passed, then a year. She was unclear on whether she was in the country illegally. The authorities had insisted on seeing her return ticket at the airport when she arrived, but she hadn't had one. This caused a fuss, but eventually they let her through. She knew she couldn't just stay indefinitely, but she hadn't figured out how visas worked. Was she supposed to have one? After the one-year mark in London, she had the idea she could only stay if she was Michael's fiancée, so she called herself that, and he went along. He was just as daft as she was about the rules. One time, she went to the UK immigration office to try to figure out the options. "I'm asking for a friend," she had said. "I'm just here on holiday." The people in the office didn't like her "asking for a friend" line.

Frightened, Sara pretended she needed to go to the bathroom and escaped out a side door.

When she thought about returning to the United States, she thought about lying right down on the pavement and going to sleep for the rest of her life. It wasn't just her family. America with its rest stops and malls, its cars and ubiquitous TV screens. It was a tremendous country, and yet it made her feel claustrophobic.

She'd have to make it work a little longer with Michael.

MICHAEL AND SARA'S FIGHTING had taken a turn for the worse this week. Of all weeks. You'd think he'd manage not to be such a lunky nobody the week that her sister got cancer and that . . . that, who knew? That Sara was going to have to fly home? On whose dime, she wanted to know? She had some money. She'd been working under the table for a frame shop Michael's friend Nancy owned. If Sara earned enough, she might have gone off on her own, tried London without Michael, but she didn't have enough, and she couldn't get more work without a permit. Sara didn't fancy using what cash she had to confess to a crime she hadn't committed. Only if she didn't, what would happen to her sister?

Michael shrugged. She'd figure it out, he said.

But that wasn't what they fought about this week. What they fought about was stupid. What they fought about was always stupid.

On Tuesday, Michael got a faux-leather lounge chair from a tenant who was moving out. It was one of the ugliest things Sara had ever seen. The arms were wooden wagon wheels, and the outline of a cowboy hat was stitched to the seatback. If Sara could have convinced herself the chair was campy and funny—something an artist might have—she might have been able to live with it. But the chair was really just ugly. It was something that fat guy her mother had married would buy and fart into while he watched TV. It was a chair that had been collecting fat guys' farts for decades, and now it was in her pretty apartment with the wood floors and the white-and-black bathroom tiles and the abandoned antique washbasin that she'd found on the street and was using as a side table.

Sara hadn't seen the chair till Wednesday morning when she woke up. She'd heard some banging around Tuesday night but hadn't thought much of it, beyond the fact that Michael was going to be exhausted in the morning. He had to get up at 4:00 a.m. for the bakery, but he hadn't arranged his sleep schedule around his new work hours. For all the bickering, she was looking forward to his coming to bed. She liked having a boyfriend. It was nice to share the bed with someone. The catch being that she didn't like having this particular boyfriend, though she wanted to. But he was sweet to her, most of the time. He did things like run out for ice cream when she wanted it after dinner. He told her she was pretty. He brought her out with his friends, who seemed to dote on her for simply being different. She liked his crowd. They laughed and were lighthearted and liked to tell funny stories.

She called him in the bakery in the morning to ask about the chair. "I hate it," she said. "Let's get rid of it."

"But Joe gave it to me."

"But I hate it."

"But Joe gave it to me."

"He's not going to know if we get rid of it."

"How are we going to get rid of it? It's so heavy. We barely got it into the apartment as is. And you know how big Joe is."

"I can't stand it. I can't stand it. It gives me the creeps."

"It's just a bloody chair, Sara."

"It's a big and ugly chair. It stands for . . . don't you understand?" she said and started to cry.

But he didn't. He didn't understand, and he didn't get how terrifying it was that Justine had cancer, and how Sara was going to have to go back to the United States and deal with all this. She'd made a joke of it on Monday night when they were out to dinner with friends—"My crazy family!"—and everyone thought it was appalling and funny both, though the cancer part certainly darkened the humor of it all. Still, what a thing for her sister to do! Give Sara's name to a cop!

"I can't listen to this," Michael said of her crying, and he hung up.

He hung up! Unbelievable. So she called him back. "How could you hang up on me? My sister's got cancer, and I . . ."

"I'm at work. I can't do this right now, Sara." Again he disconnected.

But Sara knew he was alone in the kitchen with the giant dough-mixing machine until 7:00 a.m. She called back, but the phone just rang and rang. She hung up and dialed again; she couldn't believe he wouldn't pick up. She broke the connection and dialed once more. This time the phone was busy.

So he'd taken it off the hook.

Sara got dressed and went to confront him. She knocked fiercely at the door to the restaurant—the bakery was located off the foyer inside—and eventually Michael opened the door.

"How could you just hang up?"

"I'm at work," he said, tense.

"I know you are at work," she hissed. "There's not a single person I admire who I can imagine having such a chair. It just speaks to me of stupidity and grossness and . . ."

His shirt was sprinkled with flour, as if he'd just come in from a light snowfall.

"Sara, it's OK. It's OK," he said more gently. "Things are just getting to you this week. We can get rid of the chair. It's not worth getting all bothered."

"OK," she said, her voice small and sullen. It was hard to back off her upset, now that she'd worked her way into it.

"It's all right. Just go home. I'll see you later. Give me a kiss."

She pecked his cheek, and he wrapped his arms around her.

"OK," she sniffed and turned for the door. Her body still felt angry, but he had agreed to what she wanted. She needed to stop. Sometimes the idea of killing herself didn't just attach itself to the idea of going home. Why had she gone so berserk? Sometimes it all felt like too much, and she wanted herself to go away.

THAT NIGHT, she and Michael went out with Nancy (Sara's boss from the frame shop) and Roman, Nancy's roommate. Sara couldn't tell if they were a couple as well. The four met at a corner pub. When she arrived, Sara leaned over and kissed Michael and said, "He knows I'm only using him so I can get a visa, but he puts up with me."

Everyone laughed, so Sara felt that she'd said it to be outrageous, and people knew that, and things were really OK between her and Michael. She wanted things to be OK.

"You need to become a maid," Nancy said. "Then you can have a visa for five years. That's what I hear, anyway."

"I'm not sure that's right," Roman said.

"I can clean," Sara said hopefully.

"Absolutely," Michael put in. "She likes things clean." He turned to Sara and said, "Can I give them an example?"

She shrugged an OK. She knew what he was going to tell them.

"OK," he said and began the story. One weekend, Michael and Sara had gone to the Cotswolds, and a fellow who worked at the bakery—his name was Snodgrass—had crashed at their place. Snodgrass was a big mystery to people. No one knew where he lived or slept. Sara assumed he was using the bakery job as a cover for dealing drugs. He was fat and had a long beard like a member of ZZ Top. He always wore a leather jacket and sunglasses, even in the rain. Sara hadn't wanted him to stay, but what could she say? It was Michael's apartment. When they came home, Sara saw her plastic cookie container on a table by the bed. Sara baked cookies once a week, keeping some and wrapping others in foil to give to neighbors and people at the frame shop. She liked surprising people with unexpected gifts. She had a fondness for a peanut butter cookie with a chocolate kiss pressed into it, a super-indulgent surprise. Michael opened the container and peeked inside. Then he slammed the lid down.

"What's that?" Sara had said.

"Nothing."

"What?" she insisted.

Michael cleared his throat, then said, "Snodgrass's beard."

Nancy and Roman roared when Michael got to the punch line. Michael said, "Sara went nuts. She fumigated the flat."

Sara laughed with everyone. It was funny now. Less so when she was scrubbing out the apartment. Every possible pubic hair in the bathtub had struck her as an affront. Ditto the unwiped spills and crumbs on her kitchen counter. Snodgrass's leavings. He seemed the sort of man whose body might serve as host for a variety of biting insects.

Michael followed the Snodgrass story with one about the cowboy chair. Everyone laughed, and Sara said, "I know, I know! I was being ridiculous." And she felt how crazy it was to get so worked up. It was just a chair! How could she have her priorities so out of line, especially this of all weeks?

Still, after their beers, Roman helped Michael carry the cowboy chair down to the street. Nancy and Sara waited outside while they did it. "Blimey!" Nancy said when they finally dropped the monstrosity at the curb. "It's the ugliest thing I've ever seen!" She kissed Sara good-night. "Men," she whispered. "Idiots. Every one of them." Sara started to tear up in gratitude. "Honest to God," Nancy went on. "That chair is grounds for divorce. And you're not even married."

THE CHAIR IS STILL SITTING on the curb. No one seems inclined to take it. It's not the sight of the thing that has brought Sara to Swiss Cottage, though. It's not the week of off-and-on crying, the sobs that Sara can't stop even though Michael finds her tears so unbearable. It's this very day, which started with a 6:00 a.m. phone call. Her mother, surprisingly chipper. "Things are all sorted out," Gladys said.

"What do you mean?"

"Your dad did something right for a change. He got them to throw out the charges against Justine, and it seems they'll agree to let her go if she'll enter this crazy place that he's got down there." Down there, Sara knew, meant North Carolina, where her father lived with his new wife—younger, natch; dottily Christian, ditto. "They've got some Christian rehab, and if Justine checks in and stays clean, she avoids prison. He managed to convince the neighbors not to press charges. He can do the sweet talk, I'll give him that. He told them it would be the Christian thing to do, that Justine just needs a little of the Lord's help." She snorted. "He kept the TV, though."

"What are you talking about?"

"Our TV. Your father decided he'd like to own it. A little payment for his trouble."

"But what's going to happen to Justine?"

"She's going to North Carolina. I'll keep Camille."

"Who's going to be her doctor?"

"Oh, that!" Her mother made a farting sound with her lips. "Justine doesn't have cancer. She was just saying that. So you'd feel sorry for her and help her out."

The way her mother said this, it was as if they all knew from the start that the cancer story was a lie.

"Mom. I believed her." It didn't seem like you could feel anger and gratitude at the same time, but Sara was managing it.

"Oh, I did, too. Don't you know. She really fooled me there." Her mother had a "just folks" dumbness she used when she didn't want to deal with complexity. She wasn't dumb, but sometimes it was a way to get by. Or maybe she was too relieved for outrage. "She got us both, I guess," her mother added.

"Right," Sara said, sarcastic. "That she did." Didn't her mother *care?* About what Justine had done? About what she had asked Sara to do?

Sara was relieved that Justine was healthy. She was relieved not to have to take the fall for Justine. But she was also furious. "It all worked out in the end," her mother said cheerfully, and then sensing Sara's emotion without Sara speaking, she added, "Why are you making such a big deal? You always make such a big deal."

"Yeah," Sara snarled into the phone. "*I'm* the problem here." Abruptly, before she had a chance to reconsider, she hung up.

Then she went and put on a black sleeveless dress, because it was time for Colin Gardner's funeral.

WHAT A DAY! What a lark!

(Sara had read Virginia Woolf. Well, a *little* Virginia Woolf, in her first semester at college.)

What a plunge!

(The idea of Virginia Woolf vaguely appealed. Not because Sara'd liked reading her—she hadn't really—but because Woolf had drowned herself in a river. It made Sara darkly curious. Not that Sara saw herself doing that, though sometimes when she was on the subway platform, she thought, as the train was coming, "What if I just step in? What if I just do it?")

Michael and Sara hadn't known their octogenarian landlord Colin well. Still, it was only right that they show their respects. Sara didn't know why she could mourn life's passing and daydream about offing herself at the same time. She could have that step-in-front-of-the-subway feeling and then flinch in fright when she started to stumble on a staircase. Nothing made any sense.

Today at the funeral, people would cry and talk about Colin's death as if it were a peculiar tragedy, something original Colin had done instead of something we all do sooner or later.

Sooner, Sara thought. Sooner for her, if she had to go home, if she couldn't get the right papers. She was off the hook with Justine, but not off the hook altogether.

She could not, she recited to herself for the billionth time, go home. She could not. She could not. She had this recurring dream in which Americans said, "Fries with that?" no matter the context. The postmistress as she extended a book of stamps. "Fries with that?" A beggar whose sign didn't say "Homeless. Please help," but "Fries with that?"

Michael dressed for the funeral too, and then he came into the kitchen, where Sara was polishing her shoes with a rag. He'd donned a heavy wool suit jacket, ugly and brown. It was just the sort of thing a man who owned a chair with wagon wheels might think attractive. "You can't wear that," Sara said.

"It's the only coat I have," he said.

"It's too hot. You'll pass out."

"But it's the only coat I have," he said, stubborn, annoyed.

"You don't need to wear a suit jacket," she said, her voice rising. "No one will care. You can just go in your shirt and slacks."

"I've got to wear a coat."

"No you don't," she snapped. "You'll look like a fool."

He gave her a look and said, "Of course it's all about appearances," as if he'd finally uncovered her small-minded bourgeois motives, as if heat prostration wasn't the issue here.

"I just can't believe you. I really can't believe you!" How dare he turn this into a criticism of her? "You'll look like a fool *to me.* I don't care what other people think. *I* care that you're not stupid."

"Don't call me stupid," Michael said calmly.

"I'm . . ." Sara looked around the room for something to do. Action seemed to be required. She said, "I'm taking out the trash!" She bundled it up in a fury, carried it at arm's length to prevent herself from dirtying her dress, and clattered down the stairs. Out she went, stopping once at the landing to tug her dress down before she turned for the narrow alley that led to the bins. From the landing, she could see right into the neighbor's dining room window. She often noticed the family that lived here. The kids always seemed to be drawing pictures at the table, and once Sara saw the whole family lighting Sabbath candles. It had seemed like a beautiful custom to her. Sara liked most religions that weren't her own. Sometimes she wished she were a Buddhist, other times an obsessed Catholic girl. Today, though, as she passed by the open window, she heard the mother say, "It's just been terrible. It's so, so hot, and the crazy woman next door won't stop screaming."

Instantly, Sara had that same feeling she had when her mother said Justine had breast cancer, that same growing terror.

It was she, of course. The mother was talking about her. *She* was the crazy woman next door.

Sara ran the rest of the way to the rubbish bins. She lifted a lid. Inside was a broken plastic bag, which looked like it contained—but this couldn't be—a dead *animal,* and there were maggots, hundreds of white wormy maggots, swarming all over the thing. Had someone thrown out *a dog?* Sara slammed the lid down but knew she had to pick it up again to add her bag to the heap. She lifted the lid again, tried not to look at the maggots, but looked all the same, and then ran back to the front door and quickly up the stairs. Once inside the apartment, she said, "I've got to pack. I've got to pack."

She was the crazy woman next door. Had they all heard her? Had she been *that* loud when she was yelling at Michael? When she was crying about her sister? She had to get out. But where would she go?

She started to sob. "Michael . . . Michael?"

He found her in the bedroom, put his arm around her. "What's the matter? What's the matter? It's just a coat."

"No," she said and explained what she'd heard.

"She wasn't talking about you."

"Of course she was. I can't . . ." she said. "I just can't." Then she looked around for her purse. "I can't stay here."

"It's OK. Just calm down."

"No," she said. "I can't. I can't go to the funeral. I can't do this. I'll come back later, but I've got to go now."

"I can't let you go," he said, standing in front of her, holding her arms at her sides as if protecting her from herself.

"Let go of me," she said pulling her arms away and then batting at his hands, as he made to restrain her again. "I'm fine. I've just got to go." She could not be the person who lived in this apartment for a minute longer.

She hurried down the stairs and out. *The crazy woman makes her crazy departure.* Was anyone even noticing? Oh, God, she hoped not. She wiped her face, smearing, rather than drying, her tears as she crossed the street for the subway. Down she went, wet-faced, but also reprimanding herself, *No crying in public. NO crying in public.* Though why not? When she saw people crying in public, she always stopped, asked if they were all right. Which they weren't. That was why they were crying in public. But it couldn't hurt to know someone was concerned. That's what Sara thought, though it was true people always looked horrified when she asked if they needed any help.

As a matter of habit, Sara walked to the northbound line. She was going to ride to a random stop and get out and look around. She did this a lot when she was alone, though always before with an air of adventure rather than despair. Today she was going to go to, to go to . . . she scanned the Tube map, half-laughed at the idea of getting on the Jubilee Line. Today of all days. Then she saw the words "Swiss Cottage" and thought, *Yes. OK. There.*

AT THE INDIAN RESTAURANT, David finishes up his beer. "Just need to run to the loo," he says and stands. "Then I'll take you home to meet Mattie and the kids." He heads for the back of the restaurant. Sara hasn't had much of her tea. She doesn't like tea as much as she likes the idea of being a tea drinker. She only ordered it because it seemed the sort of thing a Liesel would order. Probably the only thing Sara misses about home is the iced coffee at Dunkin Donuts.

She folds her napkin, thinks briefly of David and Mattie Burke's well-lit basement apartment, which already feels like it belongs to her. It's clean, she imagines, with its own door to a well-tended back garden. The kitchen upstairs is big and open with a central island and copper pots hanging from a ceiling rack.

Sara will be caught in this surely. The real Liesel will show up. The agency will call and ask about the missed appointment. David will try to square her American accent with whatever is on her application form. As Sara thinks this, she looks at David's papers. He has left them on the table. She grabs them, stuffs them into her purse. She will study them later. She will call the agency and say she is David's wife and apologize for not showing up at the appointed hour for the interview. She will say she has decided to go another route for her nanny. Even so, she knows this won't work. She'll slip, and something the Burkes know will contradict something she says. Police will be called. She'll end the week admitting to crimes, only now they will be crimes she has actually committed, rather than the ones her sister has committed.

David comes back from the bathroom, fishes two bills out of his wallet, then bends to look under the table.

"Ready?" Sara says, standing and making a move for the door.

"Oh," he says, "can't figure out what I did with your papers." He looks at his watch. "Never mind. I don't need the papers on Liesel Rosenthal anymore, do I? Now that I've got the real thing!"

"Right," she says. "The big trick is remembering how to spell my name. It's one *s*, and one *l* at the end."

This seems like something a Liesel might say.

This might be OK, she reassures herself. (Crazy lady begone!) This might work. This might, after all, be a whole new life.

She falls into step beside David, but in her head she isn't walking toward the Swiss Cottage stop. In her head, she is back in Michael's apartment, carefully packing her clothes. In her head, she is saying, "It's probably for the best." In her head, she is already gone.

PART TWO

9

SIP MY OCEAN

A DISHEVELED MAN—crazy? homeless?—bikes up to Daniella and Benjamin, who are standing on a sidewalk in a tony section of Copenhagen. In the storefront office behind them, Joel is renting three bikes, two young female employees handling his reservation as if it is a confusing, unaccustomed thing, though Joel is in a *bike rental shop* that plainly caters to the English-speaking world. Behind Daniella's head is a sign that reads "Bikes forrent.com." The heat of the day—could it be a hundred?—makes the wait irritating. *Let's go,* Daniella thinks, though what does it matter if they go now or later or not at all?

"Here, take this," the bicycling man shouts at Benjamin. One of the man's hands stays on his handlebar; the other extends an overstuffed backpack.

Benjamin flinches. He clearly doesn't know what to do—take it or not?—and Daniella is no help. Her impulse, like Benjamin's, is retreat. Something's the matter with the man.

"You little shit," the old man says, his lunatic beard gray and untrimmed, his dress negligibly revealing: old jeans, old shirt. "You can't help an old man," he accuses as he brings his bike to a stop, swings his backpack to the ground. "Little shit. Should learn some manners."

He is not crazy, a calibration that Daniella is only just able to make, so why should her thirteen-year-old son get there any faster than she? He is simply a nasty old man, having trouble balancing his bike.

"He was scared of you," Daniella says, furious. She can count on one hand, on one digit, the times she has gotten angry in public. "You're *scary*," she says pointedly. "And you scared him."

"That's right," the man says, mockingly, sorry for himself. "I'm an old man."

"And he's just a boy," Joel says, having arrived on the sidewalk to hear some but not all of this exchange, "so there has to be a way to meet in the middle." Normally Joel gets angry if there is a possibility of affront, but now he is placid as a Buddhist. He says something else, and all of a sudden the two men are shaking hands, agreeing to let the trouble go, talking about how the heat makes everything harder to take. Joel seems happy with the truce; not so Daniella. She's unwilling to forgive someone who scares her son, tells him he's a shit, and then lectures him on how he hasn't been brought up right. "*You* haven't been brought up by right," she wants to snap. "You don't get to decide who he is. I do." A notion that is plainly absurd, her son's identity being a complex matter and not hers to determine. Benjamin just looks unhappy. He is the reason the family has come to Denmark, and now, she knows, he wishes he were home. Or if not home, then back at computer camp, that paradise. It wasn't beastly hot there.

So far the thing Benjamin likes best about Copenhagen is the PlayStation in the rental apartment. He doesn't have one at home despite repeated requests, Daniella the resistant one. He already spends enough time blasting the enemy on the computer. Why add another platform? As it is, she doesn't like the power that combat narratives have over Benjamin's imagination. But all the teenage boys she meets are similarly entranced. Perhaps she has been unfairly holding out? Joel thinks the PlayStation is no big deal. And even Daniella has to admit that it is Benjamin's time with a screen, his super-swift computer skills, that have brought them here. Not to the bike shop, but the city. He's the one who did the sleuthing to find his half sister, Idzia, a production assistant at a film production company here. He's the reason Joel is finally going to meet his daughter.

But not yet. Idzia has agreed to meet, but not till the weekend. Benjamin, Daniella, and Joel must play tourists for a few days. They have decided to rent bikes and get their bearings in this city before they get their bearings in what might be—with Idzia in it—a whole new life.

BENJAMIN HAS KNOWN about Idzia since he was six, though he only vaguely remembers the summer day, many years earlier, when Idzia was supposed to come visit from England but never showed up. At the time, Benjamin had been as broken up as when a playdate fell through at the last moment. Which is to say, hysterical. Companionship promised then denied was always painful, all the more so when the companionship suggested a new and permanent friend. But Benjamin rebounded. At least he seemed to put Idzia out of his mind. In more recent years, though, he has grown curious again. A mystery. Someone out there who can't be accessed. Neither Joel's ex-wife nor his daughter can be found on the Internet. (Benjamin did his own search to confirm, not trusting that his parents had the Google skills to ascertain this on their own.) "Must have been aliens got them," Benjamin opined when he found nothing more on the computer than Daniella and Joel did. Daniella didn't laugh. She could never come to the story with anger or bemusement, only a sad wonder.

But in the end Benjamin *did* have skills his parents lacked. He was the one who figured out what happened to Liesel and Idzia. All he needed was his computer . . . and one extra clue.

WHEN HE ISN'T MAKING UP scenarios for video games, Benjamin is often silly. Daniella loves his sense of humor, his punning in particular. Joel is more impatient with it, calls his nattering "nonsense," and it is true that between the video game narratives and clever quips, there isn't much time for real talk. Not that Benjamin isn't capable of it. He just offers seriousness up piecemeal: to his mother in the minutes when he is settling in for sleep, to his father when they are driving. Moral, existential, and developmental dilemmas. He'll address them all, when the time is right. He's thoughtful and smart, but Thoughtful and Smart are not the countries in which he likes to live, at least in conversation. He'd rather tell a joke, do something ridiculous.

One day, in the middle school cafeteria, he stands on a chair and calls out, "I am a golden Greek god."

"Oh, you didn't," Daniella says, laughing in spite of herself when he reports this on the car ride home. Benjamin is skinny, pale, dark-haired, edging into the awkwardness and skin trouble of full-on puberty. "Didn't you get in trouble?" He didn't, but only because the lunch monitor thought it was funny, too. Sometimes Daniella realizes Benjamin's jokes aren't original. The Greek god thing came from a movie. But often enough, he'll come up with the gag himself. At a dinner with Daniella's parents, Benjamin refused the chicken Mirabella on offer by saying, "Eating. It's so been there, done that. I prefer to photosynthesize." (The cleverness got him what he really wanted, which was a microwave taco.)

It's silliness that provides the clue Benjamin needs to solve the Liesel puzzle. One day at the airport, while Joel is waiting for their bags (the family back from a weekend trip to New York), Benjamin sees a man with a baseball cap and a whistle on a string around his neck. The man has a clipboard in one hand. In the other, he holds a sign that reads "Camp Chippewa."

"I could just go over there," Benjamin says, and say, "Hey, I'm here." He plays the fantasy out further.

"Yes, hello!" the man will say. "And you are?"

"Benjamin Pearlman," I will say.

"Huh," the man will say. "Don't see your name here."

"And then," Benjamin says, "I'd go, 'Well, the sign says Camp Chippewa, and my mom said I was to look for someone with a sign saying Camp Chippewa.' My voice would get shaky, and the man would say something like, 'No worries, buddy. I'm sure it's just an oversight.' And then . . ." Benjamin holds up a finger to indicate that he needs a moment to work this plot point out. "Then they'd have to bring me to camp. They couldn't just leave me in the airport. And then . . ." Again, the finger.

"I'll tell you a story," Joel interrupts him to say. "I actually know someone who did that." They head to their car as Joel tells Benjamin the strange story of how his first wife changed her name, of how she was originally named Sara Wilson, but one day, when she was really, really upset, she walked up to a man who was holding a sign that said 'Liesel Rosenthal.'"

"At an airport?" Benjamin asks.

"No. Outside a subway station. In London. The Tube, they call it. The man was supposed to interview a babysitter by that name. He interviewed

Liesel—well, Sara—and even hired her thinking she was Liesel Rosenthal."

"So then she, like, lived with a whole false identity?" Clearly, Benjamin loves the idea.

"Not quite," Joel says. "Eventually she told her employers the truth. But she got away with it for longer than you'd think. After about four months living with the family and working as a babysitter and getting paid under the table, the family decided to go away on a trip. She was supposed to come, to watch the kids. She had to bring her passport, so she confessed. You'd think they'd flip out, and maybe they did. I guess the family liked her by then. She was a pretty terrific babysitter. Although obviously not someone you could trust."

Daniella already knows the story, but she laughs. When Benjamin was little, she'd had little luck with sitters. Would *she* go so far as to excuse such profound deceit if she had a good caretaker? Surely not.

"It was more than just not getting mad," Joel says. "The father in the family was a lawyer, and she'd been in the country too long without the right kind of visa. Whatever was wrong with her papers, he worked it all out. You'd think that once everybody knew, she'd go back to her real name, but she liked being Liesel Rosenthal better than she liked being Sara Wilson. She stayed Liesel Rosenthal until she married me. Then I helped her legally change her name, and she was Liesel Pearlman."

This is something Daniella has not considered before: that there was no reason to stick with the faux name once her employers found out, but Liesel kept it anyway.

Daniella expects Benjamin to say something when Joel finishes. Benjamin likes an outrage, livens to bad behavior. *How could Liesel prevent you from seeing Idzia!* he has insisted in the past. *She had no right to do that!* "Liesel the Weasel," he calls her, the few times he has had reason to mention her. Joel expects this story of sneakiness to confirm his perception. Or perhaps to trigger a sci-fi thought about renaming as actual shape-shifting, a new person truly born with the new moniker. He seems to be deeply thinking about something, but then his head begins to bob, and Daniella realizes it isn't deep thought. He's just listening to something on his iPod.

WHEN THEY GET HOME, Daniella starts into the laundry, and Joel goes through the mail. The usual post-trip chore split. Benjamin—his chore is entertaining himself—goes up to his bedroom to sit in front of the computer.

Fifteen minutes later, Benjamin comes downstairs and says, "I found her."

"What?" Joel says, only half-listening. He is paying a bill.

"I found your daughter. Her name is Idzia Wilson, and I think she lives in Copenhagen. Either that or she lives in Ghana. But I'm pretty sure she's the Copenhagen one. Liesel was harder—there are a lot of Liesel Wilsons out there—but I'm pretty sure your Liesel is dead."

"What? What? On the computer?" Joel says, though Benjamin is plainly not talking about something he discovered in his LEGO box. Joel runs upstairs to Benjamin's computer. Wilson? She changed her name *again?* "Where?"

Benjamin points at the screen.

"Oh, God," Joel says.

As Joel negotiates the screen, he sees that Benjamin has not pulled up an obituary but a download from the website of a London theater.

> We regret to report that the Fletcher Theatre's house manager, Liesel Wilson, died 7 July after a long battle with breast cancer. Born and raised in Schenectady, New York, Wilson lived in Geneva, Morocco and Paris, before settling in London. Prior to coming to the Fletcher, she worked for L'Atelier Bleu in Provence, the Small Arms Survey in Geneva, and the American Language School in Morocco. She leaves behind her daughter, Idzia, and many friends from the theatre.

"Oh, God," Joel repeats. This is, quite clearly, "his" Liesel.

And what year was this written? He scans the document, finally finds a faint *August 2005* in the upper left corner.

Liesel, dead. He's never even considered the possibility. She'd have only been ... what? ... in her mid-forties?

And for her to lose a breast (breasts?) before she died. He'd loved her breasts, remembers even now the feel of them in his palms. He used to stand behind Liesel, wrap his arms around her. "I'll be your bra," he'd say. She never seemed to find this particularly amusing, but he didn't stop saying it. Now he wonders why.

Oh, he'd loved her. For all the anger he has felt over the years, he's never truly forgotten that, how madly he loved her. He thinks of one of the times they made love in their first week together, how afterward she dozed atop him, her hair spread out on his chest, he stroking the back of her head. She woke sleepily to say, "I'm so happy," then dozed again. A perfect moment, even with his retrospective knowledge of how things would turn out.

And what of the rest of what is here? Her previous employers? He Googles each place, sees that Atelier Bleu (although not L'Atelier, so maybe he has the wrong website) is a consulting and development organization for cultural and tourist activities, though it is not in Provence but Paris. What expertise did she have that would serve her there? The American Language School in Morocco teaches French, English, and Arabic, so he can imagine her working there. She could teach English presumably, and her French was OK. It had served them pretty well one weekend when they'd driven up to Quebec City for a getaway. But Small Arms Survey? Its website says it serves as "the principal international source of public information on all aspects of small arms and armed violence and as a resource for governments, policy-makers, researchers and activists." What does that even mean? Liesel was rabidly anti-gun, wanted (at one point) to work to overturn the Second Amendment, an idea that came to her one evening after a bad dinner party with one of Joel's colleagues, a man who wanted to show everyone his gun collection. "You'll never convince hunters to give up their guns," Joel had told her, and she had said (this was one of their typical disagreements), "Why don't you think I can do anything?" Now in light of the horrible news of the past year—school shootings, movie theater massacres, the continued derangement of the country—*he'd* like to work to overturn the Second Amendment.

Behind him, Benjamin says, "Are you through?"

Joel turns, surprised that Benjamin is still in the room. "What?" he says, disbelieving. Can his son actually want his computer back *now?*

"Reading, I mean. Are you through reading? I can show you Idzia if you are through."

As if Joel is incapable of the feat, Benjamin leans over his shoulder and types "Idzia Wilson" into Google and up come the choices.

Idzia Wilson—Imdb

Images for Idzia Wilson

Idzia Wilson on Vimeo

Idzia Wilson/andersenfilm.dk/ZoomInfo

www.seethemermaid.dk
    Junior Producer, Idzia Wilson

www.dalgaardfilm.dk
    Production Associate, Idzia Wilson

"Go downstairs," Joel tells Benjamin.

"No," Benjamin says. "I want to see. She's my sister, after all."

"Go. Down. Stairs," Joel says.

Daniella calls up a reprimand. "Easy," she says.

"Please," he says, his voice cracking. "Please, you've got to take him."

"You think you might say thank you. I found her for you," Benjamin says and stomps out of the room.

Joel doesn't know where to start. Images? In one she's a blond with straight short hair, in another she is wearing some sort of headdress, in another she's blurry, dark-haired, and all face. But he takes this in at the same moment he takes in . . . oh, God, she has her own website. He pulls it up and finds a CV, movie trailers, and quirky photographs. A man with a robot. A woman balancing a frying pan on her head. An egg, sitting in an egg cup, with a smiley face drawn on.

It's overwhelming. Joel starts reading and clicking and then stopping and re-clicking, as if he could get it all in his head in a single moment.

Joel goes back to "Images" and finds movie shots, posters or stills, presumably the projects on which she has worked. Then he comes to an image of her face, covered in blood. "Jesus Christ," he says.

A little bit of vomit comes up in his throat. The bloodied face is not a photograph, he realizes, but a video clip, and he clicks on it.

It's not real, thank God. It's quite clearly a movie clip, excellent production values, super-saturated colors, but still it's horrible.

In it, his daughter's hair is long and crimped in even waves, mermaid-style. She is wearing a gauzy white dress, and she is walking out of a gray pillowing cloud of smoke, directly toward the camera. She's on what's clearly an urban sidewalk. The smoke obscures what must be behind her, but you can make out enough to see that people are running toward whatever she has come from. She proceeds in a steady, oddly placid way, moving evenly forward, eyes not quite focused, hair blowing back, as if she is heading into the wind. There is blood not just on her face, but smeared on her dress and one calf. She comes closer and closer to the camera. Then when her torso fills the frame, she turns her palms forward and says, "Help me." The screen goes immediately black.

As a surgeon, Joel is no stranger to blood, but his face overheats. Is he going to *pass out?* He clicks the window closed, erases the browser's history, then goes to the bathroom to splash water on his face. He shouts in the direction of the stairs, "You can have your computer back."

In his bedroom, Joel pulls his laptop out of his work backpack and finds Idzia's website again. He clicks the "Contact" link at the top of the page. Up comes a screen into which he writes, "Idzia, I am your father. I have been looking for you for years, and I have just now found you. I would like to come to Copenhagen and meet you." The only true sentence is the first sentence. The others become true in the moment of composing them. "Please," he adds, "please say you will meet me."

A WEEK PASSES with no response, and then from iwilson@dalgaardfilm .dk comes this message: "OK."

AFTER THE BIKE-RENTAL SHOP, the day's plan is to go to the Louisiana Museum of Modern Art, north of the city. All the guidebooks say it is an "absolute must," so following their advice, the family will pedal to the nearest station and load their bikes onto a train car to make the trip. Daniella is charmed that this is even possible, that all Copenhagen's streets have bike lanes, that everywhere you look bikes outnumber cars. What's more, everyone has the same type of clunky old bike that Joel is now rolling her way.

Once outfitted, they ride to the station, joining those who cycle while wearing high heels, while talking on the phone, while smoking. The only thing these Danes don't seem to do on their bikes is wear a helmet.

The ride is brief, the road flat, but they are nonetheless covered in sweat by the time they find the right track and get situated with seats. "Everyone here is in their twenties," Joel observes, meaning not just in the car's interior but in the entire city.

"I know—where are the old people?" Daniella says.

"They killed them," Benjamin puts in cheerily.

"There are cultures where they do that, you know," she says, but then can't remember what cultures do, in fact, do that. The Eskimos? Don't they leave the elderly to die on icebergs?

No one responds. Which is fine. It's too hot to talk. No air conditioning in the car, and no windows that open. A black man in the corner is sitting on the floor with an open red bottle of wine in his hand. He takes a swig. He almost looks like someone overacting the part of the drunk man. He balances the bottle between his legs, so he can take off his socks. Then he puts them back on again.

Benjamin looks at Daniella, as if for protection, and Daniella shrugs. *It's OK.* A man near them says something in Danish.

"We only speak English," Daniella says.

"Oh," the man says, quickly switching into English. "He's my friend. He's harmless. He's just a jerk."

When they arrive at the stop, their entire car seems to disembark. Daniella has the feel of a religious pilgrimage. Others appear to be continuing on foot, which makes sense, since when Daniella, Benjamin, and Joel finally arrive, they realize the museum wasn't so far away that they needed bikes. Still it feels good to get there quickly, a relief to be embraced by the cool of the museum, though they immediately head through the gift shop and out to the grounds, a grassy plateau over the ocean, Sweden in the distance, no waves crashing, just a lovely still expanse of blue under the heat-bleached sky. Wow.

Daniella would *love, love* to get into that water, and there *are* people bathing below, but when her family takes a short path through the woods and toward the water, thinking they might dip their toes in, they see that there is a fence that separates the museum grounds from the sea. As beautiful as all this is, Daniella feels an uncustomary panic about the relentlessness of the heat. She believes in global warming, has long worried about it, supports all politicians who mean to do something helpful, but her worry escalates as they head back to the gallery spaces. Will summers be like this forever and ever into the future? My God, her generation is frying—*they're frying!*—their children. She does not tend to be overemotional, but she suddenly feels like crying. *What have they done?*

Back inside, she relaxes enough to focus on the art. Louisiana is just the sort of museum she likes: big rooms, oversized works, enough (but not too much) to look at in each room, text kept to a minimum; the image is the point. Benjamin hates going to museums, and she has assumed he'd sourly insist they leave after five minutes, but he's a pleasure as they go through the rooms. In one room he even says, "That's an Andy Warhol," and she wonders how he has come to knowledge of Warhol. She hasn't taught him. A giant spider sculpture in the corner of one gallery appeals to his imagination. "They're attacking!" he cries out and pretends to recoil in horror. And there's plenty for Daniella and Joel to love: Dubuffet, Philip Guston, and Louise Bourgeois. Benjamin puts his hands to his mouth and says, "Kssht! Tiger Two-Four. This is Kilo One-Three. Be advised. We have Art inbound. Kssht." The initial rooms end at a shallow flight of stairs that lead down to a large room with video art. A double-sided monitor hangs from a ceiling in the room's center, and on both sides, a film plays of an elaborate, and seemingly unending, Rube Goldberg machine with items bursting into flames and collapsing then rolling forward. Just the thing for Benjamin. Daniella watches with him but realizes she is close to tears. It's not just the heat. She feels such a profound sense of loss. She can't even locate what this is about. She's nervous about the upcoming meeting with Idzia, even as she's eager for it. At first she thought Joel should go alone, that Idzia and he should meet one-on-one, but after an initial email saying she would meet him—a tight-lipped "OK" to his initial query—Idzia had sent a second email that said, "OK. I'll meet you, but I'm bringing my family."

You can't read tone in email. Hasn't she said as much to her office colleagues when they are getting worked up about someone's high-handedness or rudeness? But this *does* seem cold, a jab at Joel, emphasis on the fact that he is not family, never will be, no matter what he thinks. Joel should have responded, "Good. I'd love to meet them." Instead he wrote, "Sounds good. I'll bring mine." So now the plan is for Joel, Benjamin, and Daniella to meet Idzia and . . . who? Her husband and child? Children? In-laws? She's in her mid-twenties, her mother is dead. She has no siblings. How much family can she have acquired?

Joel might have emailed, asked a few questions, explained himself, got the father-daughter ball rolling in cyberspace, but when Daniella suggested as much, Joel said, "I don't know. I just get a sense that . . . no . . . I've got to take her on her terms, and her terms are I'll see you when I see you."

Already Daniella senses the meeting will not be successful, though she doesn't really know what success means in this context. Loving hugs? Promises to stay in touch? Or simply a session in which Idzia doesn't bark accusations at Joel, for surely Idzia must have inherited Liesel's impression of Joel?

Daniella's ready to move on from the Rube Goldberg video, but Benjamin insists on staying, until Joel taps Benjamin's shoulder and says, "Come on. There's something I want to show you." They disappear into an installation room around the corner.

In two days, Daniella, Joel, and Benjamin will meet Idzia at Café Wilder. "How about we meet here?" Idzia had written in an email and attached a link to the place. She added, "August 19th? 6:00?" It was the third email from her, the most loquacious. Joel, reading it in his study, forwarded it to Daniella with a note appended: "I told her yes. Love, Your Cyber-husband." He was at home upstairs, and she was downstairs when he sent the message. Daniella clicked on the link. Up came a painting of a naked woman, sitting on a floor, surrounded by a hundred open (and presumably consumed) wine bottles. As for the menu, it was a lot fancier than something Daniella pictured a young woman suggesting: wild boar and foie gras, an appetizer of "beetroot, yellow beet, candy beet, applepuré, cream and cress." Perhaps Idzia wanted to stick it to her dad by going to an expensive place?

"Mom, Mom," Benjamin calls. "Come here."

He waves her into the next room where there is a long line for an installation into which people can only enter two at a time. "Can I make up a story?" he says as they take their place in line. On two of the walls behind them, a music video is playing, the refrain of which (*I . . . don't want to fall . . . in love . . . with you*) Daniella vaguely recognizes, but in her memory the song is sung by a man instead of the slightly off-key, haunting female voice that she hears now. As she remembers it, the song was about sexual desire, now it seems bigger, more complicated. She turns and sees that the accompanying film works in a tricky way with two neighboring walls, so that duplicate images dovetail and disappear into the conjoined corner. As she watches, an enlarged and twirling eyeball resolves itself into a series of underwater images: a toy car falling through water to coral, a submerged boy holding a hand mirror, a female swimmer, and a plastic cup on the ocean floor. Everything is recognizable but quickly dissolves, with the manipulation of the camera, into pattern and abstraction. "Let's watch that," Daniella says, pointing. "This line's too long."

"No, Mom," Benjamin says. "You're going to love this. I promise."

"OK," she says, "we'll stay," but as at the bike store, she feels impatient. Is she drawn to the water images because water, on a hot day, is always a pleasure? Or does the intense melancholy of the song reflect, in an unsettling but satisfying way, her troubling mood?

"Can I make up a story?" Benjamin repeats.

"Sure," she says. She can never quite understand why he asks. The answer is always yes, though typically he launches into a pretend action drama to which she can't pay attention. Her mind will drift to chores she has to do, what she might cook for dinner, a task left unfinished at work. She will try to pay attention, to catch bits, so she can ask a question or two—*What kind of cyborg?*—but it's no good; it's as if he's speaking softly, and she can hear if she strains, but eventually the effort is too arduous, so she gives up. He catches on inevitably. *Mom, you're not paying attention.*

Now, though, she does listen—"And then the members of the Collective have three classes. There are the vipers, the drones, and the overlords"—but she keeps looking over her shoulder at the video installation.

"Don't *look* at that," he demands.

"OK, OK, I'm not looking."

But still she hears it. *What a wicked thing to do,* sings the soprano, not quite reaching the high notes, *to make me dream of you.* Daniella flashes on herself as a younger woman, to a year when she had a hopeless crush on the manager of a bookstore where she worked. She has realized since that he was probably gay, likely just starting to experiment with boys, though he was *trying* to stay heterosexual. (He'd asked her out once.) It was the beginning of the AIDS era, before people knew to protect themselves. In retrospect, it's clear that she was profoundly lucky nothing ever happened between them, but, oh, how she had ached for him at the time.

Benjamin and she have reached the front of the line. "There's water inside, so don't step on it," Benjamin instructs. The door swings open, and two people step out. Benjamin and Daniella advance into a dark, mirror-lined room in which hang hundreds (well, it seems hundreds, given the reflections) of balls of colored light. "There's the water," Benjamin says, pointing to either side of the narrow walkway on which they stand. "Can I touch it?"

She loves his pleasure, feels buoyed out of her mood. "If you want," she says. The skin of his finger touches the skin of the water in a way that strikes Daniella as magical. Perhaps this bit of misbehavior is intended as part of the experience of the installation?

When they step back outside, Daniella finally has a chance to watch the video. It's called "Sip My Ocean," and it immediately brings Daniella back to a dark place. Why is it so heartbreaking? The images are beautiful. Why is it all getting to her? That boy from the bookstore once faux-slapped her face. He wasn't trying to hit her. He was acting out a story in which he'd slapped someone else. In the story, he'd actually struck the man, but with Daniella, he'd stopped short at the last minute and run the back of his hand down her cheek. A second voice in the song's background starts to yell the lyrics in a screechy, furious voice, horrible-sounding. Daniella didn't hear this before. The refrain repeats. *I. Don't want to fall. In love. With you.* Of course, you only say that when you know you *are* going to fall in love. You only say that when you are going to fall in love, and the person you are going to fall in love with is not going to love you back.

"Mom," Benjamin tugs at her arm.

"Just a sec." She turns to find Joel at a set of stairs leaving the gallery and tells him to watch Benjamin; she needs to go to the bathroom. She wends her way back through the museum till she finds herself in front of a mirror, splashing water on her face. She dries off, closes her eyes, opens them, looks at her aging features, presses her fingers to her cheeks, in the classic posture of woe. *Enough,* she says to herself.

Obviously, it is Idzia who has made the installation so painfully powerful, for Daniella knows she is going to love her. She has known that ever since she has known there was an Idzia to love. Daniella is going to love Idzia, and Idzia is not going to want even one little sip of those waters.

10

SOURCE MATERIAL

SHE HAS THE IDEA that she still screams in her sleep. She doesn't know for sure, and Nikolaj, her roommate, never says anything, or anything directly, though in the morning, he often asks, "You OK?"

"Yeah, sure, of course. Why?"

"Nothing," Nikolaj says. "Just want to make sure you're OK."

"I am," she responds, a little defensive, but her throat is often sore. *God, how loud was she?* "I'm good. *You're* good. Right?" As if they are not talking about what they are talking about.

"Oh, yeah," Nikolaj says. "I'm great. Can I make you a coffee?" He lifts the aluminum espresso pot. She smiles. "Coffee sounds grand," then, "Mind if I shower after?"

"No problem."

Showering in the apartment is a complex business. Actually, the apartment, in its impoverishment, is a complex business. Two bedrooms: Idzia in one, Nikolaj in the other. No communal space, just the galley kitchen and the mini-bathroom: a small toilet, a tiny sink with a hose that rests on a hook over the mirror. Showering involves the hose and spraying water everywhere. It can't be done with the bathroom door closed, so Idzia and Nikolaj make a point of staying in their respective rooms when they hear water running. The intimacy of avoidance makes them intensely aware of each other's bodies, though they don't know each other that well. Earlier in the year, friends of friends put them together as roommates. For a long while the enforced closeness didn't matter. Nikolaj spent most nights at his girl-friend's, and Idzia spent long days at work, frequently going out with friends in the evening. But since the start of the summer, Nikolaj has been in the apartment most nights. Idzia assumes there's been a breakup, though Nikolaj doesn't seem downhearted. To date, the attitude they have taken with each other is that of convivial strangers who sometimes end up at the same place: a party after a ten-hour film screening at the Empire, a gathering at the Film School, or their kitchen.

But something has changed.

Last week, Idzia woke from a terrible dream to register Nikolaj stroking her back as if she was a little girl. "It's OK. It's OK," he said, and "Ssshh now. Ssshh." *Had* she been screaming? She wasn't screaming now, but he kept saying, "You're OK. You're OK." Then his hand stilled. He stopped talking. After a few moments of silence, Nikolaj kissed the top of her head and went back to his room. It was more of a paternal than a romantic kiss. If Nikolaj knew she was awake, he didn't give any indication. Idzia didn't know what to make of it.

IDZIA KNOWS NIKOLAJ KNOWS what happened to her. Probably Katie told him. Aside from Bertie back in London, Katie is the only one who knows about both parts of Idzia's life, the one before the subway bombing and the one after.

"How'd you end up in Copenhagen?" Nikolaj asked one of the first nights they were roommates.

"I kind of followed Katie here. She did a semester in London, and that's how we met." Nikolaj knows Katie, too. Everyone in the film business knows each other.

"Oh, are you two . . ." he made a rocking gesture with his fingers.

"No, no. I like boys. Katie's just a really good friend."

Sometime later, Nikolaj said, "Saw Katie tonight."

"Yeah?"

"At Bakken." Bakken is a bar in the old Vesterbro meatpacking district where people sometimes meet up.

"She told me a little about your life in London, so . . . I guess I wanted to say I was sorry."

"Thanks."

"And if you ever need . . ."

"No, thanks, I don't," she said, cutting him off.

He nodded and said, "Bar made me smell like cigarettes. I'm going to take a shower, if it's OK."

"Right," she said and went into her bedroom and closed the door.

After that first back rub, Nikolaj has been coming every night. He says what he said the first time, "Shhh. Shhh. You're OK. You're OK." She is always deep in a nightmare when he comes—not just nightmares about the bombing and immediate aftermath, but about parts of the recovery, in particular about the pieces of glass that worked their way to the surface of her skin months after she left the hospital. Each night, Idzia wakes at Nikolaj's touch, but always pretends she is asleep. It is nice, his hand. She has that little-girl feel she used to have when she still lived in Paris and her mother would bathe her and put her in the blue nightgown with little daisies, and she'd go to sleep while it was still light out, the sheets tight, the sense that things were OK, even if she was in a new apartment and her mom was with a new boyfriend.

In the morning, neither Nikolaj nor she acknowledges what has happened. But everything between them feels loaded. "Going to work?" he says one day as she is dropping her iPhone into her bag.

"Yep," she says. "That's what I do." Too much, her previous boyfriends complained. She worked too much, didn't have enough time for them.

"You enjoy it, will you?"

"OK, yeah. I mean I usually do, but OK," as if he has given her some meaningful instructions.

She works for a production company that shares a building with a few other small production companies. They all have their own offices but share a kitchen, editing room, meeting room, and screening room. It's in Christianshavn near where she lives in Amagerbro, a five-minute bike ride.

The evening of the morning that Nikolaj tells her to enjoy work, Idzia stays late, finishing off details for a shoot currently taking place in Aarhus, a city that is a lot easier (and cheaper) to film in than Copenhagen. (It's not convenient, though, being three hours west by train.) Most of the people in Idzia's company are on set—or starting their August vacation—so she's alone in the office. Finally, she turns off her computer and bikes home to what she assumes is an empty apartment. The lights are off, at any rate. "Nikolaj," she whispers softly at his bedroom door, but there is no answer. A relief. She has never whispered this way before. What would he make of it now? She makes herself a sandwich, eats it while standing in the dark kitchen, spying on neighbors in the building next door. Then she washes up and goes to bed for the horror show, which is what she calls her dream life (though only to Katie).

Her sleeping mind is in no way original. There are long tunnels she can't escape, buildings that fall on top of her, bloody bodies that must be climbed over; there is her own hand accidentally reaching into a blob of blood and tissue that was once a face; there is her mother grown into a hideous, out-sized opera star with a beach-ball head on a pipe-cleaner-thin neck. "Is this the one you want?" a woman at a fancy dress store says, but what she holds up is not an outfit but a severed leg. "I don't want it," Idzia screams. "Maybe this?" the woman says and tosses her an eyeball. Idzia screams, wakes before the eyeball strikes her cheek.

It takes her, as always, a moment to get oriented. Where is she? A room, *Yes, her own room in Amagerbro.* But she is not alone. Nikolaj is in the bed with her. She starts up. "What?"

"It's just me," he says, unthreatening, and lowers her cheek to his chest. As before, he strokes her hair and says, "You're OK." But it is not as before, because he is *in the bed* with her.

Oh, that eyeball. She feels herself start to pant, commands herself: *Forget it.* "Easy now," he says. "Just breathe."

"OK," she whispers.

For a second she thinks he hasn't heard, but then he says, "All right. You can go to sleep. Just sleep now. It's OK." She feels his bare chest, senses he is wearing boxers. She is wearing an old T-shirt and underwear, her typical nighttime outfit. Why is he here? Is he just trying to comfort her, or does he want to be her lover? She thinks to move a leg to find out if he has an erection, but she doesn't want him to intuit what she is doing. His hair-stroking hand slows and then stops altogether. He must be asleep. Idzia lies wakefully on his chest, trying to time her breathing to his. His inhalations and exhalations are longer, but she extends each of her breaths, adapts to the rhythm of his breathing. *First I'll do this with you,* she thinks peaceably, *and then,* she addresses the sparse trees outside her brick building, *we'll work this whole oxygen and carbon dioxide thing out with you.* She starts to drowse, feeling the looping efforts of Nikolaj, herself, and the trees, a Buddhist mellow overtaking her, but then a wasp buzzes at the window, and she abruptly wakes, thinks, "What now?"

IN THE MORNING, he is gone from the bed and their apartment. Probably he has an early-morning shoot. He is a cinematographer, recently graduated from the National Film School of Denmark—"that golden cradle," as Katie calls it. Soon he'll be able to afford something nicer than this, Idzia supposes. Soon he might be working for Zentropa or Nimbus or somewhere equally impressive.

Nikolaj doesn't look like a typical Dane. He is tall, broad-shouldered, fair-skinned but dark-haired with a short, cropped beard. Idzia has always liked him, found him boyishly energetic, friendly, in the realm of handsome, certainly talented, though also perhaps too committed to art. He seems like the kind of person who would refuse to film a commercial. Idzia hates that kind of impracticality. He's not snobby, though. High-minded, but definitely not snobby. The books on his shelves are about filmmakers, photographers, and maverick entrepreneurs. She's never heard him bad-mouth anyone. Still she hasn't really let herself consider him sexually till this week. Does she want that to change? Would *she* like to sleep with *him?* She probably would, if she didn't live with him. Would she want to get involved with him— with anyone—at this point?

At least she has the luxury of time to think this morning, as she is not going into the office. Or not right away. No one's there, so she's agreed to meet up with Katie at Bankerat at 10:00 a.m. Katie has a meeting at the Danish Film Institute from 9:00 a.m. to 10:00 a.m. She's going to find out what people in the Film Workshop think of the script she's working on, the one that's about Idzia. "Not *about you*," Katie corrects, when Idzia describes the project this way. "Inspired by the circumstances of your life. If I wanted it to be *about* you, I'd do a documentary. This is fiction."

"Right," Idzia says. "I get how it works. I'm source material."

Biking to Bankerat, the day already too hot, Idzia tries to come up with some joke for Katie, something where she says, "What does everyone at the Film Institute think of me, I mean of Source Material?" But the joke doesn't coalesce into anything amusing, and her head gets crowded with questions about Nikolaj. Does *he* want to sleep with *her?* Idzia assumes so. He hasn't touched her in a sexual way though. He's held her. He's put her head on his chest. You wouldn't *get in bed* with someone if you weren't expecting or offering something, would you?

Would you?

Idzia has no idea. The Danes are so odd about sex. They do it because they want to do it. They take their clothes off because there is sun in the sky or a beach nearby. They don't seem to attach the meaning to sex and nudity that Idzia does. Once, Idzia worked as a production design assistant for a Claymation porn about a swingers' club. All through the project, no one commented on what the film was *about*. You'd think it concerned Claymation figures going to the supermarket. Even the finished film seemed oddly unaware of its own content. There was something almost cute about it, right down to the gang bangs and the "oops" look of disappointment that one character has when he realizes that he's not going to be able to fuck a woman hanging by chains, her legs and arms spread, though he's waited patiently in line for this chance. Oh, no! Clay eyebrows worm in distress. He can't get it up!

Idzia's far too early for her appointment with Katie, so she locks her bike and takes a short walk in Kongens Have. This has always been her favorite of the city parks. She knows some people find it overly ordered, but that is what Idzia likes about it: the tree-lined paths, the neatly contained plants and shrubs. She doesn't know what's planted here. When people ask her what kind of tree or flower something is, she is stumped after she offers the color.

There's shade in the park, but it's not as restful as usual, simply because it's so hot. She wishes she hadn't worn a long-sleeved shirt today. She's got a camisole on underneath, but it's really underwear, not a shirt. Who really cares? Certainly no one here. She doesn't mean in the park; she means in the country, maybe in the world. Who cares how Idzia Wilson comports herself? Why nobody. It's not a happy thought. Still it brings relief, at least from the heat. She takes off her shirt, pretends not to worry that she's walking around, essentially, in a bra and a tissue. She finds her bike—a dull orange that makes it easy to locate, even in a snarl of them—and finishes her ride to Bankerat.

THOUGH IDZIA IS "MERELY" Source Material for Katie's script, she is also star of the single scene that Katie has shot. Granted, everyone involved in the production of that scene was a friend of Katie's. No money to do it, so everyone loaned effort or equipment. This is how it is for young filmmakers in Copenhagen, and the difficulty makes the community close. Maybe people compete here, like they do everywhere, but Idzia's not aware of it, if they do. What she notices most are people offering favors, or people saying, over beers, "We've got to do something together sometime." What they mean, often enough, is that they should collaborate on a ten-minute film that no one will see save the other people in the city who are producing ten-minute films that no one will see. But with Katie's scene, the favor is a little different, since Idzia plays herself. She plays herself at one of the worst moments of her life. But the final version is a little like the Claymation porn. No one talks about the content, which is of a shell-shocked, bloodied woman walking on a London street. They just say it's wonderful: the effects are amazing, the cinematography brilliant, Idzia's eerie and perfect. The produced scene won Katie a grant for script development from the Danish Film Institute as well as (just last month) admission into Super 16, a student-run film school in Copenhagen. Idzia thinks Super 16 is even cooler than the National Film School of Denmark, which is so ridiculously competitive and which rejected Katie in any case. Super 16 is more "Fuck the rules," which is just what Katie likes.

As Idzia parks her bike at Bankerat, her sense of the morning's agenda is clear. She and Katie will debrief about what the Danish Film Institute thinks of what Katie has done with the script development money, and then Idzia will dump her personal life in Katie's lap. There are people sitting, as there always seem to be, in the windows of Bankerat, looking out at the street. Idzia recognizes a man, his body covered in tattoos, his shaved head topped with a shallow porkpie hat, but she doesn't remembers how she knows him, recalls only that she doesn't like him for some reason. No customers are inside Bankerat. The usual ghoulish stuff decorates the walls: gargoyles and "real live dead stuffed animals," as Katie calls them, creatures wearing tuxedoes and evening wear. Heading first to the bathroom to wash her sweaty face, Idzia passes the small basement jail cell that is filled with stuffed animals and the glassed-in alcove that has a gopher in boxing gloves. Katie thinks Bankerat's décor is funny in a way that Idzia doesn't, but Idzia likes how reliably friendly the servers always are. Plus they always have *The Guardian,* along with *Politiken* at the bar. Once she is back upstairs, she takes *The Guardian* and a cup of coffee to the corner table where she and Katie typically sit.

SETTLING IN, Idzia fishes in her bag for her iPhone. She hasn't checked her email yet today. She gropes about but doesn't find it. Has she left it at home? She starts to take things out of her bag—her bike key, her wallet, her notebook, an opaque container with tampons, lipstick, a toothbrush, and toothpaste. There's plenty more to go. Once Katie peeked in her purse and said, "Just looking for a snack. You've got everything else in here."

"Hey!" Katie calls from the door. She's arrived atypically late. "I'm sorry. It was The Meeting with No End. I'd have left if I could." She starts her sentence in Danish but finishes in English. Idzia speaks Danish but not as well as Katie speaks English.

"It's OK," Idzia says. "I needed some time just to sit here and perspire."

Katie sniffs a laugh.

"I'm doing a really good job at it."

"I'll hug you anyway," Katie says and gives her an embrace and a kiss.

Idzia shoves everything on the table back into her bag. She'll look for the phone later.

"Good news and bad news," Katie says, but she is smiling, so whatever the bad news is, it doesn't seem to be bothering her.

"And I've got news, too. About Nikolaj."

"Really?" Katie says in a considered way, as if she's instantly aware that the news must be of the carnal variety. "Let me go get something."

Katie comes back with a refrigerated bottled juice, which she rolls over her forehead. "So fucking hot."

"I know."

"I can't decide if I want to drink this or go swimming in it."

"So what did they say?"

"No, no," Katie says. "You first. What's the news about Nikolaj?"

"No, you go."

"OK, then," Katie says, bobbing her head in an eager way that Idzia has always liked. "They love the trailer."

Katie has taken to calling the one scene they've filmed "the trailer," though originally she filmed it because she thought it was the movie's pivotal moment. "And it's your pivotal moment, too," Katie had said, back when they were first talking about it. Katie was convinced that acting would be therapeutic for Idzia. Katie didn't want her to act out the immediate aftermath of the bombing—when Idzia had blacked out briefly then woken to moaning and smoke and distant shouts—and she didn't think she should relive when she'd had to climb over bodies and follow an instructing voice down the subway tunnel to the station. Katie thinks the therapeutic moment is the one after, when Idzia asked for help. She thinks that is when Idzia's life turned around.

Katie's wrong, but Idzia doesn't tell her that. If she did, Katie would say that Idzia is just in denial.

What really happened is that after Idzia escaped the tunnel, she emerged from the station and kept going. She was heading vaguely in the direction of home, but the idea of destination was almost wholly absent; she was just leaving where she'd been. Her legs hurt, her arms, her back—she knew she was all cut up—but she kept walking in a straight line for several blocks. People must have been looking at her—a young woman with blood smeared all over her, that would attract attention—but she has no memories of solicitous concern. She doesn't even know why she finally chose to stop, when and where she did, why she turned her palms forward, and said, "Help me."

The people she'd stopped in front of were Americans in town to see their son perform at a comedy club. They didn't even know where a hospital was, but they figured it out, and they stayed with Idzia till Bertie came. "Sweetheart," Bertie said, taking her hand and stroking it. "I have some very bad news."

Later, Bertie said she only told her at that moment because she didn't think it would really be a shock—Idzia knew her mother was dying; could it be a surprise that she was now dead?—and she felt she had to tell her right away. A terrible miscalculation. Idzia screamed. One long loud top-of-the-lungs scream, and then as soon as she was done, Idzia took a breath and did it again. Nurses rushed in. She could have stopped. Idzia knew she had the power to stop even as she was shrieking, but she didn't want to. It wasn't the news so much that started her yelling, but Bertie's insistence that Idzia couldn't see her mother one last time. "You're in no shape to leave," Bertie said. And then, "You don't want to see a dead body." This in a flat voice, indicating that she'd seen plenty in her lifetime.

So Idzia screamed. Later, she wondered why she didn't tell Bertie she'd just *seen* plenty of dead bodies, and so, lucky her, was actually *prepped* for seeing another one.

In the hospital, Idzia expected Bertie to react to her yelling. Idzia wasn't so out of her head that she wasn't aware of what she was doing. But Bertie sat quietly, not even seeming to have to *endure* it—patiently waiting her out. Then she said, "At the moment, your resources for dealing with pain are unequal to your pain. The challenge, for the rest of your life, will be to change that."

Idzia looked at Bertie with hate, then tried the screaming thing again.

It didn't change anything. It stripped the vocal chords. It was all damage and stupidity, but it still got Idzia what she wanted, which was a chance to protest, useless as that protest obviously was.

IN BANKERAT, Katie continues her report, "And they were so impressed with you. Just the way you look in that scene, how you walk toward the camera. And they liked how we did the smoke, though they said there wouldn't have been any in the street, after the bomb, because that would have all been underground."

"Oh," Idzia says. It is true that her only memory of smoke is of the underground, though her sense of herself is of having walked directly out of smoke into the clear light of day.

"Also I explained that you were in the trailer, but that you weren't going to be the actress. They wanted you to be—they were enthusiastic about you—but I explained how you couldn't."

Idzia has the idea that Katie wants her to offer to play herself in the film. She'll never do that. Something occurs to her. "But wait, you already *knew* they liked this part of the film."

Katie nods. It's what got their interest in the first place. It's why they gave her the grant.

"What do they think about the new stuff?"

Idzia means the actual script. Not the scene, but what Katie's managed to build around it.

"They don't like the way the film jumps all around in time."

"It does?" Katie hasn't told Idzia what's in the script. She has an idea, of course, from the questions Katie has asked—"Remind me again, why did you and your mom go to Geneva?" "What was her job in Paris?"—but something in Idzia has been eager not to have the specifics. (The answer to Katie's question is always the same: Liesel was following a man or she had the idea that something—working for a peace organization, baking cakes—would be interesting.)

"Yeah, and they don't like the idea of leading with the trailer. They want the whole thing to be chronological, with the bombing in the dead center. And they don't like the Copenhagen section."

"Ha! They don't like my life!" Idzia is amused, not offended. *She* likes her life. She doesn't need anyone else to.

"It's not your life! It's fiction."

"Right," Idzia says. "So what do they want in the Copenhagen section?"

"Flashbacks. PTSD. All that cliché stuff. One person—not the director, don't worry—said she should have, like, a sexual addiction problem. Always needing to get close to people now that everyone she was close to is gone."

"I'll get to work on that."

"Oh, shut up," Katie says. "I agree I need something in the Copenhagen section but not that. For me this is a movie about redemption, and it's not because it's you. I just believe in my character. I said that in the meeting and one of the people there said, 'Feelings porn.'"

Idzia bristles. She's heard people say that of the Danish filmmaker Susanne Bier, who makes movies that Idzia adores beyond reason, though some people in the industry feel she's emotionally manipulative. Idzia was ready to brand it all sexism—look at how everyone in the business insists Lars Von Trier is a genius, even though no one she knows actually likes *watching* his films—but then she saw Bier's most recent film, and it was so terribly sentimental that she felt mad at Bier. How could she make the very film that the idiots had accused her of making? How could she become what *they* said she was, instead of what *Idzia* said she was?

"So anyway. That's the big news. They like it. They want to see the script again. They want me to reorder things so it's chronological, and they want me to figure out a better ending. But the other news is that there's someone at Super 16 who thinks he wants to produce this."

"Wow."

"So moving ahead, moving ahead."

Idzia checks her watch. "I should . . ."

"Not so fast. What's up with Nikolaj?" Katie asks, but she checks her watch as well.

Suddenly Idzia doesn't want to talk about it. Why had she supposed she'd want to confide? "Oh, nothing. Broke up with his girlfriend, I think. He's around a lot now. I actually have to *share* the shared apartment."

Katie says, "You've got to marry up." Katie's partner does statistical analysis for the Danish Producers' Association, and Katie is the assistant to the Oresund film commissioner. They have what no one in the business seems to have: two real salaries, and with that they've managed a small but beautiful apartment on the water in Vesterbro.

"Marrying up is the plan," Idzia says. But it's just a joke.

"Come swimming," Katie says. "Tonight? Why don't you? It's so nice." The water, she means. "And it's been so beastly."

"I will." She checks her watch. "I could get there by 7:00?"

"Perfect. We'll get dinner after."

They kiss good-bye. Outside, by her bike, Idzia fumbles in her bag and finally finds her iPhone. It's too bright on the sidewalk to check emails, so she moves to the shade across the street. The messages pop up, from this one and that one. A friend who is an intern at Zentropa; the director of the Aarhus film, who needs her to get fake license plates for the parked vehicles in the chase scene they are about to film; her boss who wants the jpeg of a film poster from last year; and Joel Pearlman, who has this to say: "Idzia, I am your father. I have been looking for you for years, and I have just now found you. I would like to come to Copenhagen and meet you. Please, please say you will meet me."

"Fuck me," Idzia says out loud.

"Happy to," says a young guy walking by, but then he waves his hand in a "Good day, good luck dealing with whatever you're dealing with" manner.

Idzia runs across the street and into the bar. Maybe Katie will still be there? *Oh, Jesus Christ. What is she supposed to do with this?* But no, Bankerat is empty. She goes back to her bike, fiddles with the lock, and then hears Katie. "Seven, don't forget," she says from where she is standing, farther down the sidewalk with her own bike.

"Oh, Katie! Look at this," Idzia says and goes toward her, phone extended.

Katie peers at the screen, using one hand to shield the sun, then looks up at Idzia.

"I mean what the fuck is this?"

Katie pulls her into a hug. "It's the end to our movie!" she says glibly.

"No, fuck you, seriously. What am I supposed to do with this?"

"You're supposed to say yes," Katie says. "How can you not?"

BUT SHE DOESN'T SAY YES. Later in the day, when she's in the office, doing a PR plan for a small animation film, her boss calls to say that they need someone else to come out to Aarhus to stand in for a location manager who's fallen ill. They are doing a street scene, and one of the residents says he's going to obstruct the shoot. They've got all the permits, and they've offered to put the residents up in a hotel, but this man doesn't care. "I could come," she offers. The only job she really hates on set is that of "continuity girl," the person who makes sure that everything in a scene—the pillows, the hair, the lighting—is the same from shoot to shoot. It's ridiculously stressful. She'd rather be a runner and fetch everyone coffee than do that. She'd rather call the police and have them come deal with this neighborhood bully than do that.

"Idzia. That would be great. Do you mind?" It's just for a week, he says, and he will put her up at the Hotel Royal. "It's where Madonna stays," he adds.

"She'll probably want to meet me," Idzia says flatly. "Tell that bitch I'm not available."

Her boss laughs. He's not really putting her up, Idzia knows. He'd never have the money to offer her anything other than the chance to crash on a friend's couch. But the production company with which they are working has endless cash. The only downside is that for the week Idzia is in Aarhus, they will be filming a car chase from 8:00 in the evening to 5:00 in the morning.

Idzia closes the office, packs some things in her apartment, and bikes to the Central Station for the next train to Aarhus.

Ordinarily there is no way Idzia would sign up for action-movie work. In her limited experience, there's nothing duller to film. As the week unfolds, her fears are borne out. A typical night: after three hours of setup and prep and people running around and nothing really happening, the director does two rehearsals then a five-second take of a car screeching down a sidewalk with another in pursuit. Three more hours pass and the car chase moves ten feet down the road. It's beyond tedious, save for those actual seconds when the cars spin out, and then Idzia, who has never enjoyed action films, is surprised by her own excitement. As for the difficult neighbor, he finally agreed to take the production company up on its offer of lodging.

Idzia and Nikolaj have never had the sort of relationship where they would report on their whereabouts. Though she is behaving normally by not giving him a heads-up about her trip, she feels strange. Should she have left a note?

She gets an email from Katie: "What happened to swimming?" Idzia types back an apology: "I forgot!" but she didn't. She never forgets anything that has to do with Katie. The part of Idzia that has a nonsexual crush on Katie, that has loved her since they were teenagers, has never gone away. Idzia has only pretended to forget, because for the first time in her life she is mad at Katie. "It's the end to our movie!" What is she thinking? Has she forgotten that Idzia is friend first, source material second? Idzia waits a few days and emails Katie again. "I'm not going to say yes." She means to her father's request for a visit.

"You have to say yes," Katie emails back. "You don't say no to something like this."

"Why not?" Idzia types.

"Because this is your father, and meeting him might be good and it might be bad, but whatever it is, you will learn something, and when you have a chance to learn something, you take it."

Idzia doesn't respond. Instead, when the week in Aarhus is up, she emails her father: "OK."

She takes the train back to Copenhagen, gets off at Central Station, but can't find her bike. Granted, there are hundreds outside, but she knows where she has left hers, and she has purposely chosen an ugly *orange* bike, because though its gears barely shift, it is easy to spot. Someone has stolen it. Someone has stolen her bike. It's worthless, she knows. But not to her.

IF NIKOLAJ COMES into her bedroom the night of her return, Idzia doesn't register it. The second night she can't fall asleep, aware she is waiting to see what will happen. She knows he has been home because there's water all over the bathroom. The third night, he doesn't come. Perhaps this only means she has been quiet: no nightmares. On the fourth night she lies in bed, eyes tearing, willing him to come, unable to sleep. She gets up and looks out the window. The brick building next door is identical to her own, and she spies on the lives there, as if watching the movies. She is curious about the man who always sits bare-chested at his dining room table. She assumes he is gay and lives with his partner—the two have a habit of standing on the balcony together whenever they are dressed for an evening out—but perhaps her suppositions are wrong, because there is also a woman who appears to live with them. A different apartment is occupied by a man whose gigantic computer screen features a spiraling screensaver. He sits in front of it at all hours of the day and night. Idzia climbs back into bed, and her eyes start to tear again. If only he would come to her. And then she hears Katie's voice, in her head, as clear as anything: "Oh, Idzia, honey. Go to him."

His door is closed, and she knocks. She cracks the door, says, "Nikolaj?" He grunts, turns over. She has plainly woken him. She walks the few steps to his bed. "It's me," she says, and he just reaches out his left hand for hers, uses the right to raise his sheet, the span enough—he has the same monastic twin bed that she does—so that she can slip in next to him. She thinks she should speak, but before she can, he starts to kiss her, rolling her under him as he does, his fingers behind and in front of her ears, then up into her hair, the kissing as satisfying and passionate as any she's ever done, his erection, no question now, poking against his boxers, and his hands pushing along her body until after a long while she feels one finger slipping into her and then a second. When he finally fucks her, it is with such focus that she goes a little out of her head, loses time, recovers herself at some moment when she realizes they've worked their way horizontally across the bed, and she is falling off head first, needs her palms to keep from slipping onto the floor. But she doesn't quite want to heave herself back onto the bed, a thrill in just having been fucked into this position, at having her throat extended, and him still pushing into her. "Nikolaj," she says finally, though, since she is about to slip completely off the mattress, and he sweeps an arm under her, pulls her whole torso back under him.

"Can I come in you?" he says, so passionately that it feels like he's saying, "I love you," and her own clinical "I'm on the Pill" would make her feel mean if it wasn't followed by the pulsing of him inside her. He drops on top of her, lies there as he falls out of her and his breathing steadies. The weight steady, then uncomfortable. She wonders if he is asleep.

But just when she assumes he must be, he says, "Now, you."

"It's OK," she says. She's always found it hard to work up interest after the big drama of a man's coming.

"No," he says, almost angry, "you," and works his kisses down her stomach and between her legs, licking there till she finally says, "I can't," because it's tough for her to come with a man, and sometimes faking it is just too exhausting. He says, "Touch yourself," which she does as he again puts his fingers inside her. He kisses her breasts, moves over her, kisses one side of her neck and then another till she does finally come, gripping his torso with her legs, holding him tightly there. "You did it," he says, as if he has intuited that having an orgasm is hard for her.

"*You* did it," she says.

He laughs, a single sniff of a laugh, kisses her right nipple, and says, "When can I do it again?"

It is 3:00 in the morning, maybe 4:00. "Whenever you want," she says.

IN THE MORNING—a Saturday, no need to rise early—they sit cross-legged with coffee cups on his bed. She says that she went to Aarhus because she didn't want to deal with stuff here.

"Me?" he says.

"No, no. I had a sort of tiff with Katie. It wasn't quite a tiff." She explains the situation with her father, the upcoming meeting, but Nikolaj completely misunderstands what she is trying to say.

"I can film it. You don't need to worry about getting a cameraman."

"No, no, I don't want to *film* it . . ."

"But if you film it, you'll know what happened."

She looks at him.

"Don't you have that thing when you are going through what is a really important moment, but it's all so intense that afterward you can't even remember what happened, just the weird little bits? We'll film it, and then you'll know exactly what it is."

"Filming it will make it weirder. No one is normal in front of a camera."

"That's not true. You know that. After a while, people forget the camera is there."

Idzia doesn't say anything.

"Or don't film it. Just have your friends come along, so they can help you remember what happened after it happens."

"Like you and Katie?"

"Sure, or whoever. Whoever you'd want to have with you. The important people in your life."

Idzia sits with this thought for a moment. The important people in her life. Katie, of course. And Bertie. Are there only two? She has a lot of friends, but maybe they are the only ones who are truly important.

"I guess if a bus hits me today, a lot of people would come to the funeral, but Katie and Bertie would be the ones to bury me."

"Who's Bertie?"

"Friend from London. Friend of my mum's. I used to live with her."

"Would she come, if you asked her to?"

"Bertie? Yeah, she'd do anything for me."

"Hit-by-a-bus litmus test. Good as any. So they're your family. You can just tell your father you'll meet him, but you're going to bring your family."

Idzia considers.

"OK," she says. And though it is far too early in whatever she and Nikolaj are going to become or not become, she says, "And can I bring you? You but not your camera, would that be all right?"

He must not like feelings porn himself, because he says, "Maybe, I'll have to ask my handler. My schedule gets pretty booked up. I'm really in demand."

"Shut up," she says.

And he does.

11

CAFÉ WILDER

CAFÉ WILDER IS NOT the posh place Joel and Daniella initially sup-posed, but a corner café favored (according to the guidebooks) by artists and intellectuals. Despite the high-end menu, it is small, somewhat grubby: four ripped leather stools pulled up to a bar, small tables lining the sidewalk or clustered in the narrow dining space that makes an L around the bar. The painting Joel saw on the website—the naked woman surrounded by wine bottles—occupies a wall at the far end of the restaurant. It is faded, the per-spective of the bottles at odds with the perspective of the nude, the effect more dingy than glamorous. A magpie hops by on the sidewalk. Joel never saw the black, white, and blue birds before Copenhagen. The girl at the bike shop had laughed when he pointed one out and asked what it was. Surely he didn't consider it special?

"Do you want a drink?" Daniella says as they sit at a small round table at one end of the bar.

Joel says, "I want six drinks," but when the waitress comes, he asks for water and explains that they are still waiting on a few people.

Daniella studies the menu. Benjamin asks for the iPhone, though with-out an international connection, the options on the small screen are not en-ticing. "What're you going to do?" Joel says. "Fruit Ninja?"

Benjamin shrugs irritably, rude-teenager style.

Joel doesn't have the energy to reprimand him, just trusts he'll be bet-ter behaved once Idzia arrives. A solitary woman enters the café, and Joel starts, but realizes, even as the jolt is subsiding, that it isn't Idzia. He sees another solitary woman on the sidewalk, talking into a cell phone. "Is that ..." he begins, but before his sentence is out, he realizes it isn't Idzia either, and in any case she said she'd be coming with others. Daniella pats his hand. "It'll be OK," she says. "She'll be here, or she won't."

"Can I download *Fast and Furious?*" Benjamin says, as he peers at the iPhone.

"No," Daniella says.

"Geez, you guys," he says, looking up. "Aren't you going to say something?"

"We're saying no," Joel says, testy. Why is Benjamin even asking? He knows they don't have an international connection.

"Aren't you going to say something to *her?* She's right there."

"Where?"

"You're looking in the wrong direction! Look! There she is!"

Joel swivels in his seat and sees Idzia on the sidewalk behind him. She is hugging her arms as if she is cold and nodding her head ferociously, apparently in agreement with something. Joel takes her in but can't quite *grasp* her. He notices things—she is medium height, curvy, *Liesel-shaped,* with straight hair pulled back in a knot—but these features don't add up to an impression exactly. What *type* is she? Arty, he supposes. Socially conscious arty. Not high-fashion arty. She wears white sneakers, a wrinkled white eyelet skirt, and a light green T-shirt, an outfit suitable for the city, a hike, or a trek through India.

He stands and lifts his hand, a salute that means, "Over here!" "Hello! Hello!" he calls.

"Geez, Dad," Benjamin says, embarrassed for him.

Idzia's round face—*his* face!—tightens into a flinch. Then she lifts her arm in a return hello. Her eyes quickly dart to the three people with her: a pregnant redhead, a blond with dramatically cropped hair, and a broad-chested young man in jeans and a black T-shirt.

As they step forward, Daniella and Benjamin stand.

"My God," Joel says. He wants to hug his daughter but doesn't want to impose the intimacy on her. His wrists twitch, then he gives in to instinct and spreads his arms. Idzia steps back, clearly refusing the gesture. He lowers his arms, but then she steps forward and raises her own. There is a comical to and fro. Everyone laughs.

"Come *on*," the young man says, and he makes a gesture with his hands that suggests closing elevator doors. "This is the big moment."

Idzia says "OK," and leans into Joel for a cautious embrace.

"I think we are going to need another table here," Daniella says to cover the silence after they separate. "And a few more chairs."

"Here, let me," the young man says and drags over two additional tables and some chairs. "Sit, sit," Daniella says, as if it is her house in which everyone has gathered. "I am Daniella, and this is Benjamin." The others offer their names in turn. Bertie, Nikolaj, Katie. Before he sits, Benjamin pockets his iPhone and puts his hand shyly forward to shake Idzia's. "It's really nice to meet you, and I . . . I just wanted to say it's really cool that you make movies."

Idzia smiles, and then there is some fussing around the pregnant woman. Would she like this seat? Or that? Is she comfortable, how far along is she, how is she handling the heat? She looks older than the others. Maybe late thirties. Possibly older.

When they are all seated, Joel can't think how to begin. He chuckles. Under the table, he feels Daniella pat his thigh. *I'll take care of this,* her hand seems to be saying.

"So, you know how we are all related, but what about you? How are you all related?" Daniella says in a party-host voice.

"Ah," says Idzia, looking at her friends, her voice primly British, "you must all explain yourselves." She presses back into her chair, as if happy, for the moment, to have no role in the conversation.

Bertie, the freckle-faced pregnant woman, says she is from London. "I'm Idzia's guardian. I took Liesel in when she had nowhere to go."

Why does she have to start with aggression? "Nowhere to go." Pregnant women are sexy now, with leggings and form-fitting shirts stretched taut over their bellies, but Bertie seems to be doing it in the old-fashioned, ungainly way, with an outsized denim jumper over a white T-shirt. She fans herself with a menu. She is a nurse, she adds, but planning to leave the hospital when the baby comes. Her husband is a cardiologist, so his hours are unpredictable. "I'm a urologist," Joel offers, but this doesn't seem to interest Bertie. "A surgeon," he adds.

Idzia says, almost as if she hasn't heard the back-and-forth between Joel and Bertie, "Also I know Nikolaj because he is my roommate. He just graduated from the National Film School of Denmark."

"Oh, great," Joel says, as if the National Film School of Denmark means something to him.

"And also Katie. She is . . ." Idzia laughs. "My best friend. We met in London, when I was still in school. She's in film, too, a director." Joel assumes Katie is gay from her bearing and her haircut, the left side of her head shaved, the hair on the right a bit longer. Idzia explains that she more or less followed Katie to Copenhagen. It is Katie, then, who must be her partner, and not Nikolaj, as Joel had first assumed. Joel flashes on something he's long forgotten: Liesel in the coat closet at their wedding reception with Allison Day, her maid of honor, snuggled into her neck. "What's going on here?" Joel had said when he came across them. Liesel said, "She's . . . Jesus Christ, get off me, Allison. She's trying to give me a hickey. She thinks it's funny." Liesel pushed the giggling Allison away. "Stop it," Liesel said and walked out of the closet. "It *is* kind of funny," Allison said and scampered away. When Liesel and Joel were still married, it *was* amusing, an anecdote to be offered at a gathering with a roll of the eye: a little bit of outrageousness on the part of Liesel's old friend. Sometimes, though, Joel wondered if it was really a clue—Trouble ahead!—and he had missed it.

"So," Daniella says cheerily. "We have so much we want to ask you!" As Katie, Nikolaj, Idzia, and Bertie respond to Joel and Daniella's initial questions, various facts of Idzia's life become clear, some of which Joel gathered from her website (the work in film) and some not. "When did you change your name?" Daniella finally asks.

Idzia says, "After the bombing, I sort of thought . . ."

"Excuse me," Joel interrupts. "What bombing?"

Idzia laughs. "Oh, right, yes, how would you know? The 2005 London subway bombing. I was in one of the cars." She smiles a little, as if to suggest that they should move on, the horrific event isn't a centerpiece story, after all, just a segue into the tale about the timing of her name change.

"What happened?" Benjamin asks.

"My God," Joel says, as Idzia elaborates. "My God." Joel shakes his head. "What you've been through."

"I changed Mom's name, too," Idzia says matter-of-factly, unable or unwilling to respond to his emotion, her words an addendum to the addendum about the bombing, all the real content of the story in the footnotes. "I mean, after she died. Not legally, but when I did her obituary for the theater where she worked. It just seemed like a way to honor her." She smiles, as if asking for approval.

Joel can't think of how to respond.

"It was a watershed moment," Idzia says, and again Joel senses a plea. What is he supposed to say?

"That's understandable," Daniella puts in, making a point, Joel thinks, of being kind, also of creating something of a pause for Joel to absorb the information.

Idzia shrugs, says she had to decide everything after that bombing. She had to decide who she wanted to be, and she decided that that was Idzia Wilson. She doesn't belabor the point, but it is pretty obvious: She didn't want to be connected to a name that had provided her nothing. She wanted to be connected to her mother.

"I see," Joel says eventually. Who can blame her?

They order, try to further assess each other's personalities through food choices. Grilled tuna salad for Daniella and Idzia, roasted potatoes for Katie (a vegan and nothing else on the menu accommodates that predilection), hamburgers for Nikolaj, Benjamin, and Joel. "Tak," Daniella says to the waitress.

"She's tried to learn a little Danish," Joel says.

"I've managed 'Kan du tale engelsk?'" Daniella says.

"I keep telling her she sounds like the Swedish Chef."

"Who?" Idzia says.

"I'm sorry. A Muppets character from the States. Do you know the Muppets? There was a chef puppet who would say, "Glada blada meatball boink boink boink.' Something like that." He shrugs. "You'd kind of have to see it yourself."

"Oh," Idzia says and looks at her napkin. Nikolaj asks, "Is it your first time in Denmark, then?"

They quickly lapse into the sort of conversation any Dane might have with any visitor. What have the Pearlmans done? What seen?

"We went to the LEGO store," Benjamin offers.

"Ah, you like LEGOs," Nikolaj says, as if impressed by Benjamin's good taste.

"And we took a boat ride through the canals," Daniella says.

"Yes," Nikolaj says. "It's a good way to see the city. You like Copenhagen?"

"Oh, yes," Daniella says. "It's beautiful."

"It's the best city in the world," Nikolaj says, and it takes a moment for Joel to realize he isn't joking.

After a while, the food arrives, the plates too full, so much for the conventional wisdom about Europeans' modest portions to Americans' piggy serving sizes. Abruptly, Joel interrupts the casual conversation; something has just occurred to him. "Your website, that clip of you walking with blood on your clothes. I thought that was a movie. *That's* the bombing?"

"A reenactment. Katie wanted to do it."

Katie shrugs.

"Why?" Joel says. His meal is in front of him, but he can't bring himself to eat. "Why would you want to reenact that? Wouldn't it be painful?"

Idzia shoots Katie a glance. "Let's talk about something else," she says. And then, "If you don't mind."

"No, whatever you want," Joel says, and everyone falls into silence. Joel picks up a French fry, puts it back down. There is a café across the street. The guidebook says that if Café Wilder is too crowded, the neighboring spot is a good second choice, but Café Wilder is largely empty, and the place across the street is bustling. Joel has a sense of having arrived somewhere after its time has passed

"I like the T-shirt," Katie says to Benjamin. Emblazoned across his chest, around a picture of an iconic British booth, is the phrase, "The Angels Have the Phonebox."

Benjamin lights up. "Do you like Dr. Who?" he says.

She laughs. "How could I like your T-shirt if I didn't like Dr. Who? What do you think of the new Doctor?" Periodically a new actor rotates into the role of the time-traveling hero, and the much-anticipated change happened just two weeks ago.

"I don't know yet," Benjamin says. "I haven't seen him in anything."

"I wanted it to be a woman. Wouldn't that be great, if for the first time ever a woman had played the Doctor?" Katie says. She seems to think this notion will challenge Benjamin, shake up his patriarchal little world, but he says, "Yeah, that would have been pretty cool." And with this interchange, Katie and Benjamin split off from the group, embark on their own conversation. It's something Joel has seen before: his son's struggle to participate in some quotidian chitchat and then the discovery of a child or adult who will meet him where he lives—in the geek world, as he might say—and everything takes off.

Daniella, sitting directly across the table from Nikolaj, must sense it is time to draw him in as well. She asks what he studied at film school. Once he tells her that he was on the cinematography track, she asks about whose work he most loves. Also about Danish film. Where should someone who knows nothing about it start? "You are asking all the hard questions," he says, rubbing his neck. "Everyone would say our first great filmmaker was Carl Dreyer. You won't get any argument there."

Feeling that there is, at last, something like a private space into which he can speak, Joel says to Idzia, "I wish there was a way I could know everything about your life all at once."

Idzia chases a lettuce leaf around her place, then puts her fork down. "I'm not trying to be rude, and I appreciate your getting in touch with me. I mean I suppose I do, but why now? I've been alive for all these years, and you never showed an interest in me. You never did anything for me. You never sent any money. You never supported me."

Joel breathes in deeply—almost *relieved*. He has expected accusations and has rehearsed his answers. "I have *always* been interested in you. I have been trying to be in touch with you your whole life."

"What are you talking about?"

"I'm talking about how your mother wouldn't let me see you."

"That's not true!" Idzia says. "That's crazy."

"I'm afraid it is true," he says. He hears Nikolaj, catty-corner across the table, say to Daniella, "Dogme, Dogme, Dogme. People are sick and tired of hearing about it. That was twenty years ago. Get over it." What could he possibly be talking about?

Idzia picks her hair up as if to put it into a ponytail, then finding no hair tie, drops it back down. It's something Liesel used to do. She looks down and then back up at her father. "I mean why should she? If you weren't helping out, if you weren't doing anything."

"I did send money."

"Since when?"

"My wages were garnished. But you are right; it wasn't enough. Still, I was willing to send whatever she wanted on the condition that she let me see you, but she wouldn't let me see you."

Idzia turns to Bertie, who doesn't seem to be part of any conversation at the table, but lost in some pregnancy fugue, where only the yet-to-be-born seem interesting. "Are you hearing this?"

"Hearing what?" Bertie says, looking up, and Joel sees she has been tapping a message into a phone on her lap. "Sorry," she adds. "I had a message." She shakes her head as if to get rid of whatever was absorbing her and to focus on what is going on in the café.

"Your mother used to call me in the middle of the night—she did this for years—demanding money, and I always told her yes, but she had to let me see you. She had to let me be your father. I had an idea she never told you. I had an idea she portrayed me as a monster, but that just isn't true. I have always wanted to know you and to be in your life."

"I . . ." Idzia looks bewildered. Nikolaj puts his hand out and lightly touches her wrist. "Things good here?"

"It's OK," Idzia says, seeming to settle into herself. Then to her father, "I just don't know where you come up with this."

"Hey, little buddy," Nikolaj says to Benjamin. "Maybe your mother and I can walk over to the canal, and I can show you the funny LEGO house. You know the one I'm talking about, Katie?"

"Oh, yeah, yeah," she says, clearly sensing Nikolaj's agenda.

Nikolaj turns to Idzia. "Maybe a few of us can go for a walk, give you a little time to . . ." he makes a back-and-forth motion with his hand.

Daniella looks uneasy.

Nikolaj says, "Oh, don't worry. It's just someone whose front door is covered with mini-figures. You know 'mini-figs'?" Benjamin bobs his head eagerly. "A funny thing. Four blocks from here. If it is OK? We'll be gone a few minutes?"

Joel nods an assent.

Daniella says, "That would be lovely." Joel has the idea she seems insipid to the others, a woman all too drawn to the platitudes of "nice" and "lovely." *But that's not fair!* he thinks angrily, aware that he is defending his wife against a criticism no one has actually voiced.

Katie, Nikolaj, Daniella, and Benjamin head for the sidewalk. Bertie starts to stand, too, but Katie puts her hand out to stop her, and Bertie sits back down. "I guess I'll just rest," Bertie says.

A waitress comes by and makes a motion to remove the plates of those who have left, but Joel says, "Just wait." Daniella and Benjamin's plates are still fairly full, but they are slow eaters, might not yet be through. Nikolaj and Katie's plates are clear.

"Your mother," Joel begins. "Sometimes she'd just call in the middle of the night and hang up. Then call again, and then again. She didn't like that I wanted to see you. It's true I would have wanted to share custody. I would have wanted to be a real father. Perhaps that scared her."

Bertie says, "I know Liesel used to call you and try to bring herself to ask you for money. But then she couldn't do it, so she'd hang up. Too proud, I think."

Joel doesn't say anything. Liesel was hardly too proud to ask for money. The notion is absurd.

"But, you know," Bertie says peaceably. "I'd tell her to do it. Other people at the theater did, too. She didn't really ask for money till she got sick."

Joel says, "I am sure this is what she told you, but it is just not true. I didn't even know that Idzia existed for the first five years of her life." Joel turns to Idzia. "When Liesel called to tell me about you, it wasn't so I could be your father, it was so I could send money. She never allowed me access to you. A simple desire for a father to see his daughter, what's more simple, and she wouldn't let it happen."

Idzia looks at him for a long moment, turns to Bertie, and returns her gaze—hooded, now hardened—to Joel. "My mother never told me you were a liar."

"I'm not a liar. Daniella can tell you about the calls. Ask her when she comes back. I have a fat file full of all the times I made a request for a visitation, and Liesel refused. There are letters to lawyers in Paris. I can show you everything. I can mail it to you as soon as I get home."

Idzia clears her throat.

And because he can see her eyes are tearing, Joel reaches across the table, squeezes her hand, and says, "The last thing I wanted to do on the day I finally meet my daughter was upset her."

"Not upset," Idzia says and turns her attention to the napkin in her lap. She is plainly about to cry.

"Last thing," Joel says.

Idzia lifts her head and says, "I need to go to the bathroom." She stands and heads for the far corner of the cafe.

Joel turns to Bertie, sensing she is the one, in the end, to whom he has to plead his case.

"Should I?" he says, meaning should he follow her.

Bertie shakes her head no. "Give her a moment, and then I'll check on her."

"Does she know anything about me?" he says.

"I don't know what she knows. I know what *I* know, which is that you were an awfully critical husband, and Liesel needed to get away from you."

"Is that what she said? Is that . . . ? She had an affair! She had an affair even though we were barely married, and then the guy she was schtupping died. I came home one day, and she was hysterical, and she couldn't tell me why, and it took me forever to figure out the truth. A friend of a friend at the theater where she was working finally told me. I was blown away. I would no more have guessed she was having an affair on me than that she was a . . . I mean it would never have even *crossed my mind*."

"Now," Bertie begins but doesn't complete her sentence.

"She was a liar! Isn't that obvious? She lied and changed her name to Liesel Rosenthal. She lied about me. She lied about everything."

"She didn't lie about you being mean," Bertie says flatly.

"I'm not being mean," he says. "I'm angry. There's a difference."

"I never heard her lie," Bertie says.

"Did you know what her real name was? It was Sara Wilson."

"I know Wilson was her maiden name," Bertie says. "I don't know what you mean about Sara."

Joel rubs his face with his hands. "Look . . ." he starts.

"It's not that I didn't know her to be . . ." Bertie begins. "She could be . . ."

Joel holds up his hand and says, "I'll explain it." He tells Bertie the story about how Liesel had been Sara Wilson up to the day she walked up to a man holding a sign at a Tube stop that said "Liesel Rosenthal."

Bertie listens and then says, "I don't know where you got that."

Joel says, "I got that from . . . It's the truth."

Idzia still hasn't come back. Bertie says, "I'm going to see what's going on."

When Nikolaj and the others return to the table, it is to Joel sitting all alone. "Where's Idzia?" Nikolaj says.

"Bathroom," Joel chokes out. "Bertie's with her."

"Everything OK?" Daniella says as she slides next to him.

He waves his hand to suggest she shouldn't pursue anything right now, but he puts his own head in his hands—melodramatically, OK, but it is a melodramatic moment.

"Dad?" Benjamin says. Then, in a panic, "Dad!"

"It's fine," Joel says. "I'm sorry. It's fine."

"But . . ." Benjamin starts. He cannot countenance his parents' low moods; their sadness terrifies him. Daniella leans toward him, starts to whisper something consoling.

Aside from the maid of honor trying to give Liesel a hickey, something else unsettling happened at Joel's wedding. When a Jewish bride and groom are under the wedding chuppah, seven blessings, Sheva Brachot, are supposed to be recited. Joel knew nothing about this tradition till his sister

Amy—always more *frum* than he—told him about it. But once she did, Joel loved the idea of asking seven different family members to recite some words. He had the words typed out in Hebrew and in transliteration. He passed them out the day before the wedding. He'd given the longest one to Amy, because she was his sister but also because she was the only one in the family who actually read Hebrew. When it was her turn, Amy stood up and began—the first words the same as any Hebrew blessing (*Baruch atah Adonai eloheinu melech h'aolem*)—but she suddenly stopped short and said, "Bless the woman who has forgotten the blessing. I am so sorry. I forgot the sheet of paper! I'm so sorry." Everyone laughed. It was one of those foibles that makes a good wedding story, but after Liesel left, and though he didn't believe in the power of the blessings, he thought back on the moment and on his sister, who sometimes seemed almost smug in the happiness of her own marriage and the choices she'd made, confidence having never been a problem for her, and decided, "You! It's your fault."

When Bertie and Idzia return to the table, Joel says, "I'm sorry."

"No, it's OK," Idzia says. She has plainly been weeping.

Bertie says, "Idzia wants me to tell you that she knows her mother had faults, but she loved her very, very much."

"Of course. Of course you did!" Joel cries. And why shouldn't she? He did, too, once. "Truly, this isn't the way I wanted things to go."

"It's all right," Idzia says.

"You know," Joel says in a cheery, let's-wipe-the-slate-clean manner. "There are some things I've always been curious about. I mean, because of all the addresses that my lawyers sent letters to." He stops for a moment. He does not mean to belabor the point of his ongoing interest in Idzia despite Liesel's efforts to thwart that interest. "I always wondered about Morocco and Geneva. I know you weren't there long, but I always wondered what took you there. What happened there."

Idzia nods, says, "Morocco was . . . it was to teach at an English language school. I don't have big memories there. Geneva was later. There was . . . a boyfriend, and he helped her get a job at a place that followed . . . I don't know how to say it . . . guns around the world. It kept track of weaponry."

"That doesn't sound like Liesel. She hated guns." And then, because he feels like he must say something nice, "I always liked that about her. That she was a peacenik, as she liked to say."

"It *was* a peace organization. She was a secretary in the office. It was just for a few months. The boyfriend didn't work out. We got stuck. There was an apartment near the office that was meant for research visitors, but no one was using it for a while, so we stayed. It was just a room with a kitchen."

So little stability, Joel thinks. It's not what she'd have been given if he'd had any say in it. "I'm sorry," Joel says. "I'm sorry I couldn't have been there for you."

"It was near the UN," Idzia adds, though Joel's not sure why

Joel says, and he's aware it's the wrong thing to say even as the words are coming out of his mouth, "I didn't give you up. You were taken from me."

"You can't say that about my mother!" Idzia explodes. "You have no right."

EVERYONE AT THE TABLE shifts focus to Joel and Idzia. Even people at neighboring tables seem to have realized eavesdropping will be profitable. The strangers think, "Why won't that man leave that girl alone?" Daniella thinks, "Down, Joel, down," as if Joel is an over-exuberant dog. Benjamin also thinks "Down, Dad, down," but he adds, in his head, a joke, "Come on, have a Daddy treat." It's what he says at home when one of his parents gets worked up. He finds a box of vanilla wafers and extends a cookie, just to make the gag work. Katie thinks, "What a fucker." Nikolaj wonders if Idzia is going to be all right. Joel just seems to shrink into himself.

Bertie remains both in the conversation and apart from it. She has for so long been involved in the drama of other people's lives, and now she has her own little drama in her belly. The baby seems to come with a clarity of vision. She sees that everyone at the table has a version of Liesel, though only half the people seated actually knew her. For Idzia, Joel's words are bringing an untrue being into the world and letting that untrue being replace the real woman her mother was. For Joel, the noble Liesel in whom Idzia believes cannot be tolerated, because she would erase the real and good man he believes he has been for all these years, a man who has made the most reasonable and loving choices he could.

As if to confirm Bertie's reading of things, Idzia says, "You can't have her," and starts to weep. Nikolaj puts his arm around her.

"I don't have her," Joel says. "You have her. I know. I know. She will always be your mother, and I'm sure you miss her. I am sorry. I am so sorry. This isn't what I wanted our meeting to be. And after all you've been through."

Bertie flashes back on the years of her friendship with Liesel. It may not be true that she never knew Liesel to lie. Years ago, Liesel told Bertie that Louise, a friend of Bertie's and now a famous actress, had said to another actress, "You have to stay away from Bertie Russell. She's evil." Upset, Bertie had confronted Louise about it, and Louise had said, "If Liesel Pearlman told you that, it's a lie." Or something like that. It's a long time ago now, and Bertie never believed Louise. After all, why would Louise know who had passed on the terrible words to Bertie? It occurs to Bertie that maybe Liesel *was* lying back then. Could she have falsely reported some ugly words? Only why would she? Bertie never stopped being troubled by the revelation: *Bertie Russell is evil.* Eventually, she went to a therapist to discuss it, though even so, she never felt fully resolved about all that happened. *Could* Joel be telling the truth? She doesn't know. It's only clear that he's not lying. He *believes* he's telling the truth.

Dead people recede. It is so hard to hold on to them, their faults and virtues magnified in their absence. You forget the everyday. So who was she? Who was she?

Bertie looks over them all. The family of Daniella, Benjamin, and Joel, the family of Katie, Nikolaj, and Idzia. Each family with its own truth. They can't agree with each other. It would be ruinous if they did. Bertie feels her baby move. Soon enough, she knows, everyone will stand, hug each other good-bye, say they want to stay in touch, though Idzia will not let Joel pursue anything, and Joel, back home, will understand that he cannot repair something so long broken.

"Hey," Benjamin says, from across the table. "I'm really glad you're my sister."

Idzia looks over at him startled. She dries her face.

"Will you be my sister forever? Will you let me know sister-type things?" His voice is silly but in earnest.

"I guess I could," Idzia says.

"Do you Skype?"

Idzia nods, says, "I always wanted a sibling."

"Me, too!" Benjamin says, as if this is a remarkable coincidence, an amazing genetic similarity. "That is what I always wanted."

And in that moment, despite what may come later, everyone just wants what the children want. And Liesel, if she were here, she would want the same. Wouldn't she?

ACKNOWLEDGMENTS

MANY PEOPLE HELPED ME with the research for this book, and though any factual errors in the book are obviously mine, I am grateful to Elaine Aresty and Holly Middleton for information about nursing, Harold Just for information about urology, Marjorie Just for information about divorce law, Mark Honan and David Timm for information about theater, Mike Morrill for information about police procedure, Gordie Stewart and Natan Tiefen-brun for information about London. Additional thanks to David Spark, Rich Weinberg, and Jennifer Wiessner for telling me stories and to Aidan Mitchell for letting me steal some of his jokes.

In Barbados, many people helped me imagine what an art opening in the 1980s would have been like, including Alison Chapman, Neville Legall, Goldie Spieler, Nick Whittle, and Nodrog Ybhsa (who even drew me pictures).

I owe an enormous debt to the unusually generous Ulrik B. Jørgensen, Film Commissioner at Oresund Film Commission/Copenhagen, who invited my family and me into his home, let me interview him on multiple occasions, and provided numerous contacts throughout Denmark. Also thanks to the many film industry professionals who spoke with me, including Rikke Tambo Andersen, Jakob Balslev, Mie Copsø, Fredrick Gottlieb, Mettelise Hansen, Amalie Lyngbo Hjort, Prami Larsen, Malte Morfar, Ves Møller Rasmussen, and Sissel Dalsgaard Thomsen.

Colby College provided three separate travel grants that allowed me to go to Copenhagen, London, and Paris for research for this novel. Years ago, they provided a travel grant to go to Barbados, for a different novel, but left-over research from that book found its way into this book. I couldn't have written this book, or my earlier one, without the school's generosity.

Thanks to dear writer friends who read the manuscript, often on repeated occasions, and provided invaluable edits and advice (not to mention emotional support): Susan Conley, Sara Corbett, Gail Donovan, Lily King, Caitlin Gutheil, Anja Hanson, Elizabeth Searle, and Monica Wood.

So grateful to my enormously grounded and kind agent, Eleanor Jackson, and to Michael Griffith, who picked *Unknown Caller* for Yellow Shoe Fiction and then gave the manuscript such an impressive and careful edit.

Finally, many thanks to all the people at LSUP who shepherded this book through production.